Daring Deception

Off The Grid: FBI Series #9

BARBARA FREETHY

Fog City Publishing

PRAISE FOR BARBARA FREETHY

"A fabulous, page-turning combination of romance and intrigue. Fans of Nora Roberts and Elizabeth Lowell will love this book." — *NYT Bestselling Author Kristin Hannah on Golden Lies*

"PERILOUS TRUST is a non-stop thriller that seamlessly melds jaw-dropping suspense with sizzling romance. Readers will be breathless in anticipation as this fast-paced and enthralling love story goes in unforeseeable directions." — *USA Today HEA Blog*

"Barbara Freethy's first book PERILOUS TRUST in her OFF THE GRID series is an emotional, action packed, crime drama that keeps you on the edge of your seat...I'm exhausted after reading this but in a good way. 5 Stars!" — *Booklovers Anonymous*

"Powerful and absorbing...sheer hold-your-breath suspense." — *NYT Bestselling Author Karen Robards on Don't Say A Word*

"I loved this story from start to finish. Right from the start of PERILOUS TRUST, the tension sets in. Goodness, my heart was starting to beat a little fast by the end of the prologue! I found myself staying up late finishing this book, and that is something I don't normally do." — *My Book Filled Life Blog*

"Freethy hits the ground running as she kicks off another winning romantic suspense series...Freethy is at her prime with a superb combo of engaging characters and gripping plot." — *Publishers' Weekly on Silent Run*

PRAISE FOR BARBARA FREETHY

"Barbara Freethy is a master storyteller with a gift for spinning tales about ordinary people in extraordinary situations and drawing readers into their lives." — *Romance Reviews Today*

"Freethy (Silent Fall) has a gift for creating complex, appealing characters and emotionally involving, often suspenseful, sometimes magical stories." — *Library Journal on Suddenly One Summer*

Freethy hits the ground running as she kicks off another winning romantic suspense series…Freethy is at her prime with a superb combo of engaging characters and gripping plot." — *Publishers' Weekly on Silent Run*

"Grab a drink, find a comfortable reading nook, and get immersed in this fast paced, realistic, romantic thriller! 5 STARS!" *Perrin – Goodreads on Elusive Promise*

"If you love nail-biting suspense and heartbreaking emotion, Silent Run belongs on the top of your to-be-bought list. I could not turn the pages fast enough." — *NYT Bestselling Author Mariah Stewart*

"Words cannot explain how phenomenal this book was. The characters are so believable and relatable. The twists and turns keep you on the edge of your seat and flying through the pages. This is one book you should be desperate to read." *Caroline - Goodreads on Ruthless Cross*

PROLOGUE

TEN YEARS EARLIER...

"It's not what we planned. It's not even close," Caitlyn Carlson said, wanting her boyfriend to refute every word.

"Life rarely goes the way we plan, but we can make it work," Quinn Kelly said.

She wanted to believe him, but she couldn't. She also didn't think it was a coincidence that he wouldn't look at her, that his sea-blue eyes were fixed on his phone.

She took a sip of the hot chocolate they'd just picked up at the coffee cart and looked toward the heavily forested hills above Bolton College, a private university located just north of San Francisco. She loved her school, which was set in a beautiful and somewhat isolated location between the mountains and the California coast. She loved the guy by her side even more.

But despite Quinn's reassuring words, there was something wrong. It wasn't just the March weather that was making her cold; it was the growing distance between them, a gap she didn't understand. In the last year, they'd become incredibly close, so close she knew he wasn't telling the truth.

Did she want the truth?

Their lives were about to change. Maybe neither one of them was ready.

Quinn tossed his empty coffee cup in a nearby trash can and frowned once more at his phone.

"Something wrong?" she asked.

"Lauren needs to change the time of our study group. They're going to meet now instead of at three."

"But we have the ribbon-cutting ceremony for the new environmental center in an hour. Will you be done by then?"

"I'm sorry, Caitlyn. I don't think I can make it."

"But it's important." Quinn was getting his master's in ocean sciences, and the new three-story building would provide environmental scientists with incredible new tools. "The facility will directly impact your research."

He finally looked at her, and she could see the conflict in his eyes, which made her feel marginally better.

"I know," he said. "But it's a group project, and I need to be there. Frankly, I think you should blow off the event, too."

"I can't do that, Quinn."

"Why not? Your family is giving it a pass. Who are they sending? Some PR rep?"

"My brother is coming, too."

"Your brother, but not your father. He's the one who should be there. He's the head of Carlson Industries, a conglomeration of companies who have done far more to harm the environment than to help it. If your family was really focused on change, they'd be doing more than just building a study center. It's easier to throw money at a problem than time and genuine commitment."

"You have a point, but the center is a good thing. It's a start. We can at least celebrate that, can't we? I don't want my family or their business to come between us, especially not now." She felt a desperate need to convince him of that. The love she felt for him was deep, overwhelming, and all-consuming. It shouldn't have gotten so serious so fast, but it had—against all odds. They came from different worlds. But when they were together, there was only one world, one island of love, and they were the only ones on it. No one else mattered.

However, as Quinn checked his phone once more, she couldn't help wondering if that was true. Maybe she was on the island alone.

"Why do you keep looking at your phone?" she demanded.

"I'm getting a lot of texts from the study group."

"Is that it? Or is there something else going on? There isn't going to be a protest, is there?" Quinn was part of an environmental activist group on campus, and there were many people in the group who weren't thrilled with Carlson Industries.

"No. There won't be a protest. I made sure of that, Caitlyn. Donovan gave me his word."

"But you still don't want to go, because you're caught in the middle between me and your friends. Isn't that the real reason you're blowing me off?"

"No. And I'm not caught in the middle. The study session is just too important. I'll see the center when it opens. Is it really that big of a deal?"

She sighed. "I guess not."

He put his hand on her shoulders and gave her a smile that made her feel immensely better. "We'll meet up later."

"You promise?"

"Of course. Why would you even ask me that?"

"I just feel like something is off."

"It's going to be all right, Caitlyn. We'll work everything out."

"Are you sure? You haven't really said what you're feeling

about all this, Quinn. I've had longer to think about it than you have. I know I sprung it on you."

"You don't have to worry. I'll take care of you."

"I'm not worried about someone taking care of me. I want you to be happy. I want us to be happy."

"You make me happy." He pulled her in for a kiss, and the heat of his mouth drove the fears away. "You're the best thing that ever happened to me."

"I feel that way, too."

"I'll see you later."

As he walked away, her gaze followed him across the quad. She felt a deep yearning to be back in his arms, to feel his lips against hers, to be connected to him, because despite his words, she could feel their connection slipping away, and it scared her.

She'd never loved anyone the way she loved Quinn. She'd fallen for him at first sight, his blue eyes capturing her heart with one look. He was incredibly handsome with his dark hair, sexy mouth, and long, lean, powerful body, but it was his passion for science, changing the world, and doing something important in his life that had really sealed the deal for her. He wasn't just a sexy scientist; he was also a fighter, and she liked that he fought for the world he wanted to live in. But she wondered sometimes if he thought she didn't fight enough. There were cracks appearing in their relationship; some she understood, some she didn't.

As Quinn reached the edge of the trees by the library, he looked back and gave her a wave, and it made her feel better, like they were connected again. Maybe her fears were all in her head. That was probably it. She waved back, watching until he disappeared.

She needed to give him time and space. He'd been through a lot in his life, losing his dad when he was eleven and his mother when he was sixteen. Quinn had been on his own ever since then, and he'd told her more than once that he'd forgotten what love felt like until he'd met her, that he was always afraid he was going to lose it. That's why he slept with his arms wrapped around her.

Well, she would keep showing him that love until he was smothered in it, until he could trust that it wouldn't disappear, that *she* wouldn't disappear.

They would work through their problems and would move forward. They would be together forever. It was what they both wanted.

Feeling better, she turned and continued on her way across campus. She had an hour before the ceremony. She could go back to her apartment and study. She had tests to worry about, too. As she checked the time, her phone buzzed, and her brother Spencer's number flashed across the screen.

"Hey, are you on your way?" she asked.

"Sorry, but I can't make it," Spencer replied.

"Are you serious? Why not?"

"I broke my tooth. I'm on my way to the dentist. I'm sorry, Caitlyn."

"I'm sorry, too, about your tooth, and the fact that I'll have to do this event alone."

"Dad said he's sending Marian down to represent the company, so you won't be completely alone."

"There should be more family members there."

"Well, it's not going to happen. You should let Marian handle it. I know you've been feeling caught in the middle between Quinn and his environmental activist friends and our family business. Why don't you skip the ceremony?"

"I think someone from the family should be there."

"Our name is on the building. It's not like anyone will forget who built it."

She frowned. "That's not the point. You were supposed to talk about how the company is changing and making efforts to go green and protect the environment."

"Yeah, Dad didn't really want me to say much. He said just cut the ribbon and raise a champagne glass."

"Sometimes, Dad really pisses me off," she said with annoyance.

"Sometimes? It happens to me more often than that. I have to go. Just bail on it, Caitlyn. Don't put yourself in the position of having to stand up for a company you don't really have anything to do with. There could be protestors. And you don't want to get caught up in that."

"I've been assured there won't be."

"Well, good, but I'm sure Quinn doesn't want to go. Why don't you hang with him, do your own thing?"

"I'll think about it. Good luck with the dentist."

"Thanks."

As she ended the call, she considered her options. She didn't really want to hang out with the dean and smile for pictures or have to say something about the company plans when she knew nothing about them. Marian was more than capable of handling the ceremony. But it still felt wrong for no one from the family to be there.

Still debating, she kept on walking. When she got to the front of the new building, which sat on a hilly rise with a perfect view of the sea, she paused, feeling proud of the new center. It would house four classrooms, three labs, a study lounge, and a small auditorium. The center wouldn't make up for the questionable business choices her family had made in the past, but it was a good move in the right direction.

She walked up the steps and opened the front door, stepping into the foyer. There was a table set with empty champagne glasses for the reception. Everything felt new: the floors polished, the walls artfully decorated, and the air clean and crisp. There was a distant murmur of conversation, probably coming from a floor up, but there was no one in sight. She stepped into the study lounge, which was also a library. It was impressively filled with an array of books.

Walking over to the nearest shelf, she ran her fingers down the spine of a new textbook. She'd always loved to read and to write, which was why she planned on being a journalist. She had a lot of questions, and that seemed to be the best way to get them answered.

The sound of ticking drew her attention to the wall, but she didn't see a clock.

She just heard a *tick, tick, tick*. An eerie feeling shot down her spine.

It suddenly felt too quiet.

She turned toward the door, but before she could take a step, a thunderous blast lifted her off her feet and threw her against the shelves behind her. The ceiling and walls collapsed around her.

She screamed as she put a protective hand against her stomach, in one last desperate attempt to save herself and her baby...

CHAPTER ONE

Dark storm clouds rolled in off the ocean and an icy chill followed Special Agent Caitlyn Carlson through her four-mile run from her LA apartment to the Santa Monica pier and then home again. She couldn't shake the feeling of foreboding shadowing her steps, and that annoyed her. She and her team had just wrapped up a three-month investigation that had taken down a dangerous cult leader and saved the lives of dozens of young women. She should be happy and relaxed.

But it was late March, and that had never been her favorite month. It reminded her of the terrible memories from the weeks she'd spent in the hospital one spring a long time ago, and the pain that had stayed with her for years after that.

Ten years, she thought, as she headed into her apartment for a hot shower.

It wasn't an anniversary she wanted to celebrate. Sometimes it felt like a long time ago; other times it felt like yesterday. But she was no longer a twenty-one-year-old college student; she was a thirty-one-year-old FBI agent. She was living a completely different life, one that was extremely satisfying. She needed to keep the past in the past.

She showered and dressed, then jumped into her car and headed to work, wondering where her next assignment would take her. They were having a team meeting at nine to discuss their ongoing cases and which investigations needed more manpower. She was looking forward to digging into something new.

She had just pulled into the underground garage when her phone buzzed with an incoming call from her mother. Frowning, she sent the call to voicemail. She rarely spoke on the phone with her mom. Occasional texts were her preferred method of communication. A text gave her the opportunity to learn what her mother wanted so she could figure out the best way to say no.

She was fairly certain that this morning's call was regarding the Carlson Foundation Gala to be held Sunday night in San Francisco. It was an event that had always meant a great deal to her family and raised vital money for many nonprofit organizations. She'd gone every year except for one when she was in London on a case, but she didn't want to go this year. They'd moved the event from its traditional May date to March, and this was the time of year when she preferred to hunker down and not socialize with anyone, especially those people who would remind her of the past.

Sliding out of the car, she took the elevator to the second floor and entered the suite of offices that housed her FBI task force. She'd worked as a special agent for over five years now, and her job was truly her life. It was where she felt in control, and that was the most important thing to her.

But as she walked past one empty cubicle after the next to find her colleagues crowded into the glass-walled conference room, she got a bad feeling in the pit of her stomach.

Something was wrong.

The meeting hadn't begun yet, but the group's attention was on the television monitor with a *Breaking News* tag running across the bottom of the screen.

As she neared the room, she could see the screen more clearly—the flames and plumes of smoke behind the reporter. There had been an explosion.

She froze, an overwhelming sense of panic hitting her from a decade ago. No matter how many times she thought she'd gotten past the trauma, it came back.

She'd get through it, just as she always had before. But her stomach twisted as she saw the next headline: *Bomb blast at Bolton College.*

Her breath came short and fast. Screams of *No! No! No!* went off in her head. It was all she could do to hold them back.

Not Bolton—not again.

The conference door opened, and one of her fellow agents, Lucas Raines, came out of the room. Lucas had brown hair and green eyes, and his usually friendly, easygoing smile had been replaced by an expression of tense concern. She didn't know what he saw in her expression, but his tall, powerful body was suddenly right in front of her, blocking her view of the screen. His hands came down on her shoulders, and his gaze commanded her attention.

"Breathe," he ordered.

"I'm breathing," she said, as she pulled herself together. She hated looking weak in front of anyone, especially her fellow agents. She'd worked hard to build a reputation as a tough, ruthless, smart agent; one who didn't let her emotions cloud her judgment. Clearing her throat, she said, "Is anyone taking responsibility?"

"Not yet. Why don't you take a minute?"

"I don't need a minute, Lucas. I need information." Determination pushed past the fear in her gut. She'd been looking for years for the bomber who had almost taken her life. It was one reason she'd joined the FBI. "Where did the bomb go off?"

"Outside the auditorium. Six injured, no fatalities yet."

She forced herself to breathe through the images flying through her head of what those injured had just gone through.

Beck Maxwell came out of the room to join them. Beck was second-in-command, and his dark eyes were also filled with concern.

"Who's leading the investigation, Beck?" she asked.

"Rob Carpenter. The San Francisco office has the case."

She wasn't thrilled with that piece of information. She'd worked under Rob for a year in Miami right after she'd become an agent, and he was too political for her taste. He was more interested in optics than in the truth. She'd also butted heads with him over her desire to investigate the Bolton blast on her own time. However, that was inconsequential now. "I need to be there. I need to work the investigation."

"Understood," Beck said. "As you know, I'm running the team while Flynn is on vacation, so I'll call Rob and let him know you're headed his way to consult. But he'll be in charge. You're too close to this, Caitlyn. You need to hang back or you'll be sent back."

She didn't want to agree with him, he was right. "I understand. I'll stay in my lane."

"I doubt that," he said dryly. "But if you need us for anything, we're here."

"I appreciate that. Thanks."

As Beck returned to the conference room, Lucas walked her back to the elevator. "If you need anything, Caitlyn, just say the word, and I'll be on a plane to SF," he told her. "I can imagine how difficult this will be for you."

She knew he didn't have to work that hard to imagine it, because she'd told him in great detail about her past experiences.

He'd also helped her look into the case file when she'd first become an agent."

"Thanks for the offer, but I'll be fine. I'm going to look at this new case as a way to get information to solve the last one."

"I just hate to see you go down that rabbit hole again."

"I can handle it. Hopefully, this rabbit hole will provide some answers."

"Good luck."

She stepped into the elevator and took it back to the parking garage, not taking a solid breath until she was locked in her car. Despite having told Lucas she could handle the situation, she was freaking out on the inside. The sounds of the blast were rocketing through her ears. She could taste the sulfur and feel the crushing weight of the bookshelves and the ceiling. She was breathing in plaster again, drowning in the thick stench of smoke and terror.

Her hand crept to her stomach and the ache that had never quite left was back, even stronger than before.

Why had the bomber waited ten years to strike again?

Was it the same person?

No one had paid for her tragic loss. Maybe now they would…

Her hand shook as she started the car, her thoughts racing down another dark path, to a man she did not want to remember, a man who had disappeared while she was fighting to recover from her injuries, a man she still didn't want to believe had had anything to do with the bomb blast that had taken the life of their child.

Quinn swam deeper into the undersea world of the Pacific Ocean off Dillon Beach, an hour north of San Francisco. The world always looked better to him underwater. It was why he spent every day as a scientific diver researching the effects of climate change on his beloved sea. And there was plenty to note, unfortunately.

With the water temperature growing warmer, an unrestricted rise in the purple sea urchin population, and harmful algae blooms hitting the California coast, the kelp beds were becoming decimated, which was an enormous problem. Kelp beds were vitally important to mitigating climate change, which was why he and six other divers had spent the last two hours thinning out the urchin population by literally taking them out of the sea.

The other divers had already gone back to their boats and returned to shore, but he was taking a final assessment and a few moments to enjoy having the ocean all to himself.

This time of the year was always the most difficult for him, and the sea had always been his best escape, a place where he could forget about the real world. He'd first discovered diving as an eight-year-old when his father had taken him on his first scuba dive off the coast of Northern Ireland. It had been one of the few things he remembered them doing together before his father had been killed.

He shook those depressing memories out of his head. He didn't want his thoughts to mar the beauty of the ocean. Unfortunately, today's escape from reality was ending. He needed to surface.

The current had picked up with an incoming storm and the choppy waves created visibility issues. He wasn't worried. He'd mapped this trip down to the last detail and had redundant safety systems with him. Sometimes it amazed him how thorough he'd become. There had been a time in his life where he'd thrown caution to the wind and leapt before looking.

He'd paid a price for that recklessness, and he'd gotten much smarter, especially when there were others depending on him. He didn't worry about his own safety, but his team would blame themselves if anything happened to him, and there was already too much guilt and regret surrounding his life. He couldn't live with any more.

When he reached the surface, he swam quickly back to the boat. Jeremiah Cooper, who had been diving with him, gave him a hand as he climbed on board. Jeremiah was a tall, blond Australian, who he'd met a dozen years ago. It was Jeremiah who'd gotten him a job on the dive team seven years ago, and he was more than grateful for the chance to combine his love of diving with his love of science. Jeremiah was married, with a baby on the way, and had a happy-go-lucky nature that made him an excellent partner. But there wasn't much sign of Jeremiah's cheerful disposition now.

There was also a look of concern in the captain's eyes. Ray Allen was a sixty-two-year-old African American with weathered skin that came from a lifetime of being on the sea.

"What's wrong?" he asked.

"You should have come up ten minutes ago," Ray grumbled. "You're always pushing the envelope. There's a storm coming."

"We have plenty of time before it hits."

"I don't like it when you don't stick to the schedule," Ray bit out.

"I don't think you're that pissed at me, so what's going on?"

"I'm worried."

"We're fine." A crack of thunder rattled the air, followed by a flash of lightning off to the east, making a mockery of his words. "Well, maybe I should have come up earlier, but we still have time to get back to shore."

"He's not talking about the storm," Jeremiah interjected.

"You're not? What's going on, Ray?"

"There was an explosion at my granddaughter's school," Ray said. "My daughter texted me a few minutes ago. She's beside herself. She can't get a hold of Brianna, and she's been trying for almost two hours."

His stomach tightened as a horrific feeling of foreboding ran through him. He knew exactly where Ray's granddaughter went to school, because he'd gone there, too. "At Bolton?" he said, barely able to get the words through his tight lips.

"Yes."

"When did it happen?"

"A couple of hours ago. It's too long for Brianna to be out of touch."

Shock and nausea ran through him as the past collided with the present. "What do you know about the explosion?" he bit out.

"Not much. It was by the auditorium. I don't think Brianna would have been over there. But I don't know. My daughter said the news is reporting injuries."

He put a hand on the rail as memories overwhelmed him.

"Brianna has to be okay. She's just eighteen—at the beginning of her life," Ray said.

"She'll be all right." He said what Ray wanted to hear, even if there was no genuine conviction to his words.

"Do you want me to take over, Ray?" Jeremiah asked quietly.

"No, I got this," Ray said, turning his attention back to the wheel.

"All right. I'm going to change," Jeremiah said, as he headed down the stairs.

Quinn moved a few feet away, staring unseeingly at the ocean, his thoughts taking him back ten years…

He stood outside the library with his phone pressed to his ear.

"Answer," he muttered, but his call went to voicemail once more, and a bad feeling ran through him. Something was going on. No one was taking his calls or answering his texts, and he didn't like it. He was out of the loop, and that was his fault. He'd been avoiding the loop, not liking the direction of the conversation, the ambition, the goals of the group that had once been a second family to him.

But they weren't his family—Caitlyn was. He needed to make sure the group knew that his priorities had changed. He was going to be a father and a husband at some point, too.

That was a terrifying thought. It wasn't what they'd planned. He was about to get his masters with thoughts of a PhD in his future. Caitlyn wanted to become a reporter after she graduated in June.

And then there was her family. The Carlsons didn't like him at all, and he had little use for them either. He and Caitlyn had grown up in different worlds, but as she liked to tell him, they had their own world now, and that was all that mattered.

He tried calling Donovan once more. No answer.

"Quinn."

He turned to see Lauren Sullivan approaching. She gave him a relieved smile. "I'm so glad you could meet now."

"It wasn't convenient, but I'm here."

"Is Caitlyn mad you won't be at the ribbon-cutting?"

"She's not thrilled. Is anything going on?" he asked. "With the ceremony?"

"What do you mean?"

"You know what I mean. I've been calling Donovan, Hank, and Wyatt. No one is answering their phones. There's no protest scheduled, is there?"

"I don't think so. I haven't heard of one. It's only ten o'clock in the morning. Those guys don't get up early. Why are you so worried?"

"I don't know. I feel like I'm missing something."

"Well, you haven't been around that much, thanks to Caitlyn."

He frowned at her sneering tone. He knew Lauren wasn't a fan, but she barely knew Caitlyn.

"Let's go inside," Lauren said. "Mitch and Tracy grabbed a conference room on the third floor."

"Okay." Before he could move, a horrendously loud bang ripped through the air. The ground shook beneath his feet. As he

looked up, a dark cloud of smoke and flames rose above the nearby trees.

He jumped to his feet, running toward that cloud, as kids poured out of buildings, moving in the opposite direction. He was pushed and shoved by the panicked crowd running for their lives, not sure where the danger was coming from. But he knew. He knew it even before he saw it. All his worst fears were coming true. He never should have left her.

When he got to the scene, shock ran through him. The new three-story building had a gaping hole in the front of it. Smoke and flames were pouring out of that hole. A man stumbled from the building covered in ash.

Sirens lit the air. The campus police were descending on the scene. He tried to get closer, but two cops held him back. He scanned the nearby crowd, desperate to see her shiny reddish-brown hair, the gray wool coat she'd been wearing over her jeans, the backpack over her shoulder that was always weighing her down. But there was no sign of her.

She wouldn't have gone inside, would she?

More fear ran through him. The ribbon-cutting wasn't supposed to start for an hour, but she'd wanted to show him the building, particularly the library dedicated to environmental science. She'd wanted him to see that her family was helping his cause. But he had wanted to see none of that.

He ran forward. He had to get into that building. He had to find her—save her.

Another cop grabbed his arm, holding him back. He struggled to get free.

"You can't go in there," the cop told him. "We don't know if there's more to come."

He stared at him in bewilderment. "More to come?"

"Yes," the man said forcefully. "Stay back."

"My girlfriend is inside."

"Then they'll find her."

He stood on the sidelines for several long minutes. As they brought each person out, his heart stopped and then started racing again when he realized it wasn't her.

As time passed, he thought maybe Caitlyn wasn't there. She could have gone back to her apartment, which was only a few blocks away. He pulled out his phone and called. She didn't answer. The truth was looking him in the eye, but he didn't want to see it.

He'd lost his father. He'd lost his mother. He couldn't lose her, too.

He felt helpless, and he hated waiting. No good ever came of waiting. He wished he could say a prayer and believe in it, but his faith had been sorely tested.

He paced around in a circle, and then he saw the firefighters bringing a body out on a stretcher.

He ran forward, ignoring the shouts to stay back.

When he got to her side, his heart stopped. Her eyes were closed, her face and clothes covered in blood and plaster. "Caitlyn!" he shouted.

A paramedic gave him a concerned but determined look. "Stay back. She's alive, but they have to get her to the hospital. You can see her there."

He watched as they put her in the ambulance. She had to be all right. She had to be.

His phone rang, but he couldn't answer it now. He was terribly afraid of what he might hear…

"Why are you standing in the rain?"

Jeremiah's question brought him back to the present. "What?" he asked in confusion, then realized the skies had opened up.

"Are you all right?" Jeremiah asked, giving him a searching look.

"Yeah," he said roughly. "Just thinking."

"About the explosion?"

"Yes."

"Me, too. I wonder who did it."

He wondered, too.

Was this blast related to the last one? If so, what the hell did that mean? And what was coming next?

CHAPTER TWO

CAITLYN FLEW into San Francisco International Airport, landing just after noon on Thursday. She rented a car, then drove forty-five minutes through the city and over the Golden Gate Bridge, weaving her way through the Marin Headlands to the campus of Bolton College, a private university of about ten thousand students. Her mother had gone to Bolton and her mother before her.

Her two older brothers had followed in the steps of their father, grandfather, and great- grandfather. They'd gone to Stanford. They'd also gone into the family business, a business that she had never wanted to be a part of, even before the explosion. Carlson Industries encompassed a dozen companies, maybe more by now, and some of those companies didn't align with her view of the world. But they were profitable, and profit had driven the Carlson empire for a hundred years. Her great-grandfather had been the first to amass a fortune, and each generation since then had contributed. Now, her brothers were doing the same.

The family, of course, made a point of giving back with the Carlson Foundation that aided thousands of charities each year.

But was it enough? She wanted to believe they were balancing the scales, because it made it easier to go to Christmas dinner. But there was a part of her that still thought they could do better. Hopefully her brothers, Baxter and Spencer, would drive the company in the right direction.

As she neared the campus, her thoughts returned to the past, to the terrible March day ten years ago. She'd lost so much: her baby, her boyfriend, and her innocence.

No one had ever paid for her losses.

Now there had been another blast. *More victims. More damage. More pain.*

Was it a coincidence that it had happened in the same month as the last one? She didn't think so.

This wasn't the first explosion she'd investigated since she'd joined the bureau. She'd been looking for answers to what had happened to her in every bomb that had gone off since then. She'd driven her fellow agents crazy with her never-ending questions about the case. Pushing that button repeatedly had gotten her into trouble with the brass, including Rob Carpenter, her first boss. He'd been happy to see her move on to New Orleans after a year under his leadership.

Despite the change in location and the fact that she had other cases to work on, she'd still found time to search for answers, but she'd discovered nothing. It still amazed her that the brick wall she'd run into had never crumbled, not even a little.

After a second year of intense obsession, her boss had pulled her aside and told her she had to make a choice. She could either let the obsession consume her and stop her career before it had even started, or she could move on and make her mark on the world in other areas.

Shortly after that, Flynn had offered her a job on his task force, and she'd taken it. For the past two years, she'd deliberately avoided any cases tied to explosives. She had wanted to move on, but today her obsession had come back to find her.

As she turned off the highway and drove down a two-lane road toward the campus, her tension rose until she was gripping the wheel so tightly, there was no blood going into her fingers. She forced herself to breathe through the raw emotions. She could do this. She *would* do this, because she had to.

Moments later, she drove through the gates leading to the campus, which was set in a picturesque location of rolling hills, thick groves of trees, and ocean views.

When she got to the first parking lot, she saw a heavy presence of law enforcement. Most cars were being waved around and sent back out through the gates, but when she showed her badge, they allowed her into the lot.

After parking, she stepped out of the car and walked toward the auditorium. Everything was so familiar, from the admissions office to the language arts building where she'd worked on the campus newspaper, to the library where she'd spent hours reading and studying. Every step took her further into the past. She almost lost it when she saw the coffee cart where she and Quinn had picked up coffees just minutes before her entire life had been blown to pieces.

She paused, remembering their conversation that morning. She'd gone over it a million times in her head. Something had distracted Quinn. He'd been checking his phone. He'd decided not to go with her to the ribbon-cutting at the last minute, because his study group had changed the time of their meeting. It was a point that the police and the FBI had grilled him about relentlessly, but his answer had never changed, and his alibi had checked out.

She had never believed he'd set the bomb. He'd been with her the night before and every second of that morning. And she couldn't stomach the idea that he would have knowingly sent her into a building that he knew was going to blow up. But the police and her family hadn't been as convinced. They might not have thought he placed the bomb, but they'd believed he knew something about it, because of his ties to the LNF Army, an environmental activist group at Bolton. LNF stood for Leave No Footprint.

The group of eco-warriors had taken part in many protests, both on campus and off, some against her family's group of businesses as well as other companies in the Bay Area with a poor record on the environment. They'd also targeted political leaders. Most of their protests had been non-violent, but some members of the group had gotten into trouble for assault, vandalism, and trespassing.

While the FBI had interrogated many members of the group, no evidence had turned up directly linking anyone in the LNF to the bomb, including Quinn.

Two months after the explosion, Quinn had left school, and he'd left her. She'd found out from a contact in the dean's office that he'd completed his finals early. After that, there was no record of him. He had disappeared off the face of the earth. As soon as she'd joined the FBI, she'd used every tool she had to find him, but she had been unsuccessful, and that was disturbing.

Why had Quinn felt the need to vanish so completely? It was one thing to walk out on her, to break up, to be done with their relationship. *But what about the rest of his life? Where had he gone and why? Had his disappearance had something to do with the explosion?*

She drew in a breath and let it out, the memories churning her stomach. She didn't need to find Quinn; she needed to find the bomber. She pulled her jacket more closely around her, feeling a chill that went deep into her bones.

Forcing herself to move, she continued down the path, seeing three girls huddled together, arms around each other. One of them was crying. They were young but so much older than they'd been yesterday when their school had probably felt like a safe place, when their biggest problems had been midterms and what to wear to parties on the weekend. Now they would be changed forever.

Her steps slowed as she neared the auditorium, the scene feeling familiar. Not that she had any personal recollection from the blast. She'd been unconscious when they'd brought her out, but she'd studied the photos in the FBI file many times.

As she neared the scene, she saw a cluster of FBI agents. In the middle of that group was Rob Carpenter. Rob was a stocky man with short, dark hair, a square face and piercing brown eyes. He was in his late forties and was a single-minded, ambitiously determined agent. Sometimes, his eye for political capital impeded his investigations. But he was a smart man, and she hoped that his promotion to running the San Francisco office had lessened his hunger for power and that they could work together. She needed in on this investigation.

Rob met her gaze and broke away from the group. "Caitlyn. I'm sorry about the circumstances, but it's good to see you again. You got here fast."

"I caught the first flight."

"I'm not surprised. When I heard about the blast this morning, your face popped into my head, along with all those conversations we had about what happened before."

"What can you tell me about today?" she asked, wanting to focus on the present.

"The device was placed in the bushes outside the front door to the auditorium. It was set off just after eight o'clock. Five students and a teacher who were standing about ten feet from the entrance were injured; none appear to be critical."

"Anyone taking credit?"

"Not yet."

"Were there events scheduled in the auditorium today?"

"Yes. There was a climate symposium supposed to start at nine. I'm not sure if the device went off prematurely or if the bomb was meant to stop the event from happening at all."

Her nerves tightened. The tie to an environmental climate symposium was disturbing. "Who was supposed to speak?"

"Representatives from three companies: the Freeman Group, Alancor, and Lexitech, as well as student leaders from Bolton's environmental group who call themselves Green Citizens for Change."

"Lexitech is a subsidiary of Carlson Industries."

"I'm aware." He glanced down at notes on his phone. "Kevin Reilly was the speaker from Lexitech. We contacted him, but he did not take our call. His assistant let us know that he'd been in the car on his way to the school when he heard about the explosion. He immediately turned around and went home. Any further questions should be directed to their corporate counsel."

"Why would he want us to talk to Lexitech lawyers when he was a potential victim?" she asked.

"My question as well. Perhaps you can use your family connections to get more information."

"Of course. I don't know if you know this, but Kevin Reilly went to school here at the same time I did. He's probably shaken up, knowing he could have been in the building."

"It sounds like you're the person to talk to him."

"What about the environmental group? Any history of violence?"

"It doesn't look that way, but the investigation has just begun. The group is local, not tied to any national organizations. According to the dean, they have approximately a hundred members. The leader is a woman, Taylor Perkins. She has already done a preliminary interview. She appeared horrified and scared. Some of the injured students were part of her group."

"I'll need access to all the interviews and the list of attendees, if there is one."

"Of course." He gave her a sharp look. "I'm happy to have your help, Caitlyn, but I need you to work closely with my team at all times. Is that clear?"

"Yes. I wouldn't have it any other way."

He gave her a small smile of disbelief. "Right. You have a tendency to follow your instinct more than your orders."

"Which has helped me solve many cases. What can you tell me about the device itself?"

"Homemade, not particularly sophisticated, which is why it didn't cause a tremendous amount of damage. This could have been worse."

She'd hated hearing that comment during her recovery. For her, the explosion had been horrific, and for those who had died as bad as it could be. But she didn't need to call Rob out on his careless words.

"Caitlyn." Emi Sakato joined them with a smile. "It's good to see you again."

"You, too." Emi was a stunning woman of Japanese descent, who had been on the team in Miami when she'd worked there. "I didn't realize you were in San Francisco."

"Since last year."

"Emi will be your contact, Caitlyn," Rob interjected. "I'll leave her to catch you up. I need to get back to the office." He gave her one last warning look. "Don't make me regret allowing you into this investigation. I remember how obsessed you were five years ago. Stay focused on what happened today, not when you were a student here."

"How are you, Caitlyn?" Emi asked, as Rob left them alone. There was a concerned gleam in her brown eyes.

"I'm hanging in there," she admitted. "I've investigated dozens of bomb blasts, but not here, not where it happened. It feels surreal."

"Maybe we'll finally get you some justice."

"I hope so. I have a gut feeling this bomb is connected to the last one. The climate symposium is a red flag. Is there any security footage of the bomber?"

"No. The cameras in front of the auditorium and nearby

buildings were hacked, so we could not see who placed the bomb, nor the moment it exploded, but we're checking every other camera on campus and in the vicinity. The cyber team is also working on the hack to see if they can trace it."

"Eyewitnesses?"

"The students who were closest to the blast are in the hospital. We haven't been able to speak to them yet, but we've talked to many who came to the area immediately after the explosion. One woman told me that her sister was here at the time of the last explosion. Her name is Allison Sullivan."

She stiffened. "There was a Lauren Sullivan in the LNF Army. Allison is her sister?"

"That's what she said. Allison said she never thought it would happen again. Did you know Lauren?" Emi asked.

"I did. And when I reopened the case five years ago, she was my first call. Lauren was the reason my boyfriend wasn't with me at the event. Lauren had changed the time of their study group. She was his alibi."

Emi's eyes widened. "That's interesting. I remember you talking about the case when we worked together, but I'm a little hazy on the details. Was Lauren cooperative when you spoke to her five years ago?"

"No, but she never liked me much. Lauren had a crush on my boyfriend, Quinn Kelly. She saw me as a rival or the reason my boyfriend wasn't spending as much of his time with the group."

"The bureau cleared your boyfriend of any involvement, right?"

"They didn't clear him, but they didn't charge him."

"And then he disappeared? Did you ever find him?"

"No. Although, I haven't actually looked for him in a few years. I had to let go of my obsession. It was dragging me down."

"I heard you're working for Flynn MacKenzie now—lucky girl."

"I am lucky. Flynn is great and our task force is amazing. We get a lot of leeway that I never had before."

"Must be nice. Rob still has a tight grip on every investigation run through our office. He meant what he said earlier, Caitlyn. If you go off on your own or step out of bounds, he'll boot you off this case without a second thought."

"I understand. But we all have the same goal. I don't expect any problems. Can you text me Allison's information? I'd like to speak to her."

"Of course," Emi replied, as they exchanged numbers. "I'll be heading back to San Francisco now. What's your plan?"

"I'm going to stay here for a while, and then I'll come in."

"See you later."

As Emi left, Caitlyn turned her gaze to the destruction. The rubble, the smoke, the damage sent another wave of nausea through her. Somewhere in her mind, the horror of what she'd gone through still lived, still plagued her, still gnawed away at any sense of control she thought she had over her life, as if to remind her that whatever she had could be taken away at any moment.

But she didn't need the reminder. She could never trust in the future. She only had this moment, this day. That was it.

As she looked away from the building, she saw a gathering crowd of onlookers, mostly students with shocked expressions, which brought her back to Allison Sullivan. *Was it simply a coincidence that Lauren's younger sister had been near the scene of this explosion?* It had to be. She would have been a little kid at the time of the first bomb.

Among the group of students was someone who didn't quite fit in.

Her heart skipped a beat. The man was tall. He had on jeans and a dark-blue jacket, a baseball cap on his head and sunglasses, although there wasn't any sun. There was something about him…the way he stood, the power of his body. His head turned. It felt like he was looking right at her. Then he suddenly swiveled around and hurried away.

Had he seen her watching him?

It took her too many seconds to move. By the time she did, he'd vanished behind the science building.

She broke into a jog. When she got to the nearest parking lot, she saw a dark SUV shoot out of the lot. She was too far away to get a license plate. But there were cameras all around the school, and one of those would have his plate.

Had it been Quinn?

Her heart pounded out of her chest at that thought.

Why would Quinn come to this scene now? Had she been wrong about him all these years? Had he been involved back then? Was he involved now?

CHAPTER THREE

As CAITLYN WALKED BACK to the auditorium, her mind raced with a million thoughts. She needed to run that license plate, but Emi had already left, and Rob would see her chasing down Quinn as a conflict of interest. She jogged back across campus, not stopping until she got to her vehicle. Once inside, she called Lucas. "I need some help," she told him. "And I need to keep it unofficial for now."

"That was fast," he replied. "What can I do?"

She appreciated his willingness to help her without asking questions, but that's how her team operated, with complete trust in each other. "I need security camera footage from Bolton."

"At the time of the explosion?"

"No, in the last hour. I'm looking for a dark SUV exiting Lot C by the science building about seven minutes ago. The driver was male, thirties, wearing a baseball cap, blue jacket, and jeans."

"I'll be in touch."

As Lucas ended the call, her phone buzzed, and her mother's name flashed across the screen. It was the sixth time her mom had called since the morning, each voicemail growing more and more worried.

"Hello, Mom," she said, picking up the call.

"Finally," her mother replied, relief in her voice. "Have you heard? Or is that a dumb question?"

"I've heard. I'm at Bolton now."

"I suspected you would be. What does the FBI know?"

"Nothing yet. There was a climate symposium scheduled today, with Lexitech on the panel."

"Your father told me Kevin was supposed to speak. Thank God he wasn't there when the bomb went off. Do you think he was the target? Was this about Lexitech, about Carlson Industries?"

"I don't know, Mom. Maybe. What does Dad think?"

"He's been at the office all day. He has said little to me except not to worry."

"He always tells you that."

"He tries to protect me," her mother admitted. "What do you think, Caitlyn?"

"I don't know, but I will find out."

Her mother sighed. "I thought you were finally done with all that. I was hoping you had moved on."

"I had moved on, but this is too close to what happened before. I need to find out if there's a connection."

"Haven't you given up too much of your life already in pursuit of a justice you may never get?"

"I'm not giving up anything. I'm doing my job."

"A dangerous job. I can't bear the thought of you getting hurt again. Your father is worried, too. He's afraid you'll let your emotions cloud your judgment."

"Well, he's never had a lot of confidence in my abilities," she said dryly. In her family, it had always been about her two older brothers, at least for her dad. Baxter and Spencer had gotten on board with the family business right out of college, while she had always wanted something different. That had put a distance between them that only increased over the years.

"That's not true, Caitlyn. Your father is very proud of you."

She let her mother's lie go untouched. "I need to go, Mom."

"If you're at Bolton, you're close. Why don't you come here tonight? We can have dinner, and you know your room is always waiting for you."

"I don't know my plans yet."

"You have to eat. Why not eat here?"

"I will try. It depends on how the investigation goes."

"Dinner will be at seven thirty. I want you to make it. And, honey…"

"What?"

"Have you been in touch with Quinn?"

"No."

"I hope it stays that way. He wasn't good for you. The way he disappeared when you were hurt…well, it just made little sense."

"You don't have to worry."

"I hope not. You saw nothing but a halo around Quinn's head, but your father and I saw the devil inside him."

"I have to go, Mom."

"I'll see you at dinner."

She ended the call without bothering to confirm. Maybe she'd make it to dinner, maybe she wouldn't. Seeing her parents was not her priority at this moment.

Her phone buzzed once more. It was Lucas. "That was fast. Did you find anything?"

"Yes. The SUV is registered to Michael Wainscott."

His words surprised her. "Really?" She'd been expecting to hear Quinn's name. Maybe she'd been wrong.

"I only did a cursory search, but his address is 16 Pomegranate Lane, Dillon Beach, CA. He has no record, no parking tickets, nothing."

"Birthdate?"

"September 5th. He's thirty-five years old."

She frowned. Quinn had been born in October and was thirty-three. Maybe it hadn't been him. Maybe her imagination had seen what it wanted to see and not what was there.

"Do you need more?" Lucas asked.

"Not at the moment. I'll take it from here."

"All right. How's it going up there?"

"It's just starting."

"The investigation or the explosions?"

His question gave her pause. *Was this a one-and-done blast? Or was there more to come?*

"I wish I knew."

"Good luck."

"Thanks." As she set her phone down on the console, she debated her options. Dillon Beach was thirty minutes away. *Would it be a fool's errand? Would she be wasting valuable time chasing down a lead to a man who might have absolutely no connection to Quinn or to the blast?*

She remembered the way he'd looked at her, then hustled away from the crowd, speeding out of the lot. Even if he hadn't been Quinn, this man might be someone worth finding out more about.

———

Quinn walked into MacDuff's, a roadside Irish pub in Dillon Beach, just before one. It was a popular stopping point for tourists and bikers heading up the coast, and for the locals of the small coastal community. He particularly liked MacDuff's, because the fish and chips and shepherd's pie reminded him of his childhood. While he hadn't had lunch, his stomach was churning too much to consider food. Instead, he settled in at the bar and ordered a shot of Jameson, his favorite Irish whiskey, from Seamus, the sixty-something bartender, who in some small way also reminded him of his dad. Not that his father had gotten anywhere close to his sixties. But that wasn't unusual for the small town in Northern Ireland where he'd grown up.

His grandfather had been in the Irish Republican Army and then the Provisional IRA, where his father had joined the cause. When Quinn was ten, those in the Provisional IRA who refused to accept the peace process splintered off to form the Real IRA. His father had been fighting for that group for a year when he was killed.

His mom had taken him to the States shortly after his father's death. She'd been exhausted by the struggles, the bloodshed, and she hadn't wanted him to get sucked into it, although at eleven, he'd already been exposed to more violence than most kids.

California had felt like an entirely different world. They'd settled into a small apartment in Watsonville, near Monterey Bay, several hours south of where he lived now. His mom had given him the one small bedroom while she'd slept on the couch. They hadn't had a lot, but what they'd had was peace. There were no late nights or long days wondering if his father would come home. There were no gunshots, no sirens, no constant beat of rebellion in the neighborhood. He hadn't realized how anxious he'd been until they were on the other side of the world.

But he had missed Ireland, their cottage with the cozy fire, and the amazing views of the sea from the cliffs where he and his friends would play. He'd also missed the food, but thankfully, Seamus's pub gave him a little taste of that when he desperately needed it.

"Here you go." Seamus set down his shot. "You okay?"

"Fine," he said shortly, downing the shot. "I'll take another."

Seamus gave him a sharp look, then refilled his glass. "Must be a woman."

He threw down the second shot, relieved at the warmth that flooded through his ice-cold veins. "You don't know what you're talking about."

"I suspect I do."

"Hit me again."

Seamus hesitated. "I don't think so. It's the middle of the day and you don't drink like this. Why don't I get you a Guinness? Slow things down a bit."

"I can take my money elsewhere."

"You'll have to do that if you want another shot. What's wrong?"

He shook his head. "That's a much bigger question than I can answer."

"Is it?" Seamus gave him a knowing look. "I've poured too many shots to too many guys who look like you. I know what love gone wrong looks like. Who is she? That pretty brunette who works at the dive shop? She was eyeing you something fierce last time you were both here."

"Melanie? No," he said with a firm shake of his head. "We have never gone out."

"I bet she'd like to."

"Stop trying to matchmake."

"Well, someone should. You're not getting any younger. Beth was saying just the other day how we should find someone nice for you."

Seamus's wife was a sweetheart, but he didn't need her help. Nor did he particularly appreciate Seamus and Beth thinking about setting him up with someone. He'd clearly been in one place for too long. People thought they knew him. They believed they were his friends. But they knew nothing about him, not even his real name.

He would finish drinking at home. He pulled a twenty out of his wallet and set it on the bar. "I'll see you later."

"Hey, now, don't run off. You got problems? I'll listen."

"It's just been a long week."

"Well, it's almost the weekend. Hopefully, you can take some time off."

He didn't want time off. Work and the sea were the two things in his life that kept him going. He got to his feet.

"One word of advice?" Seamus asked.

"I'm sure it won't be one word," he said dryly.

"Tell her. Talk to her."

"You don't know what's going on, Seamus."

"Doesn't matter. Women see things differently than we do. Only way to bridge the gap is to talk. But you're not so good at that."

"Thanks for the drinks and the bad advice."

Seamus laughed. "It's not bad advice. It's just not what you want to do."

That was true. The last thing he wanted to do was talk—to anyone—but especially to her. "I'll see you around."

As he headed out to his car, he felt only marginally more relaxed from the two shots of whiskey. His thoughts were still racing. He'd put Caitlyn and Bolton out of his mind a long, long time ago. But now they were back. He didn't know what to make of the explosion today, but he had a terrible feeling about it. It felt like something was beginning again.

Starting the engine, he turned on the radio, blasting the music to drive out the stressful memories. But since he only needed four blocks to get home, it wasn't much of a distraction.

He lived off the highway, in a small two-bedroom house set in the redwoods. There wasn't much around his home except for trees, and that's the way he liked it. He pulled into the driveway and hopped out of the car. He grabbed the mail from his box and then put his key in the lock. As he opened the door and stepped into the living room, his heart came to a crashing halt.

For a second, he thought he was imagining her.

But she was too beautiful, too angry not to be real...

He'd spent the drive home trying to tell himself that he hadn't seen her, and she hadn't seen him. But looking at her haunting brown eyes, her beautiful face, he knew he'd been wrong.

CHAPTER FOUR

"CAITLYN." Her name slipped from his lips in shock. He blinked hard, still thinking she might be a whiskey-induced mirage. But she didn't disappear, and as she raised the gun in her hands, he was even more surprised. "What are you doing here? Why do you have a gun?"

"I'll ask the questions," she said in a sharp, bitter voice that wasn't at all familiar to him.

There was edginess and anger in her eyes, as well as dark shadows that he couldn't decipher. Her hair was pulled back in a ponytail, and she seemed thinner and fitter than when they were dating. In fact, everything about her was harder, tougher.

While she'd always been able to speak her mind with him, she'd never been one to give orders. In fact, most of the time, she'd been a peacemaker, a mediator, someone who wanted everyone to get along, for the world to be a good place, and for people to do the right thing. But that idealistic, kindhearted woman didn't seem to be in this room.

"Why were you at Bolton today?" she demanded.

"I heard about the explosion. Why do you have a gun on me, Caitlyn?"

"Because you were at the scene of an explosion. Because you're driving a car registered to Michael Wainscott, and because Quinn Kelly fell off the face of the earth ten years ago."

Each statement felt like a knife going into his heart. Behind the fury in her eyes and her voice, there was pain, and he was responsible for that.

"Answer the question, Quinn. Why were you at Bolton today?" she asked.

"I heard about the explosion on the news. I couldn't get it out of my mind. I was on my way to the store and then suddenly I was on the freeway headed south. I had to see what had happened. I didn't expect to see you there. In fact, I wasn't sure it was you. I thought I might have conjured you up from my memories."

"I had a similar feeling," she muttered, for the first time letting a small crack appear in her tough armor.

"Did you follow me?" He realized that she'd not only figured out his alias and where he lived, she'd also gotten into his house. He hadn't seen a car, but maybe he had been too distracted to notice. "Did I leave the door unlocked?"

"Your lock is worthless. I got inside in two seconds."

He shook his head in bemusement. "You know how to pick locks now? Is that a skill necessary to be a journalist?"

"I'm not a journalist."

"You're not? It was all you wanted to be." For the past decade, he'd imagined her writing for some paper or working in broadcast news. He'd deliberately avoided looking at bylines or the news in case he might see her name or her face. He'd only once looked her up online, and that was about a year after he'd left. He'd seen photos showing a happy, healed woman, and that had given him some peace. He'd never looked again.

She opened her jacket and motioned toward the badge at her hip. "I'm an FBI agent."

"Seriously? Why did you give up on being a reporter?" He

wasn't sure why that was the question that came out of his mouth when there were so many other things he needed to know, but it seemed...safer.

"I was a journalist for a few years, but I didn't want to just report on the bad things that were happening in the world. I wanted to stop them."

"I can't believe you went into the FBI. You hated guns. You refused to go hunting with your father and your brothers."

"I don't believe in hunting innocent animals. But I'm very capable of taking down a criminal. Don't think I won't use this, Quinn."

Her choice of words gave him pause. "Is that what you think I am—a criminal?"

"I honestly don't know. Why did you change your name? Or is there an actual Michael Wainscott who owns the car and this house?"

He debated how much he wanted to tell her—certainly not all of it. But he had to say something, and it wouldn't take her long to figure out he was Michael Wainscott. "I changed my name. I wanted a clean start."

"From me? The first bombing? What?"

Seamus's advice to be honest ran through his head. But he couldn't tell Caitlyn the truth; he could never tell her or anyone. "Everything. I wanted to be someone else."

"Why?"

"I had my reasons."

She gave him a look filled with both disappointment and disgust. "Let's not waste any more time. Were you involved in the explosion that almost killed me and that took the life of our baby? Is that why you had to start over as someone else?"

He had to swallow hard to get past the suddenly thick and painful knot in his throat. His gut clenched at the reminder of their unborn child, someone else he had never wanted to think about again. It had been a girl. That's all he'd known about her.

Caitlyn had miscarried after the blast. She'd been eleven weeks pregnant.

"Quinn! Answer me."

Her sharp tone brought him back to the present. "No," he said, meeting her gaze. "To both." As uncertainty flashed in her eyes, he added, "You don't believe me, do you? I saw the doubt in your eyes ten years ago. The same doubt that is there now. It never went away."

"Maybe it would have gone away, if you'd stayed. But you disappeared without a good-bye, an explanation, without anything. If you had nothing to do with the bomb, then why vanish two months later? I was barely out of the hospital. I was still rehabbing. Did you not think that I might need you?"

"You didn't need me. You didn't want me around you. We were barely speaking."

Something flickered in her eyes. "I was going through a lot."

"I know. And I wasn't helping." He took a much-needed breath. "Your father also asked me to stay away from you."

"No." She immediately shook her head. "That's a lie."

"It started with a polite request. That came about a week after the explosion. When I didn't agree, threats followed. As the FBI continued to pepper me with questions about my involvement in the LNF, your father told me that their focus on me would never change, not while I was involved with you. He was a powerful man with a lot of money, and he did not want me in your life."

"You're exaggerating. My dad couldn't influence the FBI."

Despite her words, he didn't believe she was as convinced as she was pretending to be.

"I'm not exaggerating," he said flatly. "You know who your father is, Caitlyn. Don't pretend he doesn't wield tremendous power."

"If he said anything at all, he was only trying to protect me. He wouldn't have destroyed you, not if you were innocent. He couldn't make anyone arrest you without proof. Did he have proof of your involvement?"

"How could he? I wasn't involved." He tossed his keys on the table, feeling the need to change things up. "You will not like my answers, Caitlyn. So, shoot me or put down the gun, your choice. I'm going to get a beer. Do you want one?"

He walked past her into the kitchen, not entirely convinced she wouldn't put a bullet in his back. She was not the girl he'd left crying in the garden, a broken shadow of herself. She wasn't even the girl he'd known before that, the one full of optimism and hope, who believed in the innate goodness of people. He didn't really know who she was now. He just knew that his heart was pounding out of his chest, and he hadn't felt this hyped up in, well…ten years.

When he entered the kitchen, he opened the fridge and took out two beers.

She came into the room a moment later, taking a chair at the small table. As his gaze ran over her once more, he couldn't help noting how professional and businesslike she looked now in her black slacks, white blouse, and gray leather jacket. There was stress in her eyes and a pallor to her skin, but she was still beautiful. He just couldn't help missing the ripped jeans and short shorts she'd once favored, the graphic T-shirts that had always hugged her breasts, and the sexy, thick waves of her long hair that she'd almost never worn up. But when she had, he'd loved pulling the band out of her hair and running his hands through the long, silky strands, trapping her face for his kiss.

He sucked in a breath. He missed a lot of other things, too, but he couldn't let himself go any further down the path of yesterday. He couldn't remember the taste of her lips, or the curve of her hips, the way she'd said his name in a breathy, wondrous voice…

His body hardened at that memory and he told himself to get a grip.

Forcing himself forward, he walked toward the table.

She'd put her gun down, but it was within easy reach. He set a beer in front of her and sat across from her, still feeling like the entire scene was surreal. He'd never thought he would see her again, and if he had imagined catching a fleeting glimpse of her somewhere, it had never been here in his kitchen.

She took a long swig of beer and then said, "Even if my father threatened you, why didn't you talk to me about what he said? Why didn't you tell me what was going on?"

"You were shattered, Caitlyn. You weren't talking about anything back then. You could barely get through the day. You didn't need more to deal with. And, frankly, it was difficult to look at you." He drank half the bottle of beer as he finished that sentence.

"I know my injuries were bad, but—"

"It wasn't your physical injuries; it was the look in your eyes. You were so sad, so angry, and you blamed me."

"I didn't blame you."

"Yes, you did," he said forcefully, holding her gaze. "Deep down, you were furious that I didn't know about the bomb, that I changed plans at the last minute, and that I wasn't with you when it happened."

"I never wanted you to be with me, to be hurt the way I was," she denied, giving a vehement shake of her head. "But I was sad and angry. I was devastated by the loss of our baby. I know I was barely pregnant, but she was inside me, and I felt a deep, maternal connection to her. I didn't know how to process the grief, and I was in pain in a lot of other ways. I had broken bones and torn muscles. And then I lost you. Why didn't you fight for me, Quinn? Was the baby the only thing holding us together?"

"No, of course not." He finished his beer with one long, painful swallow, wishing for a way out of this horrifically awkward conversation.

"Then why?" she demanded. "Just tell me what happened.

Your actions have puzzled me for a decade, and I deserve the truth. Let's start with that morning. You were acting weird at the coffee cart. Then your study group time suddenly changed. Lauren was texting you a lot. Were you hooking up with her? Is that why you bailed on me? I could feel you pulling away from me, but I didn't understand why. I didn't know if it was because of the baby, or if you were just over me."

His gut twisted at her words. He should say yes. It would be the easiest lie, but he couldn't bring himself to tell it, to hurt her more than he already had.

"That's too long of a pause for a no," she said bitterly.

"We weren't hooking up. Lauren just needed to change the time of our study group. She had a birthday party that afternoon. You know that."

"Then why were you so distracted?"

"I had a lot on my mind with the baby news."

"Was it just that? Or did you have some hunch that there might be trouble at the ribbon-cutting? I asked you that day if you thought the LNF would protest the opening, and you said no. You told me Donovan had promised that no one would be there. Either you were wrong, or you were lying, because I'm convinced someone from that group set the bomb."

"I wasn't lying. Donovan had assured me two weeks earlier that the environmental center would not be a target."

"Even though the group believed the center had been built with my family's dirty money?"

"Yes. They agreed that the center was a positive step toward providing a place for additional research. And Donovan knew that you were important to me."

"There's a good chance your best friend betrayed you."

His lips tightened. "You don't have to tell me that."

"What about afterward? We talked about the LNF being responsible. I do remember that. You were still uncertain."

"I didn't want to believe it, but I couldn't see any other choice."

"I know the FBI grilled you about everyone in the group."

"Yes. They asked questions about the other members, but frankly they were more interested in me, in my past, my father's activities in Ireland, whether I knew how to build a bomb," he said, unable to keep out the bitterness of those memories. "Never mind that I was eleven when I left Ireland. The agent in charge was convinced that I was the most likely suspect."

She frowned. "I didn't understand why they went down that road, either, because you were really young when you lived in Ireland."

"You read the file?"

"Many, many times," she admitted. "I've memorized every word."

"Then you must know better than I who the perpetrator was."

"The case was never solved."

"You don't have a theory?"

"Of course I do. I believe someone from the LNF put the bomb in the building, probably Donovan. Whether they meant to blow me up, I have no idea. I was there early. Maybe that was just a happy accident for the bomber." She paused. "What about you, Quinn? What's your theory?"

"I thought it could have been Donovan, too, or someone who went rogue, who was more interested in violence and disruption than protecting the environment. There were several of those people in the group. But that said, I also thought it could have been targeted to your family. It was not uncommon for your father to get threats because of actions by one of his companies. There's an entire neighborhood in Southern California suffering from a cancer cluster that can be traced back to a plant owned by Carlson Industries."

"There's no connection between that neighborhood and the Bolton explosion."

"It was an example."

"I don't need an example of what my family has done wrong. I'm very aware of the blemishes on the company record, but I'm also aware of the steps that have been taken to mitigate the damage."

"I hope that's true."

"It is true," she snapped. "My father has made many changes, and my brothers will do the same as they take over the company."

"Both Baxter and Spencer are still working for Carlson Industries?"

"Yes. Baxter is further up the ladder, but Spencer is taking on more responsibility each year."

"I remember when you were getting pressure to go into the business. Your father didn't like the idea of you becoming a journalist. What does he think of you being an FBI agent?"

"He's not thrilled, but it's not up to him what I do. Let's get back to the LNF Army. If it wasn't a group decision, who would have gone rogue? You knew them better than I did. Who was at the top of your list?"

He had known the members better than her. He'd joined the LNF when he was eighteen years old and a freshman at Bolton. His roommate, Donovan Byrne, had founded the group, and almost instantly, they both had thought they'd found their tribe. The group had been composed of young, passionate ecologists and environmentalists who wanted to protect the climate and change the world. As an ocean scientist, protecting the sea was his primary concern. And for the six years that he'd belonged to the LNF, the group had been good at raising awareness and sometimes successful in encouraging companies to improve their policies.

But it hadn't just been about the environment for him. After the death of his mother two years earlier, he'd been lost. He'd needed a cause to believe in, a group to belong to, because he'd been all alone in the world. The LNF had become his second family.

That changed when he'd met Caitlyn. She'd been covering a protest for the school newspaper, and they'd fallen hard and fast for each other. The more time he'd spent with her, the less time he'd spent with the group, which was probably why he'd missed how much it was changing, how radical it had become. By the time he realized that the LNF was not the group he'd once believed in, it was too late.

"Quinn?" she pressed.

"I don't know," he said, realizing she was waiting for an answer. "Were there any suspects besides me that the FBI liked?"

"Donovan was interviewed many times, as was Hank Merchant, who was second in command. Vitaly Loucks, Lauren Sullivan, and Vinnie Caputo got some interest, as well as Gary Keniston, who had had several physical altercations during previous protests. In the end, there wasn't enough evidence to move forward on anyone. But there may be new evidence with today's explosion."

"You think they're connected?"

"Yes. The location, the type of explosion, and the climate symposium organized by eco-activists that was supposed to take place in the auditorium lead me to that conclusion." She paused. "Did you know that Lauren's sister, Allison, was a witness to the explosion and a member of the Green Citizens Group, which organized the symposium?"

His pulse jumped at that piece of information. "No. Allison was a little kid when we were in college."

"She's twenty-one now. She gave a statement to the FBI, but I need to follow up with her."

"That's strange. Or maybe it's not. She might have wanted to go to Bolton because Lauren went there, and she could be involved in an environmental group like Lauren was. Lauren was always passionate about saving the environment."

"Among other things," Caitlyn said with irritation.

"I already told you nothing was going on between us."

"She still had a huge thing for you."

"What did your FBI file have to say about her?"

"That everything she said checked out. But if anyone had had a motivation to hurt me, it was Lauren. Not only did she have a crush on you, she resented me for keeping you too busy for the group."

"She wouldn't have set a bomb, Caitlyn. She was an activist, but she was also a student. She spent hours studying. She had to get As. Her grades came before anything else."

"Of course you would defend her."

"I'm not defending her; I just don't believe she was involved."

"And yet her name comes up again today."

"Why aren't you talking to her then?"

"Because I saw you at Bolton, and I had to know why you were there."

"It really was just curiosity."

"It's difficult to believe anything you say after the way you disappeared, changed your name, and started over. Those aren't the actions of someone who is completely innocent."

"Maybe they're just the actions of someone who needed to lock the past away in order to move forward."

She gave him a hard look. "There's something missing from your story, Quinn, and I will find it."

He believed her, which meant he needed to get her out of his house and out of his life as soon as possible. "Are we done?"

"We are not even close to being done."

"What do you want from me? I have no information I can give you that will help you find out who set today's bomb or the last one. I have seen no one in ten years. I didn't just cut ties with you—I cut ties with every single person in my life."

"That might be true, but you could probably still be helpful, especially with one individual."

He didn't like the sound of that. "What does that mean?"

"The one person I can link to both blasts is Lauren. I spoke to her five years ago, when I first joined the FBI. She was not helpful at all. She gave me one-word answers and referred me to her lawyer. She would be different with you. She would talk to you about the past, and she might provide more information about her sister's environmental group."

"I seriously doubt that Lauren would want to talk to me."

"Oh, she'll talk to you. She'll be very curious if you show up at her door and will want to hear what you have to say."

"Well, I'm not interested. You want to talk to her, talk to her. I don't need to be involved in this. I have my own work."

"Which is what? I know you're in some kind of science role. I saw the research papers on your desk in the living room."

"I'm a scientific diver. I provide data to a research institute."

"How did you get that job? You changed your name, so you wouldn't have your educational credentials. Who hired you?"

"Someone who knew me at Bolton and was willing to be the conduit between me and the institute."

"Who was that?"

"You have a lot of questions."

"I'm just getting started. Even if you don't tell me, I can figure it out. I have your name now."

Which meant his career was probably over. "Fine. I work at the Oceanic Institute. I was hired by Jeremiah Cooper, who was a TA at Bolton when I was getting my master's. He knew my credentials and could appreciate the fact that I wanted no connection to the LNF, who had been branded as eco-terrorists. Jeremiah gave me a chance to do what I always wanted to do, and I'm grateful to him for that. I hope you won't punish him because of me."

"I'm not surprised you're a diver." Her gaze filled with more shadows. "The sea was your first love."

"And a constant," he said. "Every time my life spun around the ocean was there. It didn't change. It steadied me. It still does."

"I wish I had something that always steadied me," she said, revealing probably more than she wanted to. She picked up her gun. "This helps a little."

"Does it?"

"Yes. I'm in control. I have power."

"That gun wouldn't have prevented that bomb from going off."

"No, but it can prevent other bad things from happening. And, perhaps, one day it will help me get justice."

"Is that what you want—justice?" He rested his arms on the table, giving her a long, thoughtful look. "Or do you want revenge?"

She didn't flinch under his gaze, a defiant pride in her eyes. "I want both."

"What if you had to choose between one or the other? Which would you take?"

"I won't have to choose. I'll get both. I'm determined to do that, if it's the last thing I do."

"That's the problem, isn't it? It could be the last thing you do. You're going down a dangerous road."

"I am not afraid of danger, Quinn, not anymore. I am not the girl you once knew. I don't jump at spiders; I smash them. I don't run away from trouble; I run toward it."

He had to admit he was both impressed and disturbed by her words. "You're not invincible. Being an FBI agent and carrying a gun doesn't mean you can't be taken down."

"I am very good at what I do, Quinn. I can handle myself. I can handle you."

"What if I can't handle you? What if I want you to leave right now? What would you say?"

"That you've gotten to do what you wanted for the last ten years. Now, I get what I want. I need your help with Lauren, and you owe me."

A turbulent mix of emotions passed between them as their gazes clung together.

Love, anguish, doubt—the bad times—the good times: it was all there.

He saw images from their past: the first time they'd met, the instant attraction, the explosive chemistry, the overwhelming desire to be with each other when so many people would have preferred they stay apart.

He saw that last day of darkness and pain. He had gone to her house, unsure of what he wanted to do. He loved her, but they couldn't seem to connect anymore. Instead of making her happy, he made her angry and sad. Caitlyn had been in the backyard, supposedly reading, but when he'd seen her on the patio chair, he'd realized she was crying, and it wasn't just small sobs coming from her mouth, but deep, anguished, ripping cries of despair.

For two months he had tried to comfort her, to be there for her, but she kept pushing him away. Seeing her so distraught, he knew deep in his gut that leaving was the best option. He was tied to her pain. Maybe if he wasn't there to remind her, she could heal. Not that his reasons had been completely altruistic. There had been another motivation that made disappearing a good idea.

He had not seen her again—until now.

"Well?" she prodded.

"What do you want me to do?"

"Talk to Lauren about the past and about today."

"Why would she tell me anything?"

"Because you're you."

He frowned. "Like I said, it's been a long time, and there was nothing between us."

"All I know for sure is that she won't tell me anything. Maybe it's a long shot, but I have to take it. Her sister being on campus today, in the same kind of group, is too coincidental. If Lauren tells us one thing, it could all start to unravel from there."

"Now I see a hint of the optimist you used to be," he said dryly.

"Lauren lives in San Francisco. We can be there in less than an hour."

"We're just going to show up at her door?"

"Yes."

He sighed. "Do you really want to spend more time together, Caitlyn?"

"This isn't personal, Quinn. I'm not trying to spend time with you or get you back. I don't want you back. And, clearly, you were done with me a long time ago. But you and I both lost someone ten years ago. Maybe she didn't matter as much to you—"

"She did matter." He cut her off with a pointed glare. "And I have not for one second ever forgotten about her."

Caitlyn appeared taken aback by his words. "Well, how would I know that? We never talked about her, about our loss."

"You couldn't talk about it."

"You left before I was ready to discuss it. If you don't want to help me, then think of it as helping her."

"I wish we'd given her a name," he said.

Caitlyn paled at his words. "I wish we had, too." She cleared her throat. "So, what's it going to be, Quinn? Are you going to help me?"

CHAPTER FIVE

Caitlyn waited impatiently for Quinn's answer, trying not to think about what he'd just said about their baby, about wishing she'd had a name. She'd actually given their child a name, but she wasn't going to share that with him. He didn't deserve it, and she didn't trust him. She didn't know who he was anymore. She wasn't sure she'd ever known him the way she thought she had. But that didn't matter now.

She hadn't intended to ask him for help when she'd tracked him down, but it had become clear during their conversation that using Quinn might open up new leads. She'd already tried to get to the truth and had been unsuccessful. She didn't want to go down the same path. She had to try something new.

Quinn wanted her to believe that he'd had nothing to do with the bomb, that he had no knowledge of the perpetrator. He could prove that to her by cooperating.

Would he agree to help?

She could see the conflict in his deep-blue eyes. His eyes had always changed with his emotions: sometimes as dark as the sea he loved so much, sometimes light with happiness and joy. Although, she'd seen more of the dark than the light.

Actually, that wasn't completely true. For a long time, there had been light. It was only toward the end, when it had felt like everything changed, that the darkness had settled in.

The shadows in his gaze now were thick and difficult to penetrate. She couldn't read him. There was anger, pain, uncertainty, and secrets. She didn't completely buy his explanation for why he'd disappeared. There was something he wasn't telling her, and she wanted to know what that something was.

She had always been impatient with the unknown. When she sought answers, she wanted to get them right away. It had been that thirst that had driven her toward becoming a journalist. Some of that drive had also come from growing up in a family where her father made rules and statements that he never cared to explain.

She frowned as she thought about her dad. *Had he threatened and harassed Quinn into leaving?* It wasn't outside the realm of possibility. If Quinn had been the man she'd thought he was, he would have fought back. That man wouldn't have let her dad run him off. *So, was it a lie? Was there another reason for his abrupt disappearance from her life?*

She shouldn't care anymore. She'd put Quinn behind her a long time ago.

But sitting across from him made it impossible to put him back in the box she'd locked him away in. Following him had probably been a bad idea, but hopefully there would be an upside.

She just had to stay focused. That wouldn't be easy. He'd grown more ruggedly attractive over the years. His brown hair was longer but still thick and wavy. Ridiculously long black lashes framed his blue eyes. And his mouth… Her heart sped up as her gaze moved to his full, sexy lips.

God, she'd loved his mouth. *How many hours had she spent exploring it? How many times had he driven her crazy, running his mouth all over her body? And how many times had she done the same thing to him?*

"What the hell are you thinking?" he suddenly demanded.

She started, realizing she'd lost herself in memories she'd tried desperately to forget. "Nothing. Answer the question."

"Do you even remember the question?" he challenged.

She met his gaze, a little shaken by the fire she saw there now, the same fire that had burned so hot between them. She reminded herself that he'd put that fire out a long time ago. She would not restart it.

"The question is, will you help me talk to Lauren?" *Thank God, she actually had remembered the question.* "Think of it as an opportunity to prove that you want the truth as much as I do. That you don't want this latest explosion to go unsolved, too. We don't know if the bomb today was a one-off. There could be another explosion tomorrow. More people could be hurt. More people could die."

His chest rose as he blew out a breath. "All right. I'll talk to Lauren, even though I think it's a bad idea."

"Which part? Talking to Lauren or doing it with me?"

"All of it," he said sharply, as he got to his feet. "Let's go. The sooner we do this, the sooner we're done."

"Exactly." She stood up and took her gun off the table, then followed him into the living room. "I'll drive, so you don't change your mind."

"Where is your car? I didn't see it out front."

"It's around the corner. I wasn't sure who Michael Wainscott was when I first arrived. But as soon as I came inside, I knew you and Michael were the same person. I saw the photo of your parents on the table and the ocean artwork was also a giveaway."

"You're probably one of the few people who would recognize that photo."

She probably was. After his mother died, he'd kept very few

mementos from his life. "I wonder how many times you're going to start over," she murmured.

"I can't predict that."

"I sometimes feel like my life is divided into two parts. The part before the bomb and the part after. It's like I'm two people now."

There was understanding in his gaze. "I know what that feels like."

"How many people are you?"

"Four and counting. The kid in Ireland who didn't understand the violence around him, the California teenager embracing a new life only to end up completely alone, the young man who went to Bolton, who found a passion, a career, and a woman he loved more than anything. And the guy I am now, living under another name."

Her gut twisted at his words. "And who did you become as Michael Wainscott?"

"A man who does his job and doesn't get close to anyone."

"Why not? Why are you still hiding after all these years?"

"That's too long of a story, Caitlyn. And this isn't about me, is it?"

She realized she was getting distracted, and that annoyed her. She'd thought she was good at compartmentalizing, but she wasn't as good as she thought she was. "No, it's not about you. It's about our baby, getting her justice. That's it."

Caitlyn's compact sedan was way too small. Quinn could smell the scent of her perfume, a mix of florals that took him back in time. A lot about her had changed, but not that. What also hadn't changed was how his body reacted to hers. The smoking-hot look she'd given him in the kitchen had taken his breath away.

He'd never expected to see her gaze move across his face and down his body in that way.

She still wanted him!

It stunned him to think that might be true.

Not that she would act on that attraction. Caitlyn hated his guts now. Her brain was not in line with her body.

Even if she was interested, he wasn't. He couldn't get close to her again. It would be stupid and dangerous. He needed to stay in the life he'd built away from her.

But how would that be possible now that she was back in it?

He told himself he was helping her because he owed her, because he owed their baby. And that was a part of it, but it wasn't all of it. It wasn't just about duty; it was also about love, the love that had once bound them together in the deepest possible way.

He sometimes ached with the loss of that connection. He'd tried to put other women into that void, but no one had stuck.

He wondered who had made their way into Caitlyn's life. There wasn't a ring on her finger, but that might mean nothing. He wondered if she'd told anyone else at the FBI that she'd found him. He still couldn't believe she'd become an agent. He never would have imagined her taking that path.

"How did you get into the FBI?" he asked, breaking the taut silence between them. "How did you go from wanting to be a reporter to wanting to be an agent?"

"I went into journalism for a while. I worked on papers in San Francisco and then in DC. But it wasn't the career I'd imagined. I didn't feel like I was making a difference reporting on crimes that had already happened. I wanted to stop them from happening. When I was in DC, an FBI agent who knew about my family connections asked me to help him gain access to a suspect. I did more than that; I helped him break the case wide open. The agent liked my skills and my connections and suggested I consider changing jobs. The one thing my family name gave me was the power to move in circles that others can't. Here I am."

"What about the danger?"

"I'm well-trained to handle the danger, and I've discovered that I'm quite good at putting myself into situations and accessing information."

"Then why do you need me?" he said dryly.

"Because the people I need to access don't like me. And it wasn't just because they were jealous. Some didn't like me because of who I was. They thought you were sleeping with the enemy."

"It wasn't fair to tar you with your father's reputation."

"It wasn't just that they didn't like my family—they didn't like you with me. It felt like a betrayal to them. The more we were together, the less time you spent with the group. It's like I broke up the band."

"Well, that didn't matter to me. And if anyone broke up the band, it was me. I wanted to be with you."

"Do you ever regret making that choice? Were you ever sorry that we met, that we got together?"

"No. What about you? Were you ever sorry?"

She looked straight ahead at the road, then said, "Yes."

Her answer stabbed him in the heart.

They said nothing else for another fifteen minutes. When they made their way over the Golden Gate Bridge, he realized he couldn't let the silence continue. He needed more information before he spoke to Lauren. "What can you tell me about Lauren?" he asked. "You said you talked to her five years ago. I assume you know more about her life than I do. Is she married? Does she have kids? Does she work?"

"Lauren was married to Vinnie Caputo for seven years. They divorced a year ago. She's currently employed as a teacher at West Bay Community College. I believe she teaches ocean sciences. She's still your kindred spirit."

He let that bitter comment pass, more surprised by the fact that Lauren had married Vinnie. "I know she and Vinnie were dating that last year, but they always seemed to be fighting. I can't believe they got married."

"When I spoke to her five years ago, they were married and living in a nice house in St. Francis Wood. Now, she's in a flat in the Sunset neighborhood, and Vinnie has a condo in North Beach. He works in marketing for Global Eco Solutions. He has been there for six years."

"Marketing is a good fit for Vinnie. He always knew how to spin."

"Wasn't he the one who came up with slogans for LNF campaigns?"

"Yes. He had a talent for turning a complicated premise into a sound bite. I never thought he actually cared all that much about the cause, but rather was padding his resume. I might have been wrong since it sounds like he's working for an environmental company."

"Neither one seems to have been involved in any activism in the last several years, at least nothing that was documented. Today, you need to concentrate on getting Lauren to talk not only about the past but also about Allison's group at Bolton." She paused, giving him a worried look. "I should come in with you."

"If you do, Lauren will not say a word. Isn't that why I'm coming with you?"

"Okay, but you can't let her put you off. You have to challenge whatever she says, dig for details."

"I'm aware of the stakes, Caitlyn. You're going to have to trust me."

"That's not possible." She turned down Lauren's street. "This is the block. It's 426A."

"Looks like that green building. Park around the corner. I'll walk back."

She did as he suggested, squeezing the car into a tight spot.

"Quinn," she said, as he put his hand on the door.

"What?"

She gave him a long look. "Come back with something."

"I'll do my best." He got out of the car and walked down the sidewalk.

He didn't want to disappoint Caitlyn. She'd been waiting a long time for a break in the case, but he wasn't that hopeful. He had no idea how Lauren would react to seeing him. She might have liked him at one point, but the last time they'd seen each other had not ended well. He probably should have told Caitlyn that. On the other hand, she would have just thought he was trying to get out of helping her.

He had to admit he was tempted to keep on walking, to find a cab, and get as far away from her and his past as he could. But he couldn't run again. He'd thought he'd found the truth a long time ago. He'd believed that the danger for Caitlyn and everyone else was over.

Today's bomb had made him wonder if he'd been wrong. That's also why he'd agreed to help Caitlyn. It wasn't just about getting justice. He needed to know if he'd made a horrific mistake.

CHAPTER SIX

QUINN STEPPED up to Lauren's door and rang the bell before he could change his mind. When Lauren appeared on the threshold, he could instantly see the changes ten years had brought. She had always been thin, but she looked almost skeletal now, wearing jeans that probably should have been tight but hung loosely on her frame, and a green striped sweater that seemed a size too big. Her dark-brown hair was cut short and straight. Her face was pale and there were dark shadows under her eyes. She didn't look particularly well or happy. While Caitlyn hadn't aged a day, Lauren appeared closer to forty than thirty-one.

"Is it really you?" Lauren murmured, shock in her gaze. "Quinn Kelly?"

"It's me."

"I thought you were dead."

"Why would I be dead?"

"Because of what you did, Quinn. You should go." She tried to close the door, but he stuck his foot out.

"Not so fast. What do you think I did?" he challenged.

"I don't want to talk to you. Go away."

"I'm not going anywhere," he said, pushing his way into her apartment.

Lauren backed up, grabbing her phone from the coffee table in front of her couch, giving him a wary look. "I can call 911."

"Why would you need to do that? I just want to talk to you."

"About what?"

"Let's start with why you thought I was dead."

"Everyone thought that. No one could find you. You didn't even come to Donovan's funeral, and he was one of your best friends. Vinnie and some other guys thought you killed yourself over what happened to Caitlyn."

It shocked him that that was the explanation his old friends had come up with, although he supposed it was as good as any. "I just needed to start over."

"Why?" she asked, echoing the same question Caitlyn had asked earlier.

"Because I did."

"That's not an answer."

"I thought that someone in the LNF was responsible for the bomb, and I was the reason Caitlyn was hurt."

"No one ever proved that."

"I know. But I couldn't shake the feeling that the person was someone I knew. That thought wrecked me. The LNF was filled with my friends. They were my family. If anyone in the group was responsible for hurting Caitlyn and killing innocent people…well, I couldn't stand it. I needed to get away from Bolton and from everyone in that life."

"I suppose that makes sense," she said slowly. "Caitlyn came to see me several years ago. She's an FBI agent now. Did you know that?"

"I heard something about it."

"She reopened the file on the explosion. She's still searching for answers."

"Why did she come to you?"

"Because she doesn't like me. I'm the reason you weren't with her that day. But I won't apologize for that," she said, a defiant glint in her eyes. "I saved your life."

"You might have. What did you tell Caitlyn?"

"The same things I told the FBI when it happened. I changed the time of our study group because I had my roommate's birthday party that night. Caitlyn seemed to think I knew something else, but I didn't. Vinnie was angry that I spoke to her at all. He didn't like that she was digging into our lives. When she tried to talk to him, he said he had nothing to say and she could speak to his lawyer, but his lawyer never heard from her."

"It surprised me to hear you'd married Vinnie Caputo."

"Well, that wasn't the greatest idea. We had a few good years. Now we're divorced. He was cheating on me."

"Sorry."

"Why are you here, Quinn?"

"I heard about the blast at Bolton today, and I went to the campus to see what had happened."

"I didn't realize you lived in the area. You didn't go far, did you?"

He ignored her question. "When I was there, I heard one of the FBI agents talking to a female student. She said she was your sister, Allison. I couldn't believe it. When I met her years ago, she was a little kid."

"Alli is a senior at Bolton. She called me this morning. She was hysterical. Luckily, she wasn't hurt." Lauren shook her head. "I couldn't believe it had happened again. What are the odds?"

"Fairly long."

"I felt like I had PTSD when I heard about it. Suddenly, I could remember the exact sound of the blast ten years ago. It knocked us both off our feet. Remember? It was deafening."

"I remember."

"I was stunned for several minutes. But you—you immediately took off running. You knew before I did what had happened. When I got to the scene, you were fighting with the first responders. You wanted to get inside to find Caitlyn, but the building was on fire."

His mouth tightened as her words took him back again. "That was an awful moment."

"Caitlyn looked bad when they brought her out. I didn't know if she was alive."

"Neither did I."

"I tried to comfort you after the ambulance left, but you pushed me away. I couldn't blame you. You were in shock. You were angry. You were especially furious with me. You could never look at me after that. The last time we spoke, you accused me of knowing about the blast in advance. You suggested that I changed the time of our study session so you wouldn't be with Caitlyn. You threw out a lot of accusations, Quinn." Her voice hardened. "I couldn't believe that you would think those things of me."

"I was trying to find answers. I'm sorry."

"Are you?" She tilted her head, giving him a speculative look. "Why are you here now? Do you think I had something to do with this bomb, too? Because that's ludicrous. My sister goes to Bolton. She could have been killed."

"I don't think you had something to do with it," he said, realizing he was about to lose her cooperation. "When I heard your sister say her name, I thought of you, and I felt like I needed to talk to you about it. You're one of the few people who shared that experience with me."

Her gaze softened. "We do have that horrible moment in common. How did you find me? Did you ask Allison?"

"No. She was busy with the FBI. I looked you up on the internet."

"I guess nothing is private these days."

"Allison said she's involved with an environmental group."

"The Green Citizens. They're nowhere near as organized or

as passionate as we were. They make up flyers and put them up around polluting companies. They try to organize events to hold companies accountable, or at least make them more aware. They were supposed to have an event today in the auditorium, which I guess is where the bomb was located. I can't believe my sister had to live through the same thing I did. I never thought it would happen again."

"It's almost ten years to the day. Seems very coincidental. Is it possible that someone from the LNF is helping the Green Citizens?"

"I don't think so. The LNF disbanded years ago."

"And you haven't heard of any former members from our group still out there protesting?"

"I have not." She let out a sigh. "I have seen no one from the old group since I divorced Vinnie a year ago, and our so-called friends sided with him."

"Which friends were those?"

"Wyatt Pederson, Hank Merchant, and Vitaly Loucks. Sometimes Wyatt's brother, Justin."

"What are they all up to now?"

"Wyatt owns a bar in the Marina. His dad bought it for him, but he's managing it. Hank runs a gym called Evolve Fitness in Pacifica. Vitaly works for a clean energy company. Justin is an environmental lawyer."

"So, Vitaly and Justin stayed in the environment space, and Vinnie, too, right?"

"Yes, but he's a marketing guy." She paused. "Wyatt asked me about you the last time I saw him. I don't know what brought you to his mind, but it was weird to hear your name mentioned after so many years."

"What did he want to know?"

"If I'd ever heard from you, if I really thought you were dead."

"Did you think that?"

"Honestly, yes. I thought you were messed up, Quinn, and that's why you left Bolton. I even wondered if you and Donovan had made some sort of suicide pact."

"I heard Donovan fell while hiking."

"That's what the authorities said, but he was a damn good mountain climber."

"It seemed odd to me, too. Although, I wondered if he'd had some attack of conscience and just let himself fall."

She shrugged. "We'll never know."

"So, why did Wyatt bring me up?"

"He said he sometimes thought of you. He could never forget the look on your face when the firefighters brought Caitlyn out of the building. Wyatt said he'd never seen anyone look so shattered. He told me he never really got a chance to talk to you after that. And then you were gone."

Her words made little sense. "I didn't know Wyatt was at the bomb site that morning. I don't think I ever knew that."

She shrugged. "Lots of people were there, Quinn. You just couldn't see anyone but Caitlyn. Anyway, I haven't seen Wyatt since the divorce. Ditto for Hank. I ran into Vitaly a few weeks ago when I was shopping. He was polite, but he wasn't interested in chatting." She paused. "I shouldn't have been surprised when those guys dumped me after the divorce. The LNF was always about the men. They let the women in, but it was a brotherhood at the top, and you were part of that, Quinn. In fact, you were once as powerful in the group as Donovan Byrne. Then you met Caitlyn, and your passion turned to something—someone—else." She gave him a pointed look. "That's when the LNF changed. Donovan no longer had your voice in his ear; he was listening to Hank and Vitaly, Wyatt, and Vinnie, and let's not forget Gary Keniston. He brought a militancy with him that Hank and Vitaly really liked. Donovan leaned that way, too."

She was right. The group had changed when he'd met Caitlyn and started spending less time with them. They'd become more radicalized, more interested in anarchy and destruction versus reason and peaceful protests. Gary Keniston had been a big part of that, and Gary would have been at the top of his list for the bomb blast, but he'd been out of town that day at a family wedding. His alibi had been solid. Not that that didn't mean he hadn't had some knowledge or even instigated the event.

"Do you know what happened to Gary?" he asked.

"I don't. I never saw him after we all graduated. I think Vinnie might have run into him once at Hank's gym. But that's it for who we hung out with. Do you want coffee? Maybe a drink?"

"No, thanks."

"Why didn't you come to Donovan's funeral?" she asked. "He was one of your best friends."

"I didn't want to see everyone again. My emotions were too raw."

"Was that the real reason, or did you think that Donovan was responsible for the bomb? He hated Carlson Industries. And he hated that you were dating Carlson's daughter."

"Caitlyn wasn't responsible for her family."

"She didn't speak out against them."

"It's not easy to call out your family."

"You always made excuses for her."

"Do you think Donovan set the bomb?" he challenged.

She hesitated. "I would never say this to anyone else, but there's a part of me that thought he might have done it. He knew how to make things, and he was also working on some big new plan."

"What are you talking about? I never heard anything about a new plan."

"Hank told Vinnie about it at Donovan's birthday party a few days before the bombing. He said Donovan wanted to change things up, and Hank agreed that it was necessary. Hank said people in the group were going to have to get on board or get the hell out. It was time to pick a side and commit. Vinnie knew who he was talking about—you."

His stomach twisted at her words. "What was the plan?"

"No idea. After the bomb went off, Vinnie and some of the guys speculated that maybe it was part of Donovan's new plan, but Donovan wasn't talking to anyone, and Hank suddenly had nothing to say, either. The FBI were all over both of them, just like they were all over you. No one wanted to get in the middle of that."

"I remember," he said tightly. He'd tried to speak to Donovan, but his best friend had told him he had nothing to say and they shouldn't be seen talking to each other.

"You should have been at that party, Quinn. It was Donovan's birthday, but you didn't make it. I know that hurt Donovan."

"Caitlyn was sick."

"You picked her over Donovan. You abandoned the group, Quinn."

"I didn't abandon anyone. I had other priorities. We didn't take a blood oath to do everything together. It was an extracurricular group."

She gave him a disbelieving look. "It was far more than that, and you know it. We were a family."

"Families don't do everything together."

"This one did. When you veered away, Quinn, the army part of the LNF took on more meaning. People wanted to be soldiers. They wanted to fight. Donovan was right in the middle of that. He was losing faith that anything could be accomplished with peaceful protest. He thought there had to be enormous disruption, maybe even violent disruption, and he had followers who believed the same thing."

"I didn't see that."

"You were blind." She cleared her throat. "But Donovan is dead, and the LNF died with him. Even if he had something to do with the last bomb, he certainly wasn't responsible for what happened today. I can't imagine it was anyone in our group."

"It's still strange that the target of this bomb also had to do with climate change and an environmental group."

"Maybe it was a copycat. Allison knew about the previous explosion, and she said the group had talked about the LNF. Maybe someone wanted to make their own statement. Hopefully, the FBI will do a better job of solving this explosion than they did the last one. Are you sure I can't get you a drink?"

"No. I should go."

"Not yet. You haven't told me anything about yourself, Quinn. Where have you been all this time? What do you do for work?"

He hesitated, but what was the point of lying now? His cover was blown. "I work as a research diver for the Oceanic Institute."

A smile parted her lips. "That's perfect. You always loved being in the water. I'm surprised I haven't run into you before. I teach ocean sciences at a community college. We've actually had speakers from the Oceanic Institute in the classroom. Who do you work with there?"

"I work with a dive team. I doubt you'd know them."

"I never understood your love of diving. I did it once and it was so claustrophobic."

"It doesn't feel that way to me. Being underwater makes me feel free."

"I'm sure it does." She licked her lips. "Are you going to reach out to Caitlyn? She has to be investigating this new explosion."

"I'm not sure."

"You should stay away from her."

"Why?"

"Because she was never right for you. She took you away from your life."

"She didn't take me away from anything. I wanted to be with her."

"You were obsessed with her. You gave up your friends for her. She asked too much of you."

"That's not true. I know you never liked her, Lauren, but you didn't know her the way I did."

"I suppose. But in the end, you left her. Why did you?"

He shook his head. "That's between us. Do you have Wyatt or Hank's number—maybe Justin's too?"

"I have all their numbers. But they won't want to talk to you. And I'm not sure I should give out their contact information."

"Do you think they have something to hide?"

"No."

"Then what's the problem?"

She thought for a moment, then gave him a smile. "You know what? There is no problem, and I don't know why I would think about protecting them for one minute. It's not like they give a shit about me. Do you want the information for Vinnie and Vitaly, too?"

"That would be helpful." He gave her his number, and she texted back the contact information.

"I wouldn't expect anyone to throw out the welcome mat, Quinn. There was a lot of talk about you after Donovan's funeral. They couldn't believe you didn't show up for your friend's memorial service."

"People miss funerals."

"Best friends don't. Family doesn't. You don't seem to get that, Quinn. We were a family, and you turned on us. You didn't just ask me pointed questions, you asked everyone. Your suspicions were like a contagion of distrust. You were the reason we all started questioning each other, wondering if it was possible one of us was a murderer. It's a hell of an accusation to come from someone within your family."

"I spent more time in interrogation rooms than all of you

combined," he countered. "I'm fairly certain every single member in our so-called family said my name in their interview. I heard a lot of stories about me—that Caitlyn had cheated on me, and I wanted to make her pay, that I was angry with her father because he was trying to break us up, that I was using her to get inside information on Carlson Industries, and I set the bomb because she'd found out about it and was going to tell everyone. Those are just a few of the lies that were spread about me."

"I didn't realize that happened," she said in surprise. "I never made up any stories about you."

"Well, I appreciate that."

"You should let this go, Quinn. Don't get involved again. There's nothing to be gained. You started over. Don't go back."

"I'll think about it. Thanks for talking to me."

"I'm happy to talk to you more. We could meet for a drink one night."

"I have a lot of work next week, but maybe after that."

"Which probably means never, but sure, maybe after that," she said cynically. Then she walked over to the front door and opened it.

He moved into the doorway, then paused. "I wish you well, Lauren. You were a good friend to me in college. I don't know if I ever told you how much I appreciated that."

Her anger evaporated with his words.

"We understood each other," she said. "We'd both lost a parent. You helped me get through that, and I hope I helped you a little, too."

"You did. More than you know." He walked through the door and pulled it shut behind him, then hurried down the street.

When he got to Caitlyn's car, he opened the passenger door and slid inside.

"Well?" she asked impatiently. "You must have gotten something. You were gone a long time."

"Lauren was more forthcoming than I thought she would be," he admitted.

"What did she say?"

"Her first reaction was shock. Apparently, when I didn't go to Donovan's funeral, everyone thought I was dead, that I had killed myself out of guilt for what I'd done to you. Some people thought Donovan and I had had some sort of bizarre suicide pact."

Caitlyn's brow shot up. "That's crazy. Although, I am surprised you didn't go to Donovan's funeral. Why didn't you?"

"I was done with the LNF, with the past. And as we've discussed, I wasn't clear whether Donovan had had a hand in what happened to you."

"Did you ever confront Donovan? I remember you telling me you were trying to talk to him, but he was avoiding you."

"I never got much out of him, certainly not a confession. He said he was sorry that you'd been hurt. But he avoided my questions, claiming that the FBI had asked him not to speak to me, and he had to follow their orders."

"If he was sorry about what happened to me, he didn't express it. Other people sent cards. I never heard from Donovan." She paused. "What else did Lauren say?"

"Donovan had a birthday several days before the bombing."

"I remember. We didn't go because I was sick. I urged you to go without me, but you didn't want to."

He shrugged. "I didn't want to leave you alone. Apparently, at that party, Donovan and Hank were talking about some big new plan. The group was going to have to change and people needed to get on board or get the hell out of the way. Those were Hank's words."

"Sounds like Hank. He was always amped up."

"I think he had a steroid addiction back then."

"Probably now, too. I spoke to him five years ago, and his body was ripped. He also had the same angry, intense personality. But getting back to the plan, what was in it? What was it about?"

"She didn't have specifics. She just suggested that it would have been more aggressive than what we'd done in the past."

"Lauren never told the FBI that. Neither did anyone else."

"To be fair, those guys were always talking about big ideas, Caitlyn."

"True, but I suspect she didn't want to throw fuel on the fire when it came to her fellow LNF members."

"That's possible. She said everyone thought I'd abandoned the group—the family."

"That you'd chosen me over them," she said with a nod of agreement. "I knew things were getting rocky in that regard, but you didn't seem to care. I wanted to be with you, so I didn't push you to hang onto your friendships. I always thought if they were really your friends, they would be happy for you—for us."

"I thought that, too. And the LNF wasn't a family; it was a group of activists. Lauren said I was lying to myself if I believed that. Maybe I was. Perhaps my actions spurred Donovan to break his word to me."

"If he blew up a building because you missed his birthday party, he was a sick individual."

"True. I also told Lauren that I'd overheard Allison speaking to an FBI agent. I left you out of it."

"That was smart."

"She said Allison's group is nowhere near as organized or as passionate as the LNF was, that they have done little besides hand out flyers and plan that symposium."

"You know who was supposed to speak at that symposium— Kevin Reilly. He works for Lexitech now, a Carlson company."

"I had not heard that. Your family was targeted once again. What does Kevin say about the explosion?"

"Nothing. He hasn't returned my calls. Nor did he want to speak to the FBI. His assistant said he was shaken up, and he had not been on campus when it happened, so he had nothing to contribute."

That didn't make sense. "Why would he not want to talk to the FBI?"

"We're all asking that question. I'm hoping he will call me back, since we grew up together, and he works for my father."

"Your dad should be able to get him to talk."

"I hate to involve him, but I might have to. Anything else of interest come out of Lauren's mouth?"

He thought for a moment. "There was one other thing. She was talking about Wyatt, and she said Wyatt was there when they brought you out of the building, and that he had mentioned in this conversation they had a year ago that he'd never forgotten how shattered I'd looked that day. He felt bad that he'd never really talked to me about it."

"He never spoke to you after the explosion?"

"No. It became clear quickly that I was a person of interest and no one in the LNF wanted to put their face next to mine. But that's not the strange part. I never knew Wyatt was at the scene. I feel like I would have heard that before now."

"He wasn't there, according to the FBI file. Wyatt and Justin were in their father's office discussing an upcoming trip. Senator Pederson vouched for them, and their alibi checked out."

"Maybe Lauren got confused."

"Or Wyatt lied, and his father covered it up."

"That would be criminal, wouldn't it?"

"Definitely. We need to talk to Hank and Wyatt. Hank, because he knew about the plan and also because he was room-mates with Kevin, remember that?"

"Not until you just said it. But I'm not sure why that matters."

"I'm just looking for connections. We also need to talk to Wyatt, because he might not have been where he was supposed to be that day." Her eyes sparkled. "I knew you'd get something out of Lauren. Let's talk to Hank next. I want to take another look at the file before we talk to Wyatt, so I can be sure of what his statement was."

"We?" he echoed. "Don't you have a team of agents to talk to suspects like Hank and Wyatt?" He felt like he was getting sucked deeper and deeper into the quicksand that was Caitlyn, and he was torn. He wanted to find the person who'd destroyed both their lives and left them with a grief that would never completely heal. But spending more time with her would only make everything more difficult in the long run.

"The San Francisco office has a team of agents looking into the current explosion, working alongside the San Francisco Police Department and the ATF," she answered. "They're interviewing witnesses and running forensics, as well as looking for clues at the bomb site. That's all being covered." She paused. "I don't work here, Quinn. I don't know if I mentioned that, but I'm based in LA."

"You did not mention that." He'd been thinking how lucky he'd been that she hadn't found him before now since she hadn't been that far away. Apparently, she'd been farther away than he'd realized.

"I came up to consult on the investigation, because of my experience at Bolton and my knowledge of the previous case. The team here is focused on today's events; I'm looking for a connection to the past, because I'm convinced there is one."

"Maybe you're just desperate for there to be one. It could be a copycat crime—a new activist taking a page out of an old playbook. Lauren's sister obviously knew about the LNF and she's involved in this new group. That group is who you should focus on."

"That will happen, too. I'll follow the clues wherever they lead. But if it is a copycat and there was a playbook, who wrote it? Donovan? Hank? Does this plan still exist somewhere? And if it does, what's coming next? The only person who might be able to answer any of those questions is Hank, and I think you should go with me."

"Hank was not my biggest fan. You don't need me for that conversation."

"If we're together, it will shake him up, especially if he did think you were dead. That could rattle him enough to say something he might not say if it's just me."

"You're reaching."

"I don't think I am. If we want to get to the truth, this is how we do it."

"I thought I knew the truth," he muttered. "I thought it was Donovan. I thought everything died with him."

"Maybe it was him, but he might not have done it alone. And if someone else got away with it all these years, they still need to pay. Don't you agree?"

"Of course I agree."

"So, are you in or are you out?"

He made the only choice he could. "I'm in."

CHAPTER SEVEN

CAITLYN STARTED THE ENGINE, both relieved and a little wary about involving Quinn. She definitely thought he could help, but she'd also spent the past hour wondering how she was going to handle spending time with him again. She told herself it was for justice. He'd already gotten more out of Lauren than anyone else in the FBI had. She just needed to think of him as an asset, a source, someone who could help her case.

But wasn't she lying to herself?

She was curious to know more about him, and spending time with him now gave her that opportunity. It also gave her a chance to show him she wasn't the broken woman he'd left behind. She'd recovered, bounced back, and gotten stronger. She wanted him to see that.

Not that any of that was worth more than finding the bombers. But it was still something.

And she thought it might be a good idea to keep a close eye on him, anyway.

She didn't completely trust him. Quinn hadn't told her the complete truth about why he'd disappeared to start a new life. He was holding something back. She had a better chance of figuring out what that was if they kept talking. She just had to make sure she kept a wall between them. She couldn't let her guard down where Quinn was concerned. She couldn't let him weaken or confuse her. The stakes were too high.

That was easier said than done, because she was feeling all kinds of emotions being with him again. Even now, she was trying as hard as she could not to look at him, not to engage him in conversation unrelated to the bombings. But there were so many things she wanted to know, so much of his life she was curious about.

After several minutes, the silence in the car felt too tense, too thick. She had to break it. "Did Lauren say anything about her breakup with Vinnie?"

"Only that he cheated on her and that she was bitter about the fact that their college friends took his side. That might be one reason she was happy to speculate about them now. She doesn't feel as close or as protective of them as she used to."

"Maybe. Or she just felt more comfortable talking to you. I thought she would, and I was right."

He smiled.

"What?" she asked.

"You always liked to be right."

She frowned at that comment. "Everyone likes to be right," she said defensively. "But I might be a bit more extreme in that regard, because I grew up with a father who never thought I was right. According to him, I was always on the wrong path."

"Because you weren't on his path. That didn't make it wrong."

"In his eyes, it did."

"It sounds like you're doing exactly what you want to do now, or is your job driven by your desire for justice and revenge?" He glanced over at her. "What happens if you get all that? Would you still want to be an FBI agent?"

"Yes," she said with no hesitation. "I admit that the first

two years on the job, I had one goal, and that was to find the person who killed my child. I had to do it on the side, but I still found the time. I drove people crazy with my relentless questions. But then someone I respected told me I needed to make a choice, that I could let the obsession consume me, or I could choose to make more of my career. I eventually chose the job. I joined a task force run by an agent I met at Quantico, and I work on all kinds of cases now. I actually go undercover quite a bit." She smiled at the gleam of wonder and admiration in his eyes. "I'm pretty good at blending in, being someone else."

"It's difficult for me to believe you could ever blend into the shadows, not with those fiery red streaks in your hair and your beautiful face."

She felt a wave of heat run through her at his complimentary words. "I've changed my appearance occasionally, but it's not that much about looks; it's about taking on a character, becoming that person, trying to think like they would think, act like they would act. When I go deep cover, I have to stay in that persona for weeks or months at a time."

"What's the longest you've been undercover?"

"Six months. It was long enough that I started to lose track of who I was. It was good to get out and be me again before diving into another case."

"I know what that feels like."

"I guess you do, Michael Wainscott. How did you do it, Quinn? How did you create a fake ID, a fake life? You must have a different Social Security number than you used to. How did you acquire that?"

"Are you asking as an FBI agent?"

"I probably should be. I suspect you broke a few laws in your quest to become a different person, and that's what a criminal does."

A shadow passed through his gaze, but he remained silent.

"You're not going to say anything?" she asked with irritation. "I just called you a criminal. Do you have a defense?"

"Does it matter? You want my help. I said I'd give it to you. Let's talk about Hank. What do you know about his life?"

She didn't want him to change the subject, but she could see by the resolute gleam in his blue eyes that he didn't intend to answer questions about his personal life. For now, she'd let it go.

"Some of my information is a few years old," she said. "But here's what I know: Hank owns the gym in Pacifica and another one in Reno with a partner who is based in Nevada. That individual has no tie to Bolton or to our past. Hank has been arrested twice for misdemeanor assault from bar fights and a third time for vandalism. He and his neighbor had an ongoing battle about property lines and Hank got drunk and trashed the neighbor's yard one night."

"It sounds like he still has anger problems."

"I'd say so. His business encompasses both a fitness center and a boxing gym."

"Where he gets to fight all the time. I'm not surprised. Boxing was something Hank and Donovan had in common."

"Didn't you and Donovan also have that in common? You met him in the ring, didn't you?"

"When we were seventeen," he confirmed. "That gym was the only place I could pummel the hell out of my anger at being an orphan. Donovan was one of my first sparring partners. He was furious with his parents for a bitter divorce that shattered the family. We both needed an outlet, and boxing was it."

"And then you became best friends. You ended up at Bolton together. Donovan started the LNF and you were the first member. You were like brothers." She gave him another thoughtful look. "It is odd that you didn't go to his funeral."

"I had already left town and started over. I couldn't go back. And I didn't want to, because I didn't know how I felt about him anymore."

"What do you know about how Donovan died?"

"Probably not as much as you. I heard that Donovan went up to Yosemite to do some rock climbing shortly after graduation. He was pushing the limits as usual, and he slipped and fell."

"That's all I know, too. He rented a small tent cabin the night before. He was alone, by all accounts. A couple of hikers mentioned seeing him on his way up the mountain. But no one saw him fall. It apparently happened after dusk, and most people were off the mountain by then. His body was found the next morning by a hiker. Maybe he did kill himself."

"Would that give you any closure if you knew for sure?"

"No, because he wouldn't have been punished." She gave him a curious look. "Does it make you feel better? Does thinking that he was in despair somehow balance out what he might have done?"

"Definitely not," he said forcefully. "Nothing could balance out the act of that bomber—nothing. If you can't believe anything else that I say, believe that."

She saw the sincerity in his eyes, and old, intense feelings flowed between them once more. "I believe you."

"Good." He held her gaze, then let out a breath and looked out the window.

She gripped the wheel more tightly, feeling shaken by the look that had just passed between them. It was much easier to be angry with Quinn than to feel anything else.

They didn't speak again until they got to Hank's gym. By then, she had pulled herself together, ready to focus on what information they needed to get from Hank.

The gym was located in a strip mall of shops and restaurants that lined the beach. As they walked across the parking lot, Quinn gave the ocean a longing look.

The sea had always been her rival for his affection. In college, Quinn had spent hours either in the ocean or studying it.

It was a link to his childhood. He'd lived in two different worlds, but the sea connected them.

"Your real love is right there." She swept her hand toward the wide, blue sea with its crashing white waves. It had rained earlier in the day, but now there was a mix of clouds and sun.

"The ocean is always there. That's what I love about it. Not that it isn't changing every day. We're not doing a very good job of taking care of our planet."

"I know. I hope we can do better."

"Before it's too late," he said with a somewhat dire note in his voice. "Unfortunately, that might not happen. It's very difficult to change behavior or even attitudes. It's easier to just let it be someone else's problem, someone in the future, but that future is no longer as far away as it once was." He drew in a breath and looked away from the sea. "But we didn't come here to look at the water. Let's see what Hank can tell us."

He walked up to the front door and opened it for her. She smiled to herself. Quinn had always had good manners, something his mother had instilled in him a long time ago. Her friends had been so impressed when Quinn had opened her car door for her, as if that was a miraculous act. Of course, they hadn't been impressed with other things he'd done, but then they'd wanted to show their love and loyalty to her, and trashing Quinn had been part of her grieving process.

It was strange to be with him again. They weren't friends or lovers anymore, but they also weren't strangers. There really wasn't a name for what they were. They were in an odd state of relationship limbo. She didn't need to analyze it or label it, though. She just needed to use Quinn to get what she needed. It was as simple as that.

The gym smelled like men and sweat. It was a no-frills fitness center emphasizing weights and boxing. They stepped up to the front desk. A beefy young man gave them an enquiring look.

"Can I help you?" he asked.

"We're looking for Hank," Quinn replied.

"He's running a lesson in the ring right now," the man answered. "Go through the double doors, down the hall to the end. The ring is in the far back."

"Thanks."

They walked down the corridor, passing by the fitness area. At the end of the hallway was the boxing center. The large room housed a dozen large punching bags, three of which were currently being used, as well as a raised boxing ring in the center. There were two men in the ring: Hank Merchant and an older teenager.

Hank was built like a linebacker: square, muscular, and solid. He wore sweatpants and a tank top that revealed powerful arms emblazoned with tattoos. Hank had always been intimidating, with rippling muscles and tremendous power, but he seemed even more so now that he was older and stronger.

They moved toward the ring as Hank finished his lesson. When the kid stepped out of the ring, Hank turned and saw them. He froze, his reaction one of shock and paralysis. She didn't think either of those emotions had anything to do with her. His gaze was locked on Quinn.

Quinn stepped farther into the light while she hung back.

Hank jumped down from the ring, coming face-to-face with a man who had once been a friend. Quinn and Hank were the same height, but that's where the similarity ended. While Quinn had some dark shadows in his gaze, they didn't compete with the simmering anger that rose in a cloud of tension around Hank.

"So, you're not dead," Hank said, as if he wasn't happy about that. "I always figured that was too good to be true. What are you doing here, Quinn?"

"A bomb went off at Bolton today. Very similar to the last one," Quinn replied, his words cool and to the point, no trace of emotion.

"So?" Hank challenged.

"Do you know anything about it?"

Hank gave Quinn an incredulous look. "Get the hell out of my gym."

She stepped forward. "Not so fast, Hank."

Hank fell back a step, and she realized he hadn't seen her at all, not until this second. "You? You two are together?"

"We have some questions," she continued.

"I told you before, I have nothing to say to you, Caitlyn. I still don't. Leave."

"We need to talk about the past, Hank," Quinn said, not budging.

"I'm busy."

"You can take a few minutes."

"No, I can't. I have to work. You want to talk, you need to pay for my time."

"How much?" Quinn asked.

Hank hesitated, then straightened. "Ten minutes in the ring gets you ten minutes of conversation."

She was shocked at Hank's suggestion. *Why would he want to get Quinn in the ring?* She could think of only one reason. Hank wanted to fight Quinn. He wanted to do something with the anger running through him.

"Don't do it," she said, unable to stop herself.

"You still let her call the shots?" Hank drawled. "That's not surprising. You changed when you met her. You became a different person, and not one I respected."

Quinn's jaw stiffened, and he lifted his chin. "You want ten minutes in the ring, you got it."

"You'll need to be on your feet at the end of that time," Hank warned.

"If you're not on your feet, I'll take fifteen," he countered.

She frowned as the two sized each other up. "This is stupid," she said. "We don't need a fight; we need a conversation."

"This is between me and Hank," Quinn said sharply, shooting her a hard look. "Why don't you get a drink?"

"Yeah, get lost, Caitlyn," Hank added.

She did not like being dismissed. "I don't think so. And I can compel you to speak to me for longer than ten minutes, Hank."

"You can compel me to sit in front of you, but I don't have to talk," he countered.

"But you will talk to me," Quinn said, drawing Hank's gaze back to him.

"If you meet my terms."

As Quinn shed his jacket, she searched for something to say that would end this, but neither man was paying attention to her. She hoped that Quinn knew what he was doing. She couldn't imagine he'd boxed much the last ten years, although he had once spent time in the ring. But Hank made his living teaching people how to box. He had a clear-cut advantage.

And what if Hank knew nothing? Or wouldn't say anything?

Quinn could be taking punches for nothing.

"Quinn," she said, as he pushed up his sleeves. "You don't have to do this for me."

"I'm not doing it for you," he told her, and then he climbed into the ring.

CHAPTER EIGHT

CAITLYN DIDN'T WANT to watch Quinn fight Hank, but she couldn't look away. A terrible feeling of foreboding ran through her, and she felt a wave of worry and protectiveness that also bothered her. It wasn't on her to protect Quinn from anything. He'd left her to fend for herself. *Why should she care if he took a beating now?*

Unfortunately, she couldn't seem to stop herself from caring. She might not love or even like Quinn anymore, but she didn't want him to get hurt.

Not that it mattered what she wanted. Both men were eager to fight. There were layers upon layers of emotions running between them. This wasn't just about the bombings or the unanswered questions; it was about a broken relationship, a perceived betrayal. And once again, she was in the middle of it.

She'd wanted to be friends with Quinn's buddies, but the LNF members had had a built-in dislike of her because of her last name. Some had tried to be nice, probably because they liked Quinn, but others had just seen her as an embodiment of their enemy. She didn't believe they had all wanted her to die or be hurt in the blast, but at least one person had, maybe more. And while she believed Donovan had had a hand in the attack, he could have had help, and that help might have come from Hank.

She paced as the two men raised their gloved hands. She actually knew more about boxing than either of them might think. She'd been trained in hand-to-hand combat at Quantico, and she'd kept her skills up ever since then. She'd even had to use those skills a few times, although not in a ring, and not with gloves on. But neither one of these men would believe that. Neither one saw her as who she really was. Not that that mattered. This fight might be a little about her, but it was mostly about them.

A few other men gathered around as the fight grew in intensity.

She flinched as Hank landed the first blow, but it was only glancing, and Quinn was quick on his feet, landing his own right jab.

As the fight continued, she noticed that Hank favored his left. He mixed up his offensive and defensive moves, but when he was in trouble, he moved to the left.

The crowd cheered as Hank landed a harder blow and blood spurted out of Quinn's nose. Clearly, the members were rooting for Hank. This was Hank's turf. And everyone could sense that the fight was personal.

"Come on, Quinn," she yelled, the words coming out of her mouth before she could stop them.

She hadn't been on Team Quinn in a long time. In fact, she'd wanted to punch him herself, but right now, if she had to pick between the two men, she'd pick Quinn.

Quinn got off the next punishing blow. Hank stumbled backward. He pivoted toward his left, the way he'd done before. Quinn anticipated the move and hit him again, then again. He pushed forward until Hank was up against the ropes, and then delivered one quick, punishing blow after another, until Hank fell to his knees.

Quinn backed away. He glanced at the big clock on the wall. "That's ten minutes, and you're not on your feet."

Hank was breathing too hard to respond, blood dripping down his face.

Quinn stripped off his gloves.

One staffer moved toward Hank, but Hank got to his feet, motioning him away. "I'm fine," he growled.

She grabbed a towel from a nearby table and handed it to Quinn as he left the ring. He wiped the blood from his nose and then turned toward Hank, who was doing the same thing.

Hank tipped his head toward a glass-walled room behind the ring and moved toward the door.

They followed him inside. There was a table and a couple of chairs, along with a stack of flyers for an upcoming fight night.

Hank grabbed a bottle of water out of a small fridge and tossed it to Quinn.

Quinn caught it and sat down. Hank grabbed two more bottles, slid one down the table toward her and opened the other one, greedily sucking down half the bottle before he took a seat across from them.

"You've been in the ring," Hank muttered, his right eye swelling up to match his bottom lip. "You played me."

"I answered your challenge," Quinn replied. "Now, we talk, and I've got fifteen minutes. Let's start with Donovan's birthday party, a few days before the explosion."

"What?" Hank asked in wary surprise. "I thought you wanted to talk about the bombing."

"We'll get there," Quinn said. "You told Vinnie Caputo that things at the LNF were about to change in a big way, that you and Donovan had a new plan. It was going to be bold and impossible to ignore. What were you talking about?"

"I don't remember."

"I'm sure you do."

"Look, I had nothing to do with the bomb. I told her that when she was here before," he said, tipping his head in her direction.

She loved how he couldn't even say her name. Clearly, his dislike of her was as strong as it had always been, maybe even stronger now that he knew she was in the FBI and determined to solve the case.

"Did Donovan set the bomb?" Quinn asked.

Hank didn't immediately respond.

Caitlyn watched with fascination as something tense and silent passed between the two men. She had thought she'd run this show, but Quinn had taken control. And since he'd gained Hank's respect in the ring, Hank actually seemed like he might want to talk.

"I don't know for sure. He never admitted it to me," Hank said. "But I thought he did it."

"Why did you think that?" Quinn asked.

"Donovan wanted to do more than we were doing. No one was taking us seriously. We were getting nowhere. We were just college kids with a cause. We needed to make bigger and bolder statements. I agreed."

"Then there was a plan," Quinn said.

"Donovan made some notes one night. We were drinking a lot at the time, and we came up with some crazy ideas." Hank waved his hand dismissively as if it was no big deal.

"Was one of those ideas a bomb?" Quinn asked.

"Yes. Bombs, arson, vandalism…it was all discussed. But none of us were that serious. We were drunk."

"But the bomb went off," Quinn said. "That happened."

"And I was shocked," Hank replied. "Donovan told me that the grand opening was off-limits. He said you'd asked him to leave it alone for Caitlyn's sake, and that he'd agreed." Hank's hard gaze turned on her. "Even though the center was built by the dirty money that your family made by polluting the earth."

"The environmental center was a good thing," she argued. "Blowing it up didn't accomplish anything except to create sympathy for me and my family."

"Well, that's true," Hank said, taking a swig of water. "But like I said, I had nothing to do with the bomb. I think Donovan got pissed when you two didn't show up at his birthday party. He had a lot to say that night about how you were no longer his friend, Quinn. My guess is that he decided to get back at you and Caitlyn."

"It's easy to blame Donovan since he's dead," Quinn said sharply.

"That's right. That was another party you missed—Donovan's wake. You should have been there."

Quinn paled under Hank's harsh words, and she suspected there was a part of Quinn that wished he had made the service.

"Let's get back to the plan," Quinn said with determination. "What were the targets? What protests were going to take place?"

"I don't remember specifics. We were going to target structures, not people. We wanted to attack companies in the same way that they were hurting the planet. We could no longer just be a thorn in their sides; we had to attack with a knife, a fire, a gun or a bomb, whatever it would take to get their attention."

Hank spoke so pragmatically about targeted violence, she had no problem believing he would have been happy to carry out any of the acts he'd mentioned. It was odd that he was speaking so freely. He'd probably completely forgotten she was an FBI agent. He was more interested in letting Quinn know how much he'd been out of the loop.

"But we did none of it," Hank added forcefully. "It was just talk."

"Except the bomb," she reminded him.

"Like I said, that was probably Donovan. And that bomb destroyed the LNF. After the explosion, the FBI was all over us. We were being questioned repeatedly. People turned on each other and wanted to distance themselves from the group. There was a shitload of cowards in the group, more than I had imagined. By graduation, we were done."

"Do you have any proof Donovan set the bomb?" she asked.

"No. I have no evidence that Donovan did it, but based on his mood, his actions, and his unfortunate death a few months later, I believe he was guilty. I think when he realized he'd killed someone and injured a half-dozen people, including his best friend's girlfriend, that he couldn't live with the guilt."

It was a plausible story, and, in truth, only confirmed what she thought. But she needed evidence. Someone had to have something more specific than a gut feeling.

"Who else was in on the new bold, destructive plan?" Quinn asked. "You said you were sitting around drinking and plotting. It wasn't just the two of you, was it?"

"I don't want to throw anyone else under the bus. Donovan was leading the charge."

"That doesn't make sense. Donovan wasn't that radical."

"He was changing; you just didn't see it, Quinn. You were too caught up in her. Donovan was the smartest one of all of us. You really think Gary, Vitaly, Wyatt, or anyone else could have gotten away with what happened without leaving a clue behind? I don't think so."

"You're smart. Maybe you were in charge," she said.

"I wasn't," Hank replied, giving her a hard look. "I don't know what else to tell you."

"You can tell us about today," she said, bringing them back to the present.

"I've been here all day, and I haven't been to Bolton in years."

"Did you know Kevin Reilly was speaking at Bolton today?" she asked. "He could have died in that blast."

Surprise ran through Hank's gaze. "I didn't know that, but I don't see Kevin that much anymore. If you want to talk to someone about Kevin, talk to your brother, Spencer. They work together, although they don't seem to get along anymore."

"Why would you say that?" she challenged. "How do you even know Spencer?"

"We were at a party together at Vitaly's house a few weeks ago. Spencer and Kevin got into a huge fight; they almost came to blows. Vitaly had to pull them apart."

"That doesn't sound like Spencer or Kevin," she said with a frown.

"I got the feeling they were in some competition at work. You should talk to your family," Hank continued, a gleam in his eyes. "It appears that both bombings have to do with the Carlson empire."

A knock came at the door. A young staffer poked his head into the room to tell Hank his next client was waiting.

"I have to go." Hank stood up and waved them to the door. "Let's not do this again."

"I can't promise that," she said as she got to her feet. "This new explosion has changed everything."

He let out a weary sigh. "You need to find some other people to talk to. You can't keep harassing me. I don't know anything. I get that you want revenge, Caitlyn. But the person you want to punish is already dead."

"There's someone else who's not dead, who had something to do with today's explosion, and I believe they're tied to the LNF in some way."

"Well, it's not me."

"Did you know that Lauren's sister goes to Bolton. She was there today."

"I knew she went to Bolton," Hank said. "Is she all right?"

"She's fine. She's also involved in an environmental activist group on campus. Do you know anything about that?"

"No, I haven't seen Allison in a few years. If you want to know about her, talk to Lauren. Wait a second, you already spoke to Lauren, didn't you? She sent you to me." He shook his head. "She has been in a fury since Vinnie divorced her. She thinks we all deserted her."

"Did you?" she asked.

"No. We were just better friends with Vinnie than with her. I'm sorry things didn't work out for them, but I never thought they were great together from day one. I need to get to work."

She felt frustrated and restless as they walked out of the office and then out of the gym. Hank hadn't told her much that she didn't already know, although the bigger, more violent plan was new.

When they stepped outside, Quinn put a hand on her arm, and the unexpected touch made her jump.

"I need some air," he said tightly. "Let's walk on the beach."

"All right." She could use some air, too. Talking to Hank had brought back a lot of old feelings, especially when he'd looked at her with such intense dislike and reiterated how she had come between Quinn and his friends.

She also felt unsettled by Hank's mention of her brother. The fact that they had been at a party together a few weeks ago bothered her. Spencer hadn't known those guys, although he certainly did know Kevin. *But still, why would Spencer want to hang out with LNF members, people who might have been involved in an attack that had almost killed her? And what was the fight between Spencer and Kevin about?*

She needed to talk to her brother, but that wasn't a high priority. First, she had to focus on the bigger plan and figure out who had been involved in it, and/or whether that plan might have gotten into the hands of a copycat. If that were the case, there might be more than one bomb going off this time around.

She glanced over at Quinn as they walked down the path along the beach. His profile was rigid, his eyes dark with emotion, and he seemed to have nothing to say. She had no idea what he was thinking, but his thoughts appeared to be grim.

When the path ended, they headed across the sand to an outcropping of rocks that prevented them from going any farther. The cold air and icy spray made her shiver, but it also helped lift the dizzying fog of confusion swirling around her brain. As they stood at the water's edge, watching one crashing wave after another, she couldn't take the silence anymore. "What do you think, Quinn?"

As he turned to look at her, she could see the bruising around his left eye, and his nose was a bit swollen, but she didn't think he was even aware of his physical injuries. There was a deep pain in his gaze, and she knew where it was coming from.

"I was responsible."

"I didn't hear that. He said it was Donovan."

"It was Donovan because of me. The birthday party was the tipping point. Donovan started listening to crazy people. Because I didn't realize how much he had changed, you almost died." Anger tightened his lips. "He went after you to get payback. It's all so clear now. Dammit! I should have known. No one was answering my calls or my texts that morning. I had a bad feeling. I didn't act on it. And you paid the price, you and our baby."

She both wanted to stop him and wanted him to keep going. It was actually cathartic to hear the rage in his voice. She'd always felt like she was alone in her fury and her grief, even though, in many ways, she had isolated herself. She had not wanted to talk to Quinn back then. Maybe he was right. Maybe she had subconsciously blamed him for everything. And he'd tiptoed around her because of his guilt and because she was a wreck.

"There was a whole plan I knew nothing about," Quinn continued. "No one told me, because they hated me. I had betrayed them. I know someone else knew. I just know, Caitlyn."

"We'll figure out who."

"Will we? They've gotten away with it for ten years."

"But now something else has happened."

"It might not be connected to the same person."

"Or it could be," she argued. "And they didn't hate you, Quinn. They hated me for taking you away from them."

"You didn't take me away; I made the choice."

"A choice you made because I wanted to be with you. I thought we didn't need anyone but each other."

"We didn't need anyone else."

"But look what happened. Everything fell apart because we got together. And our baby—our baby died."

"I know," he said, agony in his voice. "I am so sorry, Caitlyn. I wish I could bring her back. I wish I could change what happened. I wish you had never had to suffer the way you did."

He'd said the words before, but for the first time, she actually heard him.

"I don't think I realized until just this second how much I let you suffer on your own. I was so mad. I didn't see your anger."

"It was there. It's still there," he said, his gaze boring into hers.

She could feel his pain, and he could feel hers. The wall between them came crashing down. Her heart beat faster. Her breath came shorter. She needed to look away, but she couldn't.

And then she was in his arms, and his mouth was on hers.

She didn't know who had moved first; she didn't care.

She wrapped her arms around his neck and took his hot kiss all the way in. Emotions rocketed through her, so many she thought she might keel over, but Quinn's strong arms were around her. He was holding her up, and she was holding him up.

It felt so damn good. The way it had been before but different, too.

And as they kissed, the mood changed. The grief, the anger, turned into something else, something that made her gut ache with a hollowness that only he could fill, a need that threatened to overtake everything else. It had always been that way between them. The passion had swept them away. It was doing that now.

She wanted to sink down to the sand. She wanted to wrap her body around his, to feel him all the way to her core.

But there was suddenly cold air between them.

Quinn stepped back. "What the hell are we doing?" he asked.

CHAPTER NINE

CAITLYN STARED at him in bemusement, her cheeks flushed, her brown eyes sparkling, her lips full and pink and just begging for another kiss. Quinn swallowed a knot in his throat and fisted his hands to prevent himself from grabbing her again.

He'd thought it was over between them. He'd thought she hated him.

But what had just happened sure as hell didn't feel like hate.

"I don't know," she finally said. "I don't know."

He ran a hand through his hair and then walked past her, standing at the edge of the sea, so close that the incoming tide ran over his shoes and his jeans, but he didn't care. He needed the water to calm down.

Unfortunately, the ocean wasn't able to work its usual magic. Looking out at the horizon, hearing the soothing crash of the waves, did little to calm his racing heart.

He'd just kissed Caitlyn, and he wanted to do it again and again.

But she wasn't his to kiss—not anymore, not ever again. There was so much pain between them, so much anger, distrust and…secrets.

Confiding in her wasn't an option. And he was done hurting her.

She moved closer. He turned his head to look at her, but he couldn't read her expression, and that was unsettling. He'd always been able to read her. When they were together, she'd worn every emotion on her face. She'd been open with him, and he'd been the same with her.

Now there was nothing but conflict, uncertainty, and doubt between them.

There were sparks, too.

He should have expected that the fire that had run so hot between them would instantly reignite.

"That was a mistake," he said.

"Yes."

He should be happy with her agreement, but he wasn't. "Why do you think it was a mistake?" He kicked himself for the question. They didn't need to rehash it. "Forget it."

"Forget what? The question or the kiss?"

He had to admit that he liked how direct she was now. Her confidence, her strength, were welcome traits to see. He'd been afraid that he'd destroyed her. But he hadn't. "Both."

"I don't think either of us will forget it, but it was probably inevitable, given our history. I just wish…"

He had both a desperate need to know what she wished and a desperate need to stop her from saying more.

"It doesn't matter," she said, shaking her head.

"Just say it." *Damn, why wouldn't his mouth cooperate with his brain?* "Forget I said that, too."

"That's the problem, Quinn—I have a hard time forgetting anything you've said or done. You've been haunting me for years."

"I could say the same."

"But you had a choice. You always knew where I was, or you

could have easily found me. I haven't been in hiding. I wasn't a ghost."

"Even though, it was my choice, you still haunted me, Caitlyn." He paused. "But I had to move on, and so did you. In the end, it was the right decision. Look at you now. You're this kickass woman who is brimming with intelligence, fearlessness, and confidence. You became who you were meant to be."

"Or, as my grandmother used to say, I just bloomed where I was planted."

"Well, that also proves how strong you are."

"I am strong, Quinn. And I wouldn't have been who I am if that bomb hadn't gone off, if you hadn't left me, if I hadn't had to reinvent myself. All of that is a part of who I am now. But I still wish none of it had ever happened. I wish our baby was alive."

He sucked in a breath at the reminder. "So do I."

"I also wish you hadn't hurt me the way you did," she said, her gaze holding his. "You didn't just break my heart, Quinn... you broke my soul."

Her words stabbed him once more. "I'm sorrier than you'd ever believe."

"Maybe that's true. Maybe it's not. I don't know what to think." She stared at him for a long minute. "Was it really my father who chased you away, Quinn?"

"He was part of it. My guilt was the other part. Your dad thought you would be better off without me. How could I disagree? I couldn't comfort you. I couldn't help you. You wouldn't let me. Everything I did annoyed you. You once asked me why I had to breathe so loudly. My very existence pissed you off."

Guilt floated through her eyes. "I know I was hard on you. I was having a rough time handling my emotions. And I took them out on you."

"I understood that. I just didn't know how to make things better. And deep down I knew that what had happened to you was on me. I might not have set the bomb, but I didn't see what was happening right in front of me. I didn't walk away from a group that had become militant."

"You didn't see the radicalism; you only saw your friends. To be fair, I didn't see it, either. I thought even if there was a protest that day it would just involve signs or minor vandalism. I never expected a bomb to go off. I missed the signs, too."

He couldn't allow her to blame herself for anything. "You did nothing wrong, Caitlyn. You weren't responsible for anything your family had done. You didn't force me to choose between you and my friends. You didn't drag me away from the LNF. None of it is on you," he said forcefully, needing her to believe that.

"Okay," she said with a slow nod. "But it's not all on you, either. I was hard on you after the explosion, Quinn. I have to acknowledge that." She took a breath. "I also have to say that part of the reason why I had trouble talking to you about the loss of our baby was because of the way you acted that morning before the explosion. We weren't connecting. You were on your phone. You were saying the right things, but I didn't feel the emotion behind your words. I thought that maybe you didn't want the baby, but you were trapped. You wanted to be responsible. You wanted to step up. And then when I lost her, I thought maybe you were secretly relieved."

"No! God! I wasn't relieved, Caitlyn."

"You didn't really ask about her afterward."

"I didn't know what to say. You were in so much pain, and I was, too. Sure, maybe you took me by surprise with the news. It wasn't the best timing, but I wanted to have that baby with you. You two were going to be my family." He needed to make her understand that. "I was shattered when you miscarried. But I was grateful that I hadn't lost you, too. So if I didn't express it the right way, I'm sorry. But I did want her. I swear I did."

She drew in a breath and ran the back of her hand across her eyes in a rough, defensive gesture. "The damn wind is making my eyes water."

"Mine, too."

She gave him a teary smile. "Thank you for saying that."

"It's the truth, every single word."

"I want to believe you."

"I hope you can. I might have been worried that we were young, and we weren't ready. I had a lot of debt. I had no family to lean on, and I knew your family would be furious when they found out. They were already worried that I was out to get your money or take you away from them with my radical talk. One of the last things your father said to me..." He stopped, realizing that he didn't need to tell her that. It would only hurt her more. And he had never wanted to be a wedge between her and her family. He'd lost his parents. He knew what it felt like not to have a mother or a father. He'd never wanted Caitlyn to feel that kind of isolation.

"What did he say?" she asked.

"It doesn't matter."

"Stop deciding what matters and what doesn't," she cried out in frustration. "You're not in charge of this, Quinn. You don't get to make all the choices of what is said or not said."

"Your father said it was for the best."

She paled, but she didn't immediately say he was lying. She turned her head toward the sea, the wind tugging strands of hair out of her ponytail.

He felt like an asshole for what he'd just said. But she'd wanted the truth, and he'd given it to her.

"I heard him say something like that to my mom," she muttered.

"You did?" he asked in surprise.

She turned back to him once more. "Yes. He felt badly that I had to go through it, but in the long run, he thought I'd be better off without the baby. I hated him for saying that."

"Did you ever confront him?"

"No. I've rarely confronted him about anything. Even when I try to stand up to him, he usually changes the subject or avoids me. I guess I don't press that hard, because there's no point. I'm sure you think that's cowardly."

"I think it's understandable. He's an intimidating man." He cleared his throat. "But just to say it one more time, I wasn't relieved, not one bit. I always wanted the baby, and I always wanted you."

"Okay," she said, drawing in a deep breath and letting it out. "We should get back to the car. I need to go into the office and check with my team."

"I can get a ride back to my house. You don't need to drive me to Dillon Beach."

"That would be easier." As they walked back to the parking lot, she added, "I am sorry you had to take some punches to get Hank to talk, but you were impressive."

"Hank wasn't that good."

"Oh, he was good. You were just better. Have you boxed in the last ten years?"

"As a matter of fact, I have. It's still one of my favorite workouts."

"So, you were hustling him." She gave him a small smile.

He shrugged. "Hank wanted a fight; I gave him one."

"He had a tell. You capitalized on it."

His gaze widened. "You saw it, too?"

"I've done some boxing myself since I became an agent. His defensive move was always to the left."

"You box?" he asked in disbelief, coming to a stop.

"Yes," she said with a proud smile. "It was part of my training. I found I liked it. It made me feel more powerful, more in control."

"That's important to you, isn't it? The gun, the boxing, the training, the job…"

"Yes. I'm very aware that my need for control is probably a result of what happened."

He thought about that and had to ask her a question. "How do you do it, Caitlyn? How do you go to a bomb site and walk through the rubble and not fall apart?"

"It's never easy, Quinn. Today, I felt like I was going to throw up. It was all I could do to hold it together. But I tell myself it's about finding the truth, and whatever that takes, I have to be willing to do."

"Now I'm impressed even more. I should have let you take the ring against Hank."

"I'm sure Hank would have liked to beat the crap out of me, too. Unfortunately, he had to pick one of us, and you were higher on the list. But he didn't beat you; you beat him. He wasn't expecting that. You earned his respect."

"I don't want his respect. I still don't know that he didn't set that bomb, that he didn't help Donovan do it, or that he didn't know more about it than he wanted to tell us."

"He might know more about the big plan than he told us, too. That's why we need to keep talking to people. Wyatt, Justin, Gary, Vinnie…we need to speak to all of them."

"I noticed you left your brother off that list."

She frowned. "I don't know what to think about that story, but I will speak to Spencer—maybe tonight. My mom is insisting that I come to dinner."

"Do you see them a lot?"

"Not really. It helps when I have distance, but they know I'm in town."

"Sounds like we'll have to have those other conversations tomorrow."

"Yes."

"Unless the rest of your team comes up with a suspect before then."

"That would be good, too. What are you doing tomorrow?" she asked, as they started walking again.

"I'm diving in the morning. But I'm free in the afternoon." When they reached the parking lot, he pulled out his phone. "I'll get a ride."

"All right." She licked her lips. "I'm glad we talked, Quinn."

"Me, too. Even more glad that we kissed," he couldn't help saying.

She flushed. "I don't think we should talk about that."

"Like you said, it was inevitable."

"Well, it's over now. I have to tell you one thing before we part ways."

He didn't like the change in her expression. "What's that?"

"I still think you're holding something back, Quinn. I don't know what it is, but there's a secret in your eyes. I wish you would open up to me."

"There's no secret," he denied.

"You have a tell, too. You avert your gaze when you don't want me to look too closely at you. You always did that, especially when I would bring up your family or your life in Ireland. But you never did it as much back then as you've done it today."

He had to fight not to look away from her. "I don't know what you want me to say, Caitlyn. I'm doing everything I can to help you. Let's focus on finding the bomber and figuring out the plan. That's the most important thing. I want to get justice for you and for our baby. I want to make sure no one else gets hurt." He could see the lingering doubt in her eyes, so he added, "I know you don't completely trust me, and I've given you plenty of reasons not to, but I want to find the truth. Do you believe that?"

She gave him a long look. "I do believe you want the truth, but I also believe you have a secret. However, you are helping me, so for now, I'll leave it alone."

Relief ran through him. "I'll take that."

"Hearing you open up about the loss of our baby also made

me realize that there's something I need to tell you." Indecision played through her eyes, and then she lifted her chin. "I gave her a name."

His heart stopped. That was the last thing he'd expected her to say. "You did?"

"Isabella. That was her name. It was Isabella."

He felt a rush of painful emotion. "That's the prettiest name I've ever heard."

Caitlyn's bottom lip trembled as she blinked back tears once more. "I think so, too."

Then she turned and walked away.

CHAPTER TEN

ISABELLA.

The name rocketed around Quinn's head as he got a ride home. He couldn't believe Caitlyn had named their child, but it felt absolutely right.

Isabella.

He could picture her in his mind, a little girl with Caitlyn's warm smile and curious brown eyes. She'd have Caitlyn's soft laugh, and she'd probably wave her hand in the air while she talked. She'd also have a big heart, one that could easily be hurt.

Was he describing Isabella or Caitlyn?

They felt very much the same in his mind. Not that his daughter wouldn't have gotten some of his traits, too. She probably would have been stubborn; that would have come from both of them. She would have loved the sea, because he would have made sure of that. He would have taken her swimming and diving as soon as she was old enough. He would have shown her all the wonders of the ocean.

And Caitlyn would have made their daughter watch old movies with a bowl of hot popcorn on her lap. He smiled to himself at that memory. Caitlyn had always found pleasure in the classics, especially when it came to Christmas movies, and she'd gotten him hooked on them, too. Although, he hadn't watched any in ten years because the memories had been too painful.

Caitlyn's parents, Chuck and Rebecca Carlson, would have wanted their granddaughter to have the best of everything. There would have been lessons of every kind—from ballet to horseback riding, to piano and tennis. Caitlyn had told him how booked her days had been with activities when she was growing up. Not that she blamed her parents for exposing her to so many opportunities, but sometimes she'd just wanted to stay home and read.

Books—their daughter would have had bookcases filled with stories of adventure, because books had been Caitlyn's passion even more than old movies. She'd always had at least one or two novels by her bed in college. He remembered waking up a few times to see her reading by the light on her phone. Another memory that made him smile.

Although, thinking about her in bed also made him hard, especially with the taste of her mouth so fresh on his lips. Kissing her had felt like coming home. Her mouth under his, her body in his arms, had turned the world upright again. It had felt right, even though it was wrong.

They weren't together anymore. She wasn't his woman to hold, to kiss, or to love. It had been a few moments of insanity, heated by their emotions, by memories, by fear that the past was repeating itself. It couldn't happen again. But it wouldn't be easy working with her and not touching her. The smartest thing to do would be to back off, let her go off on her own. But he'd already told her he was in. And now that she'd dragged him back into the life he'd left and made him realize that perhaps there were things he didn't know, he found himself wanting the truth as much as she did.

He'd put his past behind him after Donovan died. He'd believed that the danger to others had died with Donovan.

Clearly, it had not. It was possible that there was no connection between the two explosions. Caitlyn could be seeing a link that wasn't there. But the Lauren/Allison connection was odd. The fact that the climate symposium had included a representative from a Carlson Industries company was disturbing. Even Hank's words about Donovan's grand plan and the falling-out between Kevin and Spencer made him wonder if the plan had found a home with a new group of activists.

There was no way he could not help Caitlyn. He had to fight as hard as she was fighting. Not just for her or for himself, but for Isabella. He was glad she'd trusted him enough to tell him that she'd named their daughter. Now when he thought of their child, he had a name, and it made a huge difference. They might not have ever been a family, but love had created his daughter, and he would do whatever it took to get her the justice he'd thought he'd already gotten.

An hour later, Quinn walked into his house with a wary step, hoping he wouldn't find any other unexpected visitors, but the house was empty.

Everything was exactly the way he'd left it. At the same time, it felt completely different. He dropped his keys on the side table, his gaze catching on the photo of his parents once more. He picked up the frame and gave them a long look. "You had a granddaughter named Isabella," he murmured. "I hope her soul is with you now."

Despite his words, he didn't believe that was true. He'd been born into faith, but he'd lost it long ago.

He could almost see his mother, Erin, with her jet-black hair and blue eyes, shaking her finger at him now, telling him that was what faith was—it was what you believed in your heart, not what you could see with your eyes.

His father, Colin, with his dirty-blond hair and full, scruffy beard would be telling him the opposite, that it didn't matter what you believed if you didn't act on it. Life was about action, not about thinking. His dad probably should have thought a lot more before he acted. If he had, he might be alive.

His parents had been very different people when it came to personality and actions, but they'd had a passionate love story, starting in their teens and ending fifteen years later. Violence had stalked their marriage, but there had still been good times and a love that had never really died. Even after they'd moved to California, his mom had spoken fondly of his father, always telling him that his dad was a man who'd fought for what he believed in.

He'd tried to be a fighter, too, especially after his mom passed away. He'd found his way to the Third Street Gym, where he'd met the manager Manny Lopez, who'd taught him how to box. That's where he'd met Donovan. Boxing had become his pain relief. Speaking of which—he put a hand to his face, feeling some swelling—he probably should get some ice. But he wasn't that concerned. It had been satisfying to take Hank down, especially since Hank had completely underestimated him.

As he wandered into the kitchen, he thought once more about those early days getting to know Donovan. They'd bonded quickly because they both felt alone. Donovan's parents had gone through a bitter divorce after his mother had cheated on his father, and the family had split apart. Donovan had lived with his dad while his mom married her lover and had another child, leaving Donovan to feel completely divorced from his mother. It hadn't been much better with his dad, who traveled for work, sometimes leaving Donovan alone with a housekeeper for weeks at a time. The gym had been Donovan's second home, too.

When college came around, they'd both decided to go to Bolton. Quinn had been lucky enough to get scholarships and financial aid. While he hadn't had money, he had had his big brain. School had always been a cakewalk. Getting good grades had been easy. Even though the last few years of high school had been spent couch surfing or living on the streets, he'd still managed to get straight A's. School had been his ticket to a better life.

Donovan had not had good grades, but he did have a wealthy father, willing to donate to the school, and suddenly he was in. They'd lived together their freshman year, and their friendship had only grown stronger. Donovan wasn't much of a student, but he had a charisma and a personality that made him a big man on campus. He took his time getting through his classes. While Quinn had been finishing his master's after six years at Bolton, Donovan was finally finishing his bachelor's degree.

They were six years into their friendship when Caitlyn had come on the scene. He'd known Donovan wasn't thrilled with Caitlyn, but he hadn't cared. He was too much in love with her to care what anyone else thought. That might have been a fatal mistake.

He opened the fridge and grabbed a bag of frozen peas out of the freezer, pressing it against his face. He held it there for a few moments, wondering about all the clues he might have missed ten years ago. *Had Donovan left one of those clues behind?*

He tossed the bag of peas back into the freezer and opened the door to the basement. He hit the light and then jogged down the stairs. In the far corner of the room was a small black duffel bag. He squatted down next to it. As he opened the bag, his stomach turned over. It had been ten years since he'd looked in the duffel.

Would the items make more sense now with the new information he'd gotten?

He pulled out a spiral notebook. The first three pages contained notes from a geology class. Donovan's sprawling, messy handwriting put another knot in his stomach. After the notes were several drawings of decapitated snakes. Donovan and Wyatt had gotten tattoos with one of those snakes a few weeks before the bombing. Donovan had told him at the time that it was meant to be a reminder that there were always snakes and the only way to survive was to cut off their heads.

Thinking about it now made it seem more foreboding and gruesome. At the time, he'd thought they were both high or drunk and had gotten the tattoos in a moment of stupidity. *But had the snakes been a sign of a more deranged Donovan?*

Turning the page, he could see evidence of several pages being ripped out of the notebook. He'd noticed that before but didn't know what it meant. Maybe the missing pages were part of the grand plan Donovan and Hank had written up.

Where were those pages now? Had they survived Donovan's death? Did someone else have them?

He set the notebook aside and pulled out four loose photos. One was of Donovan and Wyatt showing off their matching snake tattoos. There were also two group photos taken at an LNF meeting. In one, Donovan was sitting at a table with Justin, Vinnie, and Hank. In the other, Lauren and Wyatt were by his side. They all looked so young in the pictures, so full of themselves and their dreams.

The final photo was of himself and Donovan. It had been taken after a climb to the summit of Squaw Valley in Lake Tahoe. They looked like they were on top of the world. He turned the photo over, and Donovan's words made his gut clench once more: *My brother from another mother.*

It was something Donovan had said often about their relationship. He'd felt the same way for a long time. But that bond had broken somewhere along the way, probably when Caitlyn had come into his life. He hadn't consciously picked her over anyone. He'd just selfishly wanted to be with her. He'd thought his friends understood.

He shoved the photos and notebook into the duffel, which also held some of Donovan's clothes. He should throw the bag away, but instead he shoved it back into the corner and left the basement. He locked the door behind him as he went into the kitchen, but that lock wouldn't keep the memories away.

They were running free and wild now, the past colliding with the present, and Caitlyn was in the middle of it all once again. He didn't know what he was going to do about her. Because she was right; he did have a secret, and if they spent more time together, there was a good chance it would come out.

As Caitlyn sat through the end of a meeting that had gone on for two hours, she was reminded of how much she hated the bureaucracy of the bigger field offices. Her team worked so much faster and more efficiently. But the one thing this office had was manpower, and they needed that now. Various teams had reported on their parts of the investigation from the explosive device, which was determined to be a pipe bomb enhanced with nails, to witness statements, symposium details, the activist group, the companies who could have been the targets, and security footage in and around Bolton.

She'd only been asked one question about Kevin Reilly and hadn't been thrilled to report that she hadn't yet reached Kevin. Rob had given her a look that suggested he might not need her on the case if she couldn't complete that simple task. She couldn't blame him. She also couldn't tell him that she'd been chasing down Quinn and other people from the past. He'd send her back to LA in a hot minute for going against his orders to stay focused on the present. But she didn't feel guilty about it. There were a lot of agents working on the present. Focusing on the connection to the past made sense, and she was the one to do it.

After the briefing, she returned to the bullpen with Emi, who told her she could work at the desk next to hers. As she logged in to the computer, she thought about everything they knew so far, which wasn't a lot. She had hoped there would be more definitive clues from today's explosion, but this case was beginning to feel very much like the last one.

Emi pulled her chair over to her desk and gave her an inquisitive look. "What have you been working on, Caitlyn? I'm asking for myself, not for Rob."

"I appreciate that. I'm not hiding information; I just don't have anything to report yet."

"But..."

"I got in touch with a couple of people from the past, Lauren Sullivan and Hank Merchant." She deliberately left out Quinn. "Lauren suggested that a copycat might be involved, someone who knew the history of the LNF at Bolton and had radicalized the Green Citizens, even though to date, they've done next to nothing in terms of protesting and definitely have no history of violence or even violent rhetoric."

"I've been looking into the group, and she's right; they have a clean slate. The group only started two years ago. The woman in charge, Taylor Perkins, is a straight-A student majoring in environmental studies. The hundred or so members seem more like a social group than anything else. It will take a while to go through everyone's history, but nothing immediately jumps out. Plus, the only injuries were suffered by members of the group."

"There could be a splinter faction."

"That's what we need to figure out. What about the other man you mentioned? What's his involvement?"

"He was a more radical member of the LNF, but he runs a gym now. He has no affiliation with any groups. He has a record, but it's for bar fights and vandalizing a neighbor's property who he had a beef with."

"Sounds like someone with an anger problem."

"Definitely. But I don't see a motive to what happened today. Ten years ago, I did, because Hank was very actively involved with Donovan Byrne, the leader of the LNF. But both Lauren and

Hank told me that the group completely fell apart after Byrne died, and I have no evidence to prove otherwise. Believe me, I've looked."

Emi gave her a smile. "I believe you. So, what's next?"

"I need to get to Kevin, and I have a secret weapon."

"What's that?"

"My father. He's ultimately Kevin's boss. I'm going to have dinner at my parents' house. I'll get my dad to call him. I know he'll pick up the phone for my dad."

"Good idea. You should know that Rob got a call from your father earlier."

She looked at Emi in surprise. "Why? What was that about?"

"He apparently wanted to put pressure on the investigation, because Lexitech is a Carlson company. He also wanted to make sure that you weren't being put in danger."

"He has no right to interfere."

"I think your father believes he has the power to do anything he wants," Emi said gently. "Rob knows your father has tremendous influence with the top brass, people who might control his career, so he'll want to solve this case as fast as possible."

"I will shut my father down tonight."

"Good. Because Rob may try to get you out of the investigation to appease your dad."

Anger ran through her at the idea that her father was trying to control her career. "I'll take care of it," she said with determination. "Thanks for the heads-up."

"No problem. I'm going to grab a salad from the café across the street. I'll talk to you later."

She picked up her phone and texted her mother: *I'm coming to dinner. See you soon.*

She immediately got back a dozen heart emojis. Her mother was happy now, but she might not be quite so happy when she got done talking to her dad.

CHAPTER ELEVEN

CAITLYN'S PARENTS lived in a three-story mansion in the Presidio, a posh, hilly neighborhood in San Francisco with views of the Golden Gate Bridge. Their stately home had iron gates at the entrance and tall trees around the front and sides of the house, while the backyard looked out at the bay. She put in a code to enter through the gates and then drove up to the home.

It was seven, and there were lights on in many of the rooms. It astounded her how lit up her parents' house always was, considering there were only two adults currently living there. While there were other staff, including a housekeeper, chef and gardener, they all lived off-site. She'd thought her parents might move to something smaller once all their kids were grown and gone, but they seemed to be comfortable where they were.

She got out of the car and moved up the steps to the grand front door. She put in her code and then entered the house, stepping into a beautiful foyer with a two-story ceiling, a sweeping staircase, and a large, round glass table holding an ornate vase of fresh flowers. Some things never changed. Her mother loved floral arrangements, especially those including lavender, and there were always fresh, colorful flowers in every room.

"Caitlyn!" her mother exclaimed, as she came down the hall from the kitchen and family room area at the back of the house.

Her mom had dark-brown hair and brown eyes that were a bit on the cool, reserved side, as were her clothes. Even when she was in her house, Rebecca Carlson was stylish and conservatively dressed in black slacks and a cashmere sweater. She was extremely fit for her sixty-six years, a result of the many hours she spent with her personal trainer doing Pilates, yoga, and weight training. She was also an avid tennis player and golfer and spent most of her free time at the nearby golf and tennis club.

"I'm so happy to see you, Caitlyn." Her mom gave her a smile, and then they exchanged a quick embrace. Hands-on affection wasn't really the Carlson way. "How are you doing?"

"I'm fine."

"You look tired."

"It's been a long day."

Her mother's sharp gaze swept her face. "You'll stay here tonight, won't you?"

"I hadn't thought that far ahead."

"I don't want you at a hotel when your room is waiting for you."

As much as she wanted to argue that she had somewhere else to go, the truth was she hadn't bothered to book a room and she might as well stay here. "All right, but just for tonight."

"I'll take it. Is there any news?"

"Today is the beginning of what will probably be another long investigation."

"With hopefully a better outcome," her mother finished.

"Hopefully. Is Dad in his study?"

"As always."

"I'm going to say hello."

"Of course. Your brothers will be arriving soon, and dinner is at seven thirty."

"You invited everyone over?" she asked in surprise. "You didn't even know if I was going to come."

"I was hopeful. But even if you couldn't make it, I felt like we needed to be together this evening. The news brought back bad memories for all of us."

"Well, it will be nice to see everyone." It had been almost a year since she'd seen her family in person. She hadn't made it home for the holidays due to work commitments. "How is Lana feeling?" she asked, referring to her brother Baxter's wife, who was four months pregnant with their first child.

"She has been having awful morning sickness. She's worried, of course, that something will go wrong since she had a miscarriage last time around."

"I hope she's all right. How is Baxter doing?"

"Honestly, I'm not sure. I think he's worn out from the stress of trying to have a child. There seems to be some tension between him and Lana, but a healthy, bouncing baby boy will be the cure for that."

"A boy? That's great."

"Another Carlson to carry on the family name. Your father is very excited about it."

"I'm sure." Her father was big on family and legacy building. The Carlson empire had been passed down from one son to the next for over a hundred years. "How is Spencer? Is he dating anyone?"

"I don't know. He doesn't tell me anything, and he's not getting along very well with your father, so he doesn't spend much time here."

"What are they fighting about now?"

"The usual—business," her mother said with a dismissive wave. "Spencer and your dad just don't think the same way. I keep telling Chuck to give Spencer a chance to find his own lane at the company. But they're always arguing about something. Anyway, you know I don't like to get involved in company matters. Why don't you see if you can get your father out of his study?"

"All right." She was happy to have an opportunity to speak to her dad before her brothers and her sister-in-law arrived.

Her father's study was located on the first floor at the opposite end of the house. As she neared the open door to his den, she heard him on the phone, and she paused, not sure she should interrupt.

"I told you, I'm not playing," her father said, a menacing threat in his voice. "I want to know what the hell happened today. If you can't do it, I'll find someone who can. Heads are going to roll."

He slammed the phone down, and she couldn't help wondering who had been at the other end of that phone call. Hopefully, it hadn't been Rob. She knew his heart was in the right place, but he wasn't helping.

She stepped forward, knocking on the door as she moved into the room. "Dad?"

Her father had been pacing the floor behind his massive desk when she entered. As soon as he saw her, the tension in his expression eased. "Caitlyn. Your mother wasn't sure you'd come."

"Here I am."

He walked around his desk to give her a hug. "I've been worrying about you all day."

"I'm okay."

He stepped back to give her a sharp look. "Are you lying to me?"

He'd asked her that question many times growing up, and her answer had always been the same: No. She'd been too intimidated to ever lie to him. He wasn't particularly tall or broad, but he had a powerful presence and a take-charge attitude that no one could ignore.

"I'm not lying," she told him. "Today's explosion brought

back some rough memories, but I'm handling them. I'm hoping this new case will not only be solved quickly but will also give us a clue to the past."

"Not if the investigators don't do a better job. I know you're one of them now, but the FBI was useless before."

"I can't entirely disagree. But this time will be different because I'm working the case, and I will get answers."

"At what cost?" He shook his head, a grim look in his gaze. "I don't like that you're getting dragged back into that darkness. It took you years to come out of it. I've never understood why you had to join the FBI, why you had to keep going back to the worst day of your life."

"My job is not just about the past. Being an agent has changed me, Dad. I'm doing good in the world, and I love that."

"I guess it's good that you like it. But I wish you would have come to work for our company. You could be running things alongside your brothers."

"It's not my thing. I like my career choice. Speaking of which, you need to back off Rob Carpenter."

"Not a chance. He needs to feel the pressure."

"He's working as hard as he can, and he's letting me help even though I'm not assigned to his office. However, if you're in his face all day long that could change, and that would be a big mistake. I know more about Bolton, eco-terrorists, and the past bombing than anyone else. I'm the best bet for solving the case. If Rob kicks me off the team, that won't happen."

"I will make sure he doesn't do that."

"I know you think you're all powerful, but you don't run the FBI."

"I have friends in higher places than Rob Carpenter. And it's not just about you. Kevin was supposed to be in that auditorium today. Carlson Industries was targeted again."

"I know. Speaking of Kevin, he's not returning anyone's calls. That's not helpful. You need to get him to talk to me."

"He's shaken, Caitlyn."

"I understand—better than anyone—but I still need to talk to him. And, frankly, his silence is making him look like he's guilty of something."

"Of agreeing to speak at his old college?" her father asked in surprise.

"People who have nothing to hide don't usually avoid our calls."

"He doesn't have anything to say; he wasn't there. He was still in his car when the bomb went off. It's the activists you should be talking to. They're the ones who always cause trouble."

"Everyone will be interviewed, Dad, but I still need to talk to Kevin. I'm concerned that he may have some knowledge of someone from our shared past that might be involved again. He went to Bolton. He was there when I almost lost my life. He shouldn't be afraid to speak to me."

"I can ask him to get in touch with you. I think he's just rattled. He feels like he had a very close call."

"Can you call him now and then hand me the phone?"

Her father hesitated. "You want me to ambush him?"

"It's hardly an ambush. Now I'm wondering why you're reluctant to call him when you're eager to get this case resolved."

"Fine." He moved back to the desk and grabbed his phone, putting in the call.

She could hear it ringing.

"He's not answering," her father said.

"Leave a message. Tell him to call me as soon as possible. That you'll expect him to make that happen tonight."

Her father frowned. He wasn't one to be ordered about, especially not by his daughter, but he did as she'd requested.

"Satisfied?" he asked.

"I appreciate your help." She swallowed hard, knowing that

she needed to bring up Quinn before everyone else arrived. "There's one more thing I need to ask you. It's about Quinn."

His demeanor shifted—his body tensing, his gaze narrowing, his jaw turning hard as a rock. "I had hoped to never hear his name again. He's the one who got you into that damn group of militants. He's the one you almost lost your life for."

"I know who he is. What I don't know is why he left. Did you tell him to get out of my life? Did you threaten him? Did you force him to leave?"

"Is that what he told you?"

"That's not an answer."

He stared back at her. "Are you seeing him again?"

"That's also not an answer. Why are you deflecting? The questions aren't difficult. Did you tell him to get out of my life or not?"

Her father lifted his chin, defiance in his brown eyes. "Yes, I told him he needed to go; he'd hurt you enough."

She'd known it was the truth even before he'd confirmed it, but she was still incredibly disappointed. "You had no right to do that."

"I'm your father; I have every right to protect you. I don't regret it. I'd do it again. I believed then and now that Quinn knew who set that bomb and he protected them instead of you. Look at his history. He practically founded the group. He came from a violent family. His father made bombs for the IRA. Quinn had more skills in that regard than anyone else. And he didn't go with you to the ceremony when he was supposed to. He conveniently had to study at a time that was suddenly changed."

Her father had certainly written an explicit narrative to explain his actions.

"Quinn was eleven when his father was killed," she said. "He didn't know how to make a bomb. That was never proven by anyone."

"The FBI liked him for a suspect."

"Was that because you kept pointing them in his direction?"

"They were following the facts. I did you a favor, Caitlyn."

"How can you say that? I loved Quinn."

"You were too young to see him for who he was. I thought you started to get it afterward. He barely came around. And when he did, you wouldn't even talk to him. He wasn't making you happy. He was making things more difficult."

"I wasn't happy whether he was there or not. I was wrecked. I was in physical and emotional pain."

"I know, and I hated seeing you like that. I missed my little girl, the one who was joyful and innocent. I wanted you to be the way you were before you met him."

"You mean before the bomb went off. Quinn didn't try to kill me, Dad. I know that."

"Well, I don't."

Their gazes clashed for a long second. "You shouldn't have sent him away. You should have let me handle it. It was my relationship, my life."

"I won't apologize. I still think it was the best decision. Have you seen him again?"

"No." She realized as she said it that this might actually be the first time she'd lied to her dad. But knowing her father was embroiling himself in the current case and his complete lack of apology for what he'd done before, she couldn't trust him not to get in the middle again.

His gaze shifted as voices rang through the house. "It sounds like everyone is here."

"I need you to promise me that you'll back off Rob Carpenter."

"Why should I?"

"Because you will not be a help—you will only be another problem that I have to deal with. I'm an agent, Dad. This is my job. And I am very good at it. Let me do it without your interference."

He stared back at her with what looked like admiration in his eyes. "I've never heard you sound so confident or determined. I used to think you were the least like me out of my three children, but maybe I was wrong." He paused. "But I wasn't wrong about Quinn. He didn't tell you everything, Caitlyn. He had secrets you knew nothing about."

She wanted to argue, but she couldn't. She didn't know if Quinn had had a secret back then, but he certainly had one now.

Dinner was awkward. Caitlyn couldn't pinpoint exactly what was wrong, but there was a lot of tension in the group. They didn't talk much about the blast, as her mother wanted to keep the conversation light, but the atmosphere was still thick with unspoken words and emotions. It reminded her of the weeks and months after the blast when everyone had tiptoed around her, not speaking of anything consequential, but the lack of discussion and acknowledgment of what had happened to her had only made things worse. It felt the same way now. After an hour of stilted conversation, she wished she hadn't come home.

She had a feeling she wasn't the only one not enjoying dinner. Her brother Baxter, who was seven years older than her, appeared more strained than normal. While he was solicitous of his wife, Lana, making sure she had everything she needed, he didn't seem to be fully present.

Lana, a tall blonde with a small baby bump, got excited when she spoke about the baby, but when the conversation moved onto other matters, she quickly lost interest. And then there was Spencer…

Spencer had light brown hair, streaked with gold. Two years older than her, Spencer was usually funny and outgoing, but tonight he was quiet. He seemed to be particularly terse with her father, but he also had little to say to her.

He caught her gaze as she finished her coffee. "Want to take a walk outside?" he asked.

She was more than happy to say yes and leave the tension behind.

They left the dining room and wandered into the backyard. A large deck offered patio seating, a built-in barbecue, and an outdoor kitchen. Beyond that was a beautifully landscaped garden, and a grotto that contained a hot tub. From the yard, she could see the lights of the Golden Gate Bridge.

She stared at those lights for a long minute. Bolton was on the other side of those lights, in the dark hills. When she'd been a student there, she'd felt like she was a million miles from home, but she really hadn't gone that far.

"This place always looks the same," Spencer murmured, digging his hands in the pockets of his khaki pants. "The world changes, but this house, this yard, never does. It's the same flowers, the same plants. Even when the patio chairs needed to be recovered, Mom just got the same material and had them redone."

"I can't tell if you're happy about that or not."

"I wouldn't mind seeing some changes around here and at work, too. The world moves on, but this family is stuck."

There was no mistaking the stress in his voice now. "Mom said you and Dad aren't getting along."

"That's an understatement."

"What's going on?"

"Dad has been running a competition for the CEO position at Lexitech since Harmon Phelps retired in January. It was supposed to be mine, but then Dad put Kevin in the running. He's a marketer, not an executive. It's ridiculous. But Kevin started undercutting me behind my back. He has been going to Dad with cool charts and graphs and convincing him that he should get the job."

"Did you talk to Dad about it?"

"Of course. He said Kevin spends more time on costs while I spend more time on dreams. He wants a CEO who can make money, as if I can't do that. We're supposed to work together for the next two months, and then Dad will pick a winner. I'm the one with the Carlson last name, not Kevin. I don't even understand why he's a possibility."

"Maybe you should work somewhere else."

"I've thought about it. But dammit, Caitlyn, how can I let Kevin take what's mine?"

She hadn't seen Spencer this worked up in a very long time. She understood his position, but she was also starting to worry that he was giving himself a very good motive for wanting to get Kevin out of his way. "Maybe you need to talk to Kevin. You have been friends for your entire lives."

"Not anymore. Kevin has changed over the past year. His ambition is off the charts. He's not the guy you knew. And he seems to think he's a Carlson. He even goes golfing with Dad, acting like he's a third son."

"You hate to play golf."

"That's not the point." Spencer gave her an annoyed look. "I thought you'd understand."

"I do. You've been at Carlson since you were twenty-one. You've put your time in."

"Exactly. I've given twelve years of my life to the company and I should be CEO of Lexitech. I'm the one who suggested Dad acquire them in the first place."

"So prove to him that you're the right choice."

"I'm beginning to think he already made his decision."

"Or he's just trying to make you do better by giving you a rival. He loves to do that. He used to pit you and Baxter against each other."

"That's true. And I have thought that was the reason, but then I see Kevin walking around all smug, and it pisses me off."

"Have you talked to Kevin since the bombing this morning?"

"No. I probably sound like an ass complaining about him when he could have been injured today."

"He could have died."

"Well, he didn't. He wasn't even there. Kevin is a golden boy. Bad luck doesn't touch him."

"I know you're angry at Kevin for trying to steal Lexitech from you, but if you talk to anyone from the FBI, do not show this bitterness."

"Why would I talk to anyone from the FBI?" he countered, a wary gleam entering his eyes. "I wasn't involved with anything at Bolton."

"You are a senior vice-president at Lexitech, same as Kevin. And if Lexitech was targeted…"

"It wasn't the only company on the panel, and we were there to talk about the environmental measures we've put into place."

"Has Lexitech received any threats recently?"

"No. Kevin wouldn't have gone if there had been threats." He paused. "I know you probably can't tell me anything, but are there any leads?"

"It's early. There's a lot of information to compile."

"And you're back in the middle of it. I can't believe going to Bolton could have been fun for you, not after another bomb went off."

"It was difficult," she admitted. "It brought back a lot of memories. There are similarities between today and ten years ago."

"You think there's a link?"

"Maybe. I spoke to Hank Merchant. He said something that surprised me."

"What's that?"

"He told me that you and Kevin were hanging out with Wyatt Pederson, Vitaly Loucks, and Gary Keniston, three of whom were prominent LNF members and suspects in the last bombing."

"Wait. What?"

"You heard me."

His brows drew together. "I think you're talking about the birthday party Vitaly hosted for his girlfriend, Shanice Lindeman. I was invited because I'm friends with Shanice. Kevin, of course, was also friends with Shanice, as well as Vitaly and Hank."

"I know Kevin has ties to the group. I just didn't realize you knew any of them."

"I've met a couple of them through Kevin and through Shanice."

"How did Shanice meet Vitaly?"

"That was through Kevin, too."

She was realizing how much of a conduit Kevin was between the past and the present. "Hank also mentioned that you and Kevin argued that night. He thought someone was close to taking a punch. That doesn't sound like you."

"I'm sure we were arguing, but it wasn't going to escalate to anything physical. What was Hank's point? What was he trying to get you to think?" Spencer challenged, his gaze narrowing. "I feel like I'm being set up or something."

"I'm not sure."

"Caitlyn, come on. Hank was obviously trying to throw shade at someone. Was it me or Kevin?"

"Maybe both of you."

"Why?"

"I don't know. That's why I brought it up."

His gaze narrowed. "Why were you talking to Hank at all? Does he know something about the bombing?"

"He says he doesn't. I'm not sure if that's true or not." She paused. "What about the organizers of the symposium? Do you know anything about the student group that invited Lexitech to participate?"

"No. Kevin was communicating with the group, not me.

Actually, one of the reasons why Kevin agreed to participate was because the girl who asked him was really hot."

"Seriously?"

"Yeah. I reminded him that he's thirty-three and I'm not sure this girl is even twenty-one, but he didn't want to hear that."

"Do you know her name?"

"I don't. Sorry. Like I said, we haven't been friends for the last several months. I wasn't that interested. I'm sure Kevin can tell you."

"He's not returning my calls. I even resorted to asking Dad to get involved, but Kevin didn't pick up the phone for him, either. I'm not sure why he's avoiding me."

"That's weird. I'm sure he'll call you back now that Dad has asked. He won't want to do anything to jeopardize his chance at becoming CEO."

"I hope he does. You should find a way to do what you want to do in business, Spencer. If it's for Dad, for Carlson Industries, great, but if it's not, that's okay, too. I know it's been ingrained in you that you should follow in the footsteps of all the great Carlson men in front of you, but that's not the only path."

"You're lucky you were born a girl," he muttered.

"I haven't had the same pressure. I know that. But we're talking about you. I haven't seen you this upset in a very long time. If you want this CEO job, then fight like hell for it, and put Kevin in his place. But if you're doing it just because you want to beat Kevin or you want to prove something to Dad, then maybe you should reconsider your goals."

"That's easier to say than to do. I've never worked anywhere else."

"It can be good."

"Do you really like what you're doing?"

"Very much. I have surprised myself with how good I am at it."

"Well, I'm glad you're happy, Caitlyn. I hope what happened

today doesn't drag you back into that dark pit of despair you spent far too much time in."

"I'm not going to let it."

"So, should I ask?"

She saw the question in his gaze. "Quinn is not a part of this." Pausing, she added, "Did you know that Dad sent Quinn away?"

Spencer stared back at her, then shook his head. "No, but I wouldn't be surprised if he did. He hated the guy, especially after the bomb went off. He blamed Quinn for everything. I have to admit, I blamed him, too. We all did. In fact, there were times when I thought you did, too."

"He wasn't responsible."

"Okay. So, what does that mean?"

She let out a sigh. "I don't know."

"Are you going to find out?"

"I'm not sure."

"Sounds like a yes to me. Have you talked to him in the last ten years?"

"I have," she said, deciding not to lie to her brother.

"Did he explain why he disappeared?"

"Not all of it."

"Enough?"

She shook her head. "Not really."

"Then maybe you should keep your distance."

"That's probably good advice."

He smiled. "You're not going to take it, are you?"

She smiled back. "Probably not."

CHAPTER TWELVE

CAITLYN WAS on her fourth cup of coffee as the clock ticked past two o'clock on Friday afternoon. She'd gotten into the office just after eight and had been working ever since, with a quick break at noon to grab a salad. They'd had two team meetings, one when she'd first arrived, and one an hour ago. Unfortunately, the developments on the case were few and far between.

She stretched her arms over her head and then turned her attention back to her computer. Before she could return to reviewing security footage from Bolton and the surrounding area, her phone vibrated on her desk.

At the text from Kevin, her heart jumped.

I'm not avoiding you, Caitlyn. I was on a plane to London. Now, I'm in a taxi. I will call you when I have a chance, but I don't know anything about the blast. I just know I could have died. I had to get out of town. I'll be in touch.

She frowned. *What the hell was Kevin doing in London?* Neither her father nor her brother had mentioned that Kevin was scheduled to leave the country.

She immediately texted Spencer: *Heard from Kevin. He's in London. What's going on? Was it a planned trip?*

She tapped her fingernails on the desk as she waited for a reply. It came quickly.

No idea. Wasn't scheduled. Ask Dad. If Kevin told anyone, it's probably him.

She didn't want to bring her father any further into the case when she'd made a point of telling him to back off. She also doubted Kevin had told her dad anything. It sounded like he'd made a panicked trip out of the country. *What was he afraid of?*

None of the other targets from the symposium had run or refused to talk to the FBI. Kevin's actions implied something; she just didn't know what. It seemed unlikely he'd set the bomb, but he had been a Bolton student ten years ago, and he had lived with Hank Merchant and been friends with other members of the LNF. Maybe that's why he was scared.

She texted Kevin back: *It's imperative that I talk to you, Kevin. Please call me ASAP.* She hesitated, then added: *I want to make sure you're safe. I'm concerned you were a target. We need to talk.*

Kevin's reply was brief. *Your family is the target. You know what that feels like. I need some time to regroup.*

I understand. But this may not be over. Spencer said you're dating one of the organizers of the symposium. Can you put me in touch with her?

She waited several long minutes. Finally, he answered: *Old news. That ended a while ago.*

What's her name? she asked.

There was no response. She waited several more minutes, but clearly, Kevin was done talking. She was surprised by his reluctance to answer a simple question about who he'd been dating. If they weren't going out anymore, there was no need for him to protect her. Yet that's exactly what he seemed to be doing.

She texted her brother again. *Kevin won't tell me the name of the woman he was seeing at Bolton. Are you sure you don't remember her name?*

Spencer replied: *I can ask his assistant.*

That would be great. Also, be careful. Make sure Lexitech's security is on point.

Don't worry. We're beefing up security at every office as well as the gala.

Dad should cancel that, she texted back.

It will probably be the safest place in the city. There will be bomb-sniffing dogs, probably wearing dog tuxes if Mom has her say.

She smiled. *Now that I might actually like to see.*

Putting her phone aside, she got on the computer again. The security cameras in the immediate area of the auditorium had been taken off-line for fifteen minutes before the explosion, so the bomb had been placed in the bushes within minutes of going off. The students who had been injured and were closest to the auditorium had not reported seeing anyone go near the area, but they'd only just arrived a few minutes prior to the blast.

She'd been looking at footage taken after the cameras went back online. For some reason, she couldn't find Quinn. He'd obviously been standing in a dead spot that hadn't been caught by any of the cameras that had been put back online. *Was that just lucky?*

She wished she didn't keep having doubts about him. She needed to find a way to think about Quinn that she could stick with, instead of going back and forth between certainty and distrust.

In her heart, she knew he hadn't set either bomb. It was just that her head kept questioning her heart, wondering if she'd been so in love with the man she just hadn't seen him for who he was. But she didn't really believe that. She had been in love, but she had also known him very well. Ten years had turned him into a stranger, but their kiss yesterday had brought him back into focus.

Letting out a sigh, she suddenly straightened, seeing a face she had not expected to see. She stopped the video, backed it up, then enlarged the screen. Her heart sped up at the appearance of the blond man wearing jeans and flip-flops. It was Wyatt Pederson, dressed the way he used to dress in college.

Why was Wyatt at the scene?

As the question ran through her mind, Wyatt left, disappearing from the scene. He'd only been there a few minutes. He hadn't spoken to anyone, and he certainly hadn't been interviewed, which made sense since it was more than five hours after the blast.

Had he gone to Bolton out of morbid curiosity?

Maybe, like Quinn, he'd just felt an inexplicable need to go to the scene.

She sat back in her seat, something else niggling at the back of her brain. Lauren and Hank had both mentioned Wyatt yesterday, and Lauren had suggested that Wyatt had been at the scene of the first explosion, which conflicted with the alibi provided by his father, Senator Pederson. *Was that a slip on Lauren's part? Or had she wanted to cast doubt onto Wyatt?*

Someone was lying. *Who?* The more she thought about it, the more she wondered if it wasn't the senator. The case file had always bothered her with its lack of depth, especially in regard to the Pederson brothers. But Agent John Bauer, who had run the investigation, had told her that they followed every fact. While they hadn't conducted more than five or six in-depth interviews with LNF members, they believed that they'd identified the persons of interest. Donovan and Quinn had been at the top of the list with Hank, Vitaly, Vinnie, Gary, and Lauren also interrogated for a possible connection to the blast.

She tapped her fingers restlessly on the desk. Had Senator Pederson put pressure on Bauer to steer the investigation away from his sons, or…

Her thoughts turned to her father. She really hoped it wasn't her dad who'd swayed the investigation, who'd been so determined to make Quinn pay for what had happened to her that he'd pressured Bauer to build his case off Quinn. However, she couldn't completely discount that possibility.

"Find something?" Emi asked.

She started as Emi appeared at her desk. "What?"

"You looked lost in thought. Did you find something?"

"Yes." She moved the footage back to Wyatt. "That's Wyatt Pederson, one of Senator Pederson's sons. He went to Bolton with me. He was part of the LNF."

Emi looked at the time stamp. "He came to the scene hours after the blast."

"And left very quickly."

A light entered Emi's eyes. "This is good, Caitlyn. I looked through the same footage, but I didn't recognize him. Nor did I find him particularly suspect. There were dozens of people who walked onto the scene and then left." Emi smiled. "You might be earning your keep after all. But..."

She saw an odd look in Emi's eyes. "What?"

"Rob will be wary of you going after a senator's son without any real proof."

"He was on the scene."

"Hours afterward. I'm not telling you not to talk to Wyatt, just tread carefully. As you know, Rob has ambitious aspirations."

"I'm aware. It was one reason why I left Miami. I'm actually surprised you wanted to work for him again."

"I needed to be here in San Francisco. My father was having health issues, and my mom needed help. I took this job so I could do that."

"How is your dad doing now?"

"Much better. In fact, his cancer is in remission, and they're planning a trip to San Diego next month. They're actually thinking of moving down south."

"Maybe you can make another move then." Emi was too good of an agent to be constrained by Rob's political handcuffs.

"I might consider that. Think you could put in a word for me with your boss? I'd love to work on a task force."

"I could do that. Flynn is always looking for good agents."

"Does Lucas Raines still work there?"

"He does. You know Lucas?"

"Our paths crossed a few years ago." Emi gave her a smile. "The man is hot."

She smiled back. "He is that."

"Is he married?"

"Nope."

"Interesting." Emi paused as a sudden hush took over the room.

She jumped to her feet as Rob walked in, followed by two senior agents. Something had happened.

Rob stepped in front of a monitor and put up an image of a building being evacuated. "This is happening now at Alancor. A board meeting was in progress when toxic fumes were released through the ventilation system. Three members of the board are on their way to the hospital."

Caitlyn caught her breath. Alancor had been scheduled to be at the symposium. That couldn't be a coincidence.

"We believe this incident may be related to the bombing at Bolton College," Rob continued. "We've notified the other symposium participants, Lexitech and the Freeman Group, to increase security and to notify us of any unusual activity. Agents Conroy and Mueller will head over to Alancor. Hazmat is already on site. Agents Johnson and Kacinzsi will go to the hospital to talk to the victims. Everyone else—do what you're doing. We need to figure out what's coming next and where. We're not just looking at bombs now."

"They're attacking by using the same pollutants they fight against," she said, her mind processing this latest attack.

"Alancor was fined two years ago for releasing toxic gas into the environment. The perpetrators hit Alancor in the same way they hit the planet."

All gazes turned to her.

"Go on," Rob said.

"Whatever the Freeman Group and Lexitech have done wrong, that will be the target."

"I've been researching that," Emi said. "The Freeman Group was sued for polluting a river in Central California."

"The water system," she said, meeting Emi's gaze. Then she turned back to Rob. "We need to make sure the water system at any office tied to the Freeman Group is secure."

He nodded. "Good idea. Agent Sakato, take the lead on that angle. Let's find the stains on the environmental records of the companies involved and see if we can get out in front of these attacks."

As the group returned to work, Rob walked over to her.

"Good insight, Caitlyn," he said brusquely.

"I hope I'm right."

"I've notified your father that Carlson Industries may also be a target, in addition to Lexitech."

"He's aware of that. He's increasing security at all offices."

"Yes, but I'm more concerned about an event that your family is holding on Sunday."

"The annual foundation gala. It's a huge fundraiser."

"I'm very aware of what it is. You need to get them to cancel it."

That might be the most difficult order Rob had ever given her. "My father doesn't bow to threats, stated or implied."

"He won't just be risking his own life; he could be risking hundreds of other lives. Talk to him."

"He might take it better from you."

"I told him what I thought. He said he's hiring extra security, that the gala will be the safest place in the city."

"Then you have your answer."

"Change his mind, Caitlyn. The mayor will be there, numerous elected officials, and heads of companies. It is a high-profile target, and we are working blind. If anything happens on my watch…"

"I'll do my best to change his mind, but I can't make any promises. Speaking of elected officials, have you had any contact with Senator Pederson?"

Something shifted in Rob's gaze. "Why do you ask?"

"His son, Wyatt, went to Bolton yesterday to look at the scene. He was in school with me. But he and his brother, Justin, were never thoroughly interviewed."

"They had an alibi. I went through the file again last night."

"I believe the alibi was bogus."

"It came from the senator. Are you saying he lied?"

"Possibly. Which is why I'm wondering if you've been in touch with him?"

"He called me yesterday," Rob admitted. "He's concerned."

"Did he mention his sons?"

"No. He was calling as a senator worried about his constituents. He wanted a progress report on the case. I gave him one. He wasn't thrilled at our lack of progress. Let's leave his son on the back burner. I do not need you accusing the senator of lying ten years ago."

"I wasn't planning on making that accusation—yet. But Wyatt could be involved in this current explosion," she argued. "He was at the scene yesterday."

"When?"

"Well, it was hours after the blast," she admitted. "However, he was there, and we need to know why. I can talk to Wyatt as an old friend. It won't be official."

His jaw tightened. "All right, but don't accuse him of anything unless you have evidence."

"Got it. I'd also like to talk to Agent Bauer. I wonder if he got pressure from the senator, if that's why the sons were not more thoroughly investigated."

Rob's expression moved from irritation to anger. "Agent Bauer is out of town. I already called him. He's on a long-awaited European trip, so that will have to wait."

"I don't think it can wait. I just need a few minutes of his time."

"His investigation doesn't matter now. I need cooperation, and if you accuse former agents and senators of obstructing an investigation, that's the last thing I'll get. Dammit, Caitlyn, don't make me sorry I brought you into this."

"I just gave you a new angle," she reminded him.

"And that was good. Look forward, not back. Stick to facts, not speculation. Cooperation is first and foremost. Everything else comes later."

"Got it."

As Rob walked away, she grabbed her bag and headed down to the parking garage. Wyatt might be a dead end, but her gut told her that he was worth talking to. The rest of the team was looking forward. But there might be an answer from the past that could lead them to the truth now, and she was the only one who could bring the two together.

CHAPTER THIRTEEN

CAITLYN HAD JUST GOTTEN into her car when her phone rang. Her heart jumped. It was Quinn. She'd been trying not to think about him for most of the day, and here he was. "Hello?"

"I was looking through some things I had from my LNF days," he said.

"And?"

"We need to talk to Wyatt."

She was surprised by his words. "I agree, but just out of curiosity, why did you come to that conclusion?"

"I found an old photo of Wyatt and Donovan. They had just gotten matching tattoos on their forearms."

"Of what?"

"A snake with its head hanging by a thread."

"That's a little disgusting. What does it mean?"

"Donovan used to say we'll never get anywhere until we cut off the heads of the snakes."

"And you think because Wyatt has the same tattoo that he shared the same thinking?"

"Yes. I also keep going back to what Lauren said about Wyatt being at the scene ten years ago."

"Which doesn't make sense because he had an alibi from the senator. It's in the file."

"Maybe Lauren lied."

"Or she didn't. Want to know something else that's interesting? Wyatt is on the surveillance footage from Bolton yesterday. It was hours after the blast, but he was there. Was he just curious like you, or did he have another reason?"

"We need to find out."

"I'm driving to his bar now."

"Don't bother. I'm sitting outside the bar. He's not there. The bartender told me he didn't come in today. Do you know where Wyatt lives?"

"Yes. 137 Dove Way, near the Great Highway."

"I'll meet you there."

She tried to tamp down the sizzle of excitement those words brought, but she wasn't particularly successful. She told herself they were just working together on the case. That was it. That was all it would be. "By the way," she added. "There was an incident at Alancor, one of the companies scheduled to speak at the symposium."

"Another bomb?"

"No, but toxic gas was piped in through the ventilation system. Several people went to the hospital because of it. Apparently, there was a board meeting going on."

"So the heads of the company were in the room," he said slowly.

"The snakes?" she queried, finishing his thought.

"Yes. And didn't Hank say yesterday that they wanted to attack the companies in the same way that they attacked the environment?"

"He did say that, and Alancor has had problems with air pollution," she said.

"Maybe Wyatt knows more about the grand plan."

"I hope he does. I'll see you soon."

A feeling of foreboding ran down Quinn's spine as he thought about the gas attack. The stakes were going up. The terrorists weren't done. They needed to get answers fast! Hopefully, Wyatt could provide some new clues. Although he wasn't sure they could trust anything Wyatt had to say. But he was curious to hear whether he'd admit to being at the scene ten years ago. Or would he stick with the alibi? It wouldn't surprise him if the senator had pulled strings. Chuck Carlson had done the same thing. Agent Bauer had clearly been susceptible to powerful persuasion, and perhaps there had also been other perks.

But while the alibi and Wyatt's snake tattoo tied him to Donovan in a weird way, it was still difficult to see Wyatt as a violent terrorist. Wyatt's passions had mostly involved beer, babes, and pissing off his father. His brother, Justin, had been the real environmental activist, but Wyatt had been more of a hanger-on, interested in the social, not the serious.

Had Wyatt's attitudes changed? Had Donovan's charismatic and persuasive personality turned the non-political Wyatt into someone else?

It took him only another five minutes to get to Wyatt's condo, which was part of a newish development perched in an area of incredibly steep streets, some with amazing views of the ocean. He had just parked when Caitlyn's car slid into a spot across the street.

As she got out and walked toward him, his stomach clenched. He'd thought he was ready to see her again, but he wasn't. She wore dark jeans today, a black sweater under the same gray leather jacket she'd had on yesterday, and a pair of low-heeled black boots. Her hair was once again pulled back in a ponytail. He itched to pull that band out of her hair and run his hands through her long, thick waves.

"Quinn?" she queried, giving him a suspicious look as he drew near. "What are you thinking?"

"Nothing."

"Are you sure?"

"You don't want to know."

Something shifted in her eyes, and the not-so-distant past played between them as her gaze dropped to his mouth. His breath caught in his chest at that look. She didn't want to want him, but she did. God help him. He felt exactly the same.

"No," she said, shaking her head.

"What was the question?"

"We're not going to kiss again."

He couldn't agree, not with his body already firing on all cylinders. It had always been that way with Caitlyn. One look and he'd gone from zero to a hundred in ten seconds.

"Let's talk to Wyatt," she said quickly. "We need to focus on what's important, and that's not us. So, stop looking at me like that."

"Like what?"

"You know what," she said, her cheeks burning.

"You're looking at me the same way," he defended.

"That's impossible. I don't like you at all anymore."

"I'm sure you don't. But that's not really what we're talking about, is it?"

She turned and marched up to Wyatt's front door, leaving him no choice but to follow.

CHAPTER FOURTEEN

WHEN WYATT OPENED THE DOOR, his jaw dropped, and amazement entered his green eyes. "Who am I looking at?" he asked.

"Not a ghost," he said.

"Are you sure? I thought you were dead, Quinn."

"That seems to be the rumor, but I'm very much alive."

Wyatt's gaze moved to Caitlyn "And you're with Quinn again? You are the last two people in the world I would have expected to ring my doorbell. Man, this is crazy."

"We weren't expecting to be here, either," he said, thinking Wyatt had changed little in the past ten years. His hair was a dark blond, his scruffy beard slightly darker. He was tan despite the winter weather, and his faded, ripped jeans and long-sleeve T-shirt with a beer-loving slogan could have been taken right out of his closet in his college apartment. The same could be said for his flip-flops.

"What are you doing here?" Wyatt asked. "Wait, this is about the bomb at Bolton yesterday, isn't it?"

"Yes," Caitlyn replied. "Can we come in and talk to you for a minute, Wyatt?"

"Sure." He waved them inside as if he didn't have a care in

the world. If he was guilty of something, he wasn't showing it. Both Lauren and Hank had gotten wary when they'd appeared, but while Wyatt was surprised, he didn't appear nervous.

"Do you want a beer?" Wyatt asked.

"No thanks," he said. That was another thing that hadn't changed. Wyatt had always preferred beer over water. And as he looked around Wyatt's apartment, he saw more images from the past: the surfing posters, the empty bag of chips on the coffee table, and the video game player on the table. Wyatt and Hank had been video game junkies. The smell of weed was also thick in the air, another reminder from the past. Wyatt might be ten years older, but he still lived like a twenty-one-year-old.

"I know. The place is a mess," Wyatt said, with an unrepentant smile and a dismissive wave of his hand. "What can I say? I don't have anyone to clean up for." His gaze grew more speculative. "When did you two get back together?"

"We're not together," Caitlyn said quickly. "We're just trying to figure out if there's a connection between yesterday's explosion and the one ten years earlier."

"I heard you're an FBI agent, Caitlyn. I have to say, I'm impressed by that. I never would have taken you for that kind of kick-ass woman. What can I help you with?"

"Why did you go to Bolton yesterday, Wyatt?" Caitlyn asked sharply.

Surprise filled Wyatt's gaze, and for the first time, he appeared more wary. "You know about that?"

"You were spotted on a surveillance camera."

"Oh. Well, I was shaken by the news of the bomb. I was supposed to be at the symposium. I heard the news just as I was getting dressed to go over there. I couldn't stop thinking about it all day, so I went in the afternoon to see what it looked like."

"Why were you going to the symposium?" Caitlyn asked.

"Kevin asked me to attend. He wanted some friendly faces in the audience. He was concerned the environmental group might try to ambush him with tougher questions than they'd promised. He was lucky he wasn't there. So was I. It's weird, because I never thought twice about going. I couldn't imagine a bomb would ever go off there again. What are the odds?"

"Pretty long," she said. "Unless the same person set both bombs."

"Who would that be?"

"I was going to ask you that," she returned.

"I have no idea."

"You know what's curious," Caitlyn continued. "I heard you were also at the bomb site ten years ago, but the FBI file says you and your brother were with your dad that morning, at his office."

Wyatt stared back at her. He ran a hand through his hair and shifted his feet. "Okay. I can explain."

"Can you?" she challenged.

Quinn had to admit he enjoyed seeing this tough side of Caitlyn. She wasn't about to let anyone run over her.

"I went to my dad's office that morning. His assistant was helping Justin and me plan a graduation trip through Europe. Justin got to Dad's office before me. He was probably talking to Caroline for about an hour before I arrived. When my dad heard about the explosion, he came to find us, and he assumed that Justin and I had arrived together, and that's what he told the FBI. When he found out I was actually at Bolton when the bomb went off, he told me not to say anything unless I had helpful information, because it would cause more trouble for me to correct him. I'd also be putting his assistant in the hot seat since she hadn't given him the right information as to when we arrived."

"That's a very long, convoluted answer, Wyatt, and I don't believe your father was confused for one second," Caitlyn said flatly.

Wyatt stared back at her and then shrugged. "You're right. He was trying to protect me. I told him I didn't need protection, but he blew right past that. He told me to keep my mouth shut, and he'd take care of the rest. I thought I'd get questioned eventually, but no one ever came to talk to me."

Quinn was surprised Wyatt was being so honest. He probably figured Caitlyn had some evidence now to prove he'd been at the bomb site ten years ago.

"Would you have had anything to say?" Caitlyn challenged. "If the FBI had talked to you?"

"No. I knew nothing. I swear, that's the truth, Caitlyn. You were a friend. Our families vacationed together. If I'd known you were in danger, I would have stepped up. I wouldn't have let you get hurt. I wouldn't have wanted to destroy the building your family funded. It was for science."

"Others didn't feel the same about that building," Quinn said. "There was a lot of talk about protesting."

"They said my family's money was dirty," Caitlyn added. "You must have heard all that."

"I didn't agree with them," Wyatt said defensively. "But it's not like anyone listened to me. I wasn't in charge of anything. You both know that. I was high most of the time in college. I only joined the LNF because Justin was into it."

"Where was your brother that morning?" Caitlyn asked.

"I told you; he was at my dad's office."

"What time did he get there?"

"Long before the bomb went off."

Quinn wondered if that were true. Did Wyatt actually know when Justin got to his father's office? They hadn't been living together that year, choosing to separate their lives more than they had previously. Justin had had his own apartment, and Wyatt had lived with Vinnie.

"You should have been honest and stepped forward with whatever information you had, Wyatt," Caitlyn said. "You should have stood up to your father."

"I have never done that. Can you honestly say you've stood

up to your dad, Caitlyn? Come on, they're both cut from the same cloth. They use their power and their money to pull strings, and they're very good at it. They protect what's theirs and that includes their kids."

"My father has never lied to the FBI about me," Caitlyn said. "There are lines that can't be crossed."

Quinn had to bite his tongue to stop himself from pointing out that while Chuck Carlson hadn't lied about Caitlyn, Chuck had lied about him to get what he wanted. But now wasn't the time to challenge Caitlyn on her dad. They needed to stay unified in front of Wyatt.

"I really didn't know anything, Caitlyn," Wyatt said.

"Who do you think set the bomb ten years ago?" she asked.

"Probably Donovan. Or Quinn. The FBI sure seemed to like you as a suspect," Wyatt added, his gaze moving from Caitlyn to him.

"I didn't do it," he said, his gaze moving to Wyatt's arms, which were covered by his long-sleeve T-shirt. "Do you still have the tattoo?"

Wyatt started at the question. "Which one?"

"The snake. The one you and Donovan got together."

Wyatt pushed up his sleeve. "I had it redone. It's not a snake anymore."

No, it wasn't. Wyatt had had the snake turned into a fire-breathing dragon. "Why did you change it?"

Wyatt met his gaze. "Because after the bombing, I thought maybe Donovan was the snake, and I'd been a fool to follow him. I believed he was a good guy fighting for a good cause, but I might have been wrong."

"What was the meaning of the snake tattoo?" Caitlyn asked.

"Donovan said that's what we needed to do—cut off the heads of the evil snakes so they couldn't keep injecting their poison into the world."

"That's dramatic," she murmured.

"It seemed cool, and I was probably high when we did it. I don't remember it that clearly. But after the bomb, I started thinking about the snake and what Donovan had said, and how he got this crazed look in his eyes when he talked about the LNF. Knowing that he might have killed you, Caitlyn, it woke me up."

"He killed people, Wyatt. I wasn't the only victim."

"I know, and that's when I was done being an activist, especially with that group. Now, it has happened again." Wyatt shook his head. "I actually told Kevin not to do the symposium. I warned him about getting involved with another environmental group, but he didn't want to say no."

"Why not?" Caitlyn asked. "Because he wanted Lexitech to show that it was being a green corporate citizen?"

"That was part of it."

"What was the other part?" Quinn asked.

"There was a girl."

"Wait," Caitlyn cut in. "I've heard about this girl. She's a student at Bolton. Spencer told me Kevin was dating someone, but he didn't know the name. Do you?"

"Sure. Allison Sullivan. And you will not believe it, but she's Lauren Sullivan's sister."

His pulse jumped at the connection between Allison and Kevin. "Are you serious?" he asked. "Kevin is dating Lauren's sister?"

"I know it's crazy," Wyatt said, meeting his gaze. "Kevin met her about six weeks ago when she reached out to book him for the symposium and he fell hard. He brought her into my bar one night and they were all over each other. I've actually been wondering about her, hoping she's all right and not one of the students who was injured. I texted Kevin, but he hasn't gotten back to me."

"She wasn't injured," Caitlyn said.

"That's good news. She's a sweet girl, not intense or edgy like Lauren. Allison is a kindhearted soul."

"What do you know about Allison's group?" Caitlyn asked.

"Not much. They aren't that active or well organized. Allison said that they've been trying to get new members, and the symposium had gotten more students excited to join, because it looked like they were actually doing something." Wyatt cleared his throat as he checked his watch. "I have to meet someone soon. Can we cut to the chase? Am I in trouble for going to Bolton yesterday, Caitlyn?"

"I wouldn't expect trouble, unless you haven't told me the entire story."

"I was there for like five minutes. It was an impulse—obviously a bad one. But seriously, Caitlyn, you know me. You both do. Can you see me making a bomb? I couldn't even pass basic chemistry. It's not in my nature. I'm a lover, not a killer."

Quinn had to admit it was difficult to see Wyatt as a bomber. This easygoing, self-deprecating attitude was how he'd always been. Wyatt had never taken himself or life that seriously. Maybe he had just been high when he'd gone with Donovan to get the snake tattoos.

"Then help us figure out who could have been helping Donovan," Caitlyn said.

"I honestly don't know. The people I've seen since then are all leading normal lives. No one is still protesting anything, not even Hank, who would have probably been my second suspect after Donovan. But Hank runs a gym now, and he spends all his time there. I don't think he cares about the environment anymore." Wyatt's gaze moved to him. "What's your role in all this, Quinn? And where have you been all these years?"

"Not that far away. I'm helping Caitlyn look for answers."

"I would think you'd have more answers than I do. You and Donovan were best friends. You knew him better than anyone."

"At one time."

"I always wondered if you'd gotten the truth from Donovan before he died. You had to be one of the last people to see him."

He stiffened, not liking the new gleam in Wyatt's gaze. "Why would you say that?"

Wyatt gave him a long look. "It doesn't matter."

"It matters," Caitlyn cut in. "Why would you think Quinn talked to Donovan last?"

"I don't want to cause trouble."

Quinn suspected that's exactly what Wyatt wanted to do.

"Just say it," Caitlyn ordered.

"Well, here's the thing. Donovan asked me to meet him in Yosemite, but I told him no. I just didn't know what was going on with him at that point. But then I changed my mind. I love to hike. And I thought to myself, what if Donovan is innocent, and everyone is abandoning him? So, I drove up there." Wyatt paused. "When I got to the campground, I was pretty sure I saw your Jeep in the lot, Quinn. I headed down the trail to where I thought Donovan would climb, and that's when I saw the crowd and the commotion. There was an area roped off and someone said a hiker had fallen and died. I had a bad feeling about it. I waited for hours to find out who it was, and it was Donovan."

"You were there, Quinn?" Caitlyn demanded. "You were in Yosemite?"

"No," he said, shaking his head. "I wasn't there. That wasn't my Jeep." He made the lie as convincing as he could.

"I guess I was wrong," Wyatt said with a shrug, but there was a sharpness to his gaze that hadn't been there before.

Maybe Wyatt's laid-back surfer dude attitude was just a front. "You just said you weren't hanging out with Donovan after the blast because you weren't sure if he was involved. Why would you suddenly decide to join him on a hiking trip?" he challenged.

"I told you why. Everyone was treating him like he had the plague, and I didn't know for sure that he was guilty. I thought it would be a good chance to talk to him. But I was too late. The park rangers said it looked like he slipped and fell. I wondered if he didn't just let go. Maybe he felt guilty for what had happened.

I don't know." He took a breath. "You should have come to the funeral, Quinn."

"I couldn't come. I couldn't mourn him that way."

"It was rough," Wyatt admitted. "Donovan was only twenty-three years old. We looked up to him, but he was a kid like us."

"I know," he said, feeling a deep pit in his stomach.

"Donovan was trying to do good things. I just think he started listening to the wrong people," Wyatt said. "Like Gary or Hank. They had a different agenda. Their motives weren't as pure as Donovan's."

"Then why don't you think Gary or Hank set the bomb?" Caitlyn challenged.

"I don't know that they didn't," Wyatt replied. "But they did nothing without checking with Donovan. He was the leader. No one made moves that he was unaware of, except maybe that last one. Maybe he realized he'd lost control."

"If he'd realized that and he wasn't involved, he could have turned someone in," Caitlyn said.

"I don't know what to say except that I'm sorry, Caitlyn. I really am. Honestly, if I had proof of who the bomber was, I would have told someone, regardless of what my father wanted." He paused as his phone rang. "Damn. Can this phone hear me talk? My dad is calling. That can't be good." He let it go to voicemail. "Is there anything else?" He'd no sooner finished speaking when the phone began ringing again. "He will not give up. I better take this. Can you see yourselves out?"

"We might need to talk to you again," Caitlyn said.

"You know where to find me." Wyatt waved them toward the door as he answered the phone.

As they walked out of the condo, Quinn didn't instantly pull the door all the way shut, as he and Caitlyn listened.

"How did you know that?" Wyatt asked, surprise in his voice. "Is someone watching me?" He paused. "Are you kidding me?"

And then his voice faded away as he moved farther into the apartment.

He pulled the door shut, meeting Caitlyn's gaze. "Sounds like Senator Pederson knows we're here. Who else at the FBI knows Wyatt was at Bolton yesterday?"

"At least two agents. My boss wasn't eager for me to pursue Wyatt because of the senator's power, and the other agent is busy with the newest attack. I can't imagine either went rushing to inform the senator." She paused, blowing out a frustrated breath. "My head is spinning. I keep going around and around in a circle and I never end up anywhere new."

"That's the problem with circles," he said dryly.

"And that's not helpful."

"What do you want to do now?"

"I'm not sure."

"How about a drink?"

"That's a great idea."

He smiled at her enthusiasm. "We could go over to the beach, hit up the Buena Vista."

She sucked in a breath. "Let's go somewhere we haven't been before. I can't take another trip down memory lane right now."

"We could head over the bridge into Sausalito."

"That's a better plan. We can go to Jake's in Tiburon. My sister-in-law said it's new and great."

"Sounds good. Shall I meet you there?" he asked, pausing by his car.

"Why don't you follow me?"

"All right." Before he could move, a loud pop made him jump, and the window of his SUV shattered. "What the—"

"Get down," she said, grabbing his arm and dragging him around the back of the car as another blast echoed through the air.

He suddenly realized what was happening. *Someone was shooting at them.*

CHAPTER FIFTEEN

CAITLYN PULLED out her gun as another shot hit the car bumper.

"What are you doing?" he asked in shock.

"Giving you cover. When I shoot, get in the car."

"Seriously."

"Trust me."

Before she could fire, the front tire of the SUV was hit. "We're not taking my car anywhere."

"We'll take my car," she said decisively. "When I shoot, run across the street."

That seemed like a bad idea. While the street was narrow, he'd be a big target. But there was no other option. They had to get away. And he needed to trust her.

"Go, now," she said, as she stood up and fired.

Her three shots covered him to the car.

Caitlyn fired off another series of shots as she ran across the street.

She jumped behind the wheel, and he got into the passenger seat. A bullet shattered the rear window. Caitlyn started the car and peeled out of the spot. There were no more shots, but as he glanced in the side-view mirror, he saw a man jumping into a black car.

"He's going to follow us," he told her.

"I see him," she said grimly.

He put on his seat belt, bracing his hand on the door as she flew around a corner. The streets were narrow and steep in this part of town and not the place you wanted to have a car chase. But Caitlyn didn't seem bothered at all. There was determination and confidence in her gaze.

"Are you okay?" she asked, flinging him a quick look.

"I'm fine. Did you get a look at the shooter?"

"He was too far away. What about you?"

"Same." He gritted his teeth as she flew past a stop sign, sliding between a bus and another car. Looking in the side-view mirror, he saw the black car behind them. There was a man in the front seat, but he couldn't get a good look at him. He squinted, trying to catch a glimpse of the license plate. He caught the first three numbers, then the rest of them, but only because the car had drawn closer. "He's catching up."

"Don't worry, I got this."

Caitlyn pressed down harder on the gas, and the car lurched forward. They weren't exactly in a race car, but she seemed able to get every bit of power and maneuverability out of the vehicle. As they came down a hill, she flew through another intersection just as the light turned red. Car horns blared as the person following them almost collided with another vehicle.

She slammed on the brakes to avoid hitting a pedestrian who jumped back so fast she landed on her ass. Then they were flying down another block. Caitlyn took a quick turn into a narrow alley and drove past dumpsters and garbage cans.

Suddenly, she slammed on the brakes, so hard he almost hit the dashboard. Then she jumped out of the vehicle.

"What the hell?" he swore, then realized she was trying to buy them some time by shoving some dumpsters into the road.

He got out to help her, and they dived back into the car as the other vehicle came down the alley, but their path was now blocked.

They'd bought a few valuable minutes.

They sped out of the alley and down three more blocks, weaving in and out of traffic, with no sign of the pursuing vehicle. "I think you lost him," he said several minutes later.

She gave him a triumphant smile. "I think so, too." She still drove quickly but lessened her speed as she headed for the Golden Gate Bridge. "But I want to get out of the city."

"The bridge could be a risk."

"We're okay. I've got this, Quinn."

"I can see that." Still, he kept a steady gaze on the mirror, not letting out a breath of relief until they had crossed the bridge and were driving north past Sausalito and Marin.

"Where are we going?" he asked as she changed lanes and took the next exit.

"I have no idea," she admitted. "I already passed the exit for Jake's."

"That's fine. We should get farther away."

"Agreed."

He looked back at the broken glass in the rear window. "Is this a rental car?"

"Yes. I'll have to get the window fixed before I turn it back in." She flung him a quick look. "Your car was damaged, too."

"Well, they can both be fixed, so I can live with that result." He paused. "Why don't we go to my house?"

She shook her head. "No. Someone just took a shot at you. Your house might not be safe."

"They could have been shooting at you. You're the FBI agent. I'm no threat to anyone."

"Unless they think you know something that they don't want exposed. Since we don't know for sure, we need to be strategic. We need to go somewhere and regroup."

He thought about that, then realized he had the perfect place. "We can go to my boat."

"If it's registered to you, even under Michael Wainscott—"

"It's not. It's registered to my captain. He's away this weekend and won't return until Monday. He went to be with his daughter and granddaughter in Santa Cruz. His granddaughter goes to Bolton, by the way. That's how I first heard about the explosion. They were panicked, but apparently the kid was fine."

"It's strange that you work with someone whose daughter goes to Bolton. Does he know you went there?"

"He does not."

"At some point, I want to hear more about how you reinvented yourself so successfully. But for now, give me directions to the boat."

"It's in the harbor by Dillon Beach."

She gave him a worried look. "I don't know, Quinn. Even if the boat isn't registered to you, it's still located where you live. It wouldn't be difficult to figure out you're a diver."

She had a good point. "We'll take it out to sea."

"We don't need to be in the harbor?"

"Not tonight. The weather is fine. And there's a quiet cove not too far north. We can anchor there." He smiled. "Trust me, Caitlyn. I can make sure we're safe on the boat."

She smiled. "I guess we both have our strengths."

"You certainly showed yours tonight." He shook his head. "I'm still trying to come to grips with what just happened. If you hadn't been able to give us cover, we could both be dead."

"But we're not. That's what matters. Don't focus on what didn't happen. Just be happy with what did."

"Is that how you get through situations like this?"

"It's one way. I also take a lot of deep breaths."

He'd been trying to do that for the past twenty minutes, but it wasn't every day someone tried to kill him. *Had they been shooting at him or at Caitlyn?* It was impossible to know. He hadn't seen anyone come out of their homes during the gunfire, but then he hadn't really had time to look. He wondered what Wyatt had thought when he'd heard the shots. *Had he known what was happening? Had he been behind it? Had the call Wyatt received from his father had something to do with what was about to happen?*

He'd thought he'd get answers by talking to Wyatt, but now he had more questions.

When they got to the harbor, the sun was slipping past the horizon. Caitlyn helped him ready the boat for departure, and it felt good to be the one giving her orders for a few minutes, to be in control. This was his world, and he knew exactly what to do and how to do it.

As they left the harbor, Caitlyn stood at a nearby rail, taking long, deep breaths. Then she gave him a much more relaxed smile. "It's nice out here. It's like we just escaped reality."

"The magic of the ocean is working already."

She turned to face him, leaning back against the rail. "You and your ocean. I was always jealous of her."

"The sea can be seductive," he said lightly.

"So, I was right to be jealous."

"No. Not even the ocean could compete with you." He paused. "I have to say, I thought you were beautiful the second I met you, Caitlyn, but now, now you're...stunning."

She flushed at his words and tucked some wind-blown strands of hair behind her ears. "I wasn't looking for a compliment, Quinn."

"I'm just telling the truth. I'm impressed, not just by your looks, but by everything about you. The way you handled yourself back there..." He shrugged. "You were right on it. No trace of fear. No concern for yourself. You saved my life."

"I did what I was trained to do. I just wish I'd hit him."

"You got us away and out of danger. That's the important thing. You drove like a madwoman. I can't believe the girl who was afraid to learn how to drive a stick shift can do what you just did."

She shrugged. "I've actually discovered I'm a really good driver."

"What can't you do?"

"I think I'll keep that to myself," she said with a small smile. "I need to call my office and fill them in and see if they can pull up any footage from Wyatt's block. If we can identify the shooter, that could be a big lead."

"Would a license plate help?"

Her jaw dropped. "You got the plate? Why didn't you say something?"

"It went out of my head until just now. I was staring at the car so hard, I memorized the plate: 7K82L6.

"That's amazing. That could be a huge clue." She threw her arms around him and gave him a hug.

He was so shocked to have her in his arms, he didn't have time to respond, to squeeze her back. And then she was moving away.

"I'm going to call Emi. She can help run this down for me." Caitlyn paused. "I have to tell her you were with me, Quinn. There will be evidence on some camera; I'm sure of it."

"I understand. Why are you worried about it?" he asked, seeing unfamiliar shadows in her eyes.

"I'm afraid you'll be a distraction, a target to derail the investigation."

"The way I was before," he said flatly.

"Yes. That's why I didn't tell anyone I'd found you. I knew eventually it would get out, and I would have to come clean, but I wanted to wait as long as I could. Maybe it was a mistake." She let out a sigh. "Maybe it was all a mistake. When I found you, when I brought you into this, I put you in danger. You could have been shot today."

"We still don't know if they were aiming at me or you." He paused. "Did you see Wyatt come out of his house?"

"I saw nothing but the shooter. You?"

"I was too busy ducking. But I'm sure Wyatt looked out his window, at the very least. He had to know we were the targets."

"I wonder if he also knew the shooter. Something to think about."

"It definitely is," he agreed.

As Caitlyn moved down the rail to make her call, he turned his attention back to the sea, wondering if he would become the focus of the investigation as he had before. But it didn't matter. He needed the truth, and this time he was going to get it, no matter who tried to get in his way.

"Are you at the office?" Caitlyn asked.

"Yes, I just got back from Alancor," Emi replied.

"Any leads?"

"Unfortunately, no. The person who got into the ventilation system did so with a stolen Alancor ID. Cameras hacked once again. A utility worker in the building was found unconscious, but he'll be all right. The same is true for the board members who went to the hospital. They should all recover, but they may experience residual lung problems."

"I'm glad no one died."

"What have you been up to?"

"I went to see Wyatt Pederson."

"Did he have anything to say?"

"A few things. I think I mentioned to you that I heard Kevin Reilly from Lexitech was dating a student at Bolton. Well, Wyatt told me that the student is Allison Sullivan."

"She did not mention that in my interview with her," Emi said. "Seems like something she would have told me, considering he was scheduled to speak. Did you hear back from Mr. Reilly?"

"Only short texts, telling me that he was in London, that he felt shaken after the bomb, and he wanted to get away."

"I guess that's understandable."

"It seems a bit of an overreaction to me. I think there's something about the relationship between Kevin and Allison that's concerning."

"Maybe he thinks she tried to kill him."

"It's possible. Wyatt said that he saw Kevin and Allison in his bar several weeks ago, and they were all over each other. I don't know what happened to end that, maybe nothing of significance, since there's a big age gap between them."

"It's worth following up on."

"Wyatt also admitted to me that his father lied when he gave him an alibi ten years ago. He had some roundabout story as to why his father wasn't really lying, but it won't hold up. I need to see what Agent Bauer has to say about this new information. But Rob keeps telling me to leave him alone, that he's on some long-awaited vacation."

"Rob doesn't want to have to address lies from the senator right now."

"I'm aware of his concerns, and I'm not eager to press the senator, but talking to Bauer is a different story. Anyway, I might try to call him tomorrow. There's one more thing and it's big."

"And you saved it for last?"

"When I was leaving Wyatt's house, someone started shooting. I fired back, but he was too far away. I jumped in my car, and he followed me through the city, but I was able to lose him."

"Are you serious? Way to bury the lead, Caitlyn."

"I was able to get a license plate: 7K82L6. Can you run it for me? And can you pull camera footage from the block around Wyatt's house? His address is 137 Dove Way."

"I'll get on this right away. This shooter could be a huge lead."

"I hope so." She took a breath, then added, "There's one more thing, and I'm just sharing this with you at the moment, Emi."

"All right. But I work for Rob, so I can't make any promises…"

"I understand. I was with Quinn Kelly at Wyatt's house. I'm with him now. We're trying to figure out if he was the target, or if I was."

"Wait a second. Quinn Kelly? Your former boyfriend and the person of interest in the first case?"

"That's the one."

"I thought you didn't know where he was."

"I found him yesterday. I wasn't ready to say anything. Last time, the investigation was derailed by an insane focus on Quinn. I don't want that to happen again. He wasn't involved then, and he's not involved now. He's helping me get to the truth."

"Are you sure he's helping you? Could he be playing you?"

"No. That's not happening. I know him, Emi."

"You used to know him. It's been ten years. And someone just tried to kill you—again."

She frowned at the reminder. "I don't know if they were aiming at Quinn or at me."

"If they were aiming at him, then he knows something."

"I don't think he does." She wished she could be absolutely positive that Quinn didn't know something, but there was something he was hiding from her. She needed to get that secret out of him before she fully committed to his innocence.

"Are you coming back to the office tonight?"

"No. I'm going to hunker down somewhere. Let me know if you find out anything."

"I will. Be careful, Caitlyn. You're personally involved, and emotions don't always lead to good decisions."

"I'm thinking clearly."

"I hope so."

As Emi ended the call, she stared out at the dark sea and hoped she was thinking clearly. But she had to admit that was difficult with Quinn nearby. Now they were alone on a boat in the middle of the ocean. That clearly hadn't been a good decision.

Why hadn't they just gone to a motel and gotten two rooms? Why had she gone along with this plan?

An annoying answer came to her mind, but she refused to accept it. It was not because she wanted time with Quinn, that she wanted to be alone with him; she'd just wanted to get them somewhere safe. Determined to stick with that reason, she walked back to Quinn.

He gave her an enquiring look. "Any news?"

"Nothing of note. Emi will run the plate. Hopefully, that will lead to at least one answer."

"You told her about me?"

"I did. I also said that I was concerned you would become a distraction. She won't lie for me, but she won't push the information out there until it's necessary."

"All right." He cut the engine. "Are you ready for a drink?"

"More than ready. Do you have drinks?"

"I do." He opened a small fridge and pulled out two beers.

"Thank you." She took the can out of his hand and popped the top. The first swallow felt incredibly good.

Quinn sat down on the bench seat, and she took a seat next to him, feeling both calm and tense at the same time.

For a few moments, they just sipped their beers, and then Quinn said, "We need to talk, Caitlyn."

"We do," she agreed. "You need to tell me what you're keeping from me."

He gave her a long, assessing look. "You haven't guessed yet?"

At his challenging words, she realized that she had guessed.

There had just been so much going on, she hadn't had a chance to process it. "It's about Donovan, about what happened in Yosemite. You told Wyatt you weren't there. You were lying, weren't you?"

"Yes. I didn't want to tell Wyatt the truth, but I think it's time I told you."

Her heart raced once more. She licked her lips as she set down her beer and folded her arms across her chest, a chill running through her. "Did you kill him, Quinn? Did you kill Donovan?"

CHAPTER SIXTEEN

CAITLYN COULD HARDLY BELIEVE the words that had just come from her mouth. But they were out now, and she wouldn't take them back.

Quinn took another draught of beer, then crinkled the empty can and set it aside. He looked at her with shadowy blue eyes that were filled with too many emotions for her to decipher.

"Yes, I killed him."

She sucked in a hard breath. She had never suspected that Quinn had had anything to do with Donovan's death. But why would she? Donovan had allegedly killed himself and Quinn had never been a violent man. He had never been a killer. "How? How did it happen?"

"Let me back up a little."

She didn't want him to back up. She was impatient to get to this part of the story. "I know the history," she protested.

"I just want to tell you everything."

"Then start talking."

"After the bombing, I tried to speak to Donovan several times but got nowhere. He wasn't willing to meet with me, and the FBI was watching both of us. Any conversation we would have could be construed as conspiring about something. I was going crazy wanting answers, wanting someone to be punished, but I was fighting for my own life at the same time. The FBI was on my ass every second of the day."

"I didn't realize that was happening."

"You were tuned out, and I couldn't blame you for that. Your hell was far worse than mine. But I knew if I wanted to get to Donovan, I would have to wait until I was no longer a suspect. When your dad told me if I agreed to disappear from your life, the FBI would disappear from mine, I decided it was the best solution for a lot of reasons. I was close to graduation, so I convinced my professors to let me take my finals early and then I left town."

"Did my father give you money to disappear?"

"He offered. I didn't take it."

She was relieved to hear that he hadn't taken money from her dad, but she was still angry that he'd let her father drive him away. "You should have fought to stay with me, Quinn. You should have been willing to keep taking the heat if it meant you could be there for me."

"It wasn't just the heat, Caitlyn. I wanted justice. No, that's not right. I wanted revenge," he said flatly. "I didn't just want the truth. I wanted someone to pay. And I knew that if I got my revenge, it had to be in a way that would never tie back to you. If I went after Donovan, and if I was successful, his followers might want to exact payback from you."

The darkness of his gaze now disturbed her. Her stomach twisted with the realization of the confession that was coming.

Did she want to hear it?

"Stop." She put up her hand. "You shouldn't tell me anything more. I'm a federal agent."

"You deserve the truth, Caitlyn."

"I'm not sure I want it anymore." She couldn't believe the words that had just come out of her mouth.

"Yes, you do. You want it more than anything. You haven't fought so hard for so long to get answers to stop me from telling you now. I'll take whatever comes of it. I can't give you much, Caitlyn, but I can give you this."

He was right. She did need to know. "Go on."

"After I left town, I waited a few weeks. I erased myself from the internet. I got a new identity. I got rid of my Jeep, by the way, so Wyatt did not see my Jeep in that parking lot. But we'll get back to him later."

She frowned. "All right. Keep going."

"I wanted the air to clear, for everyone to know that you and I were done. I wanted you to tell all your friends what an asshole I was, so the news would spread around Bolton that I deserted you and that you hated me."

"I did hate you. And I told everyone that."

"Good. That's what I was hoping. I monitored Donovan's social media from a distance. After graduation, he posted a photo from Yosemite. I knew exactly where he would be, because we went to Yosemite several times together. I drove there in a very old car I'd bought a few days earlier. I stayed in a motel outside the park and then the next morning before dawn, I went to the tent cabins where we used to stay. Sure enough, he was there. He came out around ten, and I followed him. I watched him all day, every second building my anger. He made it easier for me because he was alone, and because he went up the mountain and stayed there until dusk. He was going to camp up on the summit in his sleeping bag."

She could picture the scene so clearly. Quinn stalking Donovan throughout the day, waiting for his chance. The knot in her throat grew bigger. "What did you do next?"

"I confronted him. He was shocked to see me. For the first time since the explosion, he actually looked me straight in the eye. He knew why I'd come after him. I told him it was just me and him. He owed me the truth. I asked him if he'd set the bomb, if he'd deliberately tried to kill you or both of us."

"Did he confess?" she whispered, her heart beating so fast she couldn't breathe.

"He said he was sorry. I didn't like his answer. I hit him in the face, and he staggered backward. I thought he would hit back, but he didn't. He said he was sorry again. He'd lost himself."

"He'd lost himself?" she echoed in angry outrage. "What did that mean?"

"I don't know. I thought I wanted him to talk, but all I really wanted to do at that moment was to make him pay. I hit him again. Blood spurted from his nose, and it gave me intense satisfaction, but also filled me with more rage. I wasn't just seeing his blood; I was seeing yours. I was thinking about our baby, and the life she would never have." His jaw tightened. "I told Donovan that he had killed my child. He was stunned. He said he hadn't known you were pregnant. He apologized again. He said he'd been angry that I had betrayed him and our friendship. I told him he was the one who had betrayed me, who had lied to me, who had hurt the woman I loved and killed my baby."

Quinn's voice rose with the passion of his words, as did the tension running within her.

"Say it," she ordered.

He met her gaze. "Donovan knew what I wanted, why I'd come after him. He said he wished he'd done things differently, that he'd listened to the wrong people. He'd gotten caught up in some fever dream. I told him he had to come clean. He had to turn himself in. It was the only way. He looked at me and said I didn't want the truth, I wanted payback. I wanted him to die." Quinn's lips tightened. "He was right. I took another swing at him, but he sidestepped away from me. He said he never meant to hurt me or you. It all got fucked up. Things got out of control. And then he backed up. One step and then another. I saw it coming. I almost warned him. The words were about to come out of my mouth, but I couldn't release them."

"God," she breathed. "He went over the edge."

"One minute he was there, and then he was gone. I didn't hear him scream. I don't know if he did." Anguish filled Quinn's eyes. "All I could hear was the blood rushing through my veins. I rushed over to the side, and I looked down, but it was dark, and the canyon was deep. He was gone. I killed him."

She jumped to her feet, her body impossibly tense, her nerves on fire, her breath coming short and fast. She felt dizzy. She felt…she didn't know how she felt.

Quinn had killed Donovan!

The words went around and around in her head.

Quinn stood up, reaching a hand toward her, but then pulling it back as if he knew she wouldn't let him touch her. "Caitlyn, are you all right?"

"I—I…" She couldn't find the words. She walked around the deck, trying to breathe, trying to come to terms with what he'd just said.

Quinn's gaze followed her, but he didn't say another word.

She'd wanted to know his secret. She'd *needed* to know his secret.

Now, her mind grappled with the truth. There was a part of her that wasn't surprised. She'd known what he was going to say as soon as he said he'd been in Yosemite.

She whirled around, looking into his eyes once more. "What if he'd told you a story? What if he'd said someone else had done it? What if he'd claimed he was innocent? Would you have believed him?"

Quinn's lips tightened. "None of that happened."

"But it could have."

"It didn't. What are you trying to get me to say? That I would have just accepted some bullshit lie? No. I wouldn't have done that, Caitlyn. By the time I got to Yosemite, I was on a mission. I'd had months to think about what had happened. And I'd watched you suffer for most of that time. My anger was off the charts. I had never felt so out of control." He paused for a moment, letting that sink in, then added, "When I saw him, my rage only got worse. And when he spoke, when he apologized, there was no coming back, no change of plans. He had to pay. That's all I could think. He'd gotten away with murder. No one was going to hold him accountable. I had to do it. I had to be the one. He was my friend. And because of that, our baby was dead, and you were broken."

Her heart was still beating way too fast, but her brain was starting to work again. She believed what Quinn was saying. The truth was in his gaze. He had gone to Yosemite to get justice. And Donovan had died.

She sat back down on the bench. "Okay."

Quinn gave her a speculative look and then took a seat across from her. "That's it?"

"I'm thinking," she said sharply.

"All right. Take whatever time you need."

"I will. And I don't need your permission to do it," she snapped, anger, pain, and a myriad of other emotions running through her.

Quinn ran a hand through his hair, then folded his arms across his chest and turned his gaze toward the sea.

She went over the story in her head. It made perfect sense in some ways, but in other ways, it did not. She'd never thought of Quinn as someone who could kill another person. But then she'd never thought of herself that way, either, until after the explosion. The unbearable loss, the unanswered questions, the lack of justice had driven her crazy and reshaped her life. Even after Donovan had died, her frustration had continued, because she still hadn't known for sure that Donovan was guilty. But Quinn had known!

"How dare you, Quinn? How dare you not tell me what happened up on that mountain?"

His expression turned grim. "I couldn't tell you."

"Why not? I had a right to know what he said. You should have told me that he apologized."

"Would that have really made a difference? That he was sorry?"

"I don't know. You didn't give me the chance to find out."

"Well, I know, and it wouldn't have helped at all. It would have meant nothing to you. I figured you'd hear that he was dead, and that would give you closure."

She shook her head. "That's bullshit, Quinn. How would that give me closure?"

"You thought he was the one responsible."

"Maybe not the only one."

"Well, he didn't give up any other names," Quinn said, anger in his gaze now, too. "I know I should have asked more questions, gotten more information, but I didn't, and I can't change that. But I did make sure that he could never hurt you again."

She stared back at him for a long minute. "How did it feel? Watching him go over that edge? I need to know, Quinn. I need to know how it felt to watch him die."

"Not as good as I wanted it to feel. I thought that if he paid with his life, it would make things better, but it changed nothing."

"I wish I could have been there. I wish I could have told him what I felt in that moment." Tears burned at the back of her eyes. "I wish I could have pushed him over the side."

"I didn't want you to have to be the one to do that. That's not who you are, Caitlyn."

"It is who I am," she said. "It's who I became. I wanted vengeance as much as you did. Maybe more. But you didn't let me have that moment."

He shook his head. "You're looking at the situation now, ten

years later. You're confident, you're strong. You're more than
capable of pushing Donovan off that mountain or putting a bullet
in his head. But that's not who you were three months after the
explosion. You could barely get out of bed. You were in physical
and emotional pain. You couldn't have even made it up that
mountain. I had to take the first opportunity I could get, and that
was it. If I hadn't gone then, Donovan might have disappeared. I
might have never found him."

She knew he was right. It was still difficult to accept.

"I didn't just do it for me, Caitlyn," he continued. "I did it for
you and for Isabella, even though I didn't know her name at the
time."

Another reminder of how she had shut him out.

"What happened after he went off the mountain?"

"I left. It took me almost two hours to make my way down
the mountain. When I got back to the campgrounds, I went into
his cabin. I impulsively grabbed his duffel bag, thinking there
might be evidence in there of what he'd done."

"Wait. You have his duffel bag?"

"Yes, but there wasn't much in it, a couple of photos of me
and some other LNF members, and a notebook from school.
There were notes from a class in the front, then a drawing of
various snakes with their heads cut off. There was a quote next to
one of the snakes. It said: *Corporate greed lives like a viper in its
nest. You must kill it before it kills you.* That snake became the
tattoo that Donovan and Wyatt got together. It also appeared that
pages had been ripped out of the notebook, but I have no idea
what they contained."

"You still have the bag, don't you?"

"At my house, in the basement. I looked through the bag last
night."

"That's what reminded you of the tattoo."

"Yes."

She frowned. "You said that we'd get back to Wyatt. If you

didn't drive your Jeep there, then why would he ask you about it?"

"I think he was trying to shake me up, searching for an answer by implying he already knew the answer."

"You think he's capable of being that devious?"

"Up until that moment, I was thinking no, that there was no way Wyatt had been involved in a scheme as deadly as a bombing. It wasn't his personality. But that question gave me pause. I also don't think Wyatt was actually there."

"Why would he lie about that?"

"I don't know, but Wyatt hated to hike. It was too much work for him. He never wanted to go to the mountains with us. His story didn't ring true at all."

"I'm going to need to dig deeper into Wyatt's stories. There might be much more to find than a bad alibi." She blew out a breath. "What did you do after you left Yosemite?"

"I drove south. I didn't know where I was going to end up. When I got to San Diego and the Mexican border, I almost went across, but I ended up finding a cheap apartment near the beach. I waited for someone to come after me. It was probably a year before I thought it might not happen. But I knew I could never come out of hiding. I could never be Quinn Kelly again. Even though Donovan's death looked like suicide, there was no guarantee someone wouldn't connect my disappearance to his death. That meant I had to stay disconnected from you as well. I couldn't let anyone from my past know where I was or what I'd done. I'd made my choice. I had to live with it."

"And you never once considered telling me the truth?"

"I considered it about a hundred thousand times."

She frowned at his answer. "What stopped you? Did you think I'd give you up to the FBI?"

"No, I didn't think that. But I did believe that showing up in your life again could bring danger back to you."

"That's not the real reason."

He gave her a long look. "I looked you up online about two years after Donovan died. It was the one and only time I looked for you. I saw photos of you with your friends. You were smiling and laughing. You looked like you again. I didn't want to bring you back down by showing up and reminding you of everything you'd lost, of the pain I'd put you through."

"Do you really think you can know someone's life by looking at social media?" she challenged.

"No, but I was hopeful. I wanted you to feel better, Caitlyn. I wanted that from the beginning. I just couldn't make it happen. You couldn't decide if I was to blame or not. Sometimes, it feels like you still aren't sure."

"I have gone back and forth," she admitted. "But I don't believe you knew about the bomb or had any idea I was walking into danger."

"I'm glad."

"I still don't like the way you left me. You didn't even say good-bye."

"I did come to your house before I left. I had a whole speech planned. You were in the backyard, and you were crying. It was like you were sobbing from the depths of your soul. I didn't know how to comfort you and telling you I was leaving wasn't going to be helpful, so I just left."

"What were you going to say?"

"I was going to say we should take a break, see how we felt in a year or two. I wasn't sure at that moment that I wouldn't see you again. It wasn't until after Donovan died that I knew I'd closed that door forever."

"I guess I can kind of understand," she said slowly. "Some of it, not all of it. I need to think about it."

"I won't make the mistake of telling you to take all the time that you need."

"Good. A lot of what you did was wrong, Quinn. I can relate to your desire to get justice and revenge, because those desires have been with me every single day for the last ten years. But the way you went about it, the way you disappeared without a word, that was…"

"Unforgivable?"

"Yes. You left me when I needed you the most. That's not on my dad. That's on you."

"I know. And I'm sorry I didn't get more answers from Donovan. I really thought the danger died with him that night. Clearly, I was wrong. You told me I owed you before, and I do. But that's not why I want to help you now. I want the truth as much as you do. And if someone else needs to pay, I want that to happen, too. I want it for you, for me, and for Isabella." He cleared the sudden emotion out of his voice. "I didn't get a chance to say this before, but thank you for telling me her name, Caitlyn. You made her real again. You made her a person, and I will be forever grateful that you shared that with me."

Her eyes teared up, and she felt overwhelmed with emotion. She jumped to her feet and walked down the stairs. She sat at the table, trying to fight off the tears. She'd cried too much already. But they were pressing at her eyes, so she closed them, and she put her head in her hands and tried to hang on.

She told herself she should be happy Quinn went after Donovan. She should be happy that Donovan had said he was sorry, even though that meant nothing. But all she could feel was pain and anger that she hadn't been the one to shove Donovan off that mountain. That she hadn't been able to get payback for Isabella. That she might never get the revenge she thirsted for.

Then the tears came. She got up and walked into the cabin and closed the door. She didn't need Quinn to hear her. She didn't need him to know that deep inside she was still weak, and she was still hurting.

CHAPTER SEVENTEEN

QUINN STOOD outside the cabin door, debating what to do. The sound of Caitlyn's painful sobs tore at his heart. He wanted to comfort her. He wanted to hold her. But she'd shut him out, just like she'd shut him out before.

It had shocked him then. Those days and weeks after the explosion had been filled with anguish and anger, as well as confusion. He couldn't understand why she wouldn't let him comfort her. They'd been so close. He'd known her inside and out: all her fears, her worries, and her dreams.

But while happiness had bound them together, grief had ripped them apart. Distrust had ended their relationship. She'd blamed him and she'd doubted him. Worst of all, she just couldn't let him share or shoulder the burden of her loss, and that had made everything worse.

He'd been very much alone in his grief. He'd had no family to turn to, and his friends had disappeared. He shouldn't have been surprised to find himself completely isolated. But his college years had made him feel like he was part of something, and his relationship with Caitlyn had given him hope that he would have a family again, especially when he found out she was pregnant.

It had been too good to be true.

In his life, everything that was good eventually turned bad.

He left the galley and walked back up to the deck, letting the night air cool his heated thoughts. He had to give Caitlyn time and space, because that's what she wanted.

But was it what she needed? Was crying it all out on her own helping her?

Somehow, he doubted it.

He'd hoped she might find some small comfort in the fact that he'd gone after Donovan and while he hadn't gotten a full confession, he had gotten an apology, and Donovan had paid for what he'd done.

But she'd wanted to serve up justice. She'd wanted revenge, and he couldn't blame her, because she was the one who had been in a hospital bed for weeks, who had lost her baby, who had gone through surgery, who had been in terrible pain. But he couldn't change what had happened.

What now?

He drilled his fingers against his thighs and then he decided they'd spent enough time in the past. He needed to pull her back into the present.

Walking down the stairs once more, he paused in the galley. It sounded quieter than it had before. Hopefully, that was a good sign.

He opened up the fridge, happy to see that it was well stocked with food. He pulled out eggs, bacon, tomatoes, cheese and a package of Southwestern hash browns. His stomach rumbled, and he realized he hadn't eaten all day. Setting two pans on the small stove burners, he started cooking. Maybe the smell of bacon would draw Caitlyn out of the cabin. It had always worked before.

That thought brought a smile to his lips, as he remembered the times he'd made breakfast for her. He didn't know how to cook much else, but he'd always been good at the first meal of the day, and Caitlyn had usually woken up ravenous. He'd loved cooking for her, and he'd loved watching her walk into the kitchen wearing one of his T-shirts, her hair tangled from his fingers, her lips pink from their kisses, her eyes sleepy and happy. Sometimes, he'd have to turn off those burners and make love to her because she was so damn pretty.

He took a shaky breath at the memories. Those days were long gone, and they were never coming back. But he could still feed her. He could try to be there for her, as much as she would let him. And he would help her find out who had taken up Donovan's evil plan and made it their own.

She would never forgive him for abandoning her, and he couldn't forgive himself. Not just for the way he'd left but for not seeing what had been right in front of him. The LNF had turned into a terrorist group, and he had been oblivious. If he had been more aware, he wouldn't have let her go into that building. They wouldn't have lost their baby. Maybe they'd still be together.

Or maybe not... But at least she wouldn't have had to suffer. She wouldn't still be suffering now.

For the next several minutes, he focused on making their meal, and as he'd hoped, the door to the cabin opened when he set the plate of bacon on the table.

Her hair was mussed, her eyes and nose red, but there was a fighting light back in her eyes, and he was happy to see that.

"You cooked," she said.

"Breakfast for dinner."

"Your specialty." She snatched a piece of bacon off the plate and waved it in the air as she sat down. "This produces my favorite smell in the entire world."

"I remember." He set a plate of scrambled eggs and hash browns in front of her. "I thought you might be hungry."

"I didn't realize I was until I smelled the bacon."

He sat down across from her. "Dig in."

"You don't have to ask me twice," she said, giving him a

shaky smile as she took a bite of her eggs. "You're still an expert at scrambled eggs. I like the cheese and tomato addition. And what else is in here?"

"Green chiles. Ray likes his food spicy."

"I hope he won't mind that we've made ourselves at home."

"He won't care. We keep the fridge stocked for longer dive trips. Ray gets hungry when I'm diving."

"This is a nice boat."

"It has served me well."

She cocked her head at his words. "Past tense?"

He shrugged. "I don't know what happens in the next minute."

"Me, either." She tucked her hair behind her ear and gave him a sheepish look. "I'm a little embarrassed."

"For being human?"

"For being weak. You've heard me cry too many times."

"You're one of the strongest people I've ever met, Caitlyn."

"I haven't been very strong the last hour. I know we still need to talk about what happened on the mountain, but right now, I'd just rather eat."

"I'm good with that."

She finished off her bacon, then added, "My coworker Emi texted me some information about the car that tailed us from Wyatt's house. It was reported stolen from the home of a seventy-nine-year-old retired teacher that morning."

"So much for my brilliance in capturing the license plate."

"It was a good idea; it just didn't pan out. The woman did not have any cameras on her house, but Emi will check the neighborhood when she gets a chance. It's low priority at the moment with everything else going on."

"Why is it a low priority? You're a federal agent, and someone tried to kill you."

"True, but I can handle myself. The team needs to focus on the innocent people who could be targets of this terror group."

"Any news from Alancor?"

"Nothing of note. The next real worry is the gala on Sunday night that my family's foundation hosts. My father doesn't want to cancel. He doesn't bow to terrorists. But local and state political leaders, including our favorite senator, will be there, as well as CEO's from many companies. You might as well put a bull's-eye on the event."

"That sounds like a place we need to be."

"I will be there. You would definitely not make the invite list."

"Make me your plus one."

"We'll see. I'm still hoping I can talk my father into canceling the gala."

"Why waste your breath? It won't work. Your father does what he wants to do. Save your energy for figuring out how to get rid of that bull's-eye or protect it."

"There will be a tremendous amount of security, but it's difficult to make any event completely safe, especially when you don't know where the danger might come from."

"You should keep eating," he said. "Your eggs are getting cold."

She took another bite. "These are good. I like the spice."

"You always did like spice." She rolled her eyes, and he smiled. "I know you want us to stay in the present, but our past is part of us. Not just the bad but also the good."

"We did have some good times," she said with a sigh. "Tell me more about your life after Yosemite. How did you reinvent yourself so well? Did you buy your new identity?"

"Yes. An old friend helped me out."

"What he did was illegal."

"That's why I'll never turn that friend in."

"You're careful not to say if it was a man or a woman."

"Well, I am eating with an FBI agent."

"Who just basically heard your confession for murder. Even though…"

"What?" he asked.

She put down her fork. "I've been thinking about the sequence of events."

"I thought you didn't want to talk about it."

"Well, I changed my mind."

"Okay," he said warily. "Go on."

She stared at him for a long minute. "You didn't actually push Donovan over the edge."

"I was moving toward him."

"You said he stepped away. And then he backed up."

"Because I was coming at him," he argued.

"That's not really how you described it."

"I don't think you heard me right."

"I heard you just fine. You said he backed up. One step and then another. He was in control. He told you he never meant to hurt you or me." She shook her head. "You didn't kill him, Quinn. He killed himself. He jumped off that cliff."

"You weren't there. You don't know how fast it went."

"Maybe that's why I can see it more clearly than you can. He didn't fall. And you didn't push him. He chose to take that step. He really did kill himself."

He frowned at the conclusion she'd come up with. "If I hadn't gone there, it wouldn't have happened," he reminded her. "He fell because I confronted him. Donovan didn't go up there to commit suicide. There was no evidence of that."

"Even if your appearance, your fight, your words backed him up, I still think he took that step himself. He knew you wanted payback. Maybe there was some part of him that still loved you enough to give you what you needed most."

He didn't want to believe her version of events, but he couldn't deny that he hadn't physically pushed Donovan off that mountain. And there had been something in his eyes, some plea for understanding. But there could be no understanding of the violent, murderous act that Donovan had apologized for.

"Are you sure you're not hanging on to your view of the story because you need to believe you killed him?" Caitlyn asked. "That the revenge would not be as satisfying if it was Donovan's choice to die?"

He let out a sigh. "No, I'm not sure. I know I wanted him to suffer. I wanted him to pay for what he did."

"He didn't try to fight you. And he was a fighter; we know that."

"That part surprised me."

"He wanted you to punish him."

"Does it make it any better if we think he still had some small part of his conscience left?" he challenged.

She thought about his words. "Not for me."

"Not for me, either." He paused. "It is possible I lied to you about exactly what happened."

She met his gaze. "I knew you were lying before; you're not lying now."

"No, I'm not," he admitted. "Maybe you are right. I'm not sure we'll ever know. But I have to say that when nothing more happened after Donovan's death, no more bombs, no more news of LNF activism, I thought it was over. I was confident that he was the bomber and that was it. I never imagined it would start up again like it has."

"I never imagined it, either. I still think there's a connection. Maybe Donovan got lost, because there was a more radical voice in his ear, someone helping him with his big plan."

"Which leads us back to Hank."

"Or Wyatt. He clearly spent time with Donovan and his question about Yosemite was odd. We also can't leave out Lauren. Her sister, Allison, is dating Kevin, and Allison is part of an activist group."

"But the only injuries were to people in that group, right?"

"Yes. That could have been a bad explosive device, though. It went off before it was supposed to."

"True. We probably can't eliminate anyone, including Lauren. Although, I have to say she told me something the other day that rang true. She said the LNF was always about the guys, that the women were tolerated, but they were never really in the circle of trust, and she was right about that. I don't see Donovan trusting Lauren with his secrets."

"But Lauren did get you out of that building. I know she has stuck by her story, and the change in birthday party scheduling was all verified by third parties, but maybe she still had an inkling that something was going to go wrong, and she wanted you out of it."

"That's possible. We should also talk about some of the others: Justin, Vitaly, Vinnie and Gary. Any one of them could have been involved then and now. Justin is part of the false alibi given by his father. He should be confronted about that."

"Especially since Wyatt just confirmed it," she agreed. "We'll have to tackle Justin tomorrow." She let out a weary sigh. "Their faces are all going around and around in my head on this neverending loop. It's exhausting."

"I know. I'm on the same treadmill."

"Let's go back to your time in San Diego. What did you do for work?"

"I sold equipment at a dive shop, and I taught diving on the weekend. It was fun, but it didn't pay much, and I missed being a scientist. It was about a year later when Jeremiah Cooper walked into the shop and offered me a job. He needed scientific divers on his team up north. That was seven years ago. I've been doing the job ever since."

"And you love it?"

"I do. I'm in the water five days a week."

"What exactly do you do every day?"

"I take measurements, analyze the water temperature and the

changes in sea life and landscape. Lately, we've been physically thinning an overpopulation of sea urchins from the kelp beds which are vitally important to holding carbon and preventing it from being released into the atmosphere. But the urchins are overrunning the beds, and—" He stopped abruptly. "Sorry. You don't want to hear about sea urchins and kelp."

"It reminds me of old times," she said with a smile. "I loved hearing you talk about the ocean. You were so passionate about the environment. You came alive when you spoke about the sea, about protecting it for future generations. I know you got into the LNF for good reasons, Quinn."

"I thought I did. I thought everyone did."

"That can be the problem with activist groups. Most people get into them for good reasons, but then radicals and extremists take over, and the group changes. It doesn't make the mission bad, just the means to fulfill that mission."

"I should have seen that the LNF was changing."

"I was distracting you."

"I can't argue with that. You were one hell of a beautiful distraction."

She cleared her throat and wiped her mouth with a napkin. "What about friends? I assume you've made some as Michael Wainscott."

"A few, not many."

"Women?"

"A few, not many," he repeated, quite sure he didn't want to talk to her about other women.

"Anyone serious?"

"No."

"Because you were living under a fake name?"

"That was a part of it. A long-term relationship would require some truth-telling, and I couldn't do that."

"What was your plan? To live alone your entire life?"

"I try not to think that far ahead, because there's no point.

Life changes when you least expect it, and no amount of planning or worrying stops that from happening. It took three devastating losses to make me finally accept that."

She frowned at that comment. "That's sad, Quinn."

"It's reality. When we were together, I always had this ominous feeling that things were too good to last. I was right."

She sat back in her seat, giving him a thoughtful look. "I never believed they were too good to last. I thought they'd last forever."

"That was always the biggest difference between us. You were a glass half-full girl, and I was a glass half-empty guy. Sometimes you tempted me to come over to the light, to believe in the possibilities."

"I believed in those possibilities, too."

"I know you did. And I believed in you. But there was always this thought at the back of my mind that we were just too different. Our backgrounds were night and day."

"I didn't care that you didn't come from money; I actually liked that about you. You were different from the kids I grew up with. You had been tested in life, and you were stronger for it. You stood up for what you believed in. You even argued with my dad the first time I brought you home for dinner."

"He disliked me on sight."

"Even more so after you opened your mouth, but I didn't care. You were as strong as he was, and I hadn't seen that before. He had run off a lot of my boyfriends in high school. They were such cowards." Shadows entered her eyes. "I guess that's why it still surprises me that he ran you off, too. I thought you were a match for him."

"He only ran me off because he told me what I already thought was true."

"He's very good at knowing what buttons to push. I don't have any illusions about him, Quinn. I know he can be ruthless and cruel, especially in matters of business, but as a family man, he's very loyal and protective. He's always made sure I had what-ever I needed, well, except for you. But I'm sure that was for my own good."

It was difficult to hear Caitlyn defend her father. "Let's not talk about your dad."

"You must hate him."

"For making me the target of an FBI investigation? Yeah, I have some strong feelings."

"That was wrong." She paused. "Do you ever wonder if we would have stayed together if the bomb never went off, if we'd had Isabella and gotten married? Would we be together now?"

Her question slid through him like a knife. "I just told you I was a cynic."

"You're saying no?"

"I don't know. We can't rewrite history."

"You're right, but I wish we could do that. I'm not as opti-mistic as I once was, either, Quinn. The day that bomb went off was the last day I believed that things would last forever. And in my job, I've seen too many bad things happen to good people to not feel more cynical. On the other hand, I've also seen some amazing moments of generosity and bravery, outright sacrificial heroism. I try to hang on to those images in my head when the world starts to feel too dark."

"I'm sure the struggle is real, but in your heart, you're still an optimist. You can't fight it, and you shouldn't try. It's who you are. It's that belief that drives you to greatness. I saw heroism today—in you. You were brave as hell, Caitlyn. I hope you're proud of the woman you've become."

Her eyes sparkled. "I am proud, Quinn. Maybe I needed to go through all that fire to come out the person I am now, but I still wish it hadn't happened."

"Me, too." He paused for a moment. "I've anchored the boat in a cove. I think we should stay here tonight. You can take the cabin. I'll take the couch or sleep on the deck."

"I can sleep on the couch."

"That's not going to happen."

"You were always such a gentleman. I remember my friends were amazed at how you always opened the car door for me. Even my mother said you had nice manners when you came to the house."

"That must have been the only thing she liked," he said dryly. Rebecca Carlson had been more polite to him than Chuck, but she still hadn't wanted him for her daughter.

"Well, at least there was one thing," she said lightly, as she picked up their plates and took them to the sink. "Since you cooked, I'll wash up."

"All right," he said, sipping his coffee. It was amazing how much he liked just watching her move around the small space. It was going to be difficult to say good-bye to her again, now that she'd come back into his life in such vivid color. He would have more to remember about her, even more to like and to miss.

She came back to the table and their gazes locked for a long minute.

He didn't know what she was thinking, but the air was suddenly sizzling between them.

"Let's go up on deck," she said quickly. "I could use some air."

He wanted more than air—he wanted her. But she was already moving up the stairs, and he had no choice but to follow.

"There are a lot of stars out tonight," Caitlyn commented as she sat down on the bench next to Quinn. There wasn't much space between them, but the chilly air helped cool the hot intimacy she'd been feeling downstairs.

"It's always an amazing light show on the water. Tell me

more about your life," he said. "Who do you spend time with outside of work?"

"The same people I spend time with at work. My team is really close. It's composed of members from my Quantico class. We bonded over five years ago and we're even more closely connected now."

"They're all in LA?"

"Mostly. Our cases take us all over the country, sometimes the world. I do miss them now. I wish they were working this case."

"Why can't they?"

"Territorial issues. Rob Carpenter is the agent in charge in San Francisco, and he doesn't give up cases like this, especially not ones that involve people with power."

"Like your father."

"Yes. Rob would like to eventually end up as the hero of the day, which will help move him up the ladder."

"I'm not hearing much love in your voice for this guy."

"He was actually my first boss out of the academy. That was in Miami. He hated that I was always trying to find the Bolton bomber, even though I only worked on it when I was off work. He didn't like that I was questioning the FBI investigation. He told me to wait until I'd been on the job more than two minutes to criticize. He had a point. After a year, I transferred to New Orleans. My boss there suggested that my obsession with the Bolton case was preventing me from reaching my full potential. I realized she was right. A short time later, one of my Quantico classmates, Flynn MacKenzie created a task force, and he asked me to join. Being back with my friends really helped. Eventually, I was able to just focus on the job and not the past."

"That sounds healthy."

"Sometimes you just run out of road. That's what happened to me. I had nowhere else to go, nowhere else to look. I had hit every wall there was."

"You tried to find me, didn't you?"

"Yes, but you did a very good job erasing your life. It made me really suspicious."

"Which is why you pulled a gun on me at our first meeting."

"I didn't know what to think about you."

"Do you know what to think now? Never mind, don't answer that. Let's get back to your life. Do you have a boyfriend?"

"I never thought I'd hear that question from you."

"I had the same thought downstairs when you asked me about women."

"I shouldn't have done that, but I was too curious to leave the question alone."

"I'm curious as well."

"I have had some relationships that lasted several months. One went for a year. But it wasn't right."

"Were they agents?"

"No. They had different careers. One was a veterinarian. I met him when I was watching my roommate's dog, and he got into some chocolate. I thought that damn dog was going to die on my watch, so I took him to an emergency vet."

"And you got a boyfriend out of it," he said with a grin. "I hope the dog was okay."

"He was fine, thank goodness."

"Why didn't you and Dr. Vet last?"

"I don't know."

"You must have some idea."

"What would you like me to say? That he wasn't as good in bed as you?"

Quinn started, and she kind of liked the fact that she'd gotten a reaction out of him. Aside from the one wild kiss at the beach, he'd been holding himself in serious check.

"Yes," he said, recovering his composure. "I'm fine with you saying that."

"Well, that wasn't it," she returned. "We just weren't right for each other. We didn't like the same things. He was a nice guy, but I didn't love him."

"You probably broke his heart."

"I don't think so. He's engaged to someone else now."

"Then you did the right thing."

"Isn't it strange how it's easier to see right and wrong when it's behind you instead of when it's in front of you? We'd make fewer mistakes if we didn't have to wait for time and distance to give us clarity."

"I can't argue with that."

"Did you miss your life, Quinn? You had a lot of friends."

"Most of whom were in the LNF, and if I missed them, it was only the memory of who they'd once been to me. But I missed you, Caitlyn. I missed you a lot. It was years before I stopped thinking about you every day."

His words touched her heart and put a knot in her throat. She was grateful for the shadows surrounding them, hiding her emotions. "I missed the way we were, too, before the explosion, when we were good together. We laughed so much. Do you remember?"

"I've wanted to forget, but I haven't."

"I don't even know why we were always laughing; it's not like either one of us is particularly funny."

"You were kind of funny. You always had a story to tell from one of your classes or one of your friends. I always thought it was the writer in you. You loved books and a good tale."

"I did love to read. Remember our bad music nights?" she asked with a laugh.

The smile that spread across his lips now was probably the biggest one she'd seen since they reunited.

"Me on my guitar and you on your keyboard," he said. "But I didn't have parents who spent a fortune on guitar lessons. I was self-taught."

"You did not do a good job teaching yourself," she said candidly.

"You were pretty bad, too, especially with the Christmas carols you volunteered us to play at the apartment Christmas party. We were practically booed out of the building."

She laughed. "I think someone threw a Christmas cookie at your head."

"You ducked, and they hit me."

"Well, you were worse than me."

"I never said I was good," he declared.

"That's true."

"You, on the other hand…"

"I said I took a lot of lessons, not that I was a prodigy."

"I don't know what you were doing during those piano lessons, but they did not work."

"I actually had a big crush on my teacher, Mr. Conroy—Joel Conroy. He was like thirty and married, and I was thirteen with braces, but I saw a brilliant love affair between us. Then my mother fired him because she said I wasn't getting any better. It made me wish I had practiced more, so he could have stayed."

"That would have been a better plan," he said dryly. "But if you'd become a classical pianist, I don't think you'd be an FBI agent now."

"If a lot of things had gone differently, I would not be an agent. But life is not predictable, and I was a fool to think I could ever control any of it."

"I'm sorry you had to learn that lesson."

"It was one you learned a lot earlier than me, when your dad died, and then your mom."

"Yes. I wish I could have protected you from knowing what that kind of loss feels like."

"It wasn't your job to protect me. It's on me to do that. Now I'm better trained for it."

"What do your parents think about you being in the FBI?"

"They hate it. I'm out of touch for weeks at a time. They have to live in fear that they'll get a bad call one night. I've heard it all. I understand that my job might worry them, but it's my life, and I have to live it. I think if they knew me better, they could see that, but they just have the old version of me in their heads. I stayed in my bedroom last night. My mom has not changed a thing. It's like I was sixteen years old again."

"Does that mean the poster of Justin Timberlake is still on the wall?" he teased.

"I liked his music," she defended.

"And his abs."

"He did look good with his shirt off," she said with a laugh. "But I put the poster up when I was sixteen, so I hadn't met you or your abs yet."

"You didn't answer my question. Is the poster still up?"

"Unfortunately, yes. But I am going to rip it down the next time I'm there. That room was never really me. Maybe the posters were, but not the furniture or the décor or the pink carpet. That was my mom's vision, and I didn't fight against it. I only stayed there last night because I hadn't set up a hotel room yet, and my mom was determined to have me back in my bedroom for a night." She paused, thinking about how the people who loved her always thought they knew what was best for her. "You know what really gets to me, Quinn?"

He gave her a wary look. "I sense we're going back to our past now."

"We are. You made a lot of decisions on my behalf, and it bugs the hell out of me. Even if I can acknowledge that I wasn't in a place where you could easily talk to me, that I couldn't have made it up that mountain, or that you couldn't wait any longer to go after Donovan, I still think it was wrong to leave me out of the decisions."

"If you can acknowledge all those things, then was it really wrong?" he challenged. "What do you think you would have said if I'd told you what I was going to do. Would you have even been able to hear me through the pain? Would hearing Donovan say he was sorry have made anything that much better for you?"

She frowned, hating that he was right. She had been fragile back then. She'd been weak and shattered. She hadn't been thinking with a clear head, but she was still angry about it. "Maybe you had good reasons, but you still took the decisions away from me, and I'd already lost a lot." She got to her feet, feeling riled up once more. "I'm going downstairs. I have my gun. If there are any problems, let me know."

"I will."

"Will you? Or will that be another decision you make on your own?" she asked sarcastically.

He gave her an even look. "I'm done making unilateral decisions."

"Good. You know what's ironic? You dislike my father so much, but you both did bad things in the name of protecting me. He doesn't know what's best for me and neither do you. I'm the only one who gets to make that call. Don't forget that again."

"I won't. But please don't compare me to your father."

"Then don't act like him."

With that, she moved down the stairs and into the cabin. She threw herself on the bed and stared up at the ceiling, her brain and her body humming with emotion.

She tried to hang on to the anger as long as she could, but other emotions were coming into play. Quinn had finally been honest with her. It had taken a long time, but it had happened. Maybe she needed to be honest with herself. She had been in a bad place when most of his decisions had been made. And she didn't like to admit or remember how weak and out of control she'd felt. But he was right. She was looking at his decisions from ten years later, and he'd made those choices at a very different time; an emotional, painful, and confusing time.

He wanted her to forgive him.

She didn't know if she could get there.

Because it wasn't just anger that held her back. The real problem was that she was still attracted to him, and that bothered her on so many levels.

How could she still want him after what he'd done, the way he'd left, all of it? How could she like him even a little?

The answer was staring her in the face—love.

She'd thought that love had died with her baby. Maybe it hadn't.

But she couldn't go back down that road. She couldn't trust him again. Because if she was wrong for a second time, she didn't think she could survive it.

CHAPTER EIGHTEEN

QUINN DIDN'T SLEEP MUCH, and when dawn rose over the water Saturday morning, he was already making coffee and looking out at the horizon, not sure what to expect of a new day. They certainly couldn't stay out on the ocean, as much as he might want to. Although, he had to admit this was one of those days when land was actually beckoning. There was too much going on, and they needed to get back into action.

As he sipped his coffee, his thoughts turned once more to Caitlyn and their conversation the night before. There had been moments when it had felt good between them, like the old days, when they could smile with familiarity, laugh at a shared memory, but then the pain and the bitterness had come back.

It had hurt when she'd compared him to her father. However, the more he thought about it, the more he realized that she had a point. He had made decisions he thought would protect her, not taking into consideration what she might want. But if he had to do it over, he couldn't see himself doing anything differently. She might not remember it as clearly as he did, but her anger toward him had been a factor in his decision to leave. He wasn't making her happy. His presence just hurt her. Every time she saw him, she felt worse.

Maybe that would have changed if he'd stuck it out. But he hadn't done that. He'd left, and he'd sought revenge on a man who had once been his best friend in the world. Whether Donovan had deliberately gone over that cliff, or he'd forced him to make that terrible choice still wasn't clear in his mind. It might never be clear. But it was done. He couldn't change the past, and neither could she.

They could only go forward.

He wished to God he'd gotten more information before Donovan had slipped off that mountain. But they were where they were. They had some clues. They just didn't know how they went together. The gas attack at Alancor might provide new clues, and it fit the profile of an eco-terrorist. What didn't fit the profile was the attack on him and Caitlyn outside Wyatt's house. That had felt more personal, more specific. But that also implied that someone from the past was involved in the current events.

He turned his head as Caitlyn came up on deck with a coffee mug in her hand. Despite the early hour, she looked ready to face the day, her face shiny and clean, her hair damp from a shower.

"You found the coffee," he said.

"Like the bacon, the smell of coffee lured me out of the cabin. You know all my weaknesses." She cleared her throat. "So, Quinn…"

He tensed at the nervous look in her eyes. "Yes?"

"I'd like to start over."

He was relieved to hear that. He hadn't been sure what to expect after the way things had ended between them. And the last thing he'd wanted her to do was to kick him out of her life now. At the very least, he wanted to help her get to the truth. "I'd like to do that, too."

"There's a lot to think about going forward, and I don't want to get bogged down in the past."

"I feel the same way. So, what's the plan for today?"

"I was thinking that the only reason someone shot at us yesterday was because we made them nervous," she said, a defiant gleam in her eyes. "Today, we double down. We give people a reason to think we know something."

"You want a lure."

"Yes."

"And you want it to be me."

She met his gaze. "I didn't say that."

"You didn't have to. I'm in."

"It could be dangerous."

"I missed getting shot by about an inch; I think we've moved past playing it safe. What do you have in mind?"

"I want to start rattling cages. We could begin with Justin, see if his story matches his brother's, not only about the alibi, but also about Yosemite."

"We could plant the Yosemite question with some of the others," he said slowly. "Maybe Vitaly or Vinnie, we haven't spoken to them yet. What if we suggested that Wyatt might have killed Donovan? That would get some attention."

"That's a twist. It would be a good way to build discord, but we might be putting Wyatt in danger."

"That's true. On the other hand, we were shot at outside his house, so maybe that's not a bad thing."

"I doubt he had time to call anyone to come after us."

"I went to the bar first, and they told me he was at home. Maybe they warned him I was on the way."

"That's possible, but he sure looked surprised to see you."

"We might have been reading his chill attitude wrong, Caitlyn."

She nodded. "Okay. Then we'll sow discord everywhere we go today, with everyone we speak to, and see if anyone breaks."

"I like it. But they haven't broken in all these years. Why would they break now?"

"Because we can hit them from all sides. You're the ghost who might know more than they think. And I'm an FBI agent with a lot of resources at my fingertips."

"Sounds like we're going to be unbeatable," he said with a smile.

"I can be overconfident," she admitted.

"Don't back down. I like your confidence."

"And I like that you're willing to go on a possible suicide mission with me."

"I'm more than willing," he said, meeting her gaze. "But let's try to avoid the suicide part. We've already paid enough."

"It's someone else's turn," she agreed. "Now, I'm going to make waffles."

"I'll take us back to shore."

"Deal. I feel like I should give you a high five."

He raised his hand, but instead of tapping it, he grabbed her fingers and pulled her in for a hug.

She hugged him back, then pulled away with a flustered smile. "Do you want me to bring your waffles up here?"

"That would be great."

"Butter and syrup?"

"You know the way I like it, and I'm not just talking about waffles."

"I know we just agreed to live dangerously today, but not that kind of danger...and don't ask me what I mean, because you know exactly what I'm talking about, Quinn."

He did know. He just couldn't agree, but she was already gone, so he didn't have to tell her that they weren't on the same page at all.

He might be willing to risk everything to hold her in his arms one more time and not just for a quick hug. He wanted to be with her again. He missed the way they'd been, so perfectly in tune with each other. It had never been like that with anyone else. But it wouldn't be the same with her, either. They had too much history, too much pain. That said, he still wanted her…and he didn't know what to do about that.

CHAPTER NINETEEN

CAITLYN FELT energized as they drove back to San Francisco after making a quick stop at Quinn's house so he could grab a change of clothes and Donovan's duffel bag. She'd taken a quick look at the notebook, her stomach churning when she'd seen the snakes. But there wasn't really anything else of note besides the photos. And while those had taken her back in time, they hadn't given her any new information. She'd have to find that elsewhere.

It was a beautiful day in the city, and as she drove across the Golden Gate Bridge, she felt like she was moving toward some answers. She didn't know where they would come from, and maybe she was being too optimistic, but she was going to hang on to the hopeful feeling as long as she could.

"You look determined," Quinn commented as she drove through the toll booths and headed toward the Presidio.

"I feel determined," she said, flinging him a quick look. "It's a new day, a new start."

"The optimistic girl is back. No one can keep her down for long."

"There was a time when I stayed down way too long. That won't happen again."

He met her smile with one of his own, and her stomach did a little somersault as she turned her attention back to the road. She had a feeling some of her good mood was directly related to Quinn. He'd opened up to her last night. He'd told her his secret, and while it had been difficult to hear, she felt like a load had slipped off her shoulders.

It wasn't just that he'd been honest; it was also what he'd been honest about. He'd gone after Donovan for her, for Isabella. All this time, she'd thought he'd just run away from her and the tragedy…everything, really. But he'd had a better reason than she'd imagined. He'd tried to get justice, revenge, whatever anyone wanted to call it, and she could relate in a way that no one else could.

Quinn hadn't let his past relationship with Donovan sway him from his mission to get the truth. He'd put her and their baby ahead of all that.

She warned herself not to get too carried away. He had still left her while she was in pain. He had stayed away and out of sight for ten years. And he could have shared the truth with her a long time ago. But they were moving on. Donovan's grand plan was going down, and whoever had jumped in to copy him or make his plan their own would be caught and punished.

Her phone buzzed with an incoming text, and she glanced down at the console. It was from Kevin. She slowed down, then pulled over to the side of the road to read the text.

"What does it say?" Quinn asked.

She read aloud. "'We need to talk. Can you meet me by the carousel at Golden Gate Park at eleven?'"

"That's twenty minutes from now. It feels like an odd request," he said, concern in his gaze.

"I agree, but I need to hear what he has to say." She texted back that she'd meet him there, then pulled back into traffic.

"It could be a setup," Quinn suggested. "Someone did take a shot at us yesterday."

"It's a Saturday morning and there will be dozens of people by that carousel. It wouldn't be a great place for an ambush." She glanced over at him, knowing he wouldn't like her next thought. "I should do this alone, Quinn."

"No way, babe. We're rattling cages together."

She couldn't stop her heart from squeezing just a little when he called her babe. It had been a long time since that endearment had slipped from his lips. She pushed that thought away, focusing on the situation at hand. "Kevin works for my father, and we grew up together. I have the inside track with him. I'd rather have you wait a short distance away. You can keep an eye on things, watch my back."

He frowned. "I guess I could do that."

"Thank you."

"For what?"

"Letting me make my own decision. This is my world, Quinn. I know what I'm doing."

"I just don't want you to get hurt."

"I'm going to try to avoid that." As a smile played around his lips, she said, "What are you grinning about?"

"I was thinking about Isabella yesterday, and I could see her in my head. She would have looked just like you, and I'm sure she would have had your stubborn determination."

"You were thinking about her?" she asked, surprised and touched.

"I haven't been able to stop since you told me her name. She came to life for me. Isabella, the prettiest baby of them all."

She loved hearing the sound of their baby's name on his lips. Every time he said it, it touched her heart. "Do you like the name?"

"So much," he said, meeting her gaze. "How did you come up with it?"

"It's the name of a favorite character in a book I read when I was a child. Isabella was this courageous young girl, who got lost in the woods after a plane crash. She climbed mountains and crossed rivers, fought off wild animals, and made friends with people who could get her home. When she finally arrived, she was so happy. There was light all around her, and she felt an enormous rush of love. She was happier than she'd ever been. I liked thinking about my little girl finding her way home, being surrounded by light. It probably sounds silly."

"It sounds amazing," he said, a husky note in his voice. "I think Isabella would have been a lot like you."

"And you, Quinn. I imagined her with your dark hair and incredible blue eyes. I thought about her falling in love with the sea, going diving with you, searching for starfish in the tidal pools, wading through the surf." She shook her head. "We are getting way off track."

"Or we're getting back on track," he countered.

"There's no more track for us," she said, needing to believe that was true. She couldn't let herself go down that road again. "We're just working together to bring a terrorist down. Then we go our separate ways. You have your life and I have mine. It's never a good idea to try to recapture the past. It just doesn't work. You agree, don't you?"

"Sure," Quinn said, giving nothing away by his tone.

Despite his reply, it didn't feel like an agreement.

"Thanks for telling me the story," he added. "I forgot how much books influenced your life."

"I know I sound like a poor little rich girl, but books were my best friends for a long time."

"They were mine, too. I think Isabella would have been a big reader like you."

"And she probably would have enjoyed school, one of those annoying kids, who has to sit in the front row and get good grades all the time, like you," she teased.

"I did not sit in the front row, but I did get good grades. One thing I can say for sure—she would not have been good at softball."

She laughed. "Your arm was worse than mine. You actually hit the umpire that time we played."

"He got in the way." He paused. "We definitely would not have paid for piano lessons for her."

She laughed. "Probably not."

It felt strange to be smiling and talking about Isabella, but it also felt good. No one in her life talked about her little girl, ever. But as much as she was enjoying a break in all the pain and worry, she needed to get her focus back fast.

Kevin was finally willing to talk, and she had more than a few questions for him.

When they got to Golden Gate Park, she managed to find a spot in a parking lot not too far from the carousel. She didn't actually mind the walk. It was a nice day, and as she'd predicted, the park was teeming with people enjoying the good weather and the open space.

Golden Gate Park was huge, running at least fifteen city blocks. In addition to the carousel, there were other park attractions, including two museums and a spectacular flower garden. There were also children's playgrounds, tennis courts, basketball courts, and plenty of barbecue and picnic spaces.

The carousel was quite near to one of the kids' playgrounds. She paused by a bench next to the play structure. "Why don't you wait for me here?"

"Are you sure I shouldn't stick with you? I feel like splitting up isn't a good idea."

"We'll be twenty yards apart. I need to talk to Kevin on my own."

"All right. I'll be watching you."

She walked to the carousel, her gaze scanning the area for Kevin. She waited for five minutes, hoping Kevin hadn't decided to bail. She could see Quinn across the way. He'd left the bench, which was occupied now by a mom with a stroller and two little kids. Quinn had moved under a tall tree, his hands in his pockets, his gaze focused on her. *He really was a handsome man,* she thought idly, *even with his brilliant blue eyes covered by his sunglasses. His brown hair sparkled in the sunlight and his body...*

She cleared her throat. She did not need to be thinking about his body.

Feeling someone approaching, she turned her head and saw Kevin. He was dressed in jeans and a hoodie sweatshirt, a baseball cap on his head and glasses covering his eyes. He was walking quickly, his movements jerky and anxious.

"What's going on, Kevin?" she asked. "Why are we meeting here?"

"Someone is following me. That's why I've been hiding out."

"Were you really in London?"

"No. I lied because I'm freaked out." He took off his glasses, and she could see the panic in his eyes.

"Talk to me. Tell me why you're scared."

"Your brother."

"Spencer?" she asked in surprise. "Why would you be scared of Spencer?"

"I found out something about him, about the first explosion at Bolton."

"What are you talking about?" she asked, her stomach churning.

"Spencer was supposed to go to the opening."

"Yes, but he had to cancel. He had a dental emergency."

"Did he?"

She shook her head, unwilling to go where Kevin wanted to

take her. "I don't know what game you're playing, Kevin. If you think that somehow this ridiculous lie is going to help you beat Spencer for some job, then you're insane."

"This is not about the job. You have to believe me. It's important that you believe me. Your brother was involved in the explosion that almost killed you. He wanted to get back at your dad. He thought he'd talked you out of going that day."

"That's not true. He said the other day he hadn't tried hard enough." She stopped, frowning at the memory of that conversation.

Kevin seized on her indecision. "Because he has felt guilty all these years. But he has a problem, Caitlyn. He has rages and when he gets angry, he does stupid, dangerous shit. He's angry now with me. He hired someone to plant the bomb outside the auditorium. He wanted to kill me."

"You sound crazy, Kevin."

"I'm telling you the truth, Caitlyn. Why would I lie?"

"I don't know, but you are."

"I'm not. Spencer has mental issues. Your dad knows, and he has tried to get him help, but Spencer won't go to his therapist or take his medication."

"I don't believe you, Kevin. This is a wild story."

Kevin's lips tightened. "You need to get the FBI to back off the case. If you don't, your brother will go down for it. Your family will be destroyed."

She didn't understand the terror in his eyes. "Someone wants you to convince me of that. Who? Who are you really afraid of, Kevin? What is this about?"

He didn't reply, his gaze swinging around once more. He jumped as a basketball from the nearby court came in their direction. "Dammit," he swore.

She picked up the ball and tossed it back to the teenager who'd come running after it.

Kevin walked toward a grove of trees, his body tense and edgy. "I'm telling you the truth," he said.

"I don't think you are."

"That's because you don't want to believe your brother almost killed you. But think about it. Why did he suddenly cancel?"

"He broke his tooth."

"Call his dentist. See if that really happened."

She stared at him uncertainly. She could probably contact the dentist and find out. *But why was she letting Kevin put doubts in her head?*

"I can get you proof," Kevin said. "Just promise me, you'll slow down the investigation."

"What kind of proof?"

"Uh…" He lifted a shaky hand to his mouth, his pupils dilating.

"Are you high, Kevin?"

"People make mistakes, you know?"

She shook her head. "I have no idea what you're talking about. But it's not Spencer, is it?"

"I don't know what to do, Caitlyn—I'm trying to make things right."

"Then tell me what's really going on. Did Allison send you here? Is she involved in this?"

"Allison and I broke up." He licked his lips. "I want to tell you, but I can't."

"Why not?"

Before he could reply, something whizzed by her ear and then Kevin's jaw fell open. His eyes widened, and she stared in shock at the bloody hole in his forehead. Kevin fell to the ground, and she whirled around, instinctively dodging behind a tree as another shot hit the trunk next to her. A passerby suddenly screamed as she saw Kevin on the ground.

She pulled out her gun, not sure where the shooter was. People started running in all directions.

Then she saw Quinn sprinting down a path away from her. He must have seen the shooter and was going after him. What the hell was he thinking?

She ran after them, shouting at someone to call 911.

It wouldn't matter for Kevin. He was dead. He'd been taken out in one silent shot.

Her heart pounded against her chest. Whatever he'd been about to say had gotten him killed.

She couldn't let the same thing happen to Quinn.

She thought Quinn was chasing a guy in a navy-blue jacket, but she couldn't get a clear look. They were deep in the woods now, away from the crowds. Quinn suddenly ducked and rolled as the man turned and took a shot at him.

She sprinted forward, firing her weapon, hitting the man in the chest. The gun fell out of his hand, and he fell back onto the ground.

She ran toward Quinn. "Are you all right?"

"I'm fine," he said, getting to his feet.

"What were you thinking—going after him like that?" She punched him in the arm, anger and fear running through her at the thought of what had almost happened. "You saw what he did to Kevin, and you don't have a gun."

"I didn't want him to get away."

"It was stupid."

"So was meeting Kevin," he countered. "How do you think I felt when I saw him go down and that guy took a shot at you?"

The air between them sizzled.

"Dammit," he swore. Then he grabbed her and kissed her hard on the lips. Then he released her almost as quickly as he'd taken hold of her.

She couldn't complain. She'd needed the kiss as much as he had.

"I'm not apologizing," he told her.

"I don't want an apology." She turned away and walked over to the shooter.

His lifeless eyes were wide open. She'd had this crazy thought that she would recognize him, that he would be someone from the past, that she'd finally know something, but she had never seen the man in front of her. He appeared to be in his late thirties or forties, with a beard and a tattoo on his neck.

"Who is that?" Quinn asked.

"I have no idea."

"He looks vaguely familiar, but I can't quite place him."

She dug into the man's pocket for an ID. "Larry Simmonds. Ring a bell?"

There was an odd look on Quinn's face. "As a matter of fact, it does. He used to go to the gym where Donovan and I first met. He was an ex-soldier, a sniper, in fact. He hired himself out for people who needed muscle and someone with no conscience."

"He's a contract killer?" she asked, not really surprised, because the shot through Kevin's head had already suggested that.

"I never really knew. There was just a lot of chatter about him. Donovan was pretty intrigued by him, I have to say."

"Another connection to Donovan. Any idea why he'd kill Kevin?"

"No. What did Kevin tell you?"

She shook her head. "A lot of lies about Spencer being involved ten years ago. That he'd called me and told me not to go because he knew the building was going to blow up. He said my brother had a rage and mental problem and I needed to call off the investigation before I ruined the family. It was crazy."

"Did Spencer tell you not to go? I remember when we were at the coffee cart, you thought he was coming."

"He canceled at the last minute. He had to go to the dentist. He suggested that I should skip it, too, but he wasn't that persuasive."

"I don't think I ever heard that before, Caitlyn."

"Really? It wasn't a secret. I guess I just never thought about it. But that's not the point. I don't believe what Kevin said. He was being coerced. He was terrified. When we moved into the shadow of the trees, the shooter must have thought Kevin was going to cave. Or else he was just supposed to shoot within minutes of our conversation so there would be no time for me to get further information."

"Well, this guy is not going to talk now."

"I should have aimed lower." She pulled out her phone. "I need to call this in, and you need to leave."

"What are you talking about?"

"The police will be here soon. It will take time to clear this all up. You don't need to be involved in that. In fact, you can't be. Go now."

"I'm not going to leave you here."

"I know how to deal with this. If you're here, you'll get caught up in everything. Please, go, Quinn. We'll meet up later."

He gave her a conflicted look.

"Don't argue," she added. "We don't have time for that."

"Call me as soon as you can. I won't leave the city."

"Where will you go? You don't have a car. It's still at Wyatt's house with a flat tire and a broken window. I don't want you going back there to get it."

"You can't call all the shots, Caitlyn."

"Yes, I can."

He let out a sigh. "All right. I'll find a cab. I'll just go to the beach. Call me when you get free and we can figure out where to meet up."

"Okay." She gave him a pointed look. "Don't talk to anyone else until we meet again."

He hesitated. "I can't make that promise."

"Quinn," she protested.

"You asked me to trust you, Caitlyn. You need to do the same thing. I can promise you this—I won't talk about what happened here with Kevin, and I won't mention Spencer's name and the wild story you just got."

It wasn't exactly what she wanted, but she took it. "All right. Go." She punched in Emi's number, then said, "I have a big problem."

CHAPTER TWENTY

QUINN HATED LEAVING Caitlyn alone in the woods, but the shooter was dead, and the last thing he wanted was to get caught up in FBI red tape. He moved away from the scenes of both shootings, careful to stay in the shadow of the trees or in the middle of a crowd. He didn't want to get caught on a surveillance camera. That would only put Caitlyn in a bad position. But at the moment, his reappearance was probably the least of anyone's concerns.

As he walked, his pulse continued to race as he remembered the shock he'd felt when Kevin had fallen to the ground. He hadn't heard the shot. There must have been a silencer on the weapon. Thank God, Caitlyn hadn't been hit. She certainly could have been.

Or maybe not. Maybe there wasn't a contract on her, just on Kevin. The second shot could have simply been used as cover for the shooter's escape.

The story Kevin had given Caitlyn about her brother seemed ridiculous. He had no idea what the hell it was all about, but he needed it to be a lie. He couldn't imagine how difficult it would be for Caitlyn to have to deal with the fact that her brother had almost killed her.

On the other hand, he had never known that Spencer had called her that morning and told her not to go. No one had shared that information with him. Or if they had, it certainly hadn't stuck in his head.

It wasn't completely surprising, though. It had been a call between Caitlyn and her brother, and she hadn't been talking about anything after the blast. Spencer, like the rest of the Carlson family, had blamed him for Caitlyn's injuries. There had been no warm family moments where they'd hugged things out or talked about what had happened. He'd always been on one side of whatever room they were in, and they'd been on the other.

He frowned, not wanting to accept the premise that Kevin had made to Caitlyn. Maybe it was about derailing the investigation or turning it back on the Carlsons and promoting more terror within the family. Now Caitlyn wasn't just afraid of the next bomb or gas attack—she was terrified for her brother, for her family.

It was a clever ploy. *But why had Kevin been shot right after delivering the information? Had he simply become unnecessary? Or did he know too much?*

As those questions rolled around in his head, he left the park. He crossed the street and blended into a crowd of pedestrians that were walking down Cavanaugh Street, a block of cafés and small retailers.

He felt frustrated and restless. He needed to do something. He needed to talk to someone. Spencer would be a good choice, but Caitlyn would want to do that herself. He could call Lauren, but he wasn't sure he wanted to get more involved with her. He doubted Hank would say more than he had the day before. Same went for Wyatt, and Wyatt was a little tricky, because of the odd parts of his story, especially when it related to Yosemite.

If anyone could shed light on Wyatt's behavior and/or

involvement, it would probably be his brother, Justin, and Lauren had given him Justin's number.

Feeling like he finally had something to do that might actually be helpful, he paused in the shadow of a building and sent Justin a text: *It's Quinn. We need to meet. It's urgent.* He hesitated, then added. *Wyatt could be in trouble.*

As he waited for a reply, he continued walking, wanting to put more distance between himself and the park.

He thought Justin might reply, simply because it had always been Justin's job to protect his younger brother, who while only a year younger, had always been Justin's responsibility.

He'd actually helped Justin bail Wyatt out of a couple of bad situations in college. They'd had to get Wyatt out of a bar one night before he got the crap beat out of him for hitting on someone else's girlfriend. They'd also had to talk a woman out of calling the police because Wyatt had drunkenly gone into the wrong apartment and gone to sleep in her bed. But that was all just stupid college stuff.

Would Justin have taken steps to protect his brother from more serious situations—like the bombing? Was it possible that it wasn't the senator who had lied but rather Justin?

He let out a sigh, his frustration only relieved by the shimmering sunlight bouncing off the ocean in the distance. Fifteen minutes later, he found himself walking across the Great Highway. When his feet hit the sand, he felt almost instantly better.

He walked down to the water's edge and blew out a breath, images of Kevin falling to the ground running through his head once more. He didn't know what to think about Kevin, but seeing someone who was his age, who had once been his friend, die like that had shaken him up, reminding him how deadly the situation was.

Whoever had taken over for Donovan was fifty thousand times worse in scope and scale. The LNF looked like a kids' playgroup compared to what was happening now—cyber-attacks on cameras, bombs, toxic gas, and snipers. It was unbelievable. They were fighting a war on multiple fronts, and they didn't know where the next battle would occur.

His phone vibrated in his pocket. It was a text from Justin. *Where and when?*

He tapped out an answer. *Half hour. Ocean Beach at Vincente.*

Make it an hour.

Done.

He didn't know if it was a mistake to pick the location where he was right now, but he actually liked the wide-open beach. There was nowhere for a shooter to hide. Now he just had to wait.

Caitlyn stood back as the EMTs placed the draped body of Larry Simmonds on a stretcher. For the past hour, she'd answered dozens of questions as Rob, Emi, and a swarm of agents had descended on the park. The team was now combing both crime scenes for evidence.

She'd left out all mention of Quinn. It was probably a mistake. There would be a surveillance camera somewhere that had caught both of them as they'd entered the park, but it would take time to get that footage, and by then, hopefully she'd have some answers.

She turned her head as Emi joined her, wearing her navy-blue FBI jacket over black slacks.

"How are you doing?" Emi asked with concern.

"I'm fine. I just wish I hadn't killed Simmonds. He might have been able to give us the answers we're looking for."

"It sounds like one of you was going to die today. Better that it was him," Emi said pragmatically.

"Agreed. Hopefully, we can locate his employer, but I

suspect that transaction will be buried deep in the web and behind multiple layers of secrecy. This guy was good. He took Kevin down with one shot."

"It's almost amazing that you were able to catch up to him. Usually, those shooters disappear quickly."

"I was lucky. But Kevin wasn't." She felt a wave of anger and pain for a man who had once been a friend. "Whatever he knew died with him."

"I'm sorry. I know he's part of the Carlson family."

"He wasn't just an employee. I grew up with Kevin. He used to be a good guy. I don't know how he's involved in all this."

"It sounds like he wanted to tell you."

"He was conflicted and also terrified. Obviously, he had good reason for that fear." She had not mentioned Spencer in her preliminary statement, which could have serious consequences, but Kevin's story was bogus, and she didn't want to further the lie against her brother. Maybe she was more like her father than she'd ever believed. She was risking a lot to protect her family and Quinn. That was a disturbing thought.

"Are you coming into the office?" Emi asked.

"Not yet. I need to speak to my dad."

"Of course. Try not to get shot at again."

"I'll try." She shivered at that reminder. *How many close calls would she be able to survive before one ended her life?* But fear was what they wanted, and she wouldn't give them that.

As Justin came across the wide expanse of sand on Ocean Beach just after two o'clock, Quinn was ready. He'd had some food at the café across the street, two cups of coffee, and time to get Kevin's tragic ending out of his head, at least for the moment. Hopefully, this meeting wouldn't end with anyone being shot.

He hadn't seen Justin Pederson in ten years, but like his

brother, Wyatt, Justin hadn't changed much. Unlike Wyatt, who was more comfortable in jeans and flip-flops, Justin wore gray chinos with loafers and a button-down shirt. His brown hair was cut short and styled well, and as he drew closer, Quinn could see a neatly trimmed beard. Justin also wore sunglasses, but as he reached Quinn, he removed them.

"Quinn. I figured you'd contact me after you spoke to Wyatt yesterday. We've come full circle, haven't we? The bomb at Bolton a few days ago—it put us all back in the same place. Why are we meeting here? What is going on with Wyatt that I need to know?"

Justin had always been direct, someone who dealt in facts more than speculation, so that's what he would give him. "Kevin Reilly was shot to death in Golden Gate Park a few hours ago."

Shock flashed through Justin's brown eyes. "What?"

"He took a single bullet to the head. The shooter was probably a contract killer."

Justin's lips parted as he sucked in a shaky breath. "Why? Why would someone kill Kevin?"

"Because he's involved in what happened at Bolton. And there's a good chance Wyatt is involved as well."

"He's not."

"He went to Bolton."

"That was stupid," Justin said derisively. "But it wasn't until hours after the blast. He was curious. He had nothing to do with that bomb."

"What about the one ten years ago? I know he lied about where he was that morning. He confirmed it to me yesterday. Did you lie as well?"

Justin gave him a hard look. "I did not. In fact, I corrected the record with Agent Bauer a few days after the explosion when I realized that my father's office had made a mistake."

"That was never noted in the file."

"Did Caitlyn tell you that?"

"She did."

"Well, I told the truth. That's all I could do. It's not my fault if the FBI file is wrong. Is that it?"

"No. After we left Wyatt's house yesterday, someone shot at Caitlyn and me. Did Wyatt tell you that?"

"He said he heard gunfire. The police stopped by sometime later to ask if he'd seen anything, but he had not. It appears you were not hurt. Do you know who was shooting at you?"

Justin spoke like a lawyer, in clear, short, concise statements.

"It was probably the same man who killed Kevin today," he replied. "It's interesting that your brother never seems to hear or see anything, yet he's always very close to the action."

Justin's gaze narrowed. "Let's cut to the chase. Are you wearing a wire?"

"What?" he asked in astonishment.

"You heard me. You're hanging out with Caitlyn. She's a fed. Are you wired? Are you trying to get some kind of confession out of me?"

"No." He lifted up his shirt. "It's just you and me on this beach."

"I don't know that I can believe that."

"You can believe it," he said sharply, sensing Justin was about to bail. "I was with Caitlyn yesterday, but she doesn't trust me any more than you do. She's just using me to get answers from people who don't want to talk to her. I want answers, too. So should you." He let that sink in, then continued. "The FBI is trying to connect the two explosions at Bolton to former members of the LNF. We are going back to where we started, Justin. Your alibi will be questioned. Wyatt will be pulled into the investigation, too. He didn't just lie about where he was ten years ago, he also didn't tell anyone he was in Yosemite when Donovan died. And I did not buy his sudden desire to go for a hike in the mountains, which was always his least favorite thing to do."

Indecision played through Justin's eyes and then he gave a short nod of agreement. "All right I'll tell you the truth. Wyatt went to Yosemite, because Donovan was blackmailing him."

"What are you talking about?"

"At Donovan's request, Wyatt told Lauren to change the time of your study group."

He hadn't thought he could be surprised again, but he was. "Wyatt knew about the bomb?"

"No. I want to make that absolutely clear," Justin said forcefully. "Donovan just asked Wyatt to get Lauren to change the time of your meeting. Wyatt didn't understand the request, but he didn't question it."

"Why the hell not?"

"He was starting to feel nervous around Donovan. He thought it would be easier to just go along. That's what Wyatt does. He doesn't like conflict or confrontation."

"When did this happen?"

"The morning of the explosion, about two hours before the bomb went off."

"Lauren didn't question this request?"

"No. She just said she'd do it."

His heart thudded against his chest as he realized exactly what had happened. "You're saying that Wyatt and Lauren both knew there was a reason Donovan wanted me away from that building, and they just went along with it? Why wouldn't they warn me? I thought we were friends."

"They didn't know a bomb would go off," Justin said. "They thought there was going to be a protest and that Donovan didn't want you to get caught up in it. But Donovan also didn't want you to know about it. He thought you would try to get him to call it off."

A white fury ran through him. "And neither one chose to get Caitlyn out of the building? They left her to die. I'm going to kill them both."

"Slow down," Justin ordered. "Remember, they didn't know about the bomb. Donovan had never done anything like that before. They had no reason to suspect that kind of violence. You didn't suspect it, either."

"Because Donovan made me a promise."

"He broke it. But that's on him, not on my brother."

"Why did Donovan even involve them? Why didn't he just text me himself and tell me to meet him somewhere?"

"I don't know, but I have a theory. Donovan couldn't show that he had any inside or prior knowledge. He wanted a buffer between himself and the bomb, between you and him. He used Wyatt to get to Lauren, involving them both in his plot. If they spoke out against him later, they would be in trouble themselves. And he had manufactured evidence that would make it look like they were the bombers." Justin paused. "They were also betrayed by Donovan. You weren't the only one."

"Let's say I believe you. How was Donovan blackmailing Wyatt?"

"He'd been setting Wyatt up for days, sending him to the hardware store to pick up items that were later used in the making of the bomb. They also got the snake tattoos together and exchanged texts about their radical ideas. My brother was too high half the time to even realize what was going on. But after the explosion, it became clear. When Donovan went to Yosemite, Wyatt saw that trip as his opportunity to try to get rid of the evidence."

"And did he succeed?"

"No. He didn't find anything. Donovan was already dead, and Wyatt thought he saw your Jeep in the parking lot by Donovan's cabin in Yosemite. He thought you might have the evidence. He was scared for a long time. When nothing happened, when you didn't show up at Donovan's memorial, he thought he was home free." Justin cleared his throat. "If you try to pin anything on my brother, Quinn, everyone will know about your trip to Yosemite."

"My Jeep was not in Yosemite," he said flatly. "No matter what Wyatt says."

Justin's gaze met his. "I still believe you were there. After Donovan died and Wyatt was freaking out, I had one of my father's private investigators try to track you down. He couldn't find a trace of your existence. He said you must have reinvented yourself, because you had completely disappeared. That's what you did, isn't it? You killed Donovan and then you disappeared. Did Caitlyn know what you did, where you were? Was it all just a pretense—the breakup between you two?"

"No. That was real. Caitlyn and I had not seen each other for ten years, until last Thursday."

"How did you kill Donovan? How did you get the jump on him?"

"I didn't kill him, Justin. As far as I know, he fell, or he killed himself."

"That's difficult to believe. If you didn't kill him, why did you disappear?"

"I wanted a fresh start."

"You had more motive to kill Donovan than anyone."

"That's true, but I didn't push him off the mountain. Let's talk about what's happening now."

"I wish I knew, Quinn. But I'm in the dark."

"Did you spend time with Allison and Kevin? I know Wyatt did. He said they came into his bar a number of times."

"I never met her, and I haven't seen Kevin in at least two years. I have no idea what they were doing or why they were together. Maybe you should talk to Lauren."

"I have spoken to her. She wasn't particularly helpful."

"That surprises me. She always had a crush on you. I would have thought she'd be very cooperative in answering any question you asked."

"Well, she wasn't. But we will talk again now that I know Donovan used her to get me out of the building."

"I'd appreciate it if you would keep me and Wyatt out of that conversation."

"I'm not sure that's possible. Caitlyn will also want to talk to you, Justin, not just about now but also about ten years ago."

"I can be more helpful in an unofficial capacity. If you put me on the record, I'll deny everything, and then my father will become involved. You'll both get tied up in knots, particularly you, Quinn. You'll be spending so much time talking about Yosemite that you won't get the answers you want."

"Is that a threat?"

"It's a fact. I'm not averse to helping you track down the bomber. Wyatt and I have lived under the shadow of that explosion for too long. And whatever is happening now needs to be stopped. I have never believed in using violence to achieve environmental goals. That's why I started withdrawing from the LNF even before Donovan set off that bomb. I wasn't interested in being part of a radical group. I didn't think you were, either."

"I wasn't."

"And Wyatt—he's never had any real interest in any cause. He joined the LNF because I was in it. He thought of it like a club. He believed Donovan was his friend. Wyatt was wrecked when he realized what Donovan had done."

"But Wyatt didn't tell the FBI what he knew. Neither did you."

"I didn't know it all at the time. Wyatt didn't open up to me until after Donovan died. That's when I learned that Donovan had set Wyatt and Lauren up."

He wasn't sure he completely believed that, but he let it go.

"Wyatt is a good person," Justin continued. "He just makes bad decisions, mostly because he's not often completely sober. I know he saw Kevin and Allison a few times, but they just came into his bar. He wasn't meeting up with them. He wasn't planning anything. He's not who you need to focus on. You should be talking to Allison or Lauren, not me, not Wyatt." He paused. "Are we done?"

Justin had made a convincing argument, but then, he'd always been a great debater. "For now," he said.

"Good. Feel free to share what I said with Caitlyn. If she wants to talk more, let's do it off the books."

"I'll let her know what you said."

As Justin walked away, Quinn kept a sharp eye out for trouble, but nothing happened. After a good ten minutes, his breath came more easily. Justin was gone, and it didn't appear that anyone was going to suddenly start shooting.

His phone vibrated. It was Caitlyn.

"Where are you?" she asked.

"Ocean Beach. Can you meet me?"

"Yes. I'm just leaving my parents' house. I had to tell my dad about Kevin."

"How did he take it?"

"With great shock, concern, and anger."

"Did you tell him what Kevin said about Spencer?"

"No. I haven't told anyone that. I have to talk to Spencer first. I went by his condo on my way to my parents' house, but he wasn't there. He's also not answering his phone. I'm worried, Quinn. Actually, I'm kind of terrified."

He could hear the fear in her voice, and he wanted to put his arms around her. He wanted to comfort her and tell her everything would be fine, but at this moment, he had no idea if anything would ever be fine again. "We'll figure it out."

"We have to. And we need to do it fast. Where on Ocean are you?"

"Nearest cross street is Lincoln. I'll meet you by the corner."

"I'm glad you're safe. I had second and third thoughts about sending you away from the park. I was concerned someone might have followed you, that there might have been a second shooter."

"There wasn't, and the beach was a good place for me to go."
He paused. "It was also a good place for me to meet Justin—
open air and nowhere for a shooter to hide."

"You spoke to Justin? What did he say?"

"I'll tell you when you get here. I know what we should do
next, Caitlyn."

"I know, too. I'll be there in fifteen minutes. Oh, and I'm
driving a black SUV now. The window on the rental car is being
repaired before I turn it back in."

"See you soon."

CHAPTER TWENTY-ONE

FIFTEEN MINUTES LATER, Caitlyn saw Quinn on the corner, and her heart filled with relief. She'd known he was all right but seeing him brought that truth home.

"This is a nicer ride," he commented, as he buckled his seat belt.

"I picked it up at the office."

"How's the investigation going? Did you tell them I was in the park?"

"No. I should have, but I didn't."

He gave her a worried look. "You could have told them, Caitlyn. I don't want you to jeopardize your job trying to protect me."

"Well, you risked your life a short while ago trying to protect me. I will add you to my official written report, as I'm sure you'll be spotted on some surveillance camera somewhere. I just wanted to buy a little time." She paused. "You said you knew where we needed to go."

"Back to Bolton," he said, a gleam in his eyes. "Back to where it started."

She was in complete agreement. "Yes. We need to find Allison Sullivan. She's tied into everything: to Bolton, to Lauren, and to Kevin… She has to be involved. And it's possible Lauren is as well. What did Justin tell you?"

"More than I expected."

"I'm shocked he agreed to meet with you."

"He had something to trade."

"What's that?"

"He wanted me to be clear that if we go after Wyatt, he'll make it known that I was in Yosemite, that I killed Donovan."

She shot him a quick look. "Why would we go after Wyatt? Did he tell you something I don't know?"

"Yes, and you're not going to like it, Caitlyn. You should pull over."

"Just say it."

"Pull over first." The heavy note in his voice sent a chill down her spine.

She frowned and then changed lanes. She turned down a side street and slid into a parking spot. Throwing the SUV into park, she left the engine running. "Okay, say it," she said, steeling herself for what was coming.

"Wyatt was being blackmailed by Donovan."

"Over what?" she asked in surprise.

"Donovan asked Wyatt to have Lauren call me away from the building. This apparently happened about two hours before the blast."

She looked at him in astonishment, her heart leaping with that piece of information. "So, Lauren did change the time on purpose. What a liar she is."

"Yes. She lied. But she didn't do it for Wyatt. She knew the request had come from Donovan."

"That whole thing about the birthday party time being moved up—she had to get her roommate into the lie, too."

"Or she simply changed the time of the party. At any rate, according to Justin, neither Wyatt nor Lauren knew there was a bomb. They just believed a protest was going to happen, and Donovan didn't want me in the middle of it."

"How can we believe that's true when they lied about everything?" she asked, her head starting to pound as she processed the information.

"Justin reminded me that Donovan had never done anything violent before. They had no reason to believe an explosion would occur."

"But they knew something was going to happen. Damn them! Damn their lies! Why didn't they tell the truth afterward? Why didn't they come clean and send Donovan to jail?" She could see the answer in his gaze. "Because he had implicated them in his plot by getting them involved with your alibi."

"Exactly. He allegedly manufactured other evidence tying them to the explosion, and he used that information to blackmail them. The snake tattoos were part of that plan. If Lauren or Wyatt turned on him, they'd be turning on themselves."

She shook her head, realizing the depth of Donovan's plotting. "And Justin told you all of this, so he knew as well?"

"He said he didn't know until after Donovan died. That's when Wyatt felt free enough to tell him. Wyatt was afraid that I knew the truth and that I would come after him the way I'd gone after Donovan."

"Did you tell Justin what happened in Yosemite?"

"No. I said Wyatt didn't see my Jeep, which is the truth. Wyatt went to Yosemite to try to get the evidence away from Donovan. He thought it would be the perfect opportunity because Donovan was alone."

"That must be why the pages were ripped out of the notebook. But Wyatt said he got there after Donovan was dead, the next day. You would have been gone with the duffel bag before Wyatt got into the cabin. The timing is off."

"You're right," he said, a note of puzzlement in his gaze. "And Justin said that Wyatt didn't find anything in the cabin. So maybe he didn't get the pages. Maybe they were ripped out before either of us got there."

"Now I get why Justin thought you had something to trade. Although, I'm confused as to why Wyatt mentioned Yosemite to us yesterday. Why bring it up at all? We wouldn't have known he was there if he hadn't told us."

"I think he was trying to figure out how much I knew about his involvement. As Justin said, Wyatt doesn't always make good decisions."

"That's an understatement. I thought Wyatt was my friend." She paused, her gut twisting with anger. "He was different than Lauren or Donovan. He knew me from long before we got to Bolton, before either of us had anything to do with the LNF. But he knew something was going to happen that day. Even if I believe he didn't know there was a bomb, he still had information that he could have shared with me."

"I can't disagree."

"And then there's Lauren." She shook her head, feeling an intense desire to kick Lauren's ass. "She has lied over and over again about that damn study group. I want to arrest them both right now, sit them in a chair, and keep them there until they talk."

"I appreciate that sentiment, but I think we should move on Allison first, because she's probably more involved in whatever is happening now than either of them."

"I wouldn't be so sure of that. Lauren could easily be involved with her sister's group. Wyatt could be as well. Justin obviously wanted to protect his brother, but he could have been lying about everything."

"I don't believe he was lying about the blackmail or what Wyatt and Lauren did to draw me away from the event. It makes a lot of sense as to why no one was willing to speak up against Donovan."

"Well, I still want to interrogate each and every one of them."

He gave her a small smile. "I'm sure you'll get your chance."

"Oh, I will," she vowed. "But you're right. Allison is a priority. She was closely tied to Kevin and now he's dead. She's either dead, too, or she had a hand in it." She blew out a breath. "Thanks for getting all of that out of Justin."

"I had no idea when I contacted him that he had such significant information."

"It was a good call."

He gave her a searching look. "I'm sure that wasn't easy for you to hear."

"That Wyatt and Lauren saved you but gave no thought to me? I don't feel great about it, but I don't know why I'm even a little surprised. I always thought there was something suspect about Lauren's story. Now, I know it for sure. She will pay for her involvement. I can guarantee you that."

"I do not doubt you at all."

She put the car into drive and pulled away from the curb, a new surge of anger fueling her determination. She might have a few more answers about the past, but she still needed the complete story, the whole truth. Her payback would come later. She needed to catch whoever had taken up Donovan's plan and made it even worse. She couldn't allow anyone else to die.

Allison lived in a studio in the Seaview Apartments that consisted of two buildings, each one housing four apartments: two units on the first floor, two on the second.

As Caitlyn pulled into the parking lot and shut off the engine, she said, "It looks like we'll be taking another walk down memory lane." She'd lived at Seaview her senior year, and it was where she and Quinn had spent much of their time together. "I always knew we would have to go back in order to go forward. I knew it the instant that second bomb went off." She let out a sigh. "It looks just the same."

"When was the last time you were here?"

"The morning before the first bomb went off."

"You never returned to the apartment?"

"No. My parents took me straight home after I got out of the hospital. They sent someone to the apartment to clean out my things. There's actually a box in my old bedroom at my parents' house that has a few of your belongings in it."

"Like what?"

"Your Coldplay T-shirt."

He gave her a faint smile. "I gave that to you. It was your favorite shirt to sleep in."

She remembered that all too well. "Your cologne is in there, too, some of your books, a couple of CDs—I should get it for you sometime."

"Don't bother. Just throw it away." He gave her a quizzical look. "I'm surprised you haven't done that already."

"I moved out of my parents' house about a year after you left, and I didn't take much with me." She paused, her gaze moving back to the Seaview Apartments. "We had a lot of good times in this building." It was where they had fallen in love, where they had made love for the first time, and then spent every single night after that wrapped in each other's arms. "I didn't think we'd ever end." She cleared her throat. "This isn't getting us anywhere. We should go inside."

"For what it's worth, Caitlyn…"

"Yes?"

"Meeting you was the best thing that ever happened to me. I know it wasn't the same for you. But that's the truth."

She couldn't say the same. She was touched by the sincerity in his eyes, but she didn't want to get into another emotional discussion now. "Let's go find Allison."

He nodded, and they got out of the car. Allison lived on the first floor of building A, and since the front door was ajar, they had no problem getting inside. Her apartment was at the end of the hall. Caitlyn knocked on the door, hearing nothing but silence. In fact, the entire floor felt very quiet for a Saturday afternoon, but then a lot of students had left for the weekend, eager to get away from the fear of another bomb going off.

"I don't think she's here," Quinn said.

She opened her bag and took out a small lock-picking device. It took her less than thirty seconds to open the door.

"I guess we're going in," Quinn said dryly.

"We are."

Allison's apartment reminded her of the one she'd lived in on the second floor, although it was smaller and had no view. There was a living room and kitchen with a small café table and then a short hallway leading to a bedroom and bath.

"Being here feels weird," Quinn commented, as he wandered around. "It feels like your apartment, yet it isn't."

She moved over to the table where there were stacks of flyers for an upcoming protest in Monterey at a pesticide company. "It looks like they're scheduled to protest at this company on Tuesday morning." She grabbed a flyer, folded it, and stuck it in her pocket to review later. On the desk, she found a calculus text-book and a loose-leaf notebook. She rifled through a few pages, but they were blank. A sticky note pad had a couple of numbers written on the top. One looked like a phone number. She ripped it off and stuck it in her pocket as well. Then she pulled open the top drawer. There were pens and pencils, paper clips, and random other items but nothing noteworthy.

"I found something," Quinn said, picking up a strip of photos that were on the coffee table. "Holy shit!"

"What?" she asked, surprised by his reaction.

"This is Allison, and…I can't believe it."

She took the photo out of his hand, staring at the guy Allison was with. He was a blond, good-looking man in his early twenties, who reminded her very much of Donovan. "Who is this? How does he look like Donovan?"

Quinn stared back at her. "That has to be Donovan's brother, Tim Coulson."

His answer stunned her. "I didn't know Donovan had a brother. How did I not know that?"

"A half-brother," he corrected. "Donovan and Tim didn't grow up together. They just shared the same mother. Tim had to be at least eleven years younger than Donovan. I think he was the product of the affair Donovan's mother had, and he was born shortly after Donovan's parents divorced."

"I can't believe I didn't know this," she said, wondering why that information had not been in the FBI file. The investigation had been incredibly sloppy.

"Donovan didn't see Tim very often, because Donovan and his mother were estranged. But Donovan would take Tim on hiking trips in the summer. I met him on one of those. Tim was about eight. He seemed like a good kid, and he was thrilled to be spending time with his brother." Quinn paused. "I haven't thought about him in years. He didn't even cross my mind when Donovan died. I had a random thought for Donovan's parents at the time, but they really weren't part of his life. Neither was Tim."

She gazed back at the photo. "It can't be a coincidence that Tim is with Allison."

"Maybe Lauren introduced them," he said slowly.

"Maybe she did. And it makes sense that these two siblings of former LNF members might have wanted to follow in their footsteps. They could be working with Lauren. She could be the mastermind. Some of the other former LNF members might be involved as well."

"I'm going to knock on some doors, see if anyone in the building knows about their relationship."

"Good idea."

As Quinn left the apartment, she moved into the bedroom. The bed was unmade. There was trash on the floor. Some of the drawers were empty. When she opened the closet, she saw no sign of clothes, just more evidence that someone had left in a hurry. There were hangers on the floor, a discarded garment bag, and one worn tennis shoe.

*Allison and Tim...*she thought with disbelief. Lauren's sister, Donovan's brother, together. And in the photo, they'd looked like boyfriend and girlfriend. *But how had Kevin factored into that equation?* Maybe they'd been using him all along.

Her head ached as she searched for answers that felt so close and yet so far away at the same time. She sat down on the edge of the bed, feeling suddenly overwhelmed and exhausted. But she should be feeling energized. She finally had some real clues. Allison and Tim had left a lot of things behind. She needed to call Emi, get a forensics team to the apartment. They also needed to start looking for both of them.

She tried to get her phone out of her pocket, but her vision blurred.

"Caitlyn?" Quinn's sharp voice rang through her head, and it made the pain worse.

"Why are you yelling?"

"I'm not. What's wrong with you?"

"You have two faces."

"What the hell?"

"Now you have three. They're all so handsome."

Quinn suddenly stood up and moved away.

"Where did you go?" she slurred. "Now you have zero faces." She fell back on the bed. She was so tired. "I need to take a nap." She felt a hard hand on her shoulder. She wanted to swat it away so she could sleep, but she couldn't seem to move.

"Caitlyn, wake up. Look at me."

She blinked her eyes open. "You're back. Why are you spinning?"

He grabbed her arms and pulled them around his neck. Then he picked her up.

"Where are we going?" she asked.

"Out of here. There's some kind of toxic bleach mess in the bathroom."

"What?" she asked sleepily, her eyes feeling too heavy to keep open. "I am so tired."

"You have to stay awake. Fight it, babe."

"Your chest feels so good," she murmured. She'd always loved his chest. So strong and muscular. "I want to feel your skin against mine. Don't you want to feel that, too?"

"More than anything."

She frowned as his face spun in front of her once more. She hung on as he seemed to be running somewhere. "Are we in a hurry?"

"We are."

"I don't know if it's going to happen, us being together again."

"Oh, it will happen," he promised her.

"I want it to, but I don't want it to, you know?"

"I know."

"God, your eyes are so blue. I love your eyes. I like the way they darken when we're together." A rush of air hit her face. It pricked at her skin like tiny little knives. "It's freezing," she slurred. "I'm cold."

"Good. That will help you wake up. It's going to be okay, babe. You'll be all right." Quinn juggled her in his arms as he opened the car door and put her in the front seat.

"You're so close." She wanted to taste his sexy mouth. "You could kiss me. I could kiss you. It would be so good."

"It would be, but I have to leave you for a minute."

"I don't want you to go. I want you to stay forever."

"I wish you meant that," he said huskily. "I'll be right back. I have to warn people, get them out of the building. Don't go anywhere."

The door slammed shut. She thought she saw him running. *Why was he always running away from her?* She couldn't seem to hold on to him. But she shouldn't want to hold on to him. He'd hurt her.

He'd also made her really, really happy. She'd never been her whole self with anyone but him. She'd always been trying to be someone else. But with Quinn, it had been so real, so intimate, so honest.

She groaned against that thought. *Not honest.* He'd left her. He'd lied to her. He'd kept secrets from her. That's what she needed to be thinking about, not all the good stuff. Just the bad stuff.

But the bad stuff seemed like a long time ago. Quinn was back now. He was a good man. She liked who he'd become. She trusted him again. *Was she being stupid?*

No. She wasn't wrong. She couldn't be wrong. She just wished she didn't feel so sleepy.

Why was she so tired? The question wouldn't let her rest. A chilling cold began to seep into her bones. She blinked a few times, the view in front of her blurry. *Where was she?*

More clues began to emerge—the console in front of her, the seat belt around her body. She was in the car.

She forced her eyes all the way open. Her vision began to clear. She saw Quinn running toward the vehicle. Four people came out of the building after him. They were also running.

He opened the door and jumped in behind the wheel. "Let's get you to the hospital."

"What's going on?"

He gave her a sharp look. "Do you know where you are?"

"I'm in the car. Why am I not driving? I like to be the driver," she protested.

"Your head would have to be clear for that, and it's not."

"Why is everyone running?"

"There was poisonous gas in Allison's apartment. It made you feel the way you're feeling."

She suddenly became very aware of the way she was feeling; her head pounding like a jackhammer, and her stomach rolling with waves of nauseousness. She felt like she was awakening from a deep sleep, and the fog was lifting from her brain.

They'd gone into Allison's apartment. They'd found the photo of Allison and Tim, but she couldn't remember anything else.

Quinn rolled down the windows in the car as he drove out of the lot. "You need to breathe, Caitlyn. Fresh air. Suck it in."

"Tell me again what happened."

"There was a spill in the bathroom—bleach and ammonia…I don't know what else. It looked like someone had been mixing something. The fumes got to you."

"Why were you all right?"

"I was across the hall while you were in the bedroom. You inhaled more than I did." He shot her a quick look. "I want to get you checked out."

"I'm okay. I'm feeling better." While her head was pounding, her other symptoms were starting to recede. "I don't need to go to the hospital."

"That stuff could have damaged your lungs."

"My breathing is okay, and the hospital will take too long. Plus, I can't stand being in the hospital. It reminds me of all the weeks I was there before."

Quinn frowned. "It won't take that long, Caitlyn."

"I'm fine now. I just need to breathe." She saw the doubt in his eyes. "Really, Quinn. Let's go somewhere else and regroup. I have to call the team."

"The residents are already calling 911. I got everyone out of the building. The police will be responding soon. There's nothing you need to do right now."

"That's good. But I don't want to go to the hospital. Please, take me somewhere else."

His lips tightened as he gave her a hard look. "I should not listen to you. You were out of it a few minutes ago."

"I'm fine now. Or I will be soon," she amended. "If I feel worse, you can take me in."

"All right, but if you start to feel sick, you have to tell me, Caitlyn. I mean it."

"I'll tell you, but the nausea is going away, and so is the headache." Even though she was cold, she was happy to breathe in the crisp, fresh air.

As Quinn left the Bolton area, he got on the highway heading north away from the city. "I don't want to go to your house," she said. "Or the boat. Nothing tied to you. It's too risky."

"I know. We'll get a hotel room. At the very least, you should lie down for a bit."

"All right." Quinn took the next exit, heading toward a nice hotel.

"Rest and then food," he said, as he pulled into the parking lot. "I don't want you to get hangry on top of everything else."

She gave him a weak smile. "I have been known to do that."

"Oh, I know, trust me."

"I wouldn't mind eating something later. But not quite yet."

"Got it. You stay here; I'm going to check us in."

She sat back as Quinn headed for the office. She should probably call Emi, but she wasn't feeling on top of her game yet.

As she tried to remember everything that had happened, she started hearing words in her head. *Had she said those words out loud? Or had she just thought them?*

A wave of embarrassing heat ran through her. *Had she told Quinn she wanted to kiss him?*

But she wouldn't have done that. *Would she?*

She drew in several more breaths. There was nothing she could do now except hope her thoughts had only been in her head.

Quinn returned to the car a moment later and opened her door, offering her a hand.

"I'm okay. I can get out on my own." She felt wobbly, but she was happy that she managed to stay on her feet and not fall into his arms. "See, I'm fine," she said with determination.

"I can see how hard you're fighting to prove that you're all right," he said dryly. "You just inhaled poisonous air. It's not surprising you feel weak. I'll get the bags."

He retrieved her roller bag and his duffel out of the trunk and then they walked into the building. She felt a little seasick as the elevator lurched upward but walking down the fourth-floor hallway brought her legs back under her.

He opened the door and waved her inside. The room was comfortable and clean. There were two queen-sized beds, a TV, and a small table with two chairs. She walked over to the window and saw they had a view of the bay. The sun had set, and a quick look at her watch told her it was almost five. She didn't know where the day had gone.

"We got a view," Quinn said, as he joined her.

"Did you request it?"

"I didn't. Lucky break."

"Well, we were due for some good luck." She looked into his gaze. "Thanks for getting me out of the apartment. You saved my life and possibly the lives of everyone in that building." She paused. "Did you get any information from the other tenants?"

"I had an interesting conversation with Marc and Jana, who live across the hall. They told me that Allison changed a few months ago when her roommate moved out, and Tim moved in. They didn't care for Tim. Jana said he was creepy, and there were weird smells and noises coming from their apartment. She saw Tim come in one day with a carton of bleach. She joked that he must have a big spill to clean up, and he just glared at her and said, 'someone will have a lot to clean up.' His reply gave her chills. Marc didn't seem quite as convinced that Tim was evil, but said Tim was an intense guy and that the only conversation they'd had was about protests and disruption being the only way to stop what was happening in the world. He knew they were in an environmental group, but that was it."

"I wonder if Tim was building bombs in that apartment."

"It's possible. He was definitely doing something with the bleach. Jana also said she ran into Allison with Kevin one weekend a few weeks ago. Apparently, Tim was out of town at the time. Jana asked Allison if Kevin was her new boyfriend. She was hoping that Allison had replaced Tim. But Allison said no. Kevin wasn't her boyfriend. He was just someone who was helping her get something she needed."

"I have a feeling Kevin didn't know he was being used. What would Allison have needed from him?"

"Information on Lexitech?"

"That would make the most sense, but there haven't been any attacks at Lexitech."

"Not yet."

"Good point. Clearly, they were going to do something with the bleach, unless that's what they used in the attack on Alancor yesterday. I need to call the team and get forensics over to the apartment."

"While you do that, I'm going to get us some food."

"Thanks—for everything, Quinn."

He met her gaze, giving her a warm smile. "You're more than welcome. There's honestly nothing I wouldn't do for you, Caitlyn. You probably can't believe that, but it's true."

She was so surprised by his words that she said nothing in return. A moment later, he was gone.

She sat down on a hard chair by the table and took another breath, feeling light-headed for a different reason. But she couldn't think about Quinn now. She needed to call Emi and let them know about Allison and Tim and the potential evidence to be gathered at the apartment.

CHAPTER TWENTY-TWO

THIRTY MINUTES LATER, Caitlyn got off the phone and let out a sigh. She'd filled Emi in on everything, tying Allison and Tim to Lauren and Donovan, two generations of Bolton students, possibly two generations of terrorists. BOLOs were going out on Tim, Allison and Lauren. She mentioned that the Pederson brothers needed to be interviewed again, but Emi suggested she take that up with Rob the next day. He wanted to stay focused on the current events.

She had also told Emi that Quinn was with her at the park and at the apartment, that he'd saved her life. Whatever Emi wanted to do with that information was up to her, but she didn't believe Quinn was a person they needed to waste time on now. She also explained why she hadn't read her in earlier, that Quinn might possibly derail the investigation, and she couldn't let that happen.

Emi agreed that Quinn could be problematic, considering the focus he'd received during the first investigation, but she wasn't thrilled to have been left out of the loop as long as she had been. Caitlyn suspected it might take some work on her part to rebuild the trust, but she couldn't worry about that now.

She still hadn't mentioned Kevin's story about Spencer. That piece she would keep to herself until she had a chance to speak to her brother.

Punching Spencer's number into her phone, she gave him a call. It went to voicemail, and she left yet another message expressing extreme urgency. She didn't know why he was suddenly so unreachable. It was Saturday. Even if he was doing some work, he couldn't be that busy. *Where was he? Why wasn't he getting back to her?*

She hated the doubt building inside of her. She couldn't stand the thought of her brother being involved. Spencer was the person in her family who she was the closest to. It would be unbearable to have to accept any version of a story that involved him setting a bomb. But she needed him to call her back. Otherwise, it would be impossible to put her doubts at bay. She wanted to believe Kevin had been lying, but there had been just enough truth in his story to make her think twice.

As for Kevin, she didn't know how to feel about his death. She hadn't had time to come to terms with it. He'd once been a friend. He was close to her family. But he'd clearly had involvement with Allison, maybe Tim as well. He could have been just a mark, someone targeted to help them gain access to something, which meant the threat to Lexitech and other Carlson companies was probably very high.

Getting up, she crossed the room and then went into the bathroom and splashed cold water on her face. As she stared at her image in the mirror, she could see how pale she was. No wonder Quinn had wanted to take her to the hospital. She looked like death. But she was fine. She felt a lot better now. She dried her face with a towel, bringing the color back into her cheeks. Then she took the band out of her hair and shook it out, running her fingers through the strands.

As she walked back into the room, the door opened, and Quinn came in with two grocery bags and a pizza box.

"I'm not sure I'm that hungry," she said.

He smiled. "There's a fridge and a microwave." He set the bags down on the dresser. "I got some chocolate chip cookies, too. As I recall, chocolate chip cookies have magical healing properties for you."

She grinned. "That is still true."

"I also got a fruit bowl," he said, as he placed items in the fridge. "And a couple of green salads to balance out the pizza."

"You thought of everything."

"How do you feel?" he asked, as he closed the fridge. "Are you ready for pizza?"

"Not quite yet."

"Well, it's here whenever you want it."

"I appreciate that. I called Emi and they're sending a team to the apartment. They'll also alert law enforcement throughout the area to look for Allison, Tim, and Lauren."

"Good."

"I thought I hated Donovan the most of all, but Lauren is a close second."

He sighed, his lips turning down in an annoyed frown. "Someone else whose behavior I should have read more clearly."

"I know you don't want to believe that she knew there was a bomb, but I have serious doubts."

"You could be right. Lauren could have been Donovan's co-conspirator."

"And Wyatt, too."

He nodded. "Are they looking for him as well?"

"No, I need to talk to Rob about the Pederson brothers before we move on them. That will happen tomorrow."

"It sounds like everything that needs to be taken care of immediately is being handled. So, how are you feeling?"

"A thousand times better."

"I'm relieved. I was worried that I should have taken you to the hospital despite your protests. But I decided to let you make that decision for yourself," he added with a dry smile.

"Thank you."

"I like seeing you with your hair down."

At his words, she tucked her hair behind her ears, feeling a restlessness that she couldn't seem to tamp down. Memories were coming back into her brain and as she looked into Quinn's blue eyes, she had a feeling she'd said a few things to him that she shouldn't have. "When you were carrying me out of the apartment, did I talk to you?"

"You did. You had quite a lot to say," he said with a wicked sparkle in his eyes.

"About what?"

"How much you like…my eyes."

She was happy she hadn't referred to some other part of his body. "Well, that's true. I have always liked your eyes."

"And my chest. You had a lot to say about my chest."

She'd celebrated too soon. "Maybe we don't need to talk about it."

"Or maybe we do."

He took a step forward, and she immediately jumped back, but she ran into the wall, and Quinn was now only inches away from her.

"You said you wanted to kiss me," Quinn continued. "In fact, you begged me for one kiss."

"I'm sure I didn't beg." Although, she did remember saying something about his mouth.

"Oh, but you did." He framed her face with his hands. "You told me how much you wanted me."

"Well, I was high on fumes. You can't take what I said seriously."

"Are you still feeling high?"

"No," she said, but there were a lot of other feelings running through her now, especially as he stroked her face with his thumb and leaned in even closer. "Which is why I'm not saying anything like that."

"That's too bad. I'll talk then."

"About what?"

"How much I want you."

He dropped his gaze to her lips, and her entire body tingled.

"How much I need you," he continued, moving even closer.

Her breasts brushed against his chest, her nipples tingling through her sweater.

"I almost lost you again today," he said.

"You didn't. You saved me."

"Well, you saved me twice, so I still owe you one." His smile curved his very sexy lips. "Don't you think we should celebrate the fact that we're both alive and we're together?"

"It would complicate things."

"They're already complicated."

"I don't know…"

Disappointment ran through his gaze. "Then you do know."

He took his hands away from her face, but as he started to move away, she threw her arms around his neck. "Stop. You didn't let me finish."

"You have doubts."

"Only about how I'm going to feel later, but later doesn't matter. We don't even know if there will be a later. I'm going to stop worrying about the future." She took a breath, feeling absolutely certain of what needed to happen. "I want you, too, Quinn. I don't want it to be about the past or even tomorrow—just about now, this moment, this night."

Desire flared in his eyes. "I'm good with that."

As he lowered his mouth to hers, a sigh of pleasure escaped her lips. She really did like his mouth. And she wanted it all over her.

The sparks that had been simmering between them the last few days were suddenly blazing with heat. Their kisses were filled with hunger and desire, impatience and need. She couldn't get enough of him, and he couldn't get enough of her.

He pressed her up against the wall, and she rejoiced in the feeling of his hard body against hers. He was sweeping her away, just like he'd always done, but it was different now, because they were different.

"Gotta slow down," Quinn said, lifting his mouth to grab a breath. But almost immediately, he was kissing her neck, sliding his tongue across her heated skin, making her shiver with delight.

"I don't want to slow down. Let's go faster." She grabbed the edges of his coat and helped him off with it. Then she ran her hands under his sweater, and within seconds, that was gone, too. "I do like your chest," she said with appreciation for the muscled pecs and the fine dark- brown hair running down to the waistband of his jeans.

"Less talking. Fewer clothes," he said, impatience in his voice.

She laughed as he pulled her top up and over her head, her body tingling even more as his gaze ran across her breasts. And then his hands were on her. And she couldn't talk. She couldn't think. She could only feel.

It had been ten years, but it felt like yesterday. All the same feelings were there—the overwhelming hunger, the desperate need to get closer.

They kissed deeply and ravenously, stripping off each layer of clothing until they were bare. She ran her hands up and down his gorgeous male body while he did the same to her.

She wasn't just rediscovering his body, she was rediscovering herself, the girl she'd locked away, the girl who had loved so openly, so freely and generously, who had been willing to put her heart on the line. That girl had disappeared, but now it felt like she was coming back.

They found their way to the bed, with a quick stop to grab a condom out of Quinn's bag. She didn't question why he had packed condoms; she was just happy he had. That was one risk she couldn't take.

As she pulled Quinn down on top of her, the weight of his body was all she wanted to feel. They moved together in familiar perfection. As she looked into his beautiful darkening blue eyes, and he filled her body with his, she felt as if her broken heart was becoming whole again, as if the two parts of her life were merging back into one.

Quinn wrapped his arms around Caitlyn as they lay on their sides, facing each other. His heart was still beating out of his chest, and he doubted it would slow down any time soon.

Caitlyn brushed the hair off his forehead and gave him a satisfied smile.

"That was..." she said, searching for the right word.

"Yes?" he prodded.

"It's not easy to think of a good adjective."

"You said it was amazing a couple of minutes ago, just after you screamed my name."

"I didn't scream."

"You did, and I liked it," he told her with a smile. "I liked it all."

"We were always good together in the bedroom."

"Not always in the bedroom. In the ocean, in the library, and the elevator in the science building that somehow got stuck between floors."

She playfully punched his arm. "We promised never to speak of that."

He laughed. "I never made that promise. I was not embarrassed at all. It was one of the hottest things I've ever done."

"Me, too. You brought out an adventurous side in me back then, one I didn't know I had."

"You had it all along. You just finally let it out."

"Because I trusted you."

Her words probably weren't meant to cut, judging by the smile on her face, but they did all the same. He'd lost her trust, and he hated that.

"Don't," she said, running her fingers down his arm. "Tonight isn't about the past, remember? Or at least not the bad memories, just the good ones, like the elevator. Oh, and you forgot about the laundry room in your apartment building."

"That's right. You got very worked up over the fact that I was not separating the colors from the whites. I had to find a way to calm you down."

"I was anything but calm, and we almost got caught, remember? You were still in your boxers when that girl walked in. Not that she minded giving you a long look."

"I don't remember that, but I was only looking at you, Caitlyn. You were the most beautiful girl in the room. You were the most beautiful girl in every room."

She flushed at his words. "I'm sure not every room, but I like the exaggeration."

"I'm not exaggerating. It's the way I saw you. I was the luckiest guy in the world to be with you."

"I was lucky, too. You pushed me out of my comfort zone, Quinn. You made me try new things. You saw the world so differently than anyone in my family or in my friend group. I had been so isolated in my privileged world, but you opened it up in a huge way."

"You were good for me, too. I had buried myself in school to replace the family that I'd lost. I had my friends, of course, but when I met you, when we fell in love, it was beyond anything I'd ever felt before. You filled this deep hole in my heart that I'd thought would be empty forever."

"I wanted to fill it. I was never sure if I could ever really do that. You suffered losses I couldn't even imagine." She paused. "Well, not at that time anyway."

Shadows filled her gaze, and he could see her fighting them away. She gave him a determined smile, then moved her hand down his body. "Maybe we should leave some of this talk for later."

He caught his breath as her fingers closed around him with delicious heat. "I would have to agree. But we're going to slow down this time." He pushed her onto her back and let his gaze sweep across her beautiful curves. "I want to taste every inch of you." He ran his fingers across the slivered scars on her abdomen, the physical reminders of her deepest wound. He couldn't take away her pain, but he could give her pleasure; he could drive all the bad memories out of her head, at least for a while.

He started with a kiss on her mouth, then ran his lips down her neck, across her collarbone. He loved the light splatter of freckles on her chest. There had been a time when he'd kissed each and every one of them. Maybe he'd do that tonight, too.

But as his fingers played with her breasts, her eyes fluttered closed, and he knew what she needed. As his mouth closed around one nipple, she let out a small gasp of appreciation that made him even harder than he already was. He took his time, wanting to savor every moment that they could have together as long as he could.

It was only minutes before Caitlyn was urging him to speed up, and he couldn't deny her what she wanted—what he wanted. He'd never felt connected to anyone until he'd been with her.

As they came together once more, he felt that connection again. It was exhilarating and terrifying, because it wouldn't last. Nothing this good ever lasted.

He shoved the thought away.

He had her now, and she had him, and that was all that mattered.

It was almost ten before they got to the pizza.

"Thank goodness for the microwave," Caitlyn said, as Quinn brought her two slices of vegetarian pizza on a paper plate. She'd thrown on a T-shirt and PJ bottoms while Quinn had put on a pair of sweats, leaving his chest bare, and she was more than fine with that.

"I thought you were going to say thank goodness for me," he teased, as he sat down on the end of the bed with his own plate.

"Well, that, too. And you remembered my favorite pizza."

"Loaded with veggies, which you somehow got me to appreciate," he said with a laugh. "Before you, it was pepperoni and sausage all the time."

"At least I was a good influence in one area."

"More than one."

For the next few minutes, they ate in happy silence. It was crazy to think that this night might be one of the best nights she'd had in years. But after the last few days, she'd come to appreciate how quickly her life could cease to exist. Not that she hadn't realized that ten years ago, but it had hit her again this weekend.

She'd faced danger on the job many times, but this case was different, because it was so very personal.

"What are you thinking about?" Quinn asked.

"All the craziness that has gone down the past few days."

"I knew you were going to be trouble when you put a gun in my face."

"I knew you were going to be trouble the second I saw you at Bolton," she returned. "And you were never scared I was going to shoot you. You knew I wouldn't."

"I wasn't that sure, but I had hope."

"It feels like we've come a long way in a couple of days."

"It doesn't feel that fast when you count the ten years in between or the time we were together before that." He put his empty plate down. "When did you change your mind about me?"

"Who says I did?" she challenged.

"You did. And I want to know when and why."

She thought about that as she chewed her pizza. Swallowing, she said, "I think the first crack in my carefully built wall came when you said you wished that our baby had a name." A rush of emotion ran through her at that memory, forcing her to take a much-needed breath. "Until then, I felt like I had mourned her alone, and before you say that's because I wouldn't let you in, I already know that. But by the time I realized it, you were gone. And there was no one around me who felt what I felt. Actually, because you disappeared, I wasn't sure you did feel the way I felt. I was angry and confused and very bitter. I understand now why you did it, but I still don't know that I can forgive it—which probably seems weird after the last few hours."

Disappointment filled his gaze, but he shrugged. "I'm not asking for forgiveness. And we agreed that we wouldn't look at the past or the future. We'd just live in the moment."

"The moment has been great."

"It has."

Despite the fact that they'd just agreed on keeping the night separate from everything else, she found herself going back. "I have to say, Quinn, I never really knew how you felt about me being pregnant. You said all the right things, but the emotion behind the words was never quite real."

"Then I didn't express myself very well, because the emotions were there, and they were very real."

She wanted to believe him. "You were so distracted that last day at the coffee cart. Was it just the worry over a possible protest, knowing you weren't going to go with me to the cere-mony, or was it also about the baby?"

"You still don't know how you want to feel about me, do you?"

"What do you mean?" she asked warily.

"You hate me, you love me, you'd like to forget me… You change your mind every few minutes. You want me, but you don't want to want me. And that's a quote."

"What do you mean, that's a quote?"

"You said that to me when I brought you out of the building."

"Well, I was high."

"You were also being truthful. It's okay. I understand the conflict."

"Because you feel the same way?" she challenged.

"Yes, but not for the same reason."

"What would be your reason?"

He stared back at her. "It doesn't matter. We said we weren't going to talk about the past."

"But we are talking about it, so answer the question."

"I've loved four people in my life in a way that I haven't loved anyone else. My dad, my mom, Donovan, and you. Three out of four of those people are dead and the fourth one can never forgive me for what I did to hurt her. I don't want to want you, Caitlyn, because I fear there's nowhere for us to go. That the wound I left you with will never heal. But I'm glad we have tonight. I don't expect tomorrow. I don't expect anything."

She felt a rush of compassion for Quinn. He had lost so much in his life. She wanted to give him what he wanted—what she might want, too. But she wasn't ready. The words wouldn't come.

He had hurt her deeply, in a way only someone she'd loved as much as she'd loved him could do. *How could she risk her heart on him again?*

A buzzing sound made her start. She'd forgotten the outside world even existed. Quinn grabbed her phone off the dresser and tossed it to her.

She was surprised to see the number and quickly took the

call. "Spencer, I've been trying to reach you all day. Where have you been?"

"I just heard about Kevin," Spencer said, his voice slurred and thick with emotion.

Or was there more to it than that?

"Are you drunk?"

"Trying to get there. I can't believe someone would shoot Kevin in the middle of Golden Gate Park. And you were there? Dad said you were with him when it happened."

"I was. Kevin asked me to meet him there. When did you talk to Dad?"

"A little while ago. Do they know who did it? Who killed him?"

"No."

"What did Kevin want? What did he say to you?"

She debated how to answer that question. She couldn't believe Spencer was guilty of what Kevin had suggested. He was her brother. She knew him. But she wasn't just his sister; she was also an FBI agent, and the stakes were very high. She glanced across the bed at Quinn.

At her questioning gaze, he shrugged, and said softly, "Trust yourself."

She decided to trust herself and to trust Quinn. She put the phone on speaker.

"Kevin wanted to talk about you," she said.

"What about me? Why would he want to talk to you about me?" Spencer asked, concern in his voice. "What's going on, Caitlyn?"

"Kevin suggested that you had something to do with the bomb at Bolton ten years ago, that you didn't show up for the opening ceremony because you knew what was going to happen."

"That's insane," Spencer said loudly, amazement in his voice. "You think I let you walk into a bomb?"

"I'm telling you what Kevin said."

"I broke my tooth. I went to the dentist. You can probably call him and verify that."

"Dr. Richardson?"

"No. It was a different person. I couldn't get in to see Dr. Richardson, so a friend of mine gave me her dentist, Doctor... Damn, I can't remember the name. Wait, it was Dr. Stanyon. Yeah, I think that was it. Or Standish. I only went the one time. Her office was in Noe Valley. I can find the number, I'm sure."

He was giving her a lot of details, but she didn't like the fact that he hadn't gone to his regular dentist, that he couldn't remember the name, that his explanation wasn't as straightforward as she wanted it to be.

"I can't believe this is happening," Spencer continued. "Why would Kevin suggest such a thing?"

"He wanted me to get the FBI to drop the case. He said the trail would lead to you, that you've been plotting against Carlson Industries for years. That you hate Dad, and you want to take down everything he has built."

"That's ridiculous. You don't believe him, do you? *God!* Does anyone else know what Kevin said?"

"Not yet. I want to protect you, Spencer, but I need to figure out what Kevin was involved in. You have to try to help me."

"What can I do?"

"Did Kevin ever say anything to you about Allison or her group? Did he mention that Allison had a boyfriend named Tim?"

"What? She was dating Kevin and some other guy?"

"Not just any guy—Donovan's younger brother. I think they're involved in these new attacks, Spencer. But they're missing, and we can't find them."

"That's...unbelievable. I don't know anything about Allison or this other guy."

"I think Allison might have been using Kevin to get access to something. Has anything unusual happened at Lexitech that stands out to you?"

"There was a security breach about a week ago. It didn't appear that the thieves were able to retrieve any of our proprietary information, but the techs are still trying to figure out what happened."

"That's interesting," she said, thinking that played into her theory that Kevin had been a pawn. "What did Kevin have to say about it?"

"He was afraid it would look badly on him, that Dad would hold it against him, because he oversaw the security division. I think he would have tried to blame that on me, too, but everyone knows I know nothing about that area."

"Did Kevin do anything else you found odd?"

"I haven't really been paying that much attention to him. I told you we've been fighting for months."

"Well, you need to ramp up security at Lexitech. In fact, I'd think seriously about closing down for a few days until we can figure out what's going on."

"We already doubled the security after what happened at Bolton and then at Alancor. I don't think we can get much more secure. Dad doesn't want to shut down anything. He won't cower to terrorists."

She frowned as Spencer echoed what their father had said to her earlier in the day. "I know. He won't shut down the gala, either."

"Well, I'm not going. Neither is Baxter. He doesn't want to take any chances with Lana being pregnant."

"Good. What about Mom?"

"I told her she shouldn't go, but she said she can't let Dad down. She has to be by his side. You know she doesn't like change. They go to the gala every year. It's their tradition. And she trusts Dad to keep her safe."

"I hate that they're not taking this seriously enough."

"Well, the hotel will probably be a fortress tomorrow night. Caitlyn, I hope you don't have any doubts about me. What can I say to make you realize I would never hurt you?"

"You don't have to say anything. I believe you."

"Thank God. I really did break my tooth. I wish it had been me and not you in that explosion."

"Even if you'd come, I would have been there, too."

"I should have made sure neither one of us was there. Despite Quinn's assertion that the LNF would leave the opening alone, I had doubts. I wasn't sure I could trust Quinn. He was in deep with that group, and it's not like he hid his feelings about the environmental record of Carlson Industries when he was having dinner with us."

She saw Quinn flinch at the end of the bed. Suddenly, he was on his feet, walking to the window, his back stiff as a poker, as he looked out at the dark night.

"Quinn didn't know about it," she said.

"I know you want to believe that."

"I do believe it."

"Because you loved him."

"Yes. And I love you, Spencer, which is why I'm willing to believe in you, why I'm putting my career on the line for you."

"I appreciate that."

"Where are you now?"

"San Luis Obispo."

"What?" she asked in surprise. "Why?" San Luis Obispo was three hours south of San Francisco.

"I was feeling restless and hyped up this morning. I just got in my car and started driving. I made it to LA, spent a few hours on the beach, then started back, but I got tired, and I pulled over at a hotel. I had my phone off all day. When I turned it on, I saw all your messages as well as those from everyone else in the family. I had no idea what was going on."

She frowned, her trust in him wavering a little with this latest piece of information. On the face of it, it seemed understandable. But it was also strange that he'd been out of the city and out of touch when Kevin had been gunned down. *Was she making a mistake?* She really hoped not.

"You need to come back first thing in the morning," she told him. "Call me when you get to the city. We can meet and continue our conversation. I'd like to know more about the breach at Lexitech. Maybe my cyber techs can work with yours to trace it."

"Whatever we can do. I didn't think it was tied to Bolton, because it happened a week before that. And it's not like we haven't been hit before."

"Well, it's something to check. We'll talk tomorrow."

She ended the call. When Quinn didn't return to the bed, she got up and walked over to him, sliding her arms around his waist and resting her head on the back of his shoulders. She didn't say anything, and he didn't, either.

Finally, he turned around, his hands coming to rest on her waist as he gazed into her eyes. "Thanks for defending me."

"I told the truth." She paused. "Do you think my brother was being honest? Or am I being blinded by love and family loyalty?"

Indecision played through his eyes. "I've always been suspicious of stories with too many details."

"Me, too. But Spencer is a talker. He never uses one sentence when he can use five."

He smiled. "True. For what it's worth, I think he was being honest. I don't believe he was involved in any of these events. The play was to get you to doubt him, to spend time looking in a different direction."

"I agree. I hope we can find Allison, Tim, and Lauren soon. Maybe we should try to talk to Vinnie tomorrow. He was married to Lauren. He had to know her sister. He might be helpful."

"I'm game. I just hope tomorrow isn't too late. I feel like every minute counts."

"I know, but there's nothing more to do tonight," she said. "You're awfully amped up for someone who should be feeling a little more relaxed. I might have to do something about that."

"Oh, yeah? What would you do?"

"Let me show you." She took his hand and led him to the bed. "Lay down."

He did as she asked, and before she stretched out next to him, she grabbed the remote and turned on the TV.

"Hold on, we're watching TV?" he asked in disappointed surprise.

"You need to calm down, and I know the trick." She flipped through the channels, landing on a baking show. "Perfect. Here we go." She looked over at Quinn. "They're making scones."

He gave her a smile. "You do know the trick."

"Whenever you'd get stressed out studying, which was a lot of the time, because you were one of those annoying people who just had to get an A, we'd turn on the Food Network."

"Because it reminded me of my mom. When she had cancer, she couldn't concentrate on anything, but for some reason watching people make food made her happy. And spending that time with her made me happy."

"I was touched when you shared that memory with me, and even more when we started watching the cooking shows together. Whenever I've felt stressed the last ten years, I find myself looking for one of these shows."

"And yet it doesn't sound like you do a lot of cooking."

She laughed. "I like to watch, not necessarily cook."

"Do you think about me when you're watching the shows?" he asked.

"Far too much." She curled up next to him, resting her head on his shoulder, her hand on his chest. "Look at those blueberries. They are plump and juicy."

He laughed. "Okay, no dirty talk or the TV is going off."

She lifted her head and gave him a mischievous smile. "You don't want me to talk about how she's kneading the crust with her hands, rolling and twisting?"

"Definitely not twisting," he said with a grin. "But I like kneading. And rubbing. And anything else. Ah," he said, as her hand slid down his chest. "I thought we were going to relax."

"I changed my mind. Do you have a problem with that?"

"Not even a little bit."

CHAPTER TWENTY-THREE

SUNDAY MORNING CAME TOO FAST. Quinn woke up to the sun streaming through the window and the sound of a hair dryer. Sadly, the other side of the bed was empty. He shouldn't be surprised that Caitlyn was up. She'd always been an early riser. No doubt she was already thinking about what they needed to do today. Their momentary respite was over, but what a night it had been. He smiled to himself, thinking that he hadn't felt this happy in...well, ten years. There had been other women in his life, but no one like Caitlyn. No one who knew him as well as she did.

But the night was over, and neither one of them had made a promise for more. Although he wanted more, much more. But it had to be Caitlyn's choice. He'd made the decision to leave her. It had to be her decision if she wanted them to stay together, to have more than one night.

The dryer went off and she walked out of the room, dressed in black denim and a cream-colored sweater, her thick, reddish-brown hair falling over her shoulders, her cheeks rosy from her shower. There was a happy sparkle in her eyes, and he wanted to think he was at least partially responsible for that.

"Good morning," she said, as she came over to the bed and gave him a long, hot kiss.

He pulled her down on the mattress. "You took your shower too soon." He kissed her again. "You should have waited for me."

She gave him a regretful smile. "We need to get to work."

"Is there news?"

"No. I was just texting with Emi. Allison and Tim are in the wind, as is Lauren. There was evidence that Lauren left her house in a hurry sometime yesterday or the day before. One of the neighbors said he saw her putting a suitcase in her car Friday afternoon."

"I wonder where she went."

"And if she's with her sister and with Tim."

"It still feels surreal to think she's involved in all this. She's another person I underestimated." He cleared his throat. "What's the game plan?"

"The gala is tonight, hosted by my parents at the Vanguard Hotel. The silent auction and cocktail hour begin at six, dinner at seven. I think we should try to get a room at the Vanguard for tonight. I'm not sure if they're sold out, but if they're not, I'd like to be on site for the event. That way I can help with security. The gala would be the perfect opportunity for a terrorist group to make a big statement. The fact that everyone seems to be clearing out of their homes leads me to believe that there will be a significant attack somewhere very soon."

"Unless the gala is a decoy. It's an obvious target, and it will put a lot of security in one place, leaving other places more vulnerable. What about the Carlson Tower?"

"It will not be left unattended. It's impossible for us to cover every scenario, but those two will be fortified with security. However, with the variety of crimes that have been committed in the past several days the team is stretched thin, which I'm sure is part of the plan. Why don't you shower?" she suggested. "I'll call the Vanguard and see if I can get us a room. Then we'll get breakfast before we head into the city. I could use more than those muffins you got from the store."

"Deal." As he got out of bed, he couldn't help but notice the wistful look in her eyes as her gaze ran down his naked form. "You could take another shower," he teased. "I would make it worth your while."

"Tempting, but I need to get my head back in the game."

"Next time."

"Who said there's going to be a next time?"

"There will be," he said, wishing he felt as confident as his words.

———

Two hours later, after breakfast at a bayfront restaurant in Sausalito, Quinn slid into the passenger seat once more as Caitlyn got behind the wheel. It was half past eleven when they crossed over the Golden Gate Bridge, and with each passing mile, his mood changed from happy and relaxed to tense and uneasy. He had no idea what the day would bring, but their brief respite from the madness was over.

Caitlyn's phone started blowing up with texts, and after a quick look, she said, "I need to go into the office. I'll drop you at the hotel. You can check in, and then I'll meet you back there."

"I don't want to just sit around a hotel room," he grumbled, wishing he had his own vehicle, but it was still at Wyatt's house. "Why don't you drop me off at my car? I can call for roadside service, get the tire fixed, or get it towed to a shop."

"That will take too long. I'd rather you just went to the hotel." She gave him a pleading smile. "I promise I won't be long. When I'm done, we can talk to Vinnie together. He has a condo in North Beach. It's in the same building as Rocco's. Remember that place?"

"I do. We went there with Vinnie when we were at Bolton. It was his birthday."

"They had black ink squid linguine and I had never tried that before. I thought it was going to be disgusting, but it was delicious."

"Has anyone from your team approached Vinnie yet? He is Lauren's ex-husband."

"Not yet. Everything is happening fast." She paused. "There is something you could do for me if you're bored while you're waiting for me."

"Why do I get the feeling I am not going to like this suggestion?"

"It's just a small favor."

"What?" he asked warily.

"You could pick us up some clothes to wear to the gala tonight. You need a suit, and I need a cocktail dress. The Vanguard is near some boutiques and clothing stores."

"You want me to go shopping? Seriously?"

She laughed. "I know it sounds so mundane after all the life-and-death situations we've been in, but I do need something to wear. Otherwise, I'll have to go when I'm done at the office."

"How am I going to buy you a dress? I don't know what you would like."

She gave him a saucy look. "Then buy me something you would like to see me in."

That put a lot of thoughts into his head. "You might regret giving me that much power."

"I might, but I'm going to risk it."

While Quinn wasn't thrilled to go shopping, it was better than just waiting around. After checking into the Vanguard, he walked down the street, picking up a suit at a men's shop a block away.

Finding Caitlyn something to wear was also surprisingly easy. He hit gold at the first boutique he stopped at, finding two dresses that he thought would work. He decided to get both of them. One was a bold red, off-the-shoulder minidress that fit the image he had of Caitlyn now: confident, attractive, sure of herself, and not unwilling to stand out in a crowd. The other was black with sheer lace at the neckline. It would also look good on her, but it was definitely more conservative. Maybe she'd want that, since she was going to be working the gala, not just enjoying it. He'd let her decide.

After paying for his purchases, he returned to the hotel. Within a half hour, he was once again bored. It was almost two, and Caitlyn had been gone for a couple of hours, with only two brief texts saying she was still stuck in the office, and there was no significant news, just a lot of work that she needed to help out on.

He appreciated her focus on the case at hand, but he wanted to be in on the action, not sidelined. He thought about what he could do on his own. Caitlyn had wanted to talk to Vinnie. Maybe he should do that on his own. North Beach was less than a mile from the hotel.

Making a quick decision, he left the room, texting Caitlyn on the way: *I'm going to see Vinnie. Will fill you in on anything I learn.*

She didn't answer, which was fine. He didn't want her to talk him out of it. He and Vinnie had once been friends, maybe not as close as he'd been with some of the other guys, but they had a history, and hopefully, he could use that to his advantage.

When he got to Vinnie's building, he hit the button for Unit 3B. A moment later, a familiar voice came over the speaker.

"Yes?" Vinnie asked.

"It's Quinn. We need to talk."

After a slight hesitation, the buzzer went off. He opened the door and jogged up the stairs to the third floor. Vinnie was waiting at the door, his arms folded defensively in front of his chest, his dark eyes wary.

"I can't say I'm surprised to see you," Vinnie said. "I heard you were making the rounds."

"I probably should have started with you. Where's Lauren?"

Surprise flashed in Vinnie's eyes. "I have no idea. We divorced more than a year ago. I don't keep tabs on her. Is that why you came over here? To ask me where Lauren is?"

"It was one reason. She cleared out of her house on Friday. Her sister Allison has also disappeared from her apartment."

"You're making it sound like they're up to something."

"Oh, they're definitely up to something. Let me in, Vinnie."

Vinnie stepped aside, waving him into the apartment.

His first impression was one of clutter and chaos. There was a basketball game blaring on the television, and a pizza box on the coffee table next to a couple of beers. He faced Vinnie, not bothering to take a seat. He doubted he'd be here long enough to sit.

"What's going on?" Vinnie asked. "Wyatt said you and Caitlyn think the bombing at Bolton last week is tied to the LNF."

"It's tied to Allison and Lauren," he corrected. "And to Tim Coulson, who is Donovan's half-brother. He's been dating Allison. Did you know that?"

"I do. I ran into them two weeks ago at Union Square. I was shocked when I saw Tim. I thought I was looking at Donovan. It was like seeing a ghost. I didn't even know that Donovan had a brother. Allison said she met Tim at Bolton. It surprised me that they were together, because I'd heard from Wyatt that Kevin was dating Allison, which seemed kind of weird. But it was none of my business."

"Did you talk to Lauren about her sister being involved with Donovan's brother?"

"No. I try to talk to Lauren as little as possible. We didn't have a great marriage, and we had a worse divorce. I had no idea who she really was until it was too late."

"What does that mean?"

Vinnie's lips tightened. "She was crazy, Quinn. She had huge mood swings, and she'd get stuck on people, whether she liked them or hated them. She couldn't let go of hatred or love. It was strange."

"What would she do?" he asked curiously.

"Well, here's one instance. About a year and a half ago, right as we were divorcing, Lauren put together a photo album from college photographs. It was photos of herself with either you or Donovan. He'd been dead for ten years, and you'd been missing for longer than that. I didn't understand the sudden fascination with the two of you. And the photos were put together, like you were cut out of a picture and put next to a picture of her in it."

A tingle of uneasiness ran down his spine. "That sounds bizarre."

"It was very creepy." Vinnie shook his head in bewilderment. "She said you two were the only men who had ever really under-stood her. She had some fantasy going on in her head about both of you. Like you were the real loves of her life. I didn't get it. I knew she was trying to get back at me for cheating on her, but why she suddenly got stuck on you two didn't make sense to me."

"There was nothing between us."

"I didn't think there was anything between her and Donovan, either."

"You might be wrong about that. I recently learned that Donovan asked Lauren to change the time of our study group so that I would not be at the environmental center when it blew up. Did she ever tell you that?"

Vinnie looked shocked. "No, never. I can't believe she wouldn't have told me that. Are you sure it's true?"

"I believe it is. Wyatt was the one who asked Lauren to do

that, by the way. Are you going to tell me you didn't know that, either? That he never said anything."

"He didn't say anything. I've never heard this before." His lips tightened. "You're making it up. I don't know what your game is, but I don't want any part of it."

"It's not a game, Vinnie. Either you're lying or your friend and your ex-wife kept some big secrets from you. But let's get back to the present, because time is of the essence. Here's what I know. Allison and Tim are responsible for the latest bomb at Bolton. They're terrorists, Vinnie. The FBI thinks Lauren is helping them. You're going to become a suspect as well, because of your relationship to Lauren and Allison."

Vinnie ran a hand through his hair, giving him a tense, confused look. "It's like you're talking another language, Quinn. I don't know anything about bombs or terrorists. I can't believe Lauren or Allison would be involved. I know I said Lauren was crazy, but not like that. She's not violent."

"Maybe Tim radicalized them. He might be taking up where Donovan left off. This is not going to end well, Vinnie. If you want to give Lauren or Allison a fighting chance, you need to get them to turn themselves in. Maybe if they flip on Tim from the beginning, they can make a deal. They can save their lives and save a lot of other innocent lives."

"I can call Lauren, but I doubt she'll pick up. She hates me now. According to her, I ruined her life."

"Is she close to anyone else in the group?"

"No, not anymore. They were my friends and not hers, and since we split up, she pretty much hates them, too."

"Do you have any idea where Lauren might go if she was trying to hide in the city? You need to help me find her, Vinnie. It's imperative that we locate her as soon as possible."

"Help you?" Vinnie echoed. "What do you have to do with this, Quinn? Unless? Shit! You're not FBI, like Caitlyn, are you? Is that why you disappeared?"

"I'm not in the FBI, but I am helping Caitlyn. Where would Lauren go if she needed to hide somewhere?"

"She'd probably leave the city."

"I don't think so. The plan isn't done. There's something big coming, and it's going to be in San Francisco. Where's Lauren's mom?"

"She moved to Carmel a couple of years ago. She got remarried. Lauren and Allison don't like the guy, so they don't see much of her. They wouldn't go to their mom's house. But... Lauren's mother owns a building in China Basin. It's an arts co-op. After her mother moved, Lauren took over as property manager. They rent space to indie artists, and there is an office there."

Quinn's heart jumped. "Address?"

"2407 Howard."

"Thanks."

"You'll let Caitlyn know where you got the information? You'll tell her I'm not involved?"

"I'll let Caitlyn know. If you hear from Lauren, call me." He grabbed a pen off a nearby table and jotted down his number on the back of an envelope.

Vinnie walked him to the door. "I hope you're wrong, Quinn. Lauren was my wife, and while I don't love her anymore, I hate to think she has sunk this low."

"I'm not wrong, Vinnie. I'd watch your back. You might suddenly find yourself in a position of knowing too much." He left the apartment and jogged down the stairs. When he got to the street, he pulled out his phone and texted Caitlyn that he had a lead. She answered with a phone call.

"I was just about to text you," she said. "Did Vinnie give you something?"

"Yes. Lauren's mother owns an arts co-op in China Basin. Lauren has been managing it since her mother moved. She might be hiding out there. The address is 2407 Howard. Can you pick me up?"

"That's a great lead. But I'm sorry, Quinn. I need to go there with the team. I can't bring you along."

He groaned with frustration. "I thought I was your team."

"This is bigger than us. If all three of them are there...I need to do this the right way.

He knew she was probably right, but he didn't like it.

"I really appreciate the information," she added. "I'll let you know what we find as soon as I can. Okay?"

"All right. Be careful."

"I will be. Thanks. This could be huge."

He felt better knowing he might have done something useful. But he wanted to do more.

As he walked back to the hotel, his gaze drifted to the tall building that was a centerpiece of the San Francisco skyline, the Carlson Tower. It had been built in the seventies by Caitlyn's grandfather, and at one time it had been the tallest building in the city. It was still impressive, even though it had been dwarfed by other structures built in the last decade.

He couldn't help thinking how different the skyline would look if the tower wasn't there. It would be a spectacular target, but so would the gala. However, with those two locations so heavily guarded, was there a third location they weren't thinking about?

San Francisco was a target-rich environment. The terrorists could choose any number of locations. Hopefully, Caitlyn would find a clue, or the terrorists themselves, at the warehouse.

Caitlyn rode to the co-op with Emi, with three other agents in a car behind them. She knew Quinn was pissed at her for leaving him out of this trip, but she'd made the right decision. Hopefully, they'd find Lauren, Allison, and Tim at the warehouse, and this could all be over.

"Where did this lead come from again?" Emi asked, as she stopped at a light.

"Lauren's ex-husband, Vinnie Caputo. Quinn got the address from him."

"Quinn, huh? He seems to be everywhere."

"He's helping me."

"He's quite possibly putting your career in jeopardy," Emi said, giving her a pointed look. "You haven't been particularly forthcoming about his involvement."

"I know. I will explain everything once we get to the end of this."

"I hope you're not risking everything for this guy."

"I just want to keep this investigation focused on the right targets. Last time around, Quinn became the centerpiece for no good reason except that my father wanted him to be. There was a ridiculous amount of time spent looking into his past as a child in Northern Ireland, as if being eleven and losing his father to violence had turned him into an expert on explosives. There was absolutely no evidence to warrant that kind of intense interest."

"I agree. I was looking through the file last night," Emi said. "Agent Bauer was obsessed with Quinn. He gets more space in that file than anyone else. I also confirmed what you told me about the Pederson brothers. Their alibi goes markedly unchecked."

"Even though Justin Pederson said that he had contacted Agent Bauer to correct the file."

"That definitely was not in there."

"I called Bauer this morning."

"Really? I thought Rob wanted you to leave him alone."

"I felt it was important to reach out knowing what I know now. He didn't answer. I also did a little more digging into Bauer's life over the last week. It turns out he's not in Europe at all. I saw a photo on his social media that led me to believe he's in Germany. But I contacted the hotel, and he's not registered. In looking back through Bauer's photos, I discovered the exact same picture from five years ago. I think he went on the run as soon as that bomb went off at Bolton last Thursday. He knows his investigation won't hold up now that more people than me are looking into it."

Emi shook her head in bemusement. "That's crazy. It's not even a good cover-up—reusing an old social media post? He should have done better than that."

"I suspect he had to move quickly. Rob told me on Friday when I pressed him about bringing in Bauer that he had contacted him already, and that Bauer had told him he was on vacation. But that doesn't mean he was. I know he's a low priority right now, but when this is over, we need to find him."

"I would love to do that. I hate dirty agents more than anything in the world." Emi gave her a questioning look. "Have you ever confronted your father about his influence over the investigation?"

"Yes. He's unapologetic, which is true to form."

"Powerful men often don't see boundaries."

"That's true. But Agent Bauer shouldn't have succumbed to outside pressure, whether it came from my father or from Senator Pederson."

"Which brings us back to the Pederson brothers."

"We need to talk to them, too."

"Well, it will have to wait until tomorrow. It's all-hands-on-deck for the gala tonight."

"I know. I just hope we can keep everyone safe."

"Me, too." Emi paused. "I understand your motivation for keeping Quinn in the background. But others may not. You need to come clean sooner rather than later, at least with Rob."

"I'm not sure I can trust Rob. Look at how he told me to back off Bauer and Senator Pederson."

"He's still in charge. And you're taking a big risk to leave him in the dark."

"If we find the terrorists, the risk will be worth it."

"I hope you're right." Emi pulled up in front of a warehouse that had a very colorful mural on the outside. "This is it."

As they got out of the car, she took a look in either direction, noting mostly industrial and retail businesses on the block, many of which were closed for the weekend.

They met up with the second team, and then with guns drawn, they entered the building. Two agents cleared the first floor, which included three terrified artists who had no idea what was going on. One of the agents escorted them outside while the rest of the team made their way to the second floor. She and Emi were the first to enter a large office, but there was no one inside.

They moved into an adjacent room, and Caitlyn's heart came to a crashing halt.

Inside the room were two large tables covered with what appeared to be bomb-making materials: nails, pressure cookers, stacks of batteries, blowtorches. There were large bottles of liquids that she couldn't identify. In addition to the tables, there was a blow-up bed that looked recently slept in and a blanket thrown over a couch. There were also dozens of coffee cups and fast-food bags. Everything was a chaotic mess.

"They were here," she said, meeting Emi's gaze.

"But where are they now?"

"I wish I knew. Maybe there's a clue in this mess."

"Let's get to work."

CHAPTER TWENTY-FOUR

QUINN PACED AROUND the hotel room, making his thousandth lap of the hour. It had been two hours since he'd given Caitlyn the address of the co-op, and he'd only gotten one short text an hour ago: *No one here but lots of evidence. Will check in as soon as I can.*

He hadn't heard from her since, and he was dying to know what kind of evidence she'd found. To kill time, he'd showered and put on his suit. He'd also ordered food, which should be arriving any minute. It was past four and the gala was supposed to start at six. He didn't even know if they were still going to the gala, but he wanted to be ready if they were.

Finally, the lock clicked, and the door opened.

Caitlyn walked in, looking tired but not particularly triumphant. Whatever she'd found hadn't been a resolution.

He pulled her into his arms, wanting a kiss before anything else, which made him realize it wasn't information he'd been needing—it was her. They kissed for several minutes until she finally pulled away, giving him a happier look than she'd worn when she came in the door.

"You look handsome," she said. "Nice suit."

"Thanks. You look exhausted. What's going on? I've been going crazy here."

"I'm sorry I didn't get back to you before now. There was a lot to do. We went through the co-op, and then I just did a sweep of the ballroom and reviewed security plans for tonight."

"What did you find at the co-op?" he asked, more interested in that than the gala.

"Evidence of poisons and bomb-making materials. It looked like at least one or more of them had slept there the night before."

"Any leads on possible targets?"

"There were blueprints for this hotel and security information for the Carlson Tower. There was a list of twelve other companies that seemed like potential targets. Across the top was written: *The Dirty Dozen*."

"You did get a lot of information."

"I'm just not sure it wasn't a setup. It almost seemed purposeful in the way they'd been left out. They could have been trying to steer us in the wrong direction or just pointing us to targets that are already obvious." She paused, tucking her hair behind her ear. "There was also a really weird photo album."

His stomach twisted. "Vinnie mentioned a photo album that Lauren put together right as they were divorcing. He said she seemed to have a sick fascination with me and Donovan."

"That's what it looked like. There were photos where she literally cut herself out of a picture and then pasted herself into one that included you or Donovan. It was all very odd and unsettling. She was definitely thinking about the two of you and her relationship to both of you."

"She and I had no relationship."

"Do you think she was sleeping with Donovan?"

"No. I don't believe that. I don't think he liked her that much."

"Maybe that was it. She couldn't stand that neither of you ever wanted her."

"We need to find her and get our questions answered."

"That would be nice, but I have no idea where she is or where any of them are." Caitlyn paused. "I did some digging into Tim Coulson while I was in the office. Tim's mother, the one he shared with Donovan, died three years ago, and his father passed away three months ago. Tim inherited assets of about eight million dollars."

He let out a whistle. "I had no idea the Coulsons were that rich. I also didn't know Donovan's mother had passed away."

"She died of leukemia. She was in and out of the hospital for a couple of years. Steve Coulson died in an automobile accident. He ran his car off Highway 1 just south of Big Sur. Apparently, he was on his way to a golf tournament at Pebble Beach. The investigators speculated that he'd fallen asleep at the wheel as the accident occurred late at night. There were no witnesses."

"There never are," he said cynically, wondering if the crash had really been an accident. "Interesting that Tim inherited everything."

"He made some huge withdrawals over the past month, adding up to hundreds of thousands of dollars."

"Terrorism is expensive."

"The kind he's doing certainly is. It would explain why he was able to hire a sniper to kill Kevin."

"That adds up. When did Tim get to Bolton?"

"Three months ago. He wasn't enrolled, but he did have an apartment off campus before he moved in with Allison. We also found a storage unit in his name in LA, rented after the father died and the family home was sold. That will be gone through in great detail, but it will take time. It appears that Tim went to Bolton for the purpose of launching his terrorist attacks. Clearly, that has some connection to Donovan, but how did he get Donovan's grand plan? How did he even know about it? He was twelve when Donovan died."

"I'm sure Donovan talked about the LNF. Tim could have easily found more information as he got older. There was a lot of news coverage about the bombing. When he got rich enough, he decided to follow in his brother's footsteps."

"That makes sense." She gave him an apologetic look. "I know you were angry at me for not taking you to the co-op."

He shrugged. "I wasn't thrilled, but I'm over it. I know you have to do your job."

"I'm glad you understand."

"But don't try to leave me out of the gala," he warned. "Because I'm not staying in this room while you go downstairs."

"It would be safer if you didn't go."

"Caitlyn—"

"Fine." She put up a hand. "I won't waste my breath."

"Good. Because if two hundred other people can be there, so can I."

"You do know my parents will be there, too."

"I'm actually looking forward to that. The look on your dad's face could be priceless," he said dryly.

She gave him a warning look. "I really don't need you to get into anything with him tonight."

"I won't start anything, but I can't say I won't finish what he starts." He paused as a knock came at the door.

Caitlyn immediately pulled out her weapon.

"It's room service," he reassured her.

"Are you sure?"

"I ordered some pre-gala snacks." He checked the door to make sure there was a room service waiter in the hall, noting that Caitlyn still had her gun at the ready.

"Thanks," he said, as the man asked him if he could set it up. "I'll take it from here." He signed the sheet and handed the waiter a ten-dollar bill. Then he wheeled the cart into the room.

Caitlyn put away her gun and looked at the cart in delight. "This looks good." She picked up the bottle of champagne. "Really? Champagne?"

"Hoping we have something to celebrate later."

"That would be nice. Did you get me a dress? Or do I need to run out to a store?"

"I got you two dresses. They're in the closet."

She walked over to the closet, pulling out the dresses. "Red and black?"

"Your choice. I wasn't sure which one you'd like. I figured we could return the other one tomorrow."

"They're both beautiful. I should go with the black." She gave him a reckless smile. "But I do love red. Which one do you like?"

"You already know."

She gave him a knowing smile. "I do. Let's eat and then I'll change."

"What do you think?" Caitlyn asked an hour later as she stepped out of the bathroom in the clingy, short red dress that showed off her legs and hugged her curves.

Quinn's breath caught in his chest. She really was the most beautiful woman he'd ever been with. And it wasn't just her pretty features—it was everything about her, including the sparkle in her eyes, and the smiling confidence on her lips.

"You look spectacular," he said.

"It's the dress."

"It's you."

"You sound like a man who wants to sleep with me."

"What I have in mind doesn't involve sleeping."

She flushed. "Save that thought for later. We need to get downstairs."

"I'm ready. But first—one for the road." He pulled her in for a kiss that was meant to be brief, but one taste of her mouth had him hungering for more. He slid his tongue between her lips, needing to take it deeper, needing to tighten the connection between them.

When they broke apart, she gave him a breathless smile. "You have always been a really good kisser."

"It was never just me; it was always us together—that's where the magic comes from."

And it was magic. He was completely caught up in her spell, but he was painfully aware that the spell might not last that much longer. There would come a time when they didn't need to stay together, when this was all over, when she would go back to her life, and he would go back to his.

He couldn't imagine that life anymore. A future without her seemed too bleak to consider. *Was there really any other possible outcome?* They'd been torn apart by a bomb and brought back together by a bomb. *Would the truth, would the closure they both desperately wanted, bring an end to everything else between them?*

"Quinn?" She gave him a questioning look. "Something wrong?"

"No. Let's go."

She picked up her gun and put it in her clutch. They took the elevator down to the lobby and went through a security line for VIP guests and private law enforcement. Then they rode the escalator to the second-floor ballroom and grand hall. There were a dozen people in line at two bars set up in the hall. The silent auction was going on in a room next to the ballroom. There were a lot of pretty people in pretty clothes, and he felt very much out of place. This definitely was not his scene, not his world, but it was Caitlyn's, a reminder of their very different backgrounds.

He'd almost forgotten about the wealth and social circle she'd grown up in. When they were together, none of that had mattered. Caitlyn had not lived a big life at Bolton. She hadn't wanted to stand out. She'd wanted to live like everyone else, even if it had meant living at the Seaview Apartments with kids who'd grown up with much less than she'd had. Not that most of the students at Bolton were poor. A lot of them had come from money. He had been the one on scholarship, the one who worked extra jobs to pay the rent. And while he considered his success a freaking miracle considering where he'd come from, her parents had not been impressed with him at all.

"There they are," Caitlyn said, interrupting his thoughts. "Are you ready to face my parents?"

He followed her gaze to the very sophisticated man and woman holding court with a small circle of friends. He couldn't help the small sigh that escaped his lips. Seeing them again brought back a lot of bad memories.

Caitlyn gave him a questioning look. "I can speak to them alone."

"No." He straightened his shoulders and lifted his chin. "I'm going to enjoy seeing your father's reaction to my presence."

"I'm not sure that will be so enjoyable for me," she said dryly. "But I can give you that."

He wished she could give him a lot more than that.

As they walked over to the group, he impulsively took Caitlyn's hand in his. She stiffened for a moment, but she didn't pull away. Whether that meant as much as he wanted it to, he didn't really know, but he'd take what he could get.

Chuck Carlson's gaze changed from happy and welcoming to angry and alarmed in less than a second, especially when his gaze took in their joined hands.

Rebecca Carlson, Caitlyn's mother, appeared shocked and speechless.

The others in the group seemed to sense the tension and made muttered replies as they left them alone.

"What are you doing with him?" Chuck Carlson demanded. "Are you out of your mind?"

"Quinn is helping me with the case," Caitlyn replied evenly.

"You told me the other night you hadn't seen Quinn," Rebecca said, finally finding her voice.

"That changed, Mom."

"His name wasn't on the list. I would have noticed his name," Chuck said. "I thought you were worried about this gala putting hundreds of people in danger, Caitlyn. The last person you should be with is the man who set the bomb that almost killed you."

"I'm worried about this event but not about Quinn," she said firmly. "He had nothing to do with that bomb, and you shouldn't have any doubt about that, because you did everything you could to get the FBI to find him guilty. But they couldn't, because he was innocent. So, you need to let go of this theory you've been holding onto for so long."

It was the first time he had heard Caitlyn speak with conviction about his innocence. Her father appeared taken aback as well, and her mother looked like she wished she was anywhere else.

Caitlyn gave him a tense smile. "Would you mind getting me a drink, Quinn? I'm thirsty."

He didn't think she was thirsty; he thought she wanted to talk to her parents alone. He was fine with that. He'd made his presence known. He didn't need to spend more time with the Carlsons. In fact, shocking them hadn't been all that satisfying, because he didn't really want to come between Caitlyn and her parents. He had never wanted that. They would never believe that, but it was the truth. He'd always known how much Caitlyn loved her parents, and having lost his own parents, the last thing he would have ever wanted to do was break up her family.

"What would you like?" he asked.

"Just mineral water for me," she said, "I'm working."

"I'll be back." As he let go of her hand, he fought off a feeling of foreboding. But Caitlyn was fine. She was with her parents, and she could take care of herself.

But as he got in line for the bar, he kept his eyes on them. The three of them were now having an intense conversation. Chuck was doing most of the talking, as usual. He was probably warning Caitlyn about him once more.

A woman came up to Rebecca and pulled her away, leaving Chuck and Caitlyn to continue their conversation alone. Then one of the security agents wearing a dark-gray suit approached them.

He stiffened, hoping there wasn't a problem. No one else appeared concerned. There were two security guards standing by the top of the escalator who were completely calm.

The man spoke quietly to Chuck, and then a moment later, Caitlyn and her dad followed the agent down a side hallway.

He frowned, thinking he should get out of line and see what was going on.

Before he could move, his attention was drawn to a woman who seemed very inebriated. She was stumbling toward a nearby restroom, clutching her stomach. She didn't make it to the restroom door, heaving her guts into a potted plant.

Alarmed chatter broke out. One of the security guards went over to assist her.

And then a man suddenly started vomiting all over the cocktail table he was standing at.

More people ran toward the bathrooms. Drinks were being dropped, glasses shattering on tabletops.

What the hell was going on?

He looked toward the bar, but the bartender had disappeared. People were muttering in confusion. As a nearby woman lifted her mixed drink to her lips, he knocked it out of her hand. "Don't drink that. Don't anyone drink anything," he yelled.

Security guards and FBI agents came running up the escalators, but he couldn't wait for them. Something bad was happening, and it wasn't just in the drinks. Caitlyn had not come back. Neither had her father.

He jogged down the hall where he'd last seen them go. It led into the kitchen. He dodged past servers and cooks, seeing an open door. When he ran through it, he saw a van speeding away. The security guard who had been talking to Caitlyn and her dad was lying facedown on the ground, blood pooling under his head.

His heart stopped when he saw Caitlyn's purse a few feet away.

The truth almost knocked him off his feet.

Someone had taken Caitlyn and her father!

Agents ran up behind him. They asked him to identify himself. They forced him to his knees, hands in the air. He yelled at them that Caitlyn and her father had been kidnapped. But no one was listening. Then a female FBI agent came over. "Quinn Kelly?" she asked.

"Yes. Someone took Caitlyn and her dad. A gray van. That's all I saw."

"Get up." She waved the other security personnel away. "I'm Agent Emi Sakato."

"You're Caitlyn's friend. Help me find her." He ran his hand through his hair, feeling terrified and desperate.

Why had he left her alone with her dad?

Why had he let go of her hand?

What if he never saw her again?

"I will find her," Agent Sakato promised. "Tell me exactly what you saw."

CHAPTER TWENTY-FIVE

CAITLYN WOKE up to a searing pain in her head and a deep ache in her back and her hips. She was cold, and it was very, very dark. She blinked, trying to figure out where she was and what had happened.

She'd been talking to her dad.

One of the guys on his security team had told them there was a problem.

They'd followed him through the kitchen.

When they walked onto the loading dock, she'd felt a force behind her and then everything had gone black.

How long ago was that?

She heard someone moan. She tried to move, but her hands were in metal cuffs and locked around a pipe above her head. She squinted, trying to see where she was. As her vision cleared, she could see shapes in the darkness. It felt like they were in a storage room.

Another moan came, louder this time.

"Dad?"

"Cait…"

His voice sounded weak. Fear ran through her. "I'm here, Dad. Are you all right?"

"I—I don't know."

"Can you move?"

"No. My hands are tied behind my back. My feet are tied too. I can't get up."

"Does anything hurt?"

"My head. Someone hit me."

"Me, too. They got us when we walked onto the loading dock."

"But Kent took us out there. He's been with me for ten years." Outrage rang through his voice. "He betrayed me."

"Maybe he didn't know," she suggested, but deep in her heart she knew she was wrong. Someone had gotten to Kent. Someone had forced him to change his loyalty. *But what now? What did they want?* They weren't dead yet. *What was coming?*

Whatever it was, it was going to be big and bold. The gala had been a decoy. The real target had been her father. He'd been too arrogant, too confident in his ability to protect himself. He'd thought he had unquestionable loyalty from the people surrounding him, but that had been a false assumption.

"I'm sorry, Caitlyn," he said, regret in his voice. "I didn't think they could touch me. I bet Quinn is involved."

"No, he's not. Aren't you ever going to tire of trying to turn him into the villain you think he is? You did everything you could to get the FBI to arrest him, but there was never any evidence. What will it take for you to believe that he's innocent?"

"A lot more than your word. You were blinded by love then, and apparently now, too. I can't believe you care anything about him after the way he left you."

"You forced him to leave."

"I gave him incentive. If he'd been a better man, he would have stayed and fought for you."

She wasn't going to let him get to her. She knew now

exactly why Quinn had left and it wasn't just because her father had ordered him to do so; it was because he'd wanted to disappear and then go after Donovan. "I don't want to discuss Quinn," she said. "As I told you at the hotel, I believe the perpetrators to be two younger terrorists, siblings of people who were in the LNF. One of them dated Kevin, probably to get access to information. Spencer told me there was a security breach last week."

"You think that was tied to Kevin?"

"Yes. There's a very good chance Kevin was used and killed because he knew too much." She didn't bother to share Kevin's crazy story about Spencer with her dad. It wasn't true, and she didn't want to give more life to it.

"What do you think they want—money?"

"Maybe." But she was terrified they wanted more than that. "We need to figure out how to get out of here. Do you have any idea where we are?"

"It's hard to see, but it feels familiar. There's a scent."

"Lavender," she said. "Oh, my God! I know where we are. We're in the basement of your house."

"How can that be? It's the first place they'd look."

"No, Dad. It would be the last."

Quinn paced around a conference room in the Vanguard Hotel, where he'd spent sixty agonizingly slow minutes reiterating what he'd seen to Agent Sakato and several others. One senior agent seemed more interested in calling into question his relationship to the previous case than in hearing what he had to say about Caitlyn's kidnapping. But that agent was called away, and Agent Sakato took that opportunity to cut him loose.

She gave him her phone number, suggesting that it was possible he might hear from someone from his past, someone who could help them. He doubted anyone would call him now, but he promised to let her know if that happened.

When he finally walked back to the hall outside the ball-room, he encountered a vastly different scene than the one he'd left. All of the guests who had fallen ill had been taken to the hospital. There were about a dozen people still milling around, as well as a couple of security guards at the top of the escalators. Two of those people he recognized: Rebecca Carlson and Cait-lyn's brother, Spencer Carlson. Spencer was not in a suit. He had not been planning to attend the gala, but clearly, his mother had called him to come over. They were sitting on a bench outside the ballroom, an older couple hovering nearby, concern etched across their faces.

When Spencer saw him, he jumped to his feet and strode toward him, worry tightening his pale face. Spencer was one of those golden boys, good-looking and rich, who had been born with everything but still seemed to have trouble making some-thing out of their lives. At least, that had been his impression ten years ago. He didn't know how true it was now, but it didn't matter. Caitlyn loved and believed in her brother. He was going to trust her instincts.

"Quinn. My mom said you were back. What's going on? Do you know what's happened to Caitlyn and my dad?"

"I know they were taken away by someone in a van at the loading dock. One of your father's security guards apparently lured them out there. He's now dead."

Spencer blanched. "Oh, my God! Who was it?"

"I heard one of the agents say his name was Kent. I don't have any more details."

"Kent Wisemore has been with my dad for ten years." Spencer shook his head in bewilderment. "Why would he betray him?"

"I'm sure he had incentive. The FBI is trying to figure that out. But I'm more concerned about where Caitlyn and your father are. Do you have any idea where they might be taken?"

"How the hell would I know?" Spencer rocked back on his heels, digging his hands into the pockets of his jeans. "I'm not involved in any of this, Quinn, even though everyone keeps trying to pin the bombs on me, which is completely unbelievable. How did I get to be a target?" Spencer asked in bewilderment.

He wondered about that, too. *Why had Spencer become a target? Why had it been so important for Tim and Allison to make Caitlyn think her own brother had been responsible for the bombs?* He suddenly knew the answer. "You're being set up."

Spencer's eyes widened. "What do you mean?"

"You're going to be framed for whatever is about to happen." It all made sense now.

"How is that possible?" Spencer asked.

"Caitlyn said your company had a security breach. If Kevin was behind that, could he have accessed information about you? Could he have gained insight into proprietary information beyond Lexitech, like the other companies under the Carlson umbrella? Could he have learned about the security plans for this event or for the tower?"

"That's possible," Spencer said. "Do you think there's something else coming, Quinn? My mom is waiting for a ransom request. Is that the big play?"

His blood started to race. He shook his head. "I don't believe they're holding your father and sister for ransom." There was only one answer that made sense. "There's going to be another explosion."

"Where?"

"Maybe the Carlson Tower. The gala could have been the decoy."

"The tower has a ton of security, levels upon levels. And everything was increased several days ago. It's impenetrable."

"Even for someone with access to your security system information?"

"Damn!"

"And if Kevin planted information to make it look like you have had problems with your father or with the company or both, you could be the prime suspect for anything that happens tonight. We know they were already trying to make it look like you were responsible for the first explosion ten years ago, that you did it to get back at your father. This could be more of the same."

"It's so twisted and unbelievable. The FBI would see right through that, wouldn't they?"

"Maybe not right away, which would give the terrorists more opportunities. You need to tell the FBI what we just talked about and suggest they get over to the tower immediately. They'll be more likely to follow your direction than mine."

"All right. What are you going to do?"

"I'm heading there now. There's not a minute to waste."

"You have to save her," Spencer said, giving him a hard, desperate look. "This time you have to save her, Quinn. She can't live through that again. It almost destroyed her the first time."

"I know." He ran for the elevator. He needed a vehicle and Caitlyn had left the keys to her car in their room.

When he entered the room and saw Caitlyn's clothes on the bed, the stakes became even higher. Smelling the scent of her perfume in the air just about killed him. He could not let her die. He also could not let fear take over. He had to find her. He had to stop what was going to happen before it happened.

He grabbed the car keys from the dresser and headed back out, taking the elevator to the parking garage. He used the keys to find the car, and then he hopped inside and sped out of the garage. It had been over ninety minutes since Caitlyn and her father had disappeared. That was a long time. He hoped he wasn't too late.

As he headed toward the Carlson Tower, which loomed fifty stories high in the San Francisco skyline, he couldn't help thinking again that it was the perfect target, especially if Chuck Carlson was now inside, and Caitlyn was a bonus.

Had she even been part of the plan? Or had she just gone along with her dad to see what was going on?

The light turned green, and he pressed down hard on the gas, but there was doubt tugging at the back of his brain.

Was he on the right track?

The Carlson Tower would make for a glorious explosion. It would cause maximum damage.

But it wasn't as personal as it could be.

There were other companies in the tower; not all of them belonged to Carlson Industries. Not that he believed the terrorists cared about collateral damage. But as he thought about Donovan, about the grand plan Tim was now carrying out, he didn't believe the tower would have been on the plan.

Donovan had wanted to cut off the head of the snake. In this case, that had to be Chuck Carlson, which made the tower a good target if Chuck was there.

But then the image of the beheaded snake in his head brought forth the quote in Donovan's notebook: *Corporate greed lives like a viper in its nest. You must kill it before it kills you.*

His heart jumped. They weren't going to be at the tower. That wasn't the nest.

They were going to be at the last place anyone would expect —the Carlson home.

Who would kidnap someone and just take them home?

Maybe a very evil genius.

CHAPTER TWENTY-SIX

CAITLYN'S WRISTS were burning from the relentless scrape of the metal cuffs against her skin as she tried to get free. The only potential benefit to the fact that her hands were elevated above her head was that the blood was draining from her fingers. *Was it possible with a few twists she might be able to release her hands?* She tried to stay positive, but it was getting more difficult with each passing minute.

Her father was also struggling, grunting as he rolled back and forth, trying to loosen his ties. But he was having no more luck than she was. A few minutes ago, she'd heard footsteps upstairs, the muffled sound of voices implying at least two people.

What were they waiting for? Was someone else supposed to show up?

Whoever had grabbed them probably wasn't the boss. That would be Tim, she'd bet. *But who else was helping him? Allison? Lauren? Wyatt? Hank?* The names rolled around in her head. It disgusted her to think they might all be involved. She felt another wave of fury at herself. She shouldn't have let this happen. She'd been distracted talking to her dad. Now, they were in a terrible situation.

"It's no use," her father said, despair in his voice.

"Don't give up. We have to keep fighting. Is your phone in your pocket?"

"I can't feel it. Why?"

"I was thinking the FBI could track your phone, but the kidnappers probably tossed it as soon as they grabbed us. If you could get closer to me, maybe we could get each other free." While her hands were cuffed with metal, her ankles were zip-tied, and there could be something in the basement they could use to cut through the tie.

"I can't do it, Caitlyn."

Her dad rolled over onto his side, a good six feet from her. She could see him better now that she'd gotten used to the darkness.

"You're close," he added. "But you might as well be in the next state. I'm sorry, honey."

"It's okay. We'll figure something else out." She tugged once more at the pipe holding her captive, and to her amazement, she heard it crack. "Wait, I think something might have just broken." She pulled down hard and felt the pipe yield ever so slightly. It hadn't come loose from the wall, but there was progress. She just had to keep at it.

But then the door to the basement opened. A light went on. She blinked at the sudden brightness and stilled as two people walked down the stairs. The man who appeared first stole the breath out of her chest. Dressed in jeans and a black jacket, he looked exactly like Donovan, with his blond hair and green eyes. Tim Coulson was about the same age now that Donovan had been when she'd known him. It felt surreal to see the resemblance. But Tim's gaze differed from Donovan's. It was cold, ruthless, and evil.

"The infamous Caitlyn," he drawled. "Do you know who I am?"

"Tim Coulson. You look like your brother."

"Only I'm very much alive."

"Probably not for long," she snapped, lifting her chin in defiance despite her vulnerable position.

"I'm not worried. I have you and your father exactly where I want you. You played into my game so perfectly. In fact, you made it even easier than I thought it would be."

As he spoke, she turned her attention to the young woman hovering by the steps. Allison Sullivan was a thin brunette dressed in jeans and a gray hoodie. She didn't look exactly like Lauren, but she shared similar features. She also seemed a bit less certain of what was about to happen. Maybe the truth of what was about to occur had come too late for her.

"What do you want from us?" she asked, moving her gaze back to Tim.

"Want from you?" he echoed with a laugh. "You're not in a position to give me anything—either of you." He gazed at her father. "You look like such a small man now. How does it feel?"

Her father didn't reply.

"Answer me, old man," Tim said, taking a few steps toward her father, close enough to kick him in the gut.

Her dad moaned at the action, but he still didn't talk, and she could see Tim getting more riled up. He lifted the gun in his hand, pointing at her dad's head.

"What is this about?" she asked, wanting to distract him. "What do you want the world to know?"

Tim's gaze moved to her. "Don't you know?"

"I know what Donovan wanted. He wanted to protect the environment."

"He wanted more than that. I have his words. I know his dreams, and I've been waiting for the right time to finish what my brother started. The world will soon realize that we will not be ignored. We will not continue to let capitalists destroy our planet. We will take the power back. We will kill the greedy viper in his nest."

His words reminded her of the quote in Donovan's notebook. "Didn't Donovan write that?" she challenged. "Don't you have any thoughts of your own?"

Tim's lips tightened, and she almost regretted the taunt.

"I have far more plans than Donovan ever had," he retorted. "My brother didn't think big enough. He was afraid to go too far. But when you are fighting for a righteous cause, you must go all the way. You must hold the guilty accountable." Tim looked back at her father once more. "You had many opportunities to do better, but you were unwilling to change. Even when your daughter almost died, you continued to pollute our world."

"I've made a tremendous number of changes—"

"Shut up," Tim said, waving his gun in the air. "I have no interest in what you have to say."

"That's because you're a coward, a punk with a gun."

Her heart jolted as her dad's words incited more anger. "Dad," she pleaded. "Don't say anything else."

"Are you worried about him?" Tim asked her. "You should be. The things he has done are horrific. You've always known that, Caitlyn. You've always looked the other way."

"What's the grand plan? Where's the rest of your group?" she challenged, wanting to keep Tim talking so there was time for someone to find them. But ever since she'd realized where they were, she'd thought it was doubtful anyone would come to their rescue. The FBI would never assume that they'd be taken home by the kidnappers. She just hoped her mom hadn't come back to the house after the gala. Hopefully, the agents were keeping her safe at the hotel.

"You and your father are going to understand what it's like to suffer," Tim continued, fervor growing in his gaze. "You will know you're going to die, just like all the people who have died from the air you've polluted, the water you've poisoned."

"That's what you did this week. You poisoned the air and the water," she said. "You made innocent people sick. You're not a good person, Tim. You're a terrorist."

"I fight fire with fire."

"Who's helping you? Where's everyone else?"

"I find people to use when I need them. And then they're gone. Keeping the circle of trust small is important. Donovan didn't understand that. He built an army that was more interested in parties than in revolution."

Since he seemed interested in telling her how he was better than Donovan, she egged him on. "Why now?" she challenged. "Why did you decide to do all this now?"

"Because I had the means."

"Your father's money."

He seemed surprised that she knew about that.

"Here you are, acting like this rebel when you're a rich kid, just like me," she said. "Your father worked for a gas company. The money you're using is dirty money."

"I'm making it clean."

"You used that money to hire someone to kill Kevin. Murder isn't clean."

"Kevin was going to betray us. Traitors need to be dealt with, something else Donovan didn't understand. If he had, he would have killed Quinn."

"Tim," Allison spoke for the first time. "We need to go."

"When I'm ready," he snapped. "I've been waiting for this moment for a long time." He turned back to her. "I don't care that you're a rich kid, Caitlyn. I care that you're the reason Donovan is dead."

"How am I responsible for your brother's suicide?"

"It wasn't suicide. Quinn killed him. He killed Donovan for you. And my only regret is that your boyfriend isn't here with you. But I'll get to him. No one can stop me. I'm unbeatable. I will save the planet the way Donovan wanted. I will turn his legacy into something incredible. I will make us both gods."

The crazy was becoming more obvious. "Donovan didn't want to kill people."

"He wanted to kill you. He tried to blow you up."

"Donovan didn't want to kill me," she said. "He only wanted to destroy the building. He sent a message to Lauren to get me and Quinn out of the building, but she only got Quinn out. That wasn't what Donovan wanted. When Donovan realized he'd almost killed his best friend's girlfriend, he couldn't live with himself. Lauren is the real reason Donovan is dead."

"That's not true," Allison cut in. "Lauren told me that Donovan only wanted her to save Quinn."

"She lied to you. I have proof. I saw the message he sent her." She delivered the lies as forcefully as she could, wanting to divide them, wanting Lauren to become the wedge.

"You're the one who is lying," Allison said heatedly.

"You know I'm not." She turned back to Tim. "Lauren killed Donovan. She killed your brother, and she's making a fool of you now. Is she the one who gave you Donovan's so-called plan? Did you ever consider that it's actually her plan? That Donovan had nothing to do with it at all?"

"Shut up!" Tim shouted. "You're making this shit up. You know nothing."

"I know more than you. Quinn told me everything about Yosemite. Donovan confessed to setting the bomb. He said Lauren and Wyatt were in on it," she added, wanting to make it sound believable. "Donovan said he got lost, he listened to the wrong people. You're not following your brother's plan, Tim; you're following the plan of his so-called friends."

"Quinn is a liar, too," Tim said. "And I have very special plans for him. He will pay for what he did."

Her heart sank, but she took solace in the fact that Quinn wasn't here now.

"I should thank you, Caitlyn. I didn't know where Quinn was

until he showed up with you. But now he can be a part of this," Tim added.

"Tim," Allison said. "Come here."

He sighed and walked over to her.

Caitlyn looked at her dad and tried to send him an encouraging smile but judging by the grim expression on his face he wasn't buying into her hope. But they weren't dead yet. Tim wanted to stretch this out. That could only work in their favor.

It was quiet at the Carlson home. *Too quiet*, Quinn thought, as he crept through the trees bordering the property. There were no cars in the driveway, only one light on in the house. The iron gates were locked, which might mean that his instincts were wrong, that no one was here, that the action would be at the Carlson Tower.

But he couldn't shake Donovan's words out of his head: *Greed is found in the viper's nest.*

Chuck Carlson was the viper, and this was his home.

He saw no sign of guards, although the security system on the front gate and the tall fences surrounding the property provided a strong barrier. He knew Rebecca and Spencer were at the hotel. Baxter and his wife lived elsewhere. There might be a housekeeper inside, but it felt like the house was empty.

He walked through the side yard, coming to another gate that had a code box on it, but the gate was slightly open. His pulse leapt. There was a light on at the back of the house he hadn't seen before. There was also a person near the patio door, hovering in the shadows, perhaps looking at their phone as he caught flashes of light. In one of those flashes, he realized the person was Lauren.

He'd been right. They were here. *But where was everyone*

else? Were they inside? Had they not shown up yet? Was Lauren waiting for someone else to arrive?

He didn't know how long she'd be alone. This might be his only chance to find out what was going on. He slid into the yard, staying in the shadows of the trees, walking as quietly as he could. When he was only a few feet away, he rushed toward her, throwing her body against the wall of the house, covering her mouth with his hand as her head bounced off the stucco, her eyes bulging open when she saw him.

"Don't make a sound," he warned. He moved his hand slightly away from her mouth. "Where's Caitlyn?"

"Go away," she said breathlessly. "They'll kill you."

He put his hands on her neck, pressing his fingers against her windpipe. "Or I'll kill you."

She struggled, but she was no match for his fury or his will.

"I saved your life, Quinn. You owe me," she gasped.

"Who's inside?"

"Tim and Allison. Donovan's brother has more courage than Donovan ever had. He has a much bigger vision. When he asked Allison to introduce us, I knew he was the one I needed to give Donovan's plan to."

"You ripped the pages out of the notebook." Another piece of the puzzle clicked into place. "How did you get them?"

"I went to Yosemite with Wyatt. Donovan was blackmailing us to protect himself."

"Wyatt said he found nothing there."

"That's what I told him when I left the cabin. I decided to keep the information for myself. Wyatt was outside when I found the notebook. He was watching for Donovan."

As much as he wanted to hear that story, he needed to get to Caitlyn. "Tell me what's happening now."

"Tim is leading the fight of our lifetime."

"He's killing people, Lauren, and your sister is helping him. You're all going to end up in prison or dead."

"We're smarter than that. When I met Tim, I saw the same drive in him that I'd seen in Donovan, and I knew what I had to do. This time, I would take action. I would not be left in the shadows, out of the loop, useful only to provide someone else cover. I would be part of the bigger plan."

"Where's Caitlyn now?" he demanded, cutting off her insane ramble.

"It doesn't matter. You have to leave. They're going to blow the house up. Once again, I'm saving your life."

"Donovan told you to save both Caitlyn and me, didn't he?"

She gave him a cold stare. "Yes. But I hated her, so I didn't do it."

Her words filled him with rage. He wanted to squeeze the life out of her. He wanted to punish her, but he needed to get to Caitlyn. In a quick move, he knocked Lauren's head against the wall, and she went out like a light, sliding to the ground. He dragged her around the corner of the house and then entered the home through the back door. He could hear voices in the distance.

Using the light on his phone, he made his way through the kitchen, trying to remember the layout of the house. It seemed like the voices were coming from beneath him. They had to be in the basement. He moved toward a door off the hallway, where the voices got louder.

His pulse jumped when he heard Caitlyn's voice. She sounded strong but terrified.

"Where's Lauren?" Caitlyn asked.

"What does it matter?" a man replied.

Quinn crept down the hall. The man sounded like Donovan, which probably meant it was Tim.

"If I'm going to die," Caitlyn said, "I have a few things I'd like to say to Lauren first."

He was impressed at the determination in her voice. She was not giving up without a fight. He pulled out his phone and quickly texted Agent Emi Sakato that Caitlyn was being held at her family home.

"I know Lauren is involved in this," Caitlyn continued. "Is she too cowardly to show her face? I am shocked you'd work with someone like that, Tim."

"Lauren is dedicated to our cause."

"Lauren is the one who pointed the finger at Donovan. She's the one who told the FBI to go after him. It's in the file. I read all about it."

"She's lying," a woman said. "Lauren wouldn't betray Donovan."

Quinn took a quick breath at the new voice. Allison was clearly still alive. He had at least two people to deal with. He hadn't heard Chuck's voice, but he had to be there, too. Unless he was unconscious or worse...

"Of course Lauren would do that," Caitlyn said forcefully. "Lauren always looked out for herself. She even told me about you, Allison, about how you'd joined forces with Tim and were responsible for the bombing. She was trying to protect herself in case you were caught. She didn't want it to look like she was involved."

"I don't believe you. Lauren wouldn't sell me out," Allison retorted. "You're a liar."

"And here I was just thinking the two of you might actually be smart," Caitlyn continued. "There's probably a reason Lauren isn't here. She is going to sell you out, the way she sold out Donovan."

"Go get Lauren," Tim said sharply.

"No," Allison replied. "My sister is looking out for us. You can't believe her, Tim."

"I said, go get her," Tim repeated.

"Tim, let's just get out of here," Allison pleaded. "We don't need to prove anything to this bitch. And we have to get to the tower to meet the others. Don't get distracted from the plan."

"Don't tell me what to do. I said go get Lauren. I want to see these two face each other."

Quinn heard Allison coming up the stairs, so he moved toward the back door, grabbing a heavy vase from a kitchen counter. As Allison came around the corner, he smashed her head with the vase.

She fell with a heavy thud, no time to let out a scream. Now it was time to get Caitlyn.

Caitlyn's mind whirred with possibilities. Once Lauren came into the room, she could buy more minutes with a conversation. *What about after that?*

"Why were you trying to frame my brother?" she asked abruptly.

"Easy. I needed someone to take the fall for everything. Spencer was perfect. It's actually going to look like he was here, like he had you and your father kidnapped because your dad wouldn't give him the job he wanted. Kevin provided us with your brother's angry emails and texts. He also told us how Spencer tried to warn you away from the first bomb. At the end of the day, he'll look like the mad bomber who hated his family and everything Carlson Industries did to hurt the environment."

"It won't work," her father cut in.

"Shut up, old man. You know nothing," Tim said.

"What about Wyatt?" she asked. "Is he in on this, too? Are any of the other LNF members helping you?"

"No. This is my show. They were of no use to Donovan. Why would they be of use to me now?"

"Lauren is with you."

"She's different. She understands the vision that my brother had. And she offered me his plan in exchange for her participation. It was a fair trade. Now, I'm tired of talking. While we're waiting for Lauren to join us, because I wouldn't mind seeing you two bitches go after each other, I'll give you a little preview of what's to come."

He walked over to the bottom of the steps, drawing her attention to the large duffel bag on the floor. It didn't look like something her family would have had in the basement. As he unzipped the bag and pulled the sides away, he flipped a switch and a clock panel lit up.

It started at fifteen minutes, and it immediately began to count down. She couldn't see the explosive device that it was attached to, but it became very clear how little time they had. She looked over at her dad.

He gave her a despairing look. "I'm sorry, Caitlyn. This is my fault."

"You're right. It is your fault," Tim said, moving away from the bomb. "And you've got fifteen minutes to think about all the harm you've done, to realize that you will die with your daughter. Trust me when I say that the rest of your family will also suffer. So will your employees and your companies. Your profits will tumble, because once the head of the snake is cut off, it cannot survive."

"Let Caitlyn go," her father begged. "She has never had anything to do with the business. She is not responsible for my crimes."

"Touching," Tim said with a laugh. "Do you think I care?" As he finished speaking, he glanced toward the stairs with a growing frown of concern.

"Maybe Allison finally came to her senses and left you," she suggested.

"Shut up!" he growled, waving his gun at her. "Or I'll shoot you now."

"That would deprive you of watching me sweat."

He looked toward the stairs once more.

Something was wrong...or maybe it was right. Maybe the

FBI had figured it out. They'd grabbed Allison. She needed to keep Tim in the room.

She kicked at a nearby tower of boxes. As they came tumbling down, Tim swore and took a wild shot at her. The bullet hit the wall next to her.

Her father screamed.

She kicked at another box. Bottles of wine rolled out.

Tim jumped out of the way to avoid them.

Then someone came flying down the stairs in a blur of motion.

Quinn!

When Tim turned, he got hit in the face with a golf club. The gun dropped out of his hand as Quinn hit him again.

But Tim recovered, fighting back fast and furiously.

She yanked at the pipe once more. Harder and harder, desperate to get free so she could help Quinn.

With every ounce of strength that she had, she screamed as she pulled on the pipe. To her shock, it broke apart, and while she was still cuffed, she was no longer attached to anything.

The men were still fighting for their lives, completely unaware she was free. She crawled over to the gun and managed to pick it up.

She wasn't sure she could shoot with her hands bound, but then Quinn was shoved into the wall so hard he was stunned. Tim looked around for his gun, fury in his gaze when he saw it in her hands. He rushed toward her, and she pulled the trigger.

The bullet hit Tim in the neck. His eyes popped open in shock. Then he crumpled.

Quinn ran over to her, putting his hands on her shoulders, as his wild gaze searched her face. "Are you all right?"

"I'm fine. But there's a bomb." She tipped her head toward the device. It had ticked down to seven minutes. "Allison and Lauren are somewhere."

"I took care of them. Is there anyone else around?" he asked.

"Not that I've seen."

"Let's get out of here."

"My dad can't move."

Quinn's gaze turned to her father. "I'll get him. But I'll take you out first."

As he got her up on her feet, she said, "There isn't time. Please get my dad. I can make it up the stairs myself." She jumped forward to prove she could do it, then looked back at him. "Quinn, please," she begged.

Indecision played through his gaze. Then he ran over to her dad.

She jumped forward and again until she reached the bottom step.

"Get Caitlyn out first," her father told Quinn.

"I'm going to get you both out," he replied tersely.

Her father had some weight on him, but that didn't seem to bother Quinn. He got her father up on his knees. Then her dad leaned into him and Quinn was able to somehow lift her dad up and over his shoulder. He held him awkwardly as he moved toward the stairs, half-carrying him, half-dragging him.

Her gaze moved to the timer. *Five minutes.*

They still had to get up the stairs and out of the house. She slid toward the wall, allowing Quinn to move ahead of her. He gave her a grim look but kept on going. He moved up the steps far more quickly than she could. She stumbled while hopping onto the third step, and crashed into the wall, her heart racing with fear.

Four minutes.

She hopped up to the next step, then the next. She'd told him she could do it, and she had to be right.

Three minutes.

Three more steps to go. She jumped up another step, then crashed to her knees. She wanted to scream with frustration. She couldn't see the clock anymore.

How much time did she have left?

Quinn reappeared as she struggled to get to the top step.

"Where's my dad?" she asked.

"Outside." He swung her up into his arms and raced toward the front door.

As they left the house and hit the steps, an enormous deafening blast lifted them up in the air.

Not again...

CHAPTER TWENTY-SEVEN

IT FELT like the last time.

Caitlyn tried to hang on to Quinn, but the explosion ripped them apart. She landed hard in the middle of her mother's flowerbed as fiery pieces of wood and plaster rained down on her. Something hit her head, then her side. She winced against the pain but struggled to stay conscious. She would not die. Not like this.

Her ears screamed with pain. She could hear rumbles and bangs, but it felt like she was underwater. As the sound receded, she blinked several times, coming fully awake. The house behind her was raging with fire. One of the tall trees in the yard had broken in two, a huge branch on the ground nearby. There was so much smoke and ash in the air she couldn't see her father. She couldn't see Quinn.

"Quinn? Dad?" she screamed. "Where are you?"

Her gaze lit on a pile of rubble. She could see Quinn's shoes, and her heart crashed against her chest. She crawled over to him, her hands and feet still bound.

She managed to pull some bigger pieces of stucco off of Quinn. When she saw his face, white with ash except for the blood on his forehead, she almost lost it. *He could not be dead. He couldn't be!*

She knelt next to him. "Quinn, Quinn. Open your eyes. Please, God, open your eyes." He didn't respond. He was so still. She put her head on his chest. She thought she could hear his heartbeat. *Was that just desperation?*

She moved closer to him, putting her mouth by his ear. "I need you, Quinn. Don't leave me. Please don't leave me. I love you. I should have told you that before. Wake up. You have to live."

She almost cried when she saw his lids begin to flutter, and then his eyes—his beautiful blue eyes—were staring back at her.

"Caitlyn, are you hurt?"

She bit down on the sob that came to her lips at his generous question. "I'm fine." She kissed his mouth, needing to know that he was really okay. The heat of his lips reassured her. "What about you?"

"I'm okay. I think." He shifted and then winced as he raised his left hand. "Actually, my hand might be broken."

"Don't move. You might make it worse. I've got to find my dad." She paused, realizing she wasn't going anywhere fast. "Damn these ties."

Quinn sat up. "I put your dad on the driveway. I tried to get him far enough away. I'll go find him."

"Wait. Help me get the tie off my ankles." She tipped her head toward a shard of glass. "If you can put the edge right in the pin of the tie, it should open."

Quinn grabbed the glass with his good hand and worked the sharp edge against the tie. With enough pressure, it opened, and the tie fell apart. She jumped to her feet in relief. She'd worry about the cuffs on her hands later.

They ran toward the driveway, having to dodge flaming piles of rubble along the way.

"Dad? Dad?" she screamed, wishing the smoke wasn't so thick or so black.

"Over here," her father called out.

She blew out a breath of relief as she followed the sound of his voice. He was sitting up, staring at the house in shock.

"I didn't know if you were still in there," he said. "I thought I saw you and Quinn right before it blew up, but I wasn't sure."

"I'm okay." She knelt down beside him. "Quinn got me out in time."

Her father looked past her to Quinn. "Thank you."

Quinn nodded. "You're welcome."

"Are you sure you're not hurt, Dad?" she asked worriedly, scanning his face for any sign of injury, but he seemed to be all right.

"I'm fine," he said. "How did you find us, Quinn?"

"Donovan used to say that greed is found in the viper's nest. Everyone else was heading to the tower, but I played a hunch. When I arrived, the house was so quiet and dark, I thought I was wrong, but then I went through the side yard and the gate was ajar."

"Tim quoted that saying tonight," she told him. "It was kind of brilliant—kidnapping us and taking us home. I think I know how they got into the house, too. They used Kevin to access the security systems, the proprietary information for not only the tower but also this house, and probably how they got to my dad's personal security. One of his guards lured us to the loading dock."

"I know. That man is dead. He was killed the second they got you."

"Good," her dad said coldly. "Kent betrayed me."

"Did you see who grabbed you?" Quinn asked.

"I didn't see a thing," she replied. "Someone hit me over the back of my head." She paused. "Allison said something about people waiting for them at the tower. I need to call Emi. Do you have a phone?"

"I do," he said, patting his pockets. "I don't know where it went. But the FBI already went to the tower, and I texted Agent Sakato when I got into the house that you were here. I'm sure she's on her way."

"How did you have her number?" she asked curiously.

"We talked at the hotel after you and your father were taken. I actually saw the van leave the loading dock. I followed you down that back hall when I realized you had disappeared right as people were getting sick at the gala."

"Getting sick?" she echoed in confusion.

"The ice was poisoned."

"Oh, my God," she said, shocked by that piece of news.

"Did anyone die?" her father bit out.

"I don't know," Quinn said. "I hope not."

She shook her head. "This gets worse and worse."

"It's close to over now."

The distant sounds of sirens reassured her. But as she looked back at the house, another thought occurred to her. "You said you took care of Allison and Lauren? Were they inside the house?"

"Lauren was in the backyard. I knocked her out when I arrived. I hit Allison over the head when she went to get Lauren for you. She was by the back door. I don't know if they're alive."

"We need to find out." Before she could move, strobe lights lit up the area. Firefighters, police and FBI agents descended on the scene. She ran down the driveway and pushed the button to open the gates, then moved back to her dad and Quinn.

"You are a sight to see," Emi said, running across the yard to give her a hug. "When I saw the flames, I had a bad feeling."

"I'm okay. Quinn saved us."

Rob was right behind Emi, relief flooding his gaze when he realized both she and her father were safe. She doubted he wanted to lose such a prominent member of the corporate world on his watch.

"Mr. Carlson," Rob said. "It's good to see you, sir."

"Get these damn ties off me," her father said.

Rob motioned for one of the agents to free her dad, while Emi pulled out her key chain and used a small tool to release the cuffs locking her hands together.

She rubbed her wrists with painful gratitude when she was finally free.

"What's the status?" Rob asked. "Anyone inside?"

"Yes. Tim Coulson is in the basement," she said. "I shot him in the neck. He was dead before the bomb went off. Allison and Lauren Sullivan are unaccounted for. Quinn knocked them out. One was by the back door. The other was in the backyard. I don't know if either survived the explosion."

"We should be able to find that out soon," Rob said. "I'll let the firefighters know. I'm glad you're all okay. Although I would like to know how Mr. Kelly got here before us." He gave Quinn a sharp, suspicious look.

"How did you know where they were?" Emi asked Quinn.

"I remembered something Tim's brother used to say, about killing the viper in his nest. I took a chance," Quinn replied. "As soon as I knew I was right, I contacted you."

"You should have contacted us earlier," Rob said.

"Leave him alone," her father interrupted, cutting Rob off and surprising them all. "Quinn saved my life, and my daughter's life. We wouldn't be alive if it wasn't for him."

"All right," Rob muttered. "Can I speak to you for a moment, Mr. Carlson?"

Her father nodded, and the two of them moved toward the sidewalk.

"We were across town at the tower when Quinn texted," Emi said. "Sorry we didn't get here faster. I didn't see the text right away. We were arresting three men in a gray van. We believe they were the ones who kidnapped you and your father, Caitlyn. There were more explosives in the truck. It looked like there was a plan B."

"Allison made reference to people waiting for them at the tower," she said.

"Your brother, Spencer, told us that Kevin might have provided security information to the terrorists, so we went over there to make sure the tower was secure."

"How did Spencer know that?" she asked.

"I mentioned it to him," Quinn cut in. "We were talking after you were taken, and Spencer was wondering why he was suddenly being brought into everything. It struck me that they were setting him up, and that the breach of security at Lexitech was part of that."

"It's exactly what they were doing," she said with a nod. "Tim told me that. Do you know who the men in the van were, Emi?"

Emi pulled out her phone. "Rich Conley, Stan Huff, and David Waksman. They all have lengthy records."

"They weren't part of the current environmental group at Bolton?" she asked.

"No. They're in their thirties and forties."

"Quinn said that people at the gala got sick. Are they going to be all right?"

"So far, no one appears to be critical, but I haven't gotten an update in a while." Emi paused. "I'm going to see if the firefighters have located the Sullivan sisters."

"Thanks." When Emi moved away, she let out a breath as she met Quinn's gaze. "I think you turned my father into a fan."

"I only had to save his ass to do that," he said dryly.

"What you did was incredibly generous."

He shrugged. "I did what needed to be done. But there was a minute there when I wasn't sure I could get back to you in time, and I felt a terror very similar to the one I experienced ten years ago. I couldn't stand the idea of having the same or worse outcome."

"It wasn't the same. I'm fine."

"I know. I want to hold you, but I don't want to mess up your work reputation."

She smiled back at him. "I'm not worried about that now."

"Good to know." He put his arm around her shoulders as they watched the house burn and squeezed her tight. "Did Tim tell you how he got into all this?"

She snuggled into his side, suddenly feeling the chill as the adrenaline began to wear off. "He wanted to follow in Donovan's footsteps. It was clear he thought his brother was some kind of god. After he met Allison, Lauren gave him the pages from Donovan's notebook. She must have been in Yosemite, too. Or she took the pages at some point before that."

"She was in Yosemite. She went there with Wyatt but apparently took the pages and the blackmail evidence without telling Wyatt she'd done so. He was under the impression that she'd found nothing." Quinn paused, shifting slightly so he could look into her eyes. "I asked Lauren if Donovan had told her to get both you and me out of the building. She said yes, but she couldn't stand you, so she only got me out."

Her gut clenched at the harsh but unsurprising truth. "Deep down, I've always thought that; I just couldn't prove it."

"Lauren was as crazy as the rest of them," he said, his jaw tight, his expression grim.

She nodded. "Tim was definitely out of his mind. He looked like Donovan, but he was so evil. There was no heart in his eyes, no conscience whatsoever. He didn't care how many people he killed. He was convinced that he was some righteous warrior for the good of the planet. He was really just a criminal and a killer."

"What about Allison?"

"She didn't say much of anything. She seemed very cold, withdrawn. I don't know if Tim brainwashed her or if she was always that way. But she obviously used Kevin and had no second thought about it. Nor did she try to stop Tim from killing Kevin. I asked Tim why he had started it all now, and he said it was because he finally had the means. When his father died, and he got all that money, he knew exactly what he wanted to do with it. But he didn't want to take the time to build an army with friends and fellow believers. In fact, he thought Donovan had made a mistake turning the LNF into a social group. Tim wanted to just buy the talent he needed and then get rid of them." She paused. "I asked him if anyone else was helping him, like Wyatt. And he gave me a derisive, sneering look. He said he had no need of help from people who had failed the first time around."

"Well, I'm kind of glad to hear that. Not that it excuses anything else Wyatt may have done ten years ago."

"Agreed."

"How did your father handle what was going on?"

"He was defiant, but he was helpless. Tim loved having my father at his mercy. Tim's biggest downfall was his desire for us to know that he was bigger and better than his brother. He wanted to talk to us. He wanted to tell us everything. And he wanted to set that timer so we could watch our lives slip away minute by minute. But I knew the longer it took for him to kill us, the better chance we had."

"You were right."

"I was lucky that you were there," she corrected. "I don't think we would have been able to survive if you hadn't come." She paused as Emi came toward them.

"Both women have been found," Emi said. "They're deceased. The EMTs are bringing them out now."

She felt a conflicting range of emotions at that piece of information.

As the paramedics brought the first gurney down the drive, she knew she had to see the face for herself. She walked over to the ambulance, with Quinn on her heels, asking the EMT to wait. She wanted to ID the body.

The paramedic warned her that it was bad, but that didn't deter her.

"Show me," she ordered.

He pulled the sheet back.

She sucked in a breath as she looked at the burned face and body that was almost unrecognizable.

"It's Lauren," Quinn said quietly. "She was wearing that necklace."

The sliver of gold was one of the few things that had not burned.

Quinn put a hand on her shoulder, leaning in close. "I'm sorry you didn't get to do it yourself," he whispered.

His words would have sounded strange to anyone but her. But he knew how much she'd wanted to confront the person who had killed their baby. Lauren had certainly had a hand in that. So had Donovan.

"Ma'am?" the paramedic said, giving her a questioning look.

She nodded.

The EMT pulled up the sheet. As the next body was brought out, she shook her head and moved away from the ambulance. She didn't need to see anyone else's face.

Quinn took her hand in his. She looked into his eyes, seeing the question there. "It's enough," she said.

"Really?" He gave her a doubtful look.

"Yes. There has been so much violence, so much death. Lauren can't hurt anyone ever again. Neither will Tim or Allison. Donovan's plan has finally been extinguished. And I am tired of all of it." Her eyes blurred with tears as she saw the compassion in his gaze. "I'm not going to cry."

"You can if you want to."

"I'm a tough FBI agent now."

"Maybe later then."

"Or maybe not. I've shed way too many tears. I thought I needed to confront the person who killed our baby in order to let go of the pain, but I think maybe I just needed to confront myself. I needed to stop blaming myself for going into that building, for not protecting my daughter."

"You've been blaming yourself all this time, Caitlyn?" he asked in shock. "That is so wrong. You were a victim."

"Intellectually, I know that, but it has been hard to feel it."

He cupped the back of her head and pulled her in for a kiss, then he said, "You have brought down all the bad guys. You have gotten justice for Isabella. I hope you can let go of the pain now."

"I think maybe I can," she said with a teary smile.

"Everything okay over here?" Emi asked, as she rejoined them. "Do either of you need to see a medic?"

"Quinn needs to go to the hospital," she said. "He broke his hand."

"I don't need to go now," Quinn protested.

"You do. And I will meet you there. It looks like my mom and brother have just arrived, and I need to speak to them." She gave him a questioning look. "Is that okay?"

His smile was filled with understanding. "It's fine. I'll see you later. Take your time."

Emi walked Quinn over to the ambulance. As they left, she joined her family on the sidewalk. They hugged each other for long minutes, and then her mom's gaze swept worriedly across her face. "You're so dirty, Caitlyn. Are you hurt anywhere?"

"I'm fine, thanks to Quinn. He saved my life; Dad's, too."

"That's what your father said. I'm shocked he would do that."

"Quinn did it for Caitlyn," her father replied.

"And for you, too. That's the kind of man he is. You misjudged him horribly, Dad."

"I'm beginning to realize that."

"You are?" her mom asked in amazement.

"I am," her father said, meeting her gaze. "I have a lot of apologizing to do to both of you. Where is Quinn?"

"He's on his way to the hospital. I think he broke his hand."

"Then I'll talk to him later." He paused. "I'm going to do better, Caitlyn, not just with Quinn, with Carlson Industries. My most important job is to protect my family, and I haven't done it very well. You asked me to call off the gala, and I refused. I was so caught up in the idea that I could control everything that I couldn't see what was happening."

"You didn't want to bow to terrorists, but sometimes you have to listen to the smart people around you who are trying to keep you safe."

"You're right."

"Dad said that the guy in charge is dead, that you shot him," Spencer said.

"I did."

"She was amazing," her dad put in. "So courageous and unbelievably determined. I still don't know how you got free from that pipe, Caitlyn, or how you got Tim's gun and took a shot with your hands in cuffs."

"I just did what I was trained to do. And believe it or not, I am rather good at my job."

"I believe it. You don't have to convince me." He looked at his wife and son. "You both would have been impressed. Caitlyn worked that guy to get information, to keep him talking until help could come. She is one hell of an FBI agent."

She couldn't help but appreciate the pride in his voice. "I'm sorry I had to prove it to you in this way."

"Is it over now?" Spencer asked. "Or is there more to come?"

"It's over."

"Thank God," her mother said. "But our home…"

They all turned toward the fire that had ravaged the house.

"I can't believe it's all gone," her mom added, sadness in her voice. "It was our home, our life."

"Our life is with each other," her father said. "We'll rebuild or we'll move somewhere else. Whatever you want."

"I can't think," her mom said.

"You don't have to decide now," he told her.

"You should all go back to the hotel or maybe to Spencer's place," she suggested.

"Don't be silly," her mom said sharply. "I've already called Baxter. We'll go there. Spencer's place is small and not very clean."

"It's not that bad," Spencer protested.

"Still."

As Rob approached her parents, Spencer pulled her slightly away from them. "I'm glad you're all right, Caitlyn. I was very worried. I have to ask—did they try to tell you I was involved again?"

"Tim said he was setting you up to look like the bomber, the mastermind of all of this."

"That's what Quinn thought was happening, but it's crazy."

"I don't think the plan would have held together in the end, but they were working it hard."

"You don't believe I tried to kill you, right?"

"Not for a second; I never did. I know who all the bad guys are now, Spencer, and you are not one of them."

Relief flooded his gaze. "Good." He gave her a smile. "So, do you think Mom will rebuild the house exactly the way it was?"

"Probably," she said with a grin.

"I know I complained about nothing ever changing, but now I hope she rebuilds it exactly the same way."

"Me, too."

CHAPTER TWENTY-EIGHT

TWO HOURS LATER, Caitlyn walked into the elevator at the Vanguard Hotel with Quinn. It was almost midnight. She was exhausted but also hyped up. So much had happened. She was still trying to process everything.

After her parents had been picked up by Baxter and Lana, Spencer had headed to his place, and she'd ridden to the hospital with Emi, who had filled her in on what she'd missed at the gala and the tower. It still amazed her that Tim had been able to organize so many attacks in such a short time, proving just how dangerous he had been. She was more than happy to know he was dead.

As they entered their hotel room, she blew out a breath of relief. "I feel like a hundred years have passed since we were in this room."

"I know what you mean," Quinn said, giving her a tired smile.

"We're both filthy." Her dress was ripped, and she was covered in ash and dirt. Quinn's appearance was even more battered after his fight with Tim and his broken hand, which was now in a cast.

"We're alive," Quinn said. "That's what matters."

She took a seat on the end of the bed and kicked off the tennis shoes that Emi had generously pulled out of the gym bag in her car. Her heels had been lost somewhere between the hotel and her parents' house.

Quinn pulled two bottles of water out of the fridge and handed her one.

She took a grateful sip, her throat parched from the smoke she'd inhaled.

Quinn emptied his bottle with a couple of long thirsty gulps, then set it down and sat next to her. He slid his right hand into hers. "It's over, babe."

"I can't quite believe it," she admitted, setting her water bottle aside. "Finding the truth has driven me every single day of the last ten years. It will be strange to wake up tomorrow and not have to wonder who was responsible for the bomb that killed Isabella and almost took my life. Every day, I've thought of that blast. I've been obsessed with finding the truth, with getting justice."

"You've done that. Now you have to find a way to let the past go."

"I want to do that. I suspect it will take some time. A lot of work will need to be done to untangle the plots from ten years ago and last week. But after that…"

He smiled. "Then you'll let it go."

"Yes. What about you? How do you feel about everything?"

"I wasn't as focused on finding the truth as you were these past ten years. I thought I'd gotten my revenge when Donovan went off that mountain."

"He was the bomber. Even if he did have second thoughts about killing us, he killed Isabella and the custodian. He injured a bunch of other people. He was guilty. You weren't wrong about that."

"But his evil didn't die with him. Lauren had Donovan's

plans, and when she met Tim, she saw a chance to find glory for herself. I think it always bothered her that Donovan used her but didn't really respect her. She also hated that everyone in the group abandoned her when she divorced Vinnie. I suspect that played into her motives, too. But she was clearly out of her mind."

"How did you knock her out?"

"I smashed her head against the wall."

"I'm jealous."

"I know. I've deprived you of revenge once more."

"You did what you had to do to save me and my father. That was more important."

"I thought so. I wish I'd had time to get more information, but I was in a hurry to find you. I didn't kill her, though. She wouldn't have died if the house hadn't blown up. She got what she deserved."

"So did Allison and Tim. And we'll make sure whoever was helping them pays, too. Emi said the three guys they picked up at the tower were already starting to talk. The thing Tim didn't realize about using people just for jobs was that he would get no loyalty in return. Not that it matters now." She let out a breath. "I do wish Kevin had been able to tell me what was happening. Maybe I could have saved him."

"He should have told you, but it's possible he helped Allison more than you know and then he got caught in her web."

"That's probably what happened," she agreed. "In the days to come, we'll be calling in Wyatt, Justin, and Senator Pederson, as well as Agent Bauer. They'll have some questions to answer, too."

"Good. I'd like to see them have accountability for their lies."

"Me, too." She gave him a smile. "Are you ready to let go of Michael Wainscott and be Quinn Kelly again?"

"More than ready. I never really got used to being Michael. Sometimes, I wouldn't even answer until someone had said my name three times. And all of my relationships were limited by my inability to tell the truth."

"You can be honest now."

"I intend to be."

"Good. Me, too. I think we should start now."

"You don't want to take a hot shower first?" he asked.

"I don't want to waste another minute."

He drew in a breath and let it out. "Okay, let me have it."

As she saw him steel himself for whatever was coming, she felt bad that she hadn't said something earlier. "When I was in the basement, I kept thinking about how I hadn't told you something really important."

"Which is…"

"I was wrong."

"About what?"

"I told you on the boat that I could never forgive you. But I can forgive you, Quinn. Actually," she amended quickly. "I already have."

Hope flared in his gaze. "You don't have to say that. I know I hurt you."

"I hurt you, too. I don't think I've admitted that out loud until now. We have a lot of history between us, Quinn. Over the years, I would only allow myself to remember the way you left me and not the way you loved me. There was a time when you knew me better than anyone else. You supported my dreams. You made me think I could be whoever I wanted to be. You were my best friend." She bit down on her lip as she was filled with emotion. "I'm not going to cry through this," she said with a teary laugh.

"Can I say something?"

"Please."

"You were my best friend, too. You were my family, Caitlyn. With you, I could see a future that I hadn't believed was possible. You opened up my life as much as I opened up yours. I might have pushed you to try some new things, but you gave me back the optimism and hope that I'd lost. You made me believe again."

"Did you stop believing after we broke up?" she asked curiously.

"Yes. Those first couple of years put me back into the dark hole I'd been in after my mom died. Only it was worse, because I was responsible for that darkness. It wasn't cancer. It was me, my decisions, that had landed me where I was. And I was riddled with guilt at my inability to see what was happening in the LNF before it happened."

"Whatever you missed, I missed, too. I'm sorry that you ended up in that dark place again."

"Why would you apologize? It wasn't your fault."

"No, but I still hate knowing how much pain you were in."

"It wasn't anything compared to yours."

"Well, now we have a chance to start over. I'd like to see if we could have a future together. I don't know exactly what it would look like, but that's kind of exciting." She licked her lips. "What are you thinking?"

"I want to have a future, too."

"Are you sure that's not the pain meds talking?"

His blue eyes sparkled as a loving smile parted his lips. "I know exactly what I'm saying."

"It's happening fast. A week ago, I still hated you."

"We've packed a lot into the last several days," he admitted. "But it doesn't feel fast to me. It feels like it's taken forever for us to get back together."

"But we're not back where we were. We're starting fresh—a new you, a new me, a new us." She let that sink in and then said words she'd never believed she'd ever say to him again. "I love you, Quinn."

"I love you, Caitlyn."

He gave her a long, tender, emotion-filled kiss. Every last lingering bit of doubt and pain fell away as they wrapped their arms around each other, as they shared the love that had never really gone away. There was promise in their kiss now, too, a happier future ahead.

When they broke apart, she said, "I guess we should talk about how we're going to make our future work. We live in different cities."

He put a finger against her lips. "We've talked enough today. Let's take a shower."

"Can you get that cast wet?"

He laughed. "Were you always this practical?"

"I think I was. You've probably forgotten some of my traits that used to annoy you."

"I can't think of one." He stood up and pulled her to her feet. "We'll make it a bath instead of a shower."

"There is a spa tub with some lovely jets. I have some sore muscles from being thrown around in that van."

He frowned. "I haven't even asked you about all that."

"I don't want to talk about it now. We have time, Quinn. Lots and lots of time."

———

They slept until eleven on Monday and then ordered a massive breakfast from room service. Quinn loved watching Caitlyn demolish a veggie omelet, bacon, and French toast with fresh blueberries. He'd done the same as well, ravenous after the last few days. The stress was finally gone, and while his body felt battered, the physical pain was nothing compared to what he'd gone through the last ten years.

Caitlyn gave him a happy smile as she sipped her second cup of coffee. "I feel better."

"I can see that." His gaze roamed her face, taking in all the details, from the sparkle in her brown eyes, to the soft fullness of her mouth, and the silky shine of her hair. She wore a thick, white terry cloth robe, and he was already itching to slip it off her shoulders and explore the soft curves of her body.

"If you look at me like that, we are never going to get this day started," she warned.

"That's not a problem for me. We deserve a day off. And we need to get to know each other again."

"I feel like we're reliving the first month we were together when we had sex like three times a day for a month. We spent a lot of hours in bed."

"And elsewhere. Let's try to improve our record for the next thirty days."

"I'm not as young as I used to be, and neither are you. We're not crazy college kids anymore."

He laughed. "I think we've still got it in us."

She let out a soft sigh as she gazed back at him. "We probably do. I'm addicted to you, Quinn. I always have been."

"I'm suffering the same addiction. Only, it's not suffering at all. It's amazing. And can I just say that you're not only a bold, fast driver now, you've gotten a little more reckless in other areas, too."

She grinned. "I still have a few tricks up my sleeve."

"See, that's the problem—you shouldn't be wearing any sleeves or any clothes."

"I love this robe!" She drew it more closely around her. "It's soft and warm."

"I can make you warm."

"I know."

An intimate memory flashed between them. And unlike before, it didn't make him sad; it made him happy, because they would make more memories. They had the rest of their lives to do that.

"But," Caitlyn added, as she checked her phone that had buzzed several times in the last few minutes. "I'm getting a lot of messages. The real world wants our attention."

"What's going on?"

She flipped through her phone. "Emi says that Rob has agreed to open an investigation into Agent Bauer's conduct. They are currently trying to get in touch with him, but he is not home, and no one has seen him since last Thursday."

"That can't be a coincidence."

"No. Emi said that she picked up Wyatt this morning, and he's being cooperative. His father and brother are apparently also on their way in."

"Senator Pederson is probably bringing a team of lawyers."

"No doubt, but Wyatt is already talking, so anything his father does to stop him probably won't work."

"That's good news."

"Here's something that may not be as good," she said with a frown. She lifted her gaze to his. "Rob would also like to talk to us around three, if that works. He specifically wants you to come with me."

"Well, the FBI office is never my favorite place to be, but as long as you're there, I'm fine with it."

"You haven't done anything wrong, Quinn. You don't need to worry."

"You're forgetting Yosemite."

"I'm not forgetting it. You didn't kill Donovan. He killed himself. That's what happened."

"The FBI might not agree. And who knows what Wyatt will tell them?"

"It doesn't matter what Wyatt says. I know the truth, and I will make sure that Rob knows it, too. It won't be a problem."

He could see by the determined light in her eyes that she wouldn't let it be a problem. He was curious about something, though. "Did Tim say anything about Donovan's death? Did he believe it was suicide?"

"No. He thought you killed his brother. Tim said he had a

special plan to make you pay for Donovan's death. I was so glad you weren't with us at the gala when Kent came over."

"I was not happy about that. I was angry that I'd let go of your hand for even a second. Last night came very close to a bad outcome." His jaw tightened as he thought of what could have happened.

"We're okay now." She reached across the table and put her hand over his. "We're good, Quinn. We got justice for Isabella. And we're together again."

"You're right. That's all I'm going to think about—moving forward with you."

"So, should we try long distance for a while, maybe take vacations together?"

"Nope. Not a chance," he said with a definitive shake of his head.

"What's the alternative?" she asked with concern in her eyes. "I love my job. You love your job."

"Agreed. But last time I looked, there was an ocean in LA."

Her eyes widened with surprise. "You'd move for me?"

"I'd do anything for you, Caitlyn. I want you to believe that, really believe it. From here on out, you'll always come first. I can work anywhere. What I can't do is live without you."

"That's very generous. I could probably transfer to San Francisco, although I don't really like Rob. But I would do it, if it makes it easier for us to be together. I also cannot live without you. I know that. I've tried it for the last ten years."

"So have I. And I will not deprive your task force of their very best badass agent."

She smiled. "I can't wait for you to meet them. They're not just coworkers; they're family. I've missed them the last week. Not that Emi isn't great, or that the other agents haven't done a good job; I just don't have the same kind of relationship or trust with this group as I do with my task force."

"I do like Emi. She's cool. I'm sure the others are, too."

"They are. And you might see Emi in LA at some point. She wants to join the team. I'm going to see if Flynn can make a spot for her. By the way, there are some surfers and divers on the task force. You'll find some ocean-loving friends."

"I'm not worried. And, Caitlyn, I want to do things the right way. I want to ask your father for your hand."

Her brow shot up in surprise. "Seriously? You want to give my father permission to say no to you?"

He laughed. "If he says no, I'll still ask you to marry me. He will never run my life again. But I feel like it's something I'd like to do. I don't want to be between you and your parents and your brothers. I lost a family. I have never wanted you to feel that kind of isolation."

"That is really generous, considering what my father did to you. He tried to ruin your life."

"He didn't succeed, and I think last night was an awakening for him."

"It was definitely that. It opened his eyes to the truth about a lot of things, including you."

He squeezed her hand. "I want us to be a family. And someday, I want us to give Isabella a sister or a brother."

"Oh, my God, you are going to make me cry," she said with a sniff. "I love that you said you want to give her a sibling, and not—"

"We could never replace her."

She shook her head, meeting his gaze. "I know she was only eleven weeks old, but she was still our baby."

He felt a knot enter his throat. "Yes. She was our baby."

"But we'll have another one."

"When you're ready," he said.

"When we're both ready. We need to make all future relationship decisions together. No trying to hide things to protect each other. I watched my dad hide his whole life from my mother, keeping everything messy or scary away from her. I don't want that. I want a partner. I want my best friend. I want a man who respects me enough to tell me the truth."

"I can be all of that for you. I want the same, Caitlyn. I'm sure there will be things you can't tell me when you're on a case. I'll respect that. But outside of work—"

"You'll know everything I know. Speaking of decisions…"

He raised a brow at the mischievous sparkle in her gaze. "Yes?"

"I think we should go back to bed. We have hours before we have to go to the office."

He jumped to his feet. "I'm on board."

"You're always on board."

"I can't deny that."

Her gaze clung to his as she stood up. "I love you, Quinn."

"I love you back, and I'm going to spend the rest of my life showing you how much."

He took her into his arms and then settled his mouth over hers.

She was the one. She'd always been the one. He couldn't wait for the rest of his life.

WHAT TO READ NEXT

Don't miss the next book in the
OFF THE GRID: FBI SERIES

RISKY BARGAIN
September 21, 2021

Have you missed any books in the series?

Off the Grid: FBI Series
PERILOUS TRUST
RECKLESS WHISPER
DESPERATE PLAY
ELUSIVE PROMISE
DANGEROUS CHOICE
RUTHLESS CROSS
CRITICAL DOUBT
FEARLESS PURSUIT
DARING DECEPTION

Other thrilling romantic suspense...

Lightning Strikes Trilogy
BEAUTIFUL STORM
LIGHTNING LINGERS
SUMMER RAIN

Barbara Freethy is a #1 New York Times Bestselling Author of 69 novels ranging from contemporary romance to romantic suspense and women's fiction. With over 14 million copies sold, twenty-three of Barbara's books have appeared on the New York Times and USA Today Bestseller Lists, including SUMMER SECRETS which hit #1 on the New York Times and DON'T SAY A WORD, which spent 12 weeks on the list!

Known for her emotional and compelling stories of love, family, mystery and romance, Barbara enjoys writing about ordinary people caught up in extraordinary adventures.

She is currently writing two ongoing series: The romantic suspense series OFF THE GRID: FBI SERIES and the contemporary romance series WHISPER LAKE.

For more information on Barbara's books, visit her website at
www.barbarafreethy.com

Printed in Great Britain
by Amazon